**Everyone LOVES W**

'Brooding and atmospheric – full of mystery and twists where
nothing is quite as it seems'
**Catherine Cooper, author of *The Chalet***

'Such a great thriller with superb characterization to boot.
Hard to believe that it's a debut'
**Khurrum Rahman, author of *Homegrown Hero***

'A delicious slice of Scandi noir – such a dark, atmospheric and
compelling story! And ahh, if only those ravens could talk…'
**Jackie Kabler, author of *The Perfect Couple***

'Absolutely loved it! If you like a slow burner, Scandi Noir this
is the one for you!'
**Laure Van Rensburg, author of *The Downfall***

'The menacing, wintry heart of *Where Ravens Roost* gripped
me from the very first page! Complex, layered characterisation,
skilful writing and a twisty plot combine to create a Scandi
Noir thriller as dark as a raven's wing'
**Louise Mumford, author of *Sleepless***

'The bleak but beautiful settings are incredibly vivid (you'll
want to wear a coat while you read this) and there are twists
and turns around every corner'
**Steve Frech, author of *Dark Hollows***

'Nordin has produced an immersive tale of past secrets and
flawed family relationships, all wrapped up with a…
compelling narrative that had me glued to
my Kindle for most of the day'
**Jenny O'Brien, author of *Silent Cry***

'If this is how the series starts, I can't wait to read
whatever comes next'
**Paul Gitsham, author of *The Last Straw***

**Karin Nordin** has been a compulsive reader of thrilling stories since childhood and discovered her love of Scandinavian crime fiction during summers spent visiting family in Norway and Sweden. She has worked in healthcare and education, including as a pharmacy technician, karate instructor, and an English language teacher for the Dutch military.

Karin completed the Creative Writing MSc from the University of Edinburgh with Distinction in 2019 and also holds an MA in Scandinavian Literary Studies from the University of Amsterdam. Born in 'The Biggest Little City in the World' and raised in America's Rust Belt, she now lives in the Netherlands.

*Where Ravens Roost* is her first novel.

# Where Ravens Roost

## KARIN NORDIN

HQ
An imprint of HarperCollins*Publishers* Ltd
1 London Bridge Street
London SE1 9GF

www.harpercollins.co.uk

HarperCollins*Publishers*
1st Floor, Watermarque Building, Ringsend Road
Dublin 4, Ireland

This paperback edition 2021

First published in Great Britain by
HQ, an imprint of HarperCollins*Publishers* Ltd 2021

Copyright © Karin Nordin 2021

Karin Nordin asserts the moral right to be
identified as the author of this work.
A catalogue record for this book is
available from the British Library.

ISBN: 978-0-00-845552-1

MIX
Paper from
responsible sources
FSC™ C007454

This book is produced from independently certified FSC™ paper
to ensure responsible forest management.

For more information visit: www.harpercollins.co.uk/green

Printed and bound in the UK using 100%Renewable

Electricity at CPI Group (UK) Ltd

*For Marijke*

# Prologue

The call of the ravens was what woke him.

Stenar pulled back the curtains and peered out into the night. The clock on the nightstand read a quarter past eleven, but the engulfing darkness of the sky made it feel much later than that. Stenar rubbed his eyes and focused on the long walk between the house and the old barn thinly illuminated by the waning glow of a crescent moon. The barn and its attached rookery had been his grandfather's doing, but Stenar had learned to love those birds. Unlike members of his own species, they had been a consistent presence in his life. They understood him. They never left him.

They were his true family.

The low guttural *kraas* became more frequent and mutated into high-pitched shrieks like the phantom wails of the mythological *draug* after it tugged mariners into the sea.

Stenar went downstairs, pulled on his heavy wool-lined coat, and stepped into his mud-stained work boots. There had been an uncommon amount of rain in the last week and the distance between the house and the old barn had become a marshy length of matted grass and slick earth. His boots stuck in the mud with each step and he wrapped his arms about him to hold back the cold. Autumn had come early this year and the shorter days made

1

for cooler nights. He would be glad for winter. Then the ground would freeze and he could make this walk with less strain on his arthritic joints. There had been a time when he would have been able to bound across the yard in a matter of seconds. Now it took minutes. But the mud made it feel like hours.

The barn wasn't as sturdy as it once was. It was listing to one side and there was a hole in the roof that Stenar's son had promised to fix more than ten years ago. It hadn't been much of a hole then, but the heavy weight of snow over the years had turned it from a crack that let in an annoying amount of rain to a window-sized skylight offering a view of the stretching birch trees that surrounded the edge of the property. Stenar could see the hole as he approached the barn and the thought of it filled him with a weight of spiteful regret.

The closer he came to the barn the more flustered the caws of the ravens grew. He reached into his pocket and removed an old metal torch. His eyesight had diminished over the years and the copper red colour of the barn blended into the pitch-black of the night, concealing the edges of the door. He used to be able to find it by memory. Could reach for the handle with his eyes closed. But his memory, like his knees and his eyes, had become less reliable over the years. He pressed his thumb against the torch knob but stopped when a voice cut through the calls of the ravens.

Stenar froze, his boots sinking deeper into the mud.

Didn't he know that voice?

He slipped the torch back into his pocket and listened. The voice was muted against the high-pitched cries of the birds, but Stenar could hear anger in the speaker's tone. Anger followed by a mocking laugh that almost mimicked the provoking *toc-toc-tocs* that Stenar had heard in his youth. He slowly crept around the side of the barn, his boots mucking through the thick sludge with each step, bypassing the closed door until he came to a small broken window on the side of the rookery. He peeked in through the frosted glass but was met with the flapping of sable wings, blocking his view of whoever was in the barn. He placed one hand on the side of the building and used it to guide his steps around the back where a portion of the wooden planks had rotted away, resulting in a jagged peephole. All he could see were shadows.

Another voice, sharper and more frazzled than the first, cut through the ravens' crying and Stenar felt his heart skip a beat. He was certain he knew that voice. There was no doubt in his mind.

Stenar turned and headed back around the edge of the barn towards the door. At the corner of the building he slipped in the mud and reached out for the wall to brace himself. He impaled his hand on a loose nail. The sharp pain that tore through his palm sent him down hard on his left knee. His leg burned like it was on fire. He heard a pop and knew he'd dislocated something. He tried to stand and realised that pop was probably the hip he was supposed to have replaced last summer. A gripping cramp seized his leg but he ignored it, dragging himself through the mud towards the barn door. The birds clamoured in their pen, rattling against the mesh chicken wire and snapping at whatever intrusion had disturbed the sanctity of their barn.

He had to get up. He had to help.

The cawing of the ravens drowned out the voices. Stenar hoisted himself up on an old milk crate. The pain in his knee radiated down his calf. He took one hard step forward and his hip popped back into the socket. He winced, wiping his mud and blood-stained hand on his jacket. Then he limped back towards the door. A harsh metallic clang rang out in the night and both the sound of the voices and the birds ceased, leaving behind them an unearthly silence in the dead air. Stenar stopped. A minute passed before he heard the sound of someone shuffling inside the barn. He leaned against the wall to support himself, the wet wood splintering against his coat, and peered in through that same broken window beside the rookery. He wiped at the frost-covered window with his uninjured palm. The ravens sat still on their perches, clearing a view to the main open space of the barn.

What he saw both shocked and confused him. As he tried to process the image before him, one of the birds nearest the window craned its neck and stared at him with two dark voids for eyes. Its unnaturally hooked bill gave the impression that it was sneering. Taunting. The bird had seen what Stenar had seen, but unlike him it understood.

It understood and it would never forget.

# Chapter 1

## Onsdag | Wednesday

Kjeld's phone rang nonstop from the bustling rain-slick streets of Gothenburg to the winding frost-covered roads of Jämtland county. Even when he stopped at the Shell off the E16 near Mora to take a piss and refill his coffee amid the crowd of tourists scrambling to try an authentic Swedish cinnamon roll and purchase discounted painted horses, his phone wouldn't stop buzzing in his jacket pocket. A busload of tourists en route to the Dala horse museum caused the queue for the single toilet to curve through the gift shop and outside the front entrance. Kjeld grumbled and relieved himself on the backside of the building beside an industrial waste container.

His phone continued to vibrate against his chest, but Kjeld didn't answer. He knew who it was: Detective Sergeant Esme Jansson who had been, until recently, his partner in the Violent Crimes Division at Gothenburg City Police. That was before his suspension. It was temporary, they said. Just until the investigation into the Aubuchon murder was cleared up, but regardless of how that turned out Kjeld didn't have high expectations of the chief going easy on him. Apparently the line between good police work and breaking the law was finer than Kjeld realised and as far as the police commission was concerned, he'd not only stepped over that line, but completely ignored its existence. He didn't disagree with them that he'd made mistakes. He had. But there had been circumstances that he thought warranted those mistakes. Esme understood. She was there when the aptly named Kattegat Killer made his final demands. But she wasn't the ranking officer on the scene. He was.

His phone buzzed that he had a voicemail. He grabbed his coffee from the ledge of the trash container and retrieved his messages. *You have three new voice messages*, the soft computerised tone informed him.

There was a pause and then Esme's voice, firm and direct, was loud in his ear. But it was the increasing heaviness of her southern Scanian dialect, accented by unnecessary diphthongs and an aggressively rolled "r" that told him she was livid.

'What the hell is this about a temporary leave of absence? Don't you know we're facing an inquest in a couple of weeks? And you just up and disappear to leave me with this mess? You're a fuckin' arsehole, Nygaard. I've got the commission breathing down my neck about my statement, the Special Investigations Division is asking me to provide a witness testimony for your actions covering the entire Aubuchon case, and your neighbour called me about feeding your cat. When did I ever say you could give my number to your neighbour? I'm not your fuckin' cat-sitter. You can't just head out of town and expect other people to cover your shit for you.'

*End of first message. New message.*

Esme's voice was louder this time.

'Pick up your goddamned phone, Nygaard! I've got a shit ton of your paperwork sitting on my desk and I am not cleaning it up for you. I don't care if you're on a fuckin' beach in Tahiti, you need to get your arse back here and fix this problem. The chief

6

says you haven't turned in your deposition yet. I swear to God if I get demoted because you're an arsehole, I will never forgive you.'

*End of message. Last message.*

'Your apartment is a shit mess. You know that? Where do you keep the cat food? Call me back.'

*You have no new messages. To replay these messages, press—*

Kjeld punched the end-call button on his phone and slipped it in his pocket, walking around the petrol station and back towards his car. He felt guilty for avoiding Esme's calls, but he knew that she would try to get him to open up about everything that had happened during their last case. She would pester him until he shared his feelings and Kjeld didn't want to share them. He wanted to bury them just like he wanted to bury so many things in his past. But Esme was right. He should have told her he was going out of town. She deserved that at least. Hell, she deserved a lot more than that for covering his arse for the last four years, but Kjeld hadn't been thinking about her when he got into his car and started driving. If he was honest with himself, he hadn't been thinking about anything related to the last few months. Not her, not the chief, not the case that got him suspended, not the testimony he was supposed to give, not the possibility that he would lose his job or worse, serve time for impeding the course of a criminal investigation, not the fact that Bengt was threatening to contest his visitation rights to his daughter. Nothing.

All he was thinking about was the strange call he'd received from his father, a man he hadn't spoken to in almost twelve years. It was uncanny. Seeing his father's number pop up on the notification of missed calls was the last thing he'd expected to see that week. And his first thought was that it hadn't been his father calling at all, but someone else using the phone to give him news of the old man's death. Then he heard the familiar voice on the recording and was surprised by the severity of his gut reaction – hard disappointment.

7

He listened to the message three times, but it didn't make any sense. The context was unclear and the voice on the other end of the line was disorientated and vague, but it prickled at something in Kjeld that urged him to drive home.

Whether that prickle was hatred or sympathy, however, Kjeld didn't know. What he did know was that nothing short of an act of God would cause Stenar Nygaard to break his vow to never speak to his son again. And that act was worth driving almost ten hours across the country to confront.

'Take our picture?' a middle-aged woman asked. She was bundled up in a thick down coat with a blue and yellow Swedish football scarf wrapped around her neck. When Kjeld didn't respond right away she waved a large Nikon camera in his face. Behind her were three other women with similar short, cropped haircuts and puffy jackets, smiling with their cinnamon rolls and Daim chocolate bars.

Kjeld sighed and took the camera. He must have looked like an anomaly standing among them. While his appearance rarely stood out in a crowd of Swedes, at just over six feet, with ruddy unkempt hair, a thin scar above his top lip, and the scruff of what would be a full beard if he didn't shave soon, he was the physical antithesis of the tourists hovering around the bus. One of the women stared at the side of his head and Kjeld felt a moment of self-consciousness. She said something in a language he didn't understand. He assumed she was talking about the piece of flesh and cartilage missing from his left ear. He snapped four quick photos with the Shell petrol station in the background. The women thanked him in broken English, nodding their heads enthusiastically before hurrying off to the group conglomerating around a man waving a green flag attached to a long staff.

Kjeld quickened his pace to his car so as not to be bothered by any more tourists and pulled out of the service station just as another bus turned into the car park to continue the cycle of the never-ending toilet queue. It wasn't until he took the exit onto the E45 heading north that he realised he forgot to remove the lens cap.

* * *

November was usually a rainy month in Jämtland, but an early cold front had moved in, glossing the roads with a thin layer of ice. The gravel road that led up to Kjeld's old family home was unmaintained, interrupted with patches of long grass, fallen tree limbs, and potholes that could snap the suspension of a small car. In truth it could hardly be considered a road at all. It was more a narrow winding path cut out of the surrounding forest with so many sharp turns that Kjeld imagined his great-grandfather must have been three sheets to the wind when he decided to pave the old horse trail connecting his property to the township limits. The story was that his great-grandfather was so enamoured by the beauty of the birch and spruce trees that he refused to chop down a single one to build the drive from the town to his home. But Kjeld's impression of the story after hearing it ad nauseam during his childhood was that his great-grandfather was either too damn stubborn to cut down any trees or he just wanted to limit the possibility that anyone would visit him.

And if Kjeld looked to the other men in his family, himself included, for insight into which explanation was more likely, he would put his money on the latter.

The drive dipped downward just before reaching the house. Kjeld parked his car further up the road on the hill, not wanting to risk the possibility of getting snowed in should the weather take a turn, and walked the rest of the distance to the house. There was a bitter chill in the air that nipped at his neck and he hunched his shoulders against the cold.

It was a typical Norrland farmhouse with the red exterior and white trim, although much of the paint on the northern side had chipped and peeled over the years. Most of the clay roof tiles were covered in moss and the rain gutter on the right side had fallen and was lying in a pile of uncut brush beside the house. The picket fence that he'd painted as a child was missing some planks and someone had permanently tied the gate to an open position against the remaining pickets where it was overgrown with ragweed and arctic violets whose petals had broken off and withered due to the unnatural wetness of the season. In the distance Kjeld could see a spiral of smoke coming from the chimney of the nearest house, which was at least eight kilometres away.

He walked around a fallen garden gnome that he vaguely recognised as once belonging to his mother, and up the steps to the porch. When the doorbell didn't work, he rapped his fist against the metal screen that someone had recently fit over the yellow door. It was loosely hinged to the side of the house and made a hard clanking sound as it hit against the wooden frame.

Kjeld looked out over the yard. The disarray of weeds, abandoned garden tools buried beneath a pile of broken shutters and rotten firewood, and an overturned wheelbarrow once filled with shattered kitchen tiles caused his face to burn with anger and guilt.

What the hell was he doing here?

It was late afternoon and the sun was just beginning to dip towards the horizon, sending an orangish-yellow gleam through the trees. He was kicking himself for leaving Gothenburg in the middle of the night. It had been an impulsive decision. Now he was tired and regretting making the drive at all. If he got back in his car right now, he could probably make it to Östersund before the local businesses closed and get himself a room for the night. If he could find himself a decent cup of coffee then he could probably make it all the way back to Mora. Neither coffee nor desperation would get him back to Gothenburg before tomorrow, but at least he wouldn't be here, questioning his good sense.

He was already down two porch steps when the front door opened. Kjeld turned around and looked back at his sister as she stared at him through the mesh of the metal screen. Her expression was rigid, the age lines in her face pulled taut around thin pursed lips. After an uncomfortable pause that seemed to Kjeld to last minutes she pushed open the screen door with her hip and snorted a laugh.

'Well, I'll be damned,' she scoffed. 'It must be snowing in hell.'

# Chapter 2

Kjeld sat at the yellow Formica kitchen table and watched as his sister, Sara, peeled potatoes at the sink. He was surprised by how little had changed in the room since he was last there. Pressed flowers and plants in dusty frames still hung on the walls and his mother's hand-knit potholders were looped over the oven door and the pantry handles. The only things that were different were the padlocks on many of the cupboard doors and Sara herself. She was bigger around the middle than he remembered, but Kjeld imagined having two kids would do that to a person. Or was it three?

'Where's Dad?' he asked, running his finger along a crack at the edge of the table.

Sara shook her head, laughed again but with less amusement than when she'd seen him at the front door, and dropped a potato into a bowl on the counter. 'Really? Is that how you want to start?'

She turned and wiped her wet hands on her apron, sending him a disappointed sneer as she canted her hip to the side and weighted her balance by gripping the edge of the sink with her hand. 'Where's Dad? Seriously? When was the last time you even saw him? Ten years ago? Twelve?'

Kjeld watched as her face turned a heated shade of red. It

made her look sweaty and out of breath like she used to get when they would race each other from the back porch to the barn as children. It wasn't an attractive look on her. Then again, Sara had always been a plain-looking girl. Now she was a plain-looking woman. She had a stocky build and her hair was that same dull shade of brown their father had when he was younger. The length couldn't have been much longer than her shoulders, but it was pulled back in a messy bun making it difficult to tell. She didn't wear any make-up aside from a clumpy layer of mascara on her upper eyelashes and a slim brush of pink eye shadow. Unlike Kjeld's face, which had their mother's sharp angles, particularly around the jawline, Sara's face was round and flat. She had too much of their father in her face.

'He called me,' Kjeld said.

Sara stared at him as though using the sudden silence between them to determine whether he was telling the truth.

'What do you mean he called you?' she asked.

'I got a message from him the other day. It went straight to voicemail, but it was definitely from Dad.'

Sara took another potato out of the sink and dragged the peeler along the edge, scraping off the skin in long pieces. 'What did he say?'

'I don't know.' Kjeld sighed. 'I didn't even know he had my number.'

'What do you mean you don't know? He left you a message. What did he say?'

'It was just a bunch of nonsense. Something about the barn and the birds. It sounded like the ramblings of a drunk.'

'Dad's not a drunk,' Sara said, tossing the potato skin in the sink. 'I want to hear the voicemail.'

Kjeld took out his mobile phone, set it to play on speaker, and pulled up the message. After a pause his father's voice, frantic and confused, began to speak.

'Kjeld, it's your … It's me. You need to come home. I saw …

someone out in the barn. You must come home. I have to tell you about the ravens. They were out there. Fighting. I don't know what to do. I can't let your mother find out. She can't know. Please. You must listen to me. They were out there. I saw it. Your mother can't know. She can't. I promised her I would take care of things. They know, Kjeld. The ravens. They know.'

The message cut off.

Sara's expression hardened, her gaze fixed on the bowl of potatoes.

'Sara? Are you all right?'

She rubbed the back of her hand against her right eye as though fighting off a tear. 'I'm fine. It's just difficult to hear him talk that way. About Mum. Like she's still alive.'

'That's why I came all the way out here,' Kjeld said. 'Does he still have those damn things out in the barn?'

'The ravens, you mean?'

'Those things always creeped me out as a kid.'

Sara laughed again, honest and hearty this time. 'I remember that time you got stuck in the barn. Do you remember that? God, you must have been yelling for hours. Mum and I were upstairs with the windows closed and Dad was off doing who-knows-what so nobody heard you. I remember you were practically catatonic when he found you.' She bent down and removed a large pot from a lower cupboard, dumped the peeled potatoes into the pot, and filled it with water before setting it on the range.

'If you'd been there you would have been scared, too,' Kjeld said. He looked away from her and out the kitchen window, which offered a view of the backyard and the long empty field that led up to the barn at far end of the lot. It seemed odd to him suddenly that there would be a large treeless expanse on the property after the care his great-grandfather took to wind the road leading up to the house, but that's how it had always been.

'There's still a few out there,' she said after a pause. 'Not as many as there used to be. They're a pain in the arse to take care of. Sometimes I think about letting them all out, but that would break Dad. Those damn birds are the only thing left that he gives a shit about.'

Sara turned on the gas and tapped a dash of salt into the pot. Then she removed her apron and hung it over a hook on a wall beside a framed black orchid. The classification *Gymnadenia nigra*, the provincial flower of Jämtland, had been handwritten underneath the stem by his father years ago. She sat down at the table across from Kjeld.

'Where is Dad anyway?' Kjeld asked.

'He's upstairs. Resting.'

'At this hour?'

Sara sighed. 'Most of the time it's a miracle if I can even get him in bed at all. But I'll have to wake him up soon if he doesn't get out of bed on his own. Otherwise he'll be up all night.'

'You stay here at night?' Kjeld glanced back out the window.

'Only when he's having a bad day,' she said. 'I mean, don't get me wrong. He probably needs round-the-clock care, but I can't be here every minute of the day. It's hard enough on Tom that I'm here as much as I am. Not to mention the kids.'

'Can't you just leave him on his own?'

Sara shook her head and Kjeld could see she was trying her best not to make some kind of sarcastic remark. She looked tired. War-weary. And it was then that he noticed the dark patches of skin under her eyes and the grey hair at her temples. It had been a few years since he'd last seen her, not as long as it had been since he'd seen their father, but she seemed to have aged decades in that time.

'It's *Alzheimer's*, Kjeld.'

Kjeld looked down at the table. The message on his voicemail started to make sense. The confusion in his father's voice. The disorientated sentences. The nonsensical rambling.

Sara leaned back in the chair and crossed her arms over her chest. 'One minute he's fine and normal, talking about the good old days. The next minute he's almost burning the house down because he thinks the sofa in the living room is the old wood stove.'

'But he must have good days,' Kjeld said.

'That *would* be a good day.'

He pinched the bridge of his nose. 'How long has this been going on?'

Sara sneered. 'Chrissakes, Kjeld. I forgot how completely out of touch you were with things up here.'

'Well it's not like you ever picked up the phone to tell me. Or left me a note in one of your yearly Christmas cards. Would that have been so difficult? Happy Holidays. P.S. Dad's got dementia.'

'Don't you dare put this on me. You're never available. Besides, Bengt knew.'

Kjeld scowled at the mention of his ex-husband. He clenched his teeth behind his pursed lips, adding to his quickly building tension headache. 'Really? Bengt knew?'

'He answers his phone, Kjeld.'

A heavy thunk of something hitting the floor echoed from upstairs. Kjeld turned his attention to the doorway. Sara held her breath and for a brief moment Kjeld wondered if she was waiting for their father to fall down the stairs and solve her problems. Then a hoarse voice called out from the other side of the house.

'Sara! Sara! Would you ask your mother where she put my blue shirt? Sara!'

Kjeld raised a brow and gave his sister a questioning look.

Sara sighed and stood up. 'It starts.'

'Why is he asking about Mum?'

'Don't be daft. It's because he doesn't remember. Do us both a favour and don't talk about Mum. Please. I've got enough shit to deal with. If you bring her up then I'll never get home.'

The pot of potatoes began to boil and Sara turned down the heat. From upstairs Stenar's yelling changed from calling out Sara's name to calling out the name of their mother. Another heavy thunk, probably a dresser drawer hitting the floor, echoed down the hall.

Kjeld stood up, hooking his thumbs in his jeans pockets. 'Sara?'

'What?' she snapped. Then she took a deep breath. 'Sorry. I'm not getting much sleep. And I don't know how he's going to react to seeing you.'

Kjeld nodded. Their father had never reacted well to seeing him when he had all his faculties about him. It wasn't lost on Kjeld that him showing up unexpectedly could cause problems. He watched his sister try to keep her composure in the kitchen and thought about Esme dealing with the Aubuchon mess on her own, covering for him out of some misplaced sense of loyalty. Just like Sara taking care of their father because of some antiquated notion of familial responsibility. As if they had ever been a real family. He mentally cursed himself for driving all this way on the whim of a phone call from a demented old man.

'I have to go check on him,' Sara said, heading towards the doorway.

'Do you know why he called me?' Kjeld asked.

Sara hesitated. Then she glanced back at her brother, her brown eyes moist and her expression ambiguous. 'He got it in his head that he saw something out in the barn.'

'What did he see?' Kjeld asked.

Sara's brows creased and her lips pursed again like they did when she saw him on the front steps. When she replied her tone had lowered to a different level of seriousness. It was a tone that Kjeld hadn't heard in her voice since the night their mother died.

'A murder.'

# Chapter 3

Roland Lindqvist slammed his laptop closed and shoved it halfway across the conference-room table. At sixty-eight years old he should have been retired, spending his mornings on the golf course and his afternoons with friends, toasting the successes of their pasts and the free time of their futures over glasses of champagne while placing bets on horse races they would never watch. Standing in as temporary CEO of the family business and negotiating million-euro deals during dinnertime had never been part of that plan. Not that he was unaccustomed to the work. He'd proved himself more than capable of taking the reins from his older brother when Peter went on his sabbatical, but it was never supposed to be permanent. And it was certainly never supposed to affect his golden years.

Roland pressed the intercom at the head of the table.

'Yes, Herr Lindqvist?' the soft voice of his secretary answered.

'Ah, Hanna, you're still here. Good,' he said. 'Has Erik Norberg called?'

'No, sir,' Hanna replied.

'Anything from Jakob Holm?'

'Not since yesterday, Herr Lindqvist.'

'I suppose it would be too much to hope my brother called?'

There was a pause on the other end of the intercom and Roland imagined that Hanna was trying to determine the most appropriate means of replying to an offhanded quip about Norrmalm's elusive CEO. He saved her the awkwardness of an answer. 'Could you go down to the filing room and pull up the hard copies of the original Norrmalm ownership documents and have them placed on my desk before you leave?'

'The originals, sir? From when the company first began or after it went corporate?'

'Both, if you can find them.' Better to be overprepared.

'Yes, sir. I'll do that now.'

Roland clicked off the intercom. He smoothed down the front of his button-up shirt (an anniversary gift from his wife of forty-one years) and glanced at his watch (a gift from his mistress of twelve years). 5.27 p.m. Well past the end of the traditional workday. Which meant that Roland wouldn't hear about the rescheduling of the meeting with MineCorp until tomorrow morning if he was lucky. Early afternoon if they decided to make him sweat.

He walked over to the floor-to-ceiling glass viewing platform at the far end of the conference room. Three years ago, and at the suggestion of the board, Roland decided to physically rebrand the company's image. The dark brick walls of the building's western meeting rooms were replaced with a special UV-blocking insulated glass, which allowed the sun to shine through without inflicting damage to the skin. In the lead conference room where he now stood, overlooking the relatively untouched natural forest that bordered Norway in the west and Lapland in the north, Roland had an enclosed reinforced glass walkway built as an extension of the once unremarkable room. It was the same glass used in the construction of the ledges on the Willis Tower in Chicago and for those who dared step out onto the suspended platform, it offered an imposing view of the almost vertical drop into the original copper mine that was the bedrock of the Lindqvist legacy: Norrmalm Industries.

The environmentalists called it a blemish on the forested landscape, but to Roland it represented generations of tradition, backbreaking work, and entrepreneurial foresight. The horizon was awash in densely populated pines, interrupted by isolated patches of birch trees whose white bark trunks broke through the green like the strayed strands of silver in Roland's otherwise dark hair. Immediately adjacent to Norrmalm's corporate head-quarters, however, was a deep cavern of reddish-orange bedrock, winding dirt roads excavated into the barren vista, and, beneath that, a complex system of tunnels that had collapsed some of the nearby woodland and swallowed a small region of untouched timber into its copper jaws. That was one of the many risks of mining, but to Roland and his family it was worth it. The accidental deforestation of a patch of rarely visited wilderness didn't weigh on his great-grandfather's conscience. Nor did his grandfather or father suffer from restless nights on that account. And like them Roland slept comfortably on his interwoven silk jacquard merino wool and hand-spun 1000-count Egyptian cotton bedsheets.

He caught a glimpse of his own reflection in the glass and was surprised by how old he looked. The lines around his eyes were more pronounced now and his hair was beginning to recede. Despite the occasional aches and pains in the morning, he was in decent shape for a man pushing seventy. His doctor regularly told him that he was "fit as a horse" and would be even more so if he stayed off the whisky and cigars, but at his age those were the things worth living for.

He was getting too old for this.

Peter had taken over Norrmalm from their father after his passing thirty-four years ago. The assumption was that Peter would eventually pass it on to his own children just as the Lindqvist family had done for more than five generations. But after his wife and unborn son died in childbirth, Peter decided not to try and have any more children. He didn't even remarry.

He just buried himself in the business, allowing work to fill that familial void. And when he decided to take a leave of absence the responsibilities fell to Roland. But Roland was already preparing for retirement.

Roland remembered the day Peter told him about his need to "step away from the company for a while" like it was yesterday. The news hadn't taken him by surprise. Peter's passion for the business had diminished considerably after he turned sixty. Roland always assumed this was because their father hadn't made it to his own sixtieth birthday, but later he considered the possibility that Peter had finally felt the empty weight of investing everything into Norrmalm. Thus the revelation that Peter needed a break hadn't been a shock, but it had rattled him. And what followed was an argument that was never fully resolved because Peter refused to take an answer other than the one he'd already decided – that Roland would take over for him until his return.

A return, it seemed, that either wouldn't or couldn't occur.

On Friday it would be five years to the day that Peter left. At the time Roland understood Peter's choice. The pressures of the business had taken its toll on his brother. If Roland had been in his brother's position he would have burned out as well.

Thankfully, Peter had surrounded himself with a more than competent executive board who eased Roland into the transition. It didn't stop Roland from cursing his brother's name whenever he had to miss tee time in order to curry favour to some government official or environmental analyst, but it helped. And once the merger with MineCorp was complete, it would be worth it. Then Roland could step back from the role of director and enjoy the pleasures of retirement while still retaining a large share of future profits afforded to him and his family by birthright.

Once he got ahold of Peter and convinced him to agree to the merger, that is. That was proving to be the greatest impediment to Roland's plan. Despite Roland's attempts to contact his brother, he hadn't been able to reach him. His messages were continuously going to voicemail and there were no replies to his emails. Of course, this went along with Peter's departing wishes to be left alone during his leave of absence, but Roland thought his brother would at least make an exception for family. Peter was still Norrmalm's majority shareholder, after all. And without his signature, Roland couldn't do anything that would drastically change the arrangement of the company.

Not until Friday. On Friday Roland could file a request for a declaratory judgement for death in absentia for his brother and, as closest living relative, inherit full rights to his brother's estate. Including Norrmalm Industries.

This wasn't the time for playing it safe.

Roland returned to the table and pressed the intercom again.

'I just placed the files on your desk, Herr Lindqvist,' Hanna answered, her voice slightly out of breath on the speaker.

'Thank you, Hanna. I'm going to send you an attachment of the updated contract agreements for the proposed merger. I'd like you to forward it in an email to Jakob Holm at MineCorp before you leave for the day. And CC it to our financial adviser, as well.'

'Of course, Herr Lindqvist,' Hanna replied. 'What should I say?'

'Tell him I want their answer on the merger before noon tomorrow or I'll present the proposal to their competitor in Germany.'

'Very well, sir. Anything else?'

Roland paused. He glanced back out the window. The sun had long since dipped below the tree line and the deep red glow that spread across the orange cavern began fading into night. Two more days and it would all be his. Then he could get rid of it.

'You can politely inform him that I'm done with negotiations. This is my final offer.'

# Chapter 4

Kjeld followed Sara upstairs, the floorboards creaking with each step. While she checked on their father alone – "better that I tell him you're here before he sees you" – Kjeld stood in his childhood bedroom and observed how much it had changed. The furniture was still there, but very little of him was left. The *Dark Side of the Moon* poster that once hung above his bed had been removed, leaving behind it the remnants of sticky tack on the wall. The dresser was cleared of his model aeroplanes and lava lamp. The desk, which someone had since pushed up against the window that overlooked the front drive, was empty aside from his high school graduation photo – complete with student cap, Kurt Cobain-styled shoulder-length hair, and a toothless grin that was uncomfortably obnoxious twenty years later.

'He didn't throw everything away,' Sara said from the doorway.

'Just the stuff I liked?' Kjeld said. He regretted it almost immediately.

Sara crossed her arms over her chest and watched as her brother searched for something of himself in that room. 'There are a few boxes in the cellar. Pictures, mostly. Some school reports. Toys.'

'Toys?' Kjeld made a face.

'Excuse me, *models*. Whatever it is you used to spend hours putting together.'

Kjeld laughed. It was almost refreshing to know that they could so easily fall back into their old roles. Embrace the patterns that used to make up an almost daily ritual of antagonistic jibes between them. Squabbling siblings. Sara, the dutiful older sister with her entourage of friends, trying out new make-up styles from fashion magazines and managing high marks in her classes without really trying. Kjeld, the quiet troublemaker, building model aircraft while listening to adversarial rock music and summarily proving to be a repetitive disappointment to their father. Decades later and they were still playing their parts in a never-ending performance of familial dysfunction.

Kjeld sat on the edge of the desk and looked across the room at his sister.

'What did he see?' he asked. 'What did he tell you?'

Sara sighed and averted her gaze to the floor. 'He didn't say anything. I was in the kitchen making lunch when Inspector Ek showed up at the door saying Dad called the police.'

'*Gunnar* Ek?' Kjeld asked, surprised.

'The same. He came back to town a few years after the two of you finished police college. He took over from Ulf Arnö when he retired. That must have been seven, maybe eight years ago now.'

'Gunnar never struck me as the type to stick around,' Kjeld said.

'Not everyone was born to hate it here.'

'Not everyone was born with common sense.'

Sara pursed her lips and Kjeld could tell he'd gone too far.

'I'm sorry,' he said. 'Being here just brings back a lot of bad memories.'

'There are good memories, too, Kjeld. If you don't ignore them.'

Kjeld tried to remember the good moments, but he found that they were few and far between. Most of them involved his mother. Kjeld had always been closer to her. Always felt like she understood him better than his father did. And he'd grown up with the distinct impression that his mother expressed a kind of protective nature towards him that she didn't with his sister. Perhaps she recognised that he needed more attention than Sara. That his inarticulate struggles as a young boy with a demanding father required a gentler touch to help him cope with the conflict between himself and his father's expectations. Expectations that he would remain in Varsund, pursue a career in wildlife or forestry like his father, continue the family tradition of caring for the birds, and raise his children to do the same.

And while there had been a time in his life when Kjeld had considered doing all of those things, that time had passed. His father never could quite come to terms with the fact that Kjeld wasn't meant for a simple life in Varsund. That he needed something more. His mother had always understood him. But as much as Kjeld remembered her fondly, the last few years of her life made it difficult for him to forget the animosity between himself and his father. And that was where the understanding had ended.

'What did Gunnar say?'

Sara dropped her arms and rested her hands on her hips. 'He said Dad called the station to report a murder. He claimed to have seen someone fighting in the barn.'

'Who?' Kjeld asked.

'I don't know! Dad didn't know! He just said he saw someone get murdered out there. But Gunnar and two other officers searched all over the property. They didn't find anything. And when we tried to question Dad about it, he got confused.' Sara took a deep breath and exhaled, her lips blowing an exhausted raspberry. 'It's getting to be too much for me. I had to quit my job five years ago just to manage.'

Kjeld frowned. He opened his mouth to apologise, but the words didn't come out.

'I just couldn't do it,' Sara continued. 'Taking care of Dad and taking care of the kids. Tom. Our house. *This* house. Those stupid birds. It's too much. I don't have any time. I don't do anything else.'

Kjeld wanted to be sympathetic. He was ashamed that his sister was going through all of this without his knowledge. If he had been a better brother, he would have supported her more over the years. He might have been more involved and realised that the universe didn't revolve around him and his problems. Or maybe that was just wishful thinking. Kjeld was stubborn and selfish. In that regard he was more like their father than he liked to admit. And even if he had recognised what Sara was doing on her own, he didn't know if he would have done anything different. So resolute was the resentment between him and his father. A resentment that Kjeld thought his father might have been trying to resolve by calling him.

But that wasn't the case.

'Would it be all right if I stayed the night?' Kjeld asked.

'Are you going to behave yourself? Because I'm not joking, Kjeld. I don't want you digging around and bringing up all that bullshit from the past. Dad is ill and I'm tired,' Sara said, her eyes warning him even more than her words.

'I promise to be myself.' He smiled.

'Your better self, I hope,' she replied. 'There are clean sheets in the linen closet. Dinner is at six.'

'Yes, ma'am,' Kjeld teased.

'I'm serious. No digging into the past. Not with Dad.'

Kjeld searched her face for any sign of leniency in that matter. He couldn't promise not to ask questions, after all. Perhaps their father was only imagining things, but Kjeld couldn't get the sound of his voice on the recording out of his mind. Something had happened. Maybe not a murder, but something that caused his father to break his vow never to speak to his son ever again. And Kjeld wanted to know what that something was.

'I'll try to limit my digging to a shovel.'

* * *

26

'Dad, look who's come for dinner,' Sara said, easing Stenar into the chair beside the kitchen window.

Kjeld watched as his father sat down. Despite the extra two inches Stenar had on him, he seemed smaller than Kjeld remembered. The flannel button-up shirt that Sara had dressed him in was at least one size too big and Kjeld could tell from the way the belt was cinched unevenly around his waist that an extra hole had been added. Perhaps two. His hair, once thick and dark, always perfectly parted to one side through excessive abuse of Brylcreem and pomade, had turned thin and grey. Kjeld could see that Sara had tried to comb his hair, but without those greasy tonics it flopped over his forehead, exposing the smattering of rose-coloured age spots on his scalp. When he sat, it was with a hunch that caused him to lean to the left, and the stiffness of his posture made Kjeld wonder if he'd recently had a stroke. Or was having one now.

'Are you okay, Dad?' Kjeld asked.

'He's always a little off balance after his naps,' Sara said, pushing Stenar's chair closer to the table. 'He gets around fine most of the time. Sometimes I catch him out wandering in the woods when he should be in bed. But his shoulder cramps up if he lies on his side for too long.' She tucked a cloth napkin into the front of Stenar's shirt. 'That's why you're supposed to use the extra pillows I got you.'

'The what?' Stenar asked, breaking his stare from the window.

'I said look who came for dinner,' Sara repeated, her voice slower, more succinct.

'Who?' Stenar asked.

'It's me, Dad. It's Kjeld.' Kjeld waited for his father to look in his direction before giving a slight nod of the head.

Kjeld didn't know what he'd expected to see in his father's face. Anger? Scorn? Frustration? Disappointment? When he stormed out twelve years ago it had been with the intention of never returning. Still, he'd sometimes wondered what he would see in his father's eyes if they ever crossed paths again. He imagined countless interactions between them, all full to the brim with hatred and animosity, with years of unresolved tensions and a near-infinite amount of blame. And all of those imagined reunions ended in confrontation. Sometimes verbal. Sometimes physical. It was always an argument that never reached a resolution except the kind of resolution that the men of the Nygaard family were best at: avoidance.

So when Stenar stared back at him, his eyes blank, void of recollection, Kjeld was furious. Furious and disappointed that he'd spent all of those years hating a man who'd forgotten him.

Sara brought the bowl of boiled potatoes to the table and scooped a few onto Stenar's plate.

Stenar looked up at her, his expression suddenly bright and lucid. 'Kjeld is my son.'

'That's right, Dad,' Sara said, returning to the refrigerator for the pickled herring and the sour cream. 'And he's here for dinner.'

Stenar looked at Kjeld. Again that vacant stare. Empty of anger or hatred or disgust. Empty of any emotions. And then, with no seemingly obvious trigger, his brain perhaps latching on to some loose memory of the past prompted by a smell or sound, his mouth broke into a broad smile.

'Kjeld!' he exclaimed. 'Wonderful to see you, boy. How have you been?'

Kjeld hesitated before answering. 'I've been well.'

'Good to hear it,' Stenar said. 'Good to hear it. And work? Work is good?'

'It's steady,' Kjeld replied.

'Good, good.' Stenar removed the napkin from his shirt and placed it in his lap instead.

Sara dished out the herring onto Stenar's plate along with a large spoonful of sour cream and chives.

Stenar picked up his fork and knife and began smearing the herring into the sour cream.

'Should I cut that up for you, Dad?' Sara asked.

'Nonsense, Sara. I'm not a child.' Stenar laughed. Then he stuffed a forkful of potatoes into his mouth.

'Pickled herring for dinner? Really?' Kjeld asked.

'That's all Dad ever wants to eat,' Sara insisted. 'Every time I try to make something else, he refuses to eat it until I add pickled herring to the plate. Meatballs with herring, pancakes with herring. Last week we had pyttipanna with herring.'

'That's ridiculous,' Stenar interrupted. 'Everyone knows pyttipanna is eaten with sausages. Now, your mother, she made the best pyttipanna in all of Jämtland. She used to add silver onions with the gherkins to give it more taste. And she always made the brown sauce from scratch.'

Kjeld filled his plate with potatoes, but held off on the herring. The idea of eating something cold for dinner went entirely against his nature and he didn't want to spend the evening belching up briny fish.

'I don't remember that,' Sara said, frowning. 'Do you remember Mum making her own brown sauce?'

Kjeld shrugged. 'I have no idea.'

'It's true,' Stenar said, slurping up a piece of herring that nearly fell off his fork.

'I'll have to go through the old recipes and see if I can find that brown sauce,' Sara mused out loud, her attention wandering over to the stack of cookbooks that had occupied the counter since before she and Kjeld were born.

Kjeld continued to watch Stenar, wary and uncertain of his father's sudden clarity. A clarity that seemed not to include the fervid bitterness between them. And although it aggravated him that his father didn't return that heated resentment, Stenar's unconscious disconnection to the events that tore their family apart might make it easier for Kjeld to get to the bottom of the bizarre phone call he'd received two days ago.

'Do you remember calling me the other day?' Kjeld asked,

carefully observing Stenar for any kind of reaction that might give away the truth between the confusion.

Sara shot Kjeld a hard look.

Kjeld ignored her.

'Dad? You called me the other day. Do you remember?'

Stenar's gaze drifted from the table to the window. It wasn't fully dark yet, but the security lamp on the front of the barn was already lit. Stenar seemed transfixed by the light as though that hypnotic glow across the untamed field of weedy grass and dead thistle between the house and the barn could imbue him with answers he hadn't yet formed the questions for.

'Dad?'

'It was the birds,' Stenar said, his attention still focused out the window.

Kjeld followed his gaze outside, but didn't see anything more than an unkempt yard and a barn that should have been torn down years ago. 'What about the birds?'

'Kjeld, don't. You're going to confuse him,' Sara said.

'I just drove all the way out here because he picked up the phone and left me a message for the first time in over a decade. And then when I get here you tell me he claims to have seen a murder. I think that's reason enough to try and get him to explain what he saw.' Kjeld glared. Although his relationship with his father had always been difficult, he thought that he and Sara at least had something of an amiable rapport. He wasn't blind to the fact that circumstances put her in an awkward position when it came to balancing their father and himself, but the revelation that she hadn't called him about any of this left him confounded. 'Tell me about the birds, Dad.'

Stenar directed his attention back to Kjeld, a look of honest bewilderment across his face. 'The what?'

'You called me to tell me something about the birds. Something you saw in the barn. Something you didn't want Mum to know. What is it you wanted to tell me?' Kjeld insisted.

Stenar furrowed his brows, staring at Kjeld with an uncontrolled incomprehension. He clearly couldn't remember the conversation.

'What did you see in the barn?' Kjeld said, leaning over the edge of the table in the hope that it might focus Stenar's attention. He could see a thought on his father's face, but Stenar remained silent.

'Kjeld, stop! Leave him alone.' Sara reached over to place a comforting hand on Stenar's arm. 'Are you all right, Dad?'

Stenar jerked his arm away from her, knocking the edge of his plate and spilling his dinner all over his lap. The plate hit the floor with a crash and broke into large jagged pieces. The sound sent Stenar into a panic. He fought against the edge of the table, trying to push out his chair to get away. His foot caught on one of the chair legs and tilted him backwards.

Sara leaped forward and caught the back of Stenar's chair before it could fall.

Kjeld stood up, unprepared for the outburst and uncertain of how to help. He'd never been very skilled at comforting the emotional distress of others. Or himself, for that matter. And the involvement of family only seemed to heighten his discomfort. Nevertheless, at the risk of causing more upset he moved around the edge of the table to offer what little help he could.

But Sara wasn't having it.

'Just stop! Just go away! You're going to make things worse,' she yelled. Then she lowered her voice to a soft, calming tone. 'It's all right, Dad. It's nothing. A plate fell is all. Just relax. I can get you a new plate.'

Stenar shoved her to the side, pushing her into the corner of the table. Then he began to pull at the buttons on his shirt in a disorientated attempt to remove it.

Kjeld took another step forward. 'Let me help, Sara. I can—'

'Get *out*. I said get out!' she yelled, wincing against the searing pain in her hip where the corner of the table stabbed her. She would have a bruise in the morning. 'You've done enough.'

Kjeld backed away, watching the scene unfurl before him as if he were a stranger to the players involved. In a single snap he saw his father go from a normal adult conversation to grunting like a temperamental four-year-old, flailing his arms as though he were drowning. He knew this man, but he didn't recognise him. It occurred to him then that Sara was probably right. Their father hadn't seen anything in the barn. He was just confused, the memories of the past and the present merging into an incongruous mess that his mind couldn't make sense of.

Kjeld walked to the kitchen door and wondered if it was too late now to drive to Mora. He was tired, physically and emotionally. It would be safer to wait until morning, assuming Sara let him stay after their father's outburst. If he left early enough, he could even make it all the way back to Gothenburg before Esme left work to feed his cat.

He was halfway through the door when Stenar broke into tears.

'It wasn't just me,' he said, his face wet and his mouth blubbering as bits of herring caught at the crusty corners of his lips. 'I wasn't the only one who was there. The birds were there. The birds saw everything.'

\* \* \*

What was he doing here?

While Sara tried to calm their father down from his fit, Kjeld went out for a smoke.

It was cool outside, colder than normal for the time of year but certainly not as frigid as the feelings in the family home, although that wasn't saying much. The Norrland weather, not unlike the Nygaards, was just as unpredictable in autumn as it was in summer, and it could turn on a dime. So while it wasn't usually the kind of weather that necessitated a winter coat, Kjeld wished he'd had the foresight to bring a heavier jacket. Just in case. Then again, it probably wouldn't be necessary. He'd all but decided that he'd be heading back to Gothenburg in the morning. Coming home hadn't been the worst decision he'd made in recent months, but it was up there.

Curiosity, however, nagged at him.

He finished two unfiltered cigarettes, burned down almost to his fingertips, before he decided to cross the quiet field to the old barn. When he stepped inside, flipping the switch to light the hanging industrial lamps, he expected to see more signs of recent activity. Aside from a steady path, however, forged into the dirt floor from decades of repetitious behaviour by the bird-crazed men of the Nygaard family, which led from the door to the rookery, there was very little indication that anyone had been in the barn. No one but his father, sister, and the lone officer who could find no trace that something inauspicious had taken place on the property.

Nothing worse than a serious lack of upkeep, that is.

It wasn't one of those massive, commercial-sized buildings meant to service an entire farm as was common in the southern provinces, but it was a decent-sized structure for the north. His great-grandfather had built it after moving to Sweden following the prolific industrialisation of Denmark that demolished much of the natural landscape surrounding the economic epicentres. That's what inspired him to seek the solace of serene isolation in a region that, by measure of its hard-to-reach location and unforgiving winters, promised never to host a population with more than three people per square kilometre. Likewise, that isolation was what inspired him to invest in the birds.

Like the kitchen with its odes to the past in the form of his mother's kitsch salt and pepper shakers, hand-knit potholders, and rose-print valance curtains that probably could have been sold online as retro were they not stained yellow from forty years of his father's cigar smoke, the barn was like a snapshot of an earlier time. On the wall opposite the door hung shovels, rakes, the old hand plough from when the clearing between the house and the barn was a vegetable garden, a pickaxe, a frayed rope looped over a rusty nail, and various other equipment typical of an unused outbuilding. The floor along the edges of the barn was equally dishevelled. A collection of broken pails, rolls of chicken wire, the old outhouse door, the remains of Sara's wooden childhood rabbit hutch, and a heavy dust-collecting tarp that Kjeld knew was covering the engine of his own '78 Saab Turbo, which even without the frame probably still held the record for most speeding tickets in the entire province.

And on the far side of the barn were the birds.

Just thinking about them made him shiver.

At the height of the rookery's capacity there had been at least thirty ravens packed into the back of the barn, but Kjeld's father had always insisted to him that his father before him once had a colony of nearly fifty birds after a particularly prolific mating season with a breed of *Corvus varius* that had travelled east from the Faroe Islands and interbred with the current stock. That was why many of the birds that Kjeld remembered from his youth were less glossy and had distinct whitish coloured feathers at the base of their necks. He remembered being disappointed by that as a young boy, as though that minor morph of colouration somehow ruined the sweeping uniformity of a colony of otherwise near-identical birds. They were smaller than the crows he'd see in the summer foraging along the coast of Hammarstrand where Kjeld often celebrated Midsommar with extended family on his mother's side, and it etched in him an inaccurate assumption that the ravens in the rookery were somehow defective.

It wasn't until much later while he was sitting in a biology lecture at the university that he realised those white feathers weren't a sign of weakness or deficiency, but the result of a very specific genetic drift and allelic mutation in a species that was currently extinct. Perhaps his father's ravens had even been the last of that subspecies, slowly breeding themselves back to the more dominantly homogenous and recognisable shade of black.

34

Now there were little more than a dozen ravens in those nests, most of which were beyond their years, bald patches between their feathers and scruffy plumage denoting their age and aggression towards each other.

They looked just as bad as his father and Kjeld almost laughed at the absurdity of it all. To think he'd once feared these creatures as much as his father's disappointment.

The birds were quiet and placid as Kjeld approached them. He watched as they pruned their feathers on the small wooden perches and shot him sharp, seemingly systematic glances as though expecting him to do something threatening. Only one of the birds kept a consistent gaze on Kjeld as he peered into the rookery. He was a large bird, assertive in appearance, with deep-set eyes and a strong beak that curved into an abnormal hook at the end. He eyed Kjeld like a bouncer at an elite club, paid to keep out the riffraff. But he also had an almost mocking gleam to his expression, as though he knew something that Kjeld did not. Kjeld imagined that cheeky scorn he thought he saw on the bird's face had something to do with the rookery itself; the sole scene of cleanliness in the entire barn. The only thing cared for. The rookery and its sable-hued residents were his father's true pride and joy, after all. Even with Stenar's scattered memory those damn birds still took precedence over his own children. Kjeld knew that. And the large steel-eyed raven knew that too.

Kjeld touched his ear where a scarred indentation broke the curve of his helix and grimaced.

This was a waste of time.

Kjeld's phone buzzed in his pocket, scaring some of the birds nearest the chicken-wire wall into flying back into the nests they'd built in the high corners of the rookery. It was Esme again, insisting for the umpteenth time that he call her back. He texted her a quick message. Something light-hearted but nondescript. Enough to let her know that he was alive. Not enough to let her know when he'd be back.

He was about to leave when the large raven cawed at him. It craned its neck unnaturally and then picked at a mess of dried grass and twigs that made up its nest. As it dug its hooked beak into the debris, a shiny glimmer reflected off a low-hanging light bulb. Kjeld edged closer to the rookery door to get a better look. He squinted his eyes, peering into the shadowy corner of the nest. When that didn't help he tapped the torch button on his phone and shined a bright light onto the spot. Many of the ravens flew to the darker sides of the rookery, but the large bird did not. It held its ground as it rearranged the nest, revealing a single tooth beneath the brush.

A human tooth. With a silver filling.

# Chapter 5

## Torsdag | Thursday

'Goddamn, Nygaard. You got old.'

Kjeld reached over the desk and shook the hand of Gunnar Ek, county police inspector for the north-west district of Jämtland and Kjeld's childhood friend. 'You should try looking in the mirror sometime. At least I've still got all my hair.'

Gunnar laughed and ran his fingers back through his thinning blond thatch.

Kjeld recalled the thick head of hair that Gunnar had during their academy days. It was like something out of a magazine, evenly styled and coiffed to add an inch to his slightly shorter than average height. It hadn't fooled anyone, but it had been a source of pride for the man. Now he had to comb it over to the side just to give the illusion that it wasn't falling out. Except that illusion wasn't working out so well.

'My general practitioner suggested a multivitamin and a biotin supplement, but I just bought a volumising shampoo. It's cheaper and it still gives what hair I have left a glossy shine.' Gunnar smirked. 'And sometimes that's all it takes to get my Tinder matches to swipe right. You'd be surprised how many of the ladies are going for the bald look these days. Maybe I'll shave it all off. It worked for Bruce Willis.'

'Sure it works. In the movies,' Kjeld said.

'Well, we can't all be born with good looks *and* good hair.' Gunnar waved to the chair across from the desk. 'I can't believe you're here. If someone told me that Kjeld Nygaard would be back in Varsund before I reached the age of retirement, I would have eaten my hat.'

'Then you'd have to rely on your comb-over to hide your not-so-secret hair loss,' Kjeld joked, sitting down in the chair across from Gunnar's desk.

'Guess it's a good thing I didn't make that bet then.'

Kjeld chuckled and glanced around Gunnar's office. It was a small room. Simple like the rest of the police station, which was little more than a collection of offices and a two-celled drunk tank extending off the side of the local community centre. On the back wall hung a framed certificate of Gunnar's promotion to county inspector. Beside that were a few pictures of him with friends and local businessmen. The most prominent of the photos was one of him standing between two tuxedo-clad gentlemen at what must have been an awards ceremony, followed by another of him fly-fishing with an older fellow who Kjeld couldn't place, but thought looked familiar. And although it was clear that Gunnar took pride in these images, judged by the thorough dusting over the frames, there was nothing extravagant or particularly noteworthy about the rest of the room. Not like the offices of Kjeld's higher-ups in Gothenburg, which displayed row after row of plaques, supercilious certificates, and the usual rewards for expected bravado. Probably because there was little need for extravagance in a town the size of Varsund. But also because the budget for county police was limited. Nothing ever happened in Varsund, after all. Or, at least, nothing that warranted an official report.

Gunnar sat in the vinyl chair behind the desk and leaned back like he was some kind of local big shot. Kjeld supposed that in a town like Varsund he probably was. But Kjeld remembered Gunnar from childhood and it was hard to reconcile the image he had of the boy who filled the girls' toilets with fresh lobsters as a senior prank with the man shaking hands with Varsund Kommun council members in those photographs. He also felt a thorny unease being in Gunnar's presence. But whether that was brought on by the uncomfortable nostalgia of being in the presence of someone he recognised but didn't really know anymore or by his own reluctance to remember the events that ended their friendship, Kjeld couldn't say. Maybe it would have been easier to talk to Gunnar if he still had that blond pompadour.

'I didn't expect to be here,' Kjeld said.

'This is about your old man, isn't it?' Gunnar asked, reaching across his desk to reposition a heavy glass paperweight a few millimetres to the right.

'He says he saw something out in the barn.'

Gunnar sighed. 'I hate to break it to you, Kjeld, but your dad is not all there. Now we went up there the day he called us. I can't tell you the shock it gave your sister when we showed up on the front porch. She had no idea about any of it. Didn't even know Stenar had called us. But we looked around. Gave the barn and the back half of the yard a good once-over. Couldn't find anything to corroborate what he said he saw.'

'And then?'

'And then we left. What do you want me to say? Someone says they've seen a murder, the very least I would expect to find is some evidence of a struggle. There wasn't anything. Place looked like it hadn't been touched in years.'

Kjeld searched Gunnar's face for any sign of that sarcastic jokester he knew from school, but he didn't see anything. Gunnar was being honest. And why shouldn't he? What did he have to hide aside from the fact that his police skills were rubbish and he was suffering the emasculating effects of male pattern baldness?

'Did he say who he saw in the barn?' Kjeld asked.

Gunnar shook his head. 'Like I said. Your dad isn't all there. Sara used to bring him into town once a week to do some shopping and get a bite to eat at the snack bar, but he lost it on one of the waitresses once and she stopped bringing him.'

Kjeld raised a brow. 'What'd he do?'

Gunnar took a deep breath and breathed out his nose. 'He threw a cup of coffee at her. She got second-degree burns on her arm.'

'Sounds like the coffee was too hot to begin with.'

Gunnar shot Kjeld a cold stare. 'I'm serious, Kjeld. She could have filed a report against him. Could have pressed charges. You can thank Sara she didn't. She agreed to pay for the girl's medical costs. That couldn't have been easy for her.'

Kjeld frowned. 'Why do you say that?'

'Well, Tom got laid off last year. You didn't know? He's been doing some temporary work on and off in Östersund and some work-from-home stuff, but nothing long term. Shit. You didn't know, did you?' Gunnar laughed. 'Damn, you really did cut off all ties when you left.'

'Not all ties,' Kjeld insisted.

'Right,' Gunnar said. 'Just the big ones.'

Kjeld sat forward in his chair and removed a small Ziploc bag from his jacket pocket, placing it on top of the desk beside the paperweight.

'What's this?' Gunnar asked, picking up the bag and eyeing the silver-capped tooth inside.

'I found it in the barn.'

Gunnar stared at him and Kjeld imagined he could see the wheels in his mind turning. Gunnar never did like being proven wrong. It was one of the reasons why he played the role of the big fish in the little pond while Kjeld had worked his way up the ranks in the city. That's how it had always been with the two of them. Friends because they both had similarly shitty childhoods in the same small town, but when it came to the way they approached their professions they couldn't have been more different. Gunnar knew that and Kjeld knew that. And although they'd never said it out loud, it hovered there between them like a neglected wound that had begun to fester.

And then there was that falling-out they'd had during their last term at the police academy, but Kjeld liked to think that was all water under the proverbial bridge by now.

Gunnar shrugged. 'This could be anything. This could be your dad's.'

'It's not,' Kjeld said.

'This isn't enough to prove a murder, Kjeld. You know that.'

'But it is proof that something happened out there. Something brutal enough to knock out a person's tooth.' Kjeld unconsciously raised his voice a few decibels. Not in anger, but sincerity. And while he still wasn't entirely certain that he accepted his father's account that he'd witnessed a murder in the barn, he didn't dismiss the fact that something had happened out there.

'You're making assumptions. Someone could have walked into a pole or a beam. Where did you find this tooth anyway? This might be the sticks, but we know how to inspect a potential crime scene. And we searched that place damn good.' Gunnar's tone also increased, frustrated.

Kjeld lowered his voice, knowing his response carried more doubt than confirmation. 'In one of the raven nests.'

Gunnar snorted. 'Come on, Kjeld. Seriously? Who knows where the hell one of those birds picked that up? That could have come from anywhere.'

'I don't believe it did. I know my father isn't as coherent as he used to be—'

'That's an understatement.'

'But I think it's enough to open an investigation.'

'Well, I can't open a murder investigation on your belief.' Gunnar pushed the plastic bag with the tooth back across the

41

desk. 'And even if I wanted to, I'd need more than just a tooth. I'd need a *body*. Or at the very least someone missing a body. And the only person around here who—' Gunnar cut himself off.

'Is someone missing?'

Gunnar's response took one second longer than it should have. 'You know how it is out here. Out-of-towners sometimes go out in the woods unprepared. There's always someone missing in the national park. And ...'

'And?'

'Well, it's not exactly a missing person's case, but the Drunken Bear did disappear a few years back.'

'The who?'

'Valle Dahl. The old alkie who used to hang around outside the ICA begging for handouts. You remember. He's been around since we were kids.'

Kjeld did remember, but he hadn't thought about the man in years. He'd become something of a joke around Varsund. The kind of person who teenagers liked to tease and mothers shied away from. Kjeld couldn't recall the man ever doing anything wrong. He was just a staple of the community. The kind of person other people tried not to notice because they were either embarrassed that they didn't know how to help or ashamed they didn't try. He was the one person who everyone in town recognised, but no one actually knew. Or so it had always seemed.

'He just left?'

'I suppose so. Didn't notice it myself, if I'm being honest. One day someone just said they hadn't seen the Drunken Bear in a while and that's when we all realised he wasn't around anymore.'

'And no one thought to look into it?'

'Like I said, there haven't been any bodies.'

Kjeld shoved the bag back into his pocket. Then he stood up and made his way towards the door.

Gunnar leaned forward in his chair, resting his forearms on the desk. He looked up at Kjeld with a knowing grin. 'You know we're not all just a bunch of dumb hicks out here. We read the news.'

Kjeld stopped and glanced back at his old friend. 'What's that supposed to mean?'

'You're something of a celebrity, you know. Strange how that situation with the Kattegat Killer went down. I've read all the news articles on it and I can't seem to figure out what happened. There seem to be a lot of holes in that investigation,' Gunnar said, folding his hands together. 'Almost like he got help from someone on the inside.'

Kjeld narrowed his eyes. He could feel the muscles in his right arm tense, fingers clenching into a fist at his side as though waiting for Gunnar to make a formal accusation. One that could warrant a punch to the face.

But Gunnar just gave a smug smirk and shrugged his shoulders. His thin hair rolled to the side and revealed a small bald patch near the crown of his head. 'It's probably just sloppy journalism.'

'Probably,' Kjeld said.

'You gonna drop this?'

Kjeld didn't hesitate. 'No.'

'No body. No evidence. And an unreliable witness. There's nothing to find here, Nygaard.'

This time it was Kjeld's turn to grin, a wry curl of his lips to match the sneer in his eyes. 'Then I guess I'll just have to talk to the more reliable witness.'

Gunnar's expression fell. 'What other witness is that?'

'The bird,' Kjeld said. Then he left.

# Chapter 6

Kjeld was halfway through the front door from his disappointingly unhelpful trip to the police station when Sara started laying into him. She was still angry with him from the night before. By the time she'd calmed their father down from the fit Kjeld had sent him into and put him to bed it was well past midnight and rather than risk waking up her husband and the kids by coming home in the middle of the night, she decided to sleep over. Now she was curt, exhausted, and told Kjeld in as few words as possible that she was going home. And when Kjeld didn't jump to his own defence right away she took out her anger on her coat, pulling up the zipper so hard it nearly snapped.

'You're doing what?'

'I'm taking a break for a few days.'

Sara shoved past her brother and stormed out the front door. Kjeld followed.

The temperature had dropped considerably that morning and had only seemed to get worse as the day went on. The frigid air sent a chill through Kjeld's body. He shoved his hands into the pockets of his jeans and watched as Sara continued down the front steps.

'What does that mean exactly?' he asked.

'It means that I'm taking some time for myself. And for my family. I feel like I spend every waking minute here, Kjeld. I'm tired. I need to recover,' Sara said, shoving the ends of her scarf down the front of her coat. 'And since you're sticking around for a few days I don't see any reason to be here.'

Kjeld continued after her, mentally cursing himself again for not bringing a heavier coat. 'What about Dad?'

'You can take care of him,' Sara replied, crossing the yard to the twisting drive that led away from the house. A thin layer of frost coated the uncut grass.

Kjeld scoffed, a bitter huff of breath that expressed his discomfort better than any honest exchange of words could ever do. She wouldn't leave him alone with their father. She knew that was a recipe for disaster. 'You've got to be kidding.'

'Do I look like I'm kidding?'

Sara fumbled with her key. Her car, an early Nineties model Volvo station wagon that had seen more than its fair share of brutal winters, was parked a short distance from the house. The wheel wells were rusty on both the front and rear panels and there was a layer of mismatched paint on the driver's side door where someone had tried to cover up a scratch. In the back seat was a mess of sports bags and children's toys. The interior was frayed, probably where one of her kids had picked at a small gash in the fabric until it turned into a gaping hole, exposing the yellowing cushion underneath. The disarray told Kjeld more about his sister's state of mind than any of the previous night's argument and he suddenly felt guilty for taking out his frustration on her.

Sara jiggled the key. Eventually she managed to push it into the lock and unlatch the door.

'This damn car,' she muttered, tossing her purse into the passenger seat.

Kjeld caught the door and held it open. 'Are you serious, Sara? I don't know a damn thing about taking care of someone with—'

'With what, Kjeld? Dementia? Yeah, I know. Maybe if you

45

hadn't run off and ignored us you might have learned a thing or two about it.' She climbed into the driver's seat.

'You know that's not fair.'

'*Life* isn't fair. Do you think I enjoy coming out here every day? No, of course not. But he's our dad. That's what you do. A few days won't kill you.'

'That's not what I mean and you know it,' Kjeld insisted.

Sara looked up at him, her gaze only slightly apologetic. 'I've left a list of his medications on the kitchen counter. As well as a schedule for keeping him calm. As long as you don't deviate too much from his normal routine everything should be fine.'

The seatbelt wheezed from overuse as she stretched it across her lap. 'Oh, and don't let him go wandering off into the woods by himself. The mine has been expanding into the northern part of the forest. It's not safe up there.'

Sara tugged on the car door and Kjeld let go to avoid getting his fingers caught. She snorted a laugh as though it were part of a game they'd been playing. A game that had been going on for decades. She turned the key in the ignition and the old Volvo slowly rumbled to life.

'What if he freaks out like he did last night?' Kjeld said through the glass. 'What am I supposed to do then?'

Sara shrugged, putting the clutch in gear. 'If it's too much for you, do what anyone would do in an emergency.'

Kjeld stared at her, anticipating her words before she even said them and knowing he deserved far worse.

'Call the police,' she said. Then she jerked the car into gear and drove off.

\* \* \*

Kjeld strode back into the house, slamming the door shut behind him.

What was Sara thinking leaving him alone with Dad? Was she

46

just doing it to get back at him? He supposed he couldn't blame her. Hell, he might have done the same were he in her position. As siblings they'd always been good at holding grudges against each other. Never anything too deliberate, of course. Just the usual annoyance between a brother and sister that led to a minor reprisal later on. Kjeld's abandonment of the family, however, was more than just a simple aggravation and inconvenience for Sara. His leaving had inadvertently determined both of their futures and Kjeld hadn't exactly said or done anything to redeem himself since he arrived, unwanted and unannounced. So even though he half expected Sara to show up the next morning having given him a taste of his own medicine, he also realised that this might have transcended their normal level of sibling retaliation.

She very well might have plans to leave him there for days on his own.

'Sara? Are you home?' Stenar called out.

Kjeld followed his father's voice into the living room.

'Oh,' Stenar said, looking up from an aviary atlas on Northern European birds. 'It's you.'

There was split second where Kjeld thought he saw something more in his father's eyes. Not simply recollection, but a knowing aggravation he used to harbour whenever Kjeld came home for a visit. A prickling irritation like the one that led to their last argument. The one where they'd both said something unforgivable.

Did his father remember the argument? Kjeld couldn't tell.

'Yeah, it's me,' Kjeld said, slumping into one of the wing-backed armchairs beside the couch.

Stenar turned the page.

'What are you reading?' Kjeld asked.

'The mating displays of *Podiceps cristatus*,' Stenar replied, not looking up from his book.

'Which one is that?'

'The great crested grebe.'

Kjeld couldn't recall what that was.

47

Stenar interpreted Kjeld's silence as ignorance. 'You saw one on that trip to Hässleholm. The one where your sister confused hand lotion with sunscreen.'

Kjeld reached back into his memory, but he was drawing a blank. The irony wasn't lost on him.

'It snatched that fish you caught at Store Damm.'

'Oh! The one with the mohawk?' Kjeld said.

'It's commonly referred to as a crest or a plume.'

'Looked like a mohawk to me.'

Stenar harrumphed, licking the end of his finger to help him turn the next page.

Kjeld watched his father, silently struggling to reconcile his own memories of the man with the person who sat before him. If he hadn't been there the previous evening for his dad's fit he never would have believed that the man was losing his mind. Sitting there on the sofa his father looked as he always did: the consummate researcher whose twigs, flower petals, and precious crows took precedence over his own kin. Seeing Stenar there and knowing that he wasn't the same man he was when Kjeld was growing up, not mentally at least, infuriated Kjeld. Even more so because he knew that any argument with his father would be futile. Stenar wouldn't remember it later. And Kjeld would just be frustrated with himself for allowing an old man to control his feelings.

'How can you remember that?' Kjeld asked.

'What do you mean?' Stenar replied, his attention still focused on the full-colour photographs of the great crested grebe.

Kjeld resisted the urge to raise his voice. 'How can you remember some random bird we saw on holiday when I was eight but not what happened in the barn?'

Stenar stopped reading. He placed his palm on the glossy page of the book, covering an image of a two-egg nest perched in the high grass on the edge of a lake. After a thoughtful pause he closed the book and looked at Kjeld.

'It was your sister's birthday. We were supposed to go up to your uncle's summer cabin that weekend, but your cousin broke her ankle two days before and they stayed in the city. Your mother suggested we go to the south instead. You complained most of the drive there,' Stenar said, his expression staunch. Serious. For him the memory was clear as day.

'And the barn?'

Stenar didn't answer.

Kjeld leaned forward in the chair. 'Come on, Dad. You've got to remember something. Anything.'

Stenar clenched his fingers around the edge of the atlas until his knuckles turned white. His stare was distant but unwavering, his mind searching for an answer in the murky confusion of his memory.

'I went out there and had a look around,' Kjeld continued. 'I found something.'

'You did?' Stenar hesitated.

Kjeld stood up from the chair and sat down on the couch beside his father. He reached into his pocket and removed the plastic bag with the tooth, setting it atop the bird atlas so Stenar could get a better look.

'I need my glasses.' Stenar reached over to the side table to grab his bifocal lenses. Then he picked up the plastic bag and held it close to his eyes, scrutinising the silver-capped tooth inside as he would a small fragment of bone or an unfamiliar leaf found in the wilderness.

'Do you recognise it?' Kjeld asked.

'Should I?'

Kjeld sighed. 'I found it in the rookery. One of the birds was hiding it in its nest.'

'Which one?'

'The big ugly one with the hooked beak.' The one that looked like it would be first in line to peck Kjeld's eyes out if the opportunity ever arose.

49

'Hermod,' Stenar said.

It took Kjeld a moment to realise that his father was referring to the bird and not to the owner of the tooth. 'You named a bird Hermod?'

'No, your mother did.'

Kjeld shook his head in disbelief. 'That would make that bird more than nineteen years old, Dad.'

'Thirty-two,' Stenar insisted. 'The oldest known living *Corvus corax* in the wild was twenty-three years and three months, but researchers at the Tower of London have observed captive ravens living well past the age of forty.'

Stenar handed the bag back to Kjeld.

'Sounds like a cushy life for a bird,' Kjeld said, shoving the bag and the tooth back into his pocket.

Stenar reopened his avian atlas to the section on the great crested grebe. 'If you don't mind giving up the ability to fly.'

'Come again?'

'The Tower ravens all have one flight wing clipped to prevent them from flying away should they accidentally get out. They can fly short distances to perch, but if they were ever to get out in the wild they wouldn't be able to depend on flight for survival.' Stenar removed his glasses. 'But they're treated like royalty. Waited on by servants. Served fresh meat from one of the most expensive butchers in the country. So, I guess it's a matter of perspective. Would you rather live like a king or be able to fly?'

Kjeld didn't know how to respond. His father's clarity both discouraged and frustrated him. He remembered reading once that patients with dementia could often times speak just as coherently as any other person, leading to so many late diagnoses of Alzheimer's. Apparently, it was easier on the family members to convince themselves that their ageing parent was simply absent-minded than to believe that they were suffering from a debilitating mental disease. But that didn't lessen Kjeld's feelings of being stonewalled in his attempts to discover what it was his father saw.

Assuming he had seen anything. The only thing that was clear was that Stenar's passion for birds was one of those topics that solidified him in the moment.

Then again, birds were less complicated than people. And it made Kjeld wonder what his own brain would latch on to when he was old and his memory began to erode. He could only hope it was something as intellectual as ornithological behaviour and lifespans, but with his luck it would probably be the nutritional content of his cat's preferred brands of cat food or useless trivia picked up from old episodes of *Jeopardy*.

'Where would Hermod find a tooth?'

Stenar kept his eyes on the page. He looked as though he were reading the same sentence over and over again. 'Where do they find anything?'

'In the barn?'

'I don't let them out as much as I used to. Sara doesn't like to help with the birds. She's waiting for us to die.'

Kjeld gave Stenar a quizzical look. That struck him as an odd thing to say, but according to the websites Kjeld had skimmed in bed the night before, it wasn't uncommon for people with dementia to make misplaced comments. His dad probably didn't even know what he was saying. Nor did he realise how hurtful his words might have sounded.

'That's not true, Dad.' Kjeld felt his phone vibrate against his thigh. He glanced down to see another message notification from Esme. He would call her back soon. 'Sara is just stressed out. She's always been highly strung.'

Stenar's expression clouded over. 'She didn't get that from your mother.'

'I guess not.'

'Your mother was always very calm,' Stenar said.

'I think she had to be.'

The antique Mora clock on the opposite wall ticked away the seconds, the weight-driven pendulum swinging from one side to the other within the rounded longcase. It was hand-painted a light green, which had faded and cracked over the years, embellished with gold. The tall floor-standing clock had been given to his mother as a wedding gift and it struck Kjeld as being the only feminine object in the room. Like his mother had been, its presence was almost entirely unnoticed until the room was silent.

'Did you know that female great crested grebes usually only lay two eggs?' Stenar asked, removing a handkerchief from his shirt pocket to blow his nose.

'I don't think I know anything about them except that they have plumes,' Kjeld said.

'There's too much competition in the clutch if they have more than two hatchlings. After they hatch, the parent grebes, both the male and female, will identify which of the hatchlings is their favourite and they'll care for that single hatchling alone. They focus all of their attention on that individual hatchling, feeding it and teaching it everything it needs to know to survive to adulthood. So, in a clutch of more than two eggs, the others very often don't make it.'

Kjeld craved a cigarette. His phone buzzed in his pocket again. This time he didn't look to see who it was. 'What if the parents have the same favourite?'

Stenar raised his gaze from the book to stare at Kjeld. His brows lowered, causing the lines around his eyes to deepen. 'Then that chick has to wait until the other is fed and satiated.'

'And then?'

'And then hope that the parents haven't forgotten about him.'

# Chapter 7

The conversation with his father left Kjeld confused. He needed someone to confide in. Someone outside of the situation who could help him see past his own anger and biases. When he looked at his phone he realised he had a voicemail from Bengt and he briefly considered calling him. Bengt always had the ability to see through Kjeld's problems, perhaps because he'd spent so many years working through them. But helping Kjeld come to his senses wasn't Bengt's job anymore. That was a commitment he'd quickly and rightfully relinquished when they separated. Besides, all of their recent conversations had turned into arguments. And the last thing Kjeld needed was another squabble that went unresolved.

Kjeld scrolled to his recent calls and tapped the name at the top. The minute he heard Esme's voice bellowing on the other end of the line, loud enough for Kjeld to hear her clearly while holding the phone at arm's length from his ear, he regretted calling at all.

'Do you realise that I've been trying to get ahold of you for two days? Seriously, you can't even respond to your texts? Where are you?' she asked.

Kjeld could hear in her tone that she didn't expect him to give her an honest reply.

'I'm in Varsund.'

'Where the hell is Varsund?'

'Jämtland.'

'Jämtland?' Esme said in disbelief. 'What in the world could possibly be going on in Jämtland?'

'I had a family emergency,' Kjeld said. He sat down on the edge of the bed in the room that used to be his but wasn't anymore.

There was a pause on the other end of the line and Kjeld imagined that Esme was trying to determine whether or not he was being truthful. In the background he heard the sound of a dish being set on the counter.

'Is it Tove?' Esme's voice lowered. 'Is she all right? Did something happen?'

Kjeld rarely spoke about his private life with his colleagues, but Esme was the exception. It was therefore no surprise to him that her first thoughts would go to his daughter. For a while, before things soured between him and Bengt, Esme had spent a lot of time with Tove. In that almost hazy memory of the past before Kjeld had irreparably ruined the situation between him and his husband, Esme had become a sort of honorary aunt, always around to ease the tension. The four of them would picnic in Kungsparken or wander through the greenhouses of the botanical gardens where Kjeld would try to recall the scientific names of the northern plants he'd learned in his youth. His success rate seemed to diminish exponentially with each passing year.

Once, while Kjeld and Bengt were at an appointment with a marital counsellor, Esme took Tove to Liseberg. They rode the carousel so many times that Esme had gotten sick and spent half the afternoon lying in the grass while Tove stuffed her face with peppermint sticks and scared other children in the house of mirrors. To this day Tove still claimed that it was the best day of her life. Kjeld didn't have the heart to tell her that was the day he and Bengt decided to separate.

'Tove's fine. It's my dad.'

'Your dad?' Esme hesitated as though she were unsure of what to say. 'I didn't know your dad was still alive.'

'His health isn't that good. He has Alzheimer's. Sometimes he's clear as day and sometimes it's like talking to a brick wall. We haven't spoken in a long time. Too long, probably. And then he called me out of the blue the other day and I just had to come up here to see what was going on.'

'I'm sorry, Kjeld. I— Well, I honestly thought you'd just bailed on me because of what happened with the case. I didn't realise.'

Kjeld could hear the sound of water running from a tap on her end, but it was quickly cut off by another clinking of a dish. 'No, I should have called you. I should have told you. I just couldn't deal with anyone from work. And the thing with my dad—'

The stairs creaked as someone reached the top stop. Kjeld felt a surge of that age-old instinctual worry bred into all teenage boys that their parents might hear what they were saying in confidence to their friends. Not unlike the persistent and sometimes irrational fear from his adolescence that his father might walk in on him while he was looking through that conspicuously hidden box of magazines he kept under his bed. But then he realised he didn't cut himself off because he was concerned that Stenar might hear what he was saying. Kjeld was listening to make sure he made it safely to the top step. He counted the creaks of the old wooden floorboard until he knew Stenar was on the landing.

'Kjeld?' Esme's voice interrupted his thoughts.

'Sorry. There's something odd going on here, but I can't tell if it's something real or if it's just me looking for something to explain all the shit that I remember about this place.'

'What's odd? Your dad's health?' Esme asked. A cat meowed in the background.

'He called the police last week because he thought he saw a murder on his property.'

'You're kidding.'

'I wish I were. Anyway, the local police checked everything

out, but they couldn't find anything. Dad called me, rambling, and I didn't know what to think. So, I just drove up here,' Kjeld said, realising how ridiculous the entire thing sounded when he said it out loud.

'And? Do you think he really witnessed a murder?'

Did he? It was no secret in the Nygaard family that Kjeld had never gotten along with his father, but as far as he knew his father had never lied to him. And although Kjeld recognised that dementia could cause Stenar to say things that weren't true or were skewed by inaccurate recollection, he didn't feel like this was some kind of fabrication. It wasn't an intentional lie. Kjeld believed that his father's insistence on having seen something was based on an event that actually occurred. What that event was, however, Kjeld couldn't say.

'I think he saw something. Something that affected him enough to reach out to me despite our differences.' Kjeld let out an audible exhalation as he stared at the dried remnants of sticky tack over his bed that used to hold up his music posters. 'To be honest, I don't know what to think. I know it's insane, but I can't help but feel like there's something more going on here. I found something, too. It's probably nothing. A fluke or a coincidence. But things just don't seem right.'

'What did you find?' Esme asked.

'A human tooth.'

'What the hell, Kjeld? Have you taken this to the local police?'

'I did, but I've got history with the guy in charge here and he's none too pleased to see me.'

Esme paused and Kjeld assumed she was carefully thinking through her response. She'd always been more cautious of the words she used, which had saved them in numerous interview sessions over their years of working together. Esme had a knack for reaching out to people and for knowing when they wanted to say more than they did. In the beginning it had been a problem for Kjeld, who preferred doing things his own way. A way that

56

normally involved taking a big leap without looking to see if there was sturdy ground to land on. But they'd both learned to find a balance between each other. Now she was not only his most trusted colleague, but his best friend as well.

After a lengthy silence she asked, 'Are you okay?'

'Yeah,' Kjeld replied. 'Being here is just more difficult than I remembered.'

'Look, I have to meet with the chief tomorrow to talk about my report on the Aubuchon investigation. The media has turned this thing into a monster. Now that Nils is well enough to go to trial, the prosecution is trying to fast-track the case. Meanwhile the defence is arguing to get the date pushed back on the grounds that some piece of paper wasn't filed properly or something. But if you want me to come up there, I will.'

'Thanks, Esme, but I don't think I'm going to be here much longer. Unless my dad can tell me something more, I'm at a dead end.' A dead end that not only included his father's unprovable memory, but their relationship as well.

'Just let me know if things change and you want me to— Shit!' Esme said.

'What is it?' Kjeld asked, holding the phone further from his ear.

'I just cut myself.'

'Cut yourself?'

'I sliced my finger on a can,' she said. She breathed a heavy sigh into the phone, muddling the sound of a wince as she ran the cut under the tap.

'What are you doing?'

'What do you think I'm doing?' she said. 'Trying to feed your damn cat.'

# Chapter 8

## Fredag | Friday

Erik Norberg, private lawyer for the Lindqvist family for going on forty years, watched as Roland reread the document. It was an official request for a declaratory judgement of death in absentia for one Peter Lindqvist. Legally there was precedent, but Erik couldn't help but feel a sense of betrayal when he wrote up the request. It didn't seem right. Not without a more thorough investigation into Peter's last communications. But Roland had insisted. And whether Peter was actually dead or just off the grid, didn't really matter. His absence was enough to prove him incapable of performing his corporate duties under Norrmalm's company guidelines.

'I just sign here?' Roland asked.

'And initial on the first page,' Erik said.

Roland scrawled his signature across the bottom of the document, clicked his pen, and pushed the papers across the desk.

Erik removed a stamp and ink pad from a drawer. 'You're sure you want to go through with this?'

'If I'm not sure now then I will be after we secure this merger with MineCorp,' Roland said, glancing down at his watch.

Erik hesitated. 'What if he shows up after this?'

Roland sent him an admonishing glare. 'Then I'll split my half with him as I'm legally obligated to do.'

Erik nodded his head. The law was very particular when it came to estates. Both Roland and Peter had inherited Norrmalm Industries upon their father's death, giving them each half of the company, an even fifty-fifty. If Peter had had any children, his half would have then passed on to them. But since he had no children, his share would revert to the next closest living family member: Roland.

'And you're sure you want to sell it?' Erik asked, rolling the stamp over the ink pad. 'Norrmalm has been in your family for—'

'Generations,' Roland finished. 'I know. But the future isn't in mining. I don't want it. My kids don't want it. And if Peter wanted it then he'd be here, but he isn't. Besides, there won't be another deal like this.'

Erik glanced down at the document, swallowed his shame, and pressed the stamp over Roland's signature. Then he signed in the witness box.

'I'd offer my congratulations, but it doesn't feel right.'

Roland reached over for the whisky decanter on the edge of Erik's desk and poured them both a glass. 'Don't worry. It'll feel better after you get paid.'

* * *

The darkness was deceiving. It stretched on disproportionate to the day, distorting a person's sense of time and reality. Scientists claimed it was something a man could get used to, but Roland had spent much of his life in Varsund and it still felt unnatural. The human condition was not made for long nights and short days.

Roland stood on the wraparound porch that he and Peter had built after Roland's daughter was born. Although they'd each had legal share to half the house, Peter had moved out shortly after his wife passed, leaving it to Roland and his family. He stared out into the pitch-black forest. It was uncommonly cold and he feared that winter would be longer and harder this year than was expected. That was always a burden on Norrmalm Industries. While the industrial aspects of mining didn't change much in the winter months, the persistent cover of darkness and the bone-chilling temperatures were hard on the workers. Not the people in the office, who curled up in their cubicles continuing their easy day-to-day chores and checklists, but the employees who worked on site. The miners, labourers, foremen. The people who braced themselves against the weather conditions, no matter how unpleasant, and earned their paycheques with each physically and mentally exerting task set upon them. And with little complaint.

Granted, Swedish labour laws were some of the best in the world. But that didn't change the fact that the work was hard. Arduous. Roland remembered working alongside the miners as a young man. Sweating, swearing, spending the evenings soaking his muscles in the bath to ensure they wouldn't be too tight and wooden to continue the next morning. His father had insisted that he and Peter understand the physical energy and mental fortitude that went into the job so that when they were in charge they would know on whose backs the company was upheld.

Roland never insisted that his children go through the same process and he regretted it. Particularly with his son, David. He blamed himself for their selfishness, their ego and their entitle-ment. He should have been stricter like his father. Like Peter.

He puffed on a cigar, watching as the end glowed a hazy amber hue before darkening. The air outside was crisp, biting, and he knew he wouldn't be able to stand out there much longer, but he enjoyed the solitude. He'd never been the social butterfly that Peter was. He didn't have that same knack for drawing people in and captivating their attentions. Peter had always been the life of the party, with his charming smile and plethora of waiting compli-ments, while Roland was the more introverted, practical-minded brother. He preferred being in the background, which was why he'd been so furious with Peter when he decided to leave. Roland was never meant to lead a company. If given a choice, he probably would have preferred working alongside the miners as opposed to sitting in on budget meetings. But that's not how things turned out. And it didn't matter anymore. He'd inherited the company and now he was about to give it away.

Although he secretly wished that Peter had been around to make that decision for him.

*Damn you, Peter.*

His phone jingled the familiar email tone and he opened his inbox expecting to see an invoice from Erik Norberg. What he saw, however, left him speechless.

Roland set the cigar on the railing so he could hold the phone with both hands. His eyes squinted at the bright shine of the screen. He must have read the name of the sender and the title of the email five times before he opened it. And even then he couldn't believe it. It was impossible.

Less than four hours after Roland had proclaimed him dead, Peter decided to make contact.

# Chapter 9

The house was suffocating and Kjeld needed space to breathe. He needed to escape the overwhelming sensation of being smothered by the past and by his father's unintentional reminders that Kjeld had failed him as a son. Kjeld did feel a pang of guilt as he headed out of the house, leaving his father on his own, but that guilt was nothing compared to the anger he kept close to his chest. Anger that he needed to vent before he said something he would really regret.

The Gruva was the only pub in Varsund and it wasn't even a good one. It was dirty, the floor permanently stained orange from the copper dust that the miners trucked in on their boots, and the walls were coated in cigarette smoke even behind the corners where the paper began to peel. The beer was watered down, probably past date, and the only thing they served in bottles was a cheap Polish brand that was well known for smelling like cat piss. But it was the only joint open after eleven o'clock except for the bowling alley and after spending two hours trying to get his dad to go to sleep Kjeld didn't want to deal with that crowd. He had enough stressors as it was without adding the irritating combination of bored teenagers and the din of crashing pins.

Kjeld sipped his beer and winced at the taste. Flat.

He took out his phone and played the message from Bengt that he'd been ignoring since yesterday.

'Kjeld, I seriously need you to answer my calls. There have been reporters outside of Tove's school all week trying to get a sound clip about you and – I can't even fuckin' say his name – the goddamn Kattegat Killer. So stupid. Honestly, the media makes him sound like a villain in a comic book.' Bengt sighed. The sound was probably louder than intentional, but it felt like he was blowing in Kjeld's ear. 'Please call me. Talk to Tove. She misses you. And if you can do anything to get these vultures off our backs … Yeah, that's all I wanted to say.'

Kjeld clicked off the voicemail without deleting the message. He took another sip of beer. Somehow it tasted worse the second time around.

'A little bird said you were in town, but I didn't believe it.'

Kjeld looked up from his beer to the woman on the stool beside him.

The woman crossed her legs and rested her elbow on the countertop. She was dressed in a black turtleneck and a pair of light-coloured form-fitting jeans that tapered to the ankles. The outfit was flattering but practical, aside from the high-arched cheetah-print heels, which while adding a playfulness to her appearance did not seem sensible for the time of year. Then again, Kjeld made the drive to Varsund without a coat, so he wasn't the best judge of sensible clothing. She was tall, probably nearing his own height, although it was difficult to tell while she was seated. Her hair, tight and curly in a style that reminded him of the late Eighties, was free around her dark face and it bounced when she tilted her head to the side to return his intrusive stare. She wasn't old, but she looked much younger than she was thanks to the delicate application of contour and blush around her cheeks, which provided her otherwise round face with a more angular dimension. Her lashes were fake, but not overbearing, and her eyeliner drew out to thin points beyond her lids, giving her eyes a cat-like appearance. Compared to the rest of the bar's patrons, who consisted mainly of smudge-faced miners wasting their paycheques on enough cheap swill to leave them hungover until the Monday morning whistle, she was overdressed. She leaned forward over the counter and snatched a thin straw from behind the bar. Kjeld was certain he knew her, but her name escaped him.

'I scarcely believe it myself,' he said, bringing the beer to his lips in a small sip. 'Do I know this little bird you're speaking of?'

The oddly familiar woman placed the straw into the glass of her negroni, stirring the ice around the orange peel. Then she nodded to a group of three ladies sitting at a corner table, cheering on a pot-bellied man with a bushy blond beard who was drunkenly trying to hit a dartboard mounted on the wall. His aim wasn't even close.

'Is that Camilla Aaberg?' Kjeld could hardly believe his eyes. Camilla had been a close friend of his sister's when they were younger and was considered, by most of the boys in Kjeld's class, to be a looker. She was bigger than he remembered, pear-shaped, and her hair was dyed a shade of red that looked more plum in the yellow fluorescent lighting. Her roots were showing on her scalp. And if it weren't for that abrasive laugh, Kjeld might not have recognised her.

'The witch cackle gave her away, didn't it?' The woman smirked. 'And that's Stina Carlson, Jenny Frisk, and the impressive dart-thrower over there is Åke Hjorth.'

'No.' Kjeld's jaw dropped. 'Seriously? That guy was *the* athlete in school. Everyone said he was a shoo-in for the national football team. Wasn't he scouted?'

'Yeah, but he threw his back out in the first year of training. Never healed properly. Came back home. Started drinking. You know how it goes.'

Kjeld did know. Varsund was like a black hole. A stagnant place that was reluctant to change. It was almost a time-honoured tradition to return to Varsund after failing to make it in the world beyond that insignificant blip of a town. Kjeld only hoped that when it came to trying to make a successful life outside of his hometown that he would be the exception to the rule. He would never survive returning to Varsund permanently.

Kjeld watched the woman beside him as she shook her head at the group on the other side of the room. Her name was on the tip of his tongue.

'We dated in high school, you know.'

Kjeld laughed. 'I think I would remember if I'd dated you.'

She continued to stir the straw in the drink, the ice cubes clinking against the sides of the glass. 'Well maybe making out behind the ticket booth of the spring fair doesn't exactly count as dating, but it certainly left an impression.'

Kjeld set his glass down on the counter, brows furrowing together near the centre of his forehead, and looked at her again. Then it hit him. 'Hanna? Hanna Eklund?'

'Have I changed so much?' She took a sip of her drink, leaving a lipstick print on the edge of the glass.

'No,' Kjeld said, shaking his head. 'Well, if I'm being honest you're—'

'Slimmer?' Hanna interrupted.

'I was going to say taller than I remember.'

Hanna tucked a chunk of curls behind her ear. 'It's okay to say it. I was fat.'

'I wouldn't say fat.'

'Heavy, then.'

'Not heavy.'

'Are you kidding? I was twice the size I am now.' Hanna scoffed.

'I guess I didn't notice,' Kjeld replied.

'Plump. Chubby.'

'Built.'

Hanna threw her head back and laughed. It was a nice sound. It was more familiar to Kjeld than her appearance, although now

65

that he had a name to go with the face, he was beginning to see a reflection of the girl he'd once known.

'If that isn't a diplomatic way of putting it then I don't know what is,' Hanna said, raising her glass towards Kjeld's beer. 'Skål.'

'Skål,' Kjeld toasted.

Hanna puckered her lips and dabbed her fingers against them, wiping away a few drops of the drink that missed her mouth in an attempt to preserve her lipstick. Kjeld had the impression that she was doing it intentionally to keep his attention, but he was probably off the mark.

'How long has it been?' he asked.

'Since high school or since the spring fair?'

'Either. Both.'

The bartender came by and placed a bowl of nuts on the counter between their drinks.

'Oh, goodness. Who knows anymore? I try not to think about it,' she said, waving her hand in the air. 'It just makes me feel old.'

'Well, you look great,' Kjeld said. He picked through the bowl of nuts until he found a cashew and tossed it in his mouth.

'You're not looking so bad yourself. Filled out a bit more in the chest, I see. Not that you were in bad shape back in school, but you were kind of skinny.'

'I had ridiculous aspirations of playing for IFK Göteborg.'

'Göteborg? Boo. Malmö FF forever.'

'You're not just saying that because they always win, are you?'

'Are you kidding?' Hanna reached over and took a handful of nuts from the bowl. 'I'm just saying that because they always have the best-looking players. I watch for the aesthetic, not for the score.'

'I guess it could be worse.'

'You're right. You could have said you were a Helsingborg fan.'

Kjeld snorted. 'I wouldn't dream of it.'

'Good,' Hanna said. 'Then at least we share that in common.'

'At least,' Kjeld said, wondering what else they might have in common. He needed a distraction from the last few days. That was the main reason why he was malingering in Varsund's only pub, after all. Home had too many memories that he wasn't ready to face. And if anything, having a moment away from his father gave him the opportunity to collect his thoughts and cool his temper. It might save him from saying something he would regret for another twelve years. Maybe longer.

Hanna finished her drink and waved the bartender over for another. When he looked at Kjeld, Kjeld shook his head. One was enough. Besides, he had to make the drive back to his dad's house and those winding roads were unforgiving in the dark.

'So, what are you doing here anyway?' Hanna asked, fetching herself a new straw from behind the bar for her drink.

'Here at Gruva or in Varsund?'

'I forgot you thought you were something of a wise guy. Looks like some things never change.'

'Just looking in on family.' Kjeld sipped at his beer. He should have ordered something from a bottle.

'Your sister?'

'My dad. Sara, too, I suppose. Can't really come to Varsund and not run into everyone.'

'Ain't that the truth.' Hanna nodded. 'I see her in town sometimes. She always looks like she's tackling all the world's problems at the same time.'

'Kids'll do that to you.'

'Oh, I don't know. I don't let mine run me ragged.'

'You've got kids?' Kjeld asked. He couldn't say exactly why he was surprised by the fact that she had children. Maybe it was just his memories of her as a teenager that conflicted with Kjeld's image of motherhood. Or maybe he just had difficulty imagining the people from his past as anything other than what they were in his memories. Figures frozen in time and place. 'I thought only models and movie stars got figures like that after kids.'

'Models, movie stars, and anyone willing to spend their

'alimony on a personal trainer instead of a new house.' She paused as though she didn't find her own joke very amusing.

'Whatever works,' Kjeld said. 'How many kids do you have?'

'Two incredibly headstrong boys. But they spend most of their time with their father in Örebro.' She raised her left hand and wiggled her fingers, making the absence of a ring impossible to miss. 'Which is fine by me. The schools are better down there anyway. I get them every other weekend and during the summer holidays.'

'How old are they?'

'Fourteen and seventeen. Which means they aren't interested in what their mum has to say anyway,' Hanna said. Kjeld couldn't help but notice a hint of bitterness in her tone.

'I have a daughter,' Kjeld admitted after a pause. 'She'll be turning seven next year. But her dad and I have been on the outs almost since the day she was born.'

'Her dad?' Hanna raised her brows over the brim of her glass. 'Don't tell me you're playing for the other team now.'

Kjeld grinned. 'I wouldn't dream of taking sides.'

Hanna laughed and the corner of her lip turned upward into a more interested smile. Kjeld imagined he'd said something right.

She took a sip. 'It's a tough game, marriage. You won't catch me signing up for that again. From now on I'm keeping it simple.'

'Performing one night only?'

'I'd consider making an exception for IFK Göteborg's next goalkeeper.' She winked.

'Centre midfielder,' Kjeld corrected.

'See, now we've got a problem. I like to watch the players dive for the ball.' Hanna stared at him, breaking eye contact only to blink.

A rush of heat seeped through Kjeld's cheeks, causing his pale skin to flare a reddish hue. 'I probably can't run the length of a field anymore anyway. Suppose I could try a different position.'

'I don't know if I believe that. Rumour has it you're quite the experienced policeman these days. Or are we supposed to say police officer?'

'I prefer detective or inspector.'

'Isn't running part of a detective's job description?'

Kjeld grinned. 'Honestly, I'm probably due for a physical.'

'If I didn't know better, I'd say you've become more agreeable in your old age.'

'Not too agreeable, I hope.'

'I guess that remains to be seen.'

To say Kjeld was relieved to have come across someone who didn't make him feel like his youth had been nothing but gloom and disappointment was an understatement. Hanna was easy to connect with. It was unfortunate he hadn't been secure enough in himself when he was younger to recognise that. If he hadn't been so desperate to escape Varsund he might have made a life-long friend in her.

Kjeld finished his beer and placed a few hundred-kronor bills on the counter for both their drinks. He stood up from the stool and pulled on his jacket, nodding his head to the door. 'You wanna go out for a smoke?'

Hanna glanced back to the trio of women drinking and laughing. Åke had given up on darts and was trying to impress them by chugging a pint of beer.

'Unless you have to get back to the gossip party,' Kjeld said.

Hanna stood up, grabbing her coat and purse off the stool beside her. 'I'd rather catch up with an old friend.'

'I'm glad to hear that.' Kjeld smiled. He motioned towards the exit. 'After you.'

# Chapter 10

## Lördag | Saturday

Kjeld stood on the APM Terminals port in Gothenburg, facing off against Nils Hedin, his good friend and the recently outed Kattegat Killer. They were surrounded by countless rows of stacked shipping containers. The company names – Scania, Maersk, CNA – were painted over with haphazard graffiti tags and dimly illuminated by the security lamps. They looked more like angry street art and menacing shadows than corporate logos. Kjeld held his breath as the sweat trickled down the back of his neck and puddled beneath his collar, leaving a damp cold spot. His grip tensed on his service weapon as he waited for Nils, posed to shoot with a steadier hand than his own, to make the first move. Esme shouted behind him. A gun went off.

A metallic crash jolted Kjeld awake.

He sat up, his head woozy from the night before, and looked down at the figure beside him. He had a vague recollection of being a teenager again. Driving down to the only late-night service station in the county, buying a pack of low-alcohol beer – discount German weizenbock – and a few bottles of pear cider, laughing as Hanna sang along to the radio as it played the pop classics of the early Nineties, and struggling to make love in a single bed.

Hanna rolled over onto her side. The sheets slipped down from her shoulder to expose her naked skin. It looked even smoother than he remembered last night. She mumbled something in her sleep.

Kjeld crawled out of bed. His body ached from trying to make love like he was twenty years old and from the unconscious politeness of giving Hanna more of the small mattress so she could rest easier. His back cracked as he pulled on his jeans. He picked up the shirt he was wearing yesterday from the floor, sniffed the armpits, decided it was too rank for breakfast, and stretched a hooded sweatshirt over his head instead. Then he went downstairs, careful to walk on the right side of the staircase so the steps wouldn't creak.

Stenar stood in the kitchen wearing nothing but a pair of long thermal underpants and an untied robe. On the floor was a large cast-iron pan and two broken eggs.

'What the hell, Dad?'

'I wanted eggs,' Stenar said.

Kjeld stepped around the eggshells and picked up the pan, setting it on the stovetop.

'I just wanted eggs,' Stenar said.

'I know, Dad. It's fine,' Kjeld replied, grabbing a roll of paper towels from the counter. 'Just have a seat. I'll make you some eggs.'

Stenar walked over to the window, stepping into some of the splattered egg yolk with his slippers and dragging it across the kitchen floor.

Kjeld sighed.

'Where's Sara? Sara should be here.'

Kjeld bent down and began wiping up the egg from the floor. 'We've had this conversation, Dad. Sara's taking a break. She's spending time with the kids.'

Stenar continued to stare out the window and into the yard,

71

where a fine layer of snow covered the ground. It wasn't fully light out. It wouldn't be until midday. But there was a hazy morning glow that peeked through the trees and caused the unbroken snow to shimmer. In the distance a chorus of cawing rang out from the barn.

Kjeld wasn't used to the shorter days. While Gothenburg also saw a shift towards darkness in the winter months, it was never quite as pervasive as in the north. He'd forgotten how gloomy it could be. Even the snow, which was far too early in the season to be sticking to the ground, felt foreboding. He missed the faithfulness of the rain in Gothenburg. It was much more predictable.

'I need to feed the birds,' Stenar said.

'The birds can wait, Dad. Just sit down.'

'No, I have to go out there. They're waiting for me.'

Kjeld tossed the paper towels in the waste basket and washed his hands in the sink.

Stenar made his way to the door, slippers smearing a path of raw egg across the space that Kjeld had just cleaned up.

'For Chrissakes, Dad!'

'I can make eggs,' said a voice from the doorway.

Kjeld glanced over at Hanna who leaned against the entranceway. She wore one of his clean undershirts, the few that he'd brought with him, paired with her jeans from the night before.

Stenar, on the other hand, didn't seem to notice anything peculiar in an unfamiliar woman standing in his kitchen. Perhaps he thought she was Sara or Mum. Maybe he didn't notice her at all. Kjeld had trouble keeping up with his father's manic recollection.

'Don't worry about it. I can make eggs,' Kjeld insisted. 'Dad, this is Hanna. Hanna, Dad.'

'How do you like your eggs?' Hanna asked, as she helped Stenar into a chair at the table. 'Over easy? Scrambled? You look like an over-easy man to me.'

Stenar smiled. 'I like the way Sara makes them.'

'How does Sara make them?' Hanna asked.

Kjeld ruffled through a pile of papers beside the bread box. 'Sara said there was a list here with instructions.'

The cawing of the ravens in the barn began to increase and Stenar's attention was once again drawn out the window.

Hanna walked over to the counter, leafing through the pages that Sara left while Kjeld wet a rag in the sink to clean the floor with.

'Wow,' Hanna said, skimming over the checklist. 'Someone is organised.'

'Yeah, tell me about it,' Kjeld groaned, wiping up the last of the egg that Stenar had dragged across the floor. He'd deal with the slippers later.

'Over easy! I knew it. It's like a sixth sense I have.'

'A sixth sense about eggs?' Kjeld scoffed.

'You tell me, Mister Hard-Boiled.' Hanna smirked.

'Stick to the egg fortune telling. Your *yolks* need a little work.'

Hanna winced at Kjeld's bad play-on-words and then blew him a mocking kiss before taking the butter dish out of the refrigerator and setting it on the counter. Then she sat down at the table beside Stenar.

'I need to feed the birds,' Stenar said.

'I heard a bunch of birds when I was in the bathroom. They sounded kind of agitated,' Hanna said.

'They're always agitated.' Kjeld set a plate of crisp bread on the table.

Hanna immediately proceeded to dip a knife into the butter dish and spread it across a piece of crisp bread for Stenar.

Kjeld cracked two eggs into the pan. He idly recalled that Bengt and his mother had both been able to crack an egg with one hand. He'd never managed to learn how to do that.

The eggs sputtered and sizzled in the melted butter and Kjeld turned down the heat.

'Would you like some coffee?' Hanna asked Stenar.

Stenar's empty gaze didn't drift from the window.

When he didn't hear a response, Kjeld turned his head. 'Dad? Coffee?'

'There's someone in the barn,' Stenar replied.

'What?' Kjeld stepped over to the window and stared out towards the barn.

'He's right,' Hanna said. 'I think I see something.'

At first he didn't see anything. Nothing but an unmarred stretch of fresh snow and the shadow of the birch trees reaching out over the old red building that housed the rookery and years of collected junk. Then the shadows changed. The door was open.

'I'll be damned,' Kjeld muttered.

'What if they let out the birds?' Stenar stood on shaky legs. 'They're not fit to be let out.'

Kjeld rushed to the door, slipped on his boots, and headed out into the yard.

\* \* \*

The biting chill of the air stung his face and Kjeld immediately regretted not grabbing his dad's heavy work coat on his way out the door. His boots crunched against the snow, which had partially frozen over, leaving a thin tier of ice crystals between his tread and the hard ground underneath. He pulled his hood over his head and wrapped his arms around his chest as he crossed the stretch of land between the house and the barn. He could feel the expectant eyes of Hanna and his father watching from the kitchen window, boring holes into the back of his head.

He reached his hand out to the barn door, preparing to fling it wide open, when someone from the inside shoved their entire body against it. The door slammed into Kjeld's face and pushed him into the outside wall, momentarily disorientating him and blocking his view of the figure who then raced out into the woods.

Kjeld scrambled around the door and followed suit.

When he was a boy, he used to know those woods like the

back of his hand. He could have mapped out every stone, rabbit hole, fallen branch, and thorny bramble. But Kjeld was beginning to realise that not everything in his past was as he remembered it. And the overgrown tract of forest behind the property was no exception.

The figure darted through the trees. They weren't moving quickly, but they manoeuvred the array of birch and pine better than Kjeld. They'd been here before.

Less than a few metres into the woods Kjeld tripped over a tree root that had snaked itself above ground, sending him stumbling into the snow and brush. He picked himself up and cut across a patch of less dense foliage to catch up.

'Stop! Police!' Kjeld yelled. His chest burned from the combination of physical exertion and cold air. He felt like he was breathing in ice cubes that numbed the back of his throat when they melted. He pushed on harder, dodging low-hanging branches and jumping fallen logs, but the ache only increased his rate of inhalation and made it worse.

The figure ahead of him began to tire, but their familiarity with the woods continued to give them the advantage in the chase. Kjeld tried to catch a glimpse of their face as they weaved to the left, but all he could see was their dark-coloured back as they zigzagged through the trees. The figure continued on towards higher ground, grasping at birch trunks to help propel their weight forward.

Kjeld followed despite the stabbing pain in his chest. He really needed to stop smoking.

Kjeld slowed down in order to avoid the rocky ground made all the less manoeuvrable by the blanket of slippery snow. The wind picked up and white flakes began to fall from the sky. Then the flakes thickened. Within a minute he could barely see a few metres in front of him and the dark outline of the suspect blurred into the swirling snowfall.

Kjeld quickened his pace, skidding over the slick ground and shielding his gaze with his arm. He no longer knew which direction he was running in and his fingers were beginning to stiffen from the cold. Still he forged on, wincing against the whirling snow until he had to stop running for fear that his lungs might shatter.

He fell against a birch tree. The sharp papery bark jabbed into his back as he coughed up a chunky mouthful of phlegm. The hairs in his nostrils became uncomfortably hard and the mucus that ran down his front lips tasted acrid. He wiped the snot on his sleeve. His body throbbed, more from the cold than the sudden exercise, and he was about to give up the chase when a heavy crack of branches echoed through the quiet forest.

Kjeld broke into a straight run with no regard for what the snow might have been covering on the ground. When he caught sight of the footprints it kicked him into gear and he increased the length of his strides. He winced, his vision obscured by the falling snow. To compensate he stretched his arms out in front of him to prevent inadvertently going headfirst into a tree. He was getting closer. He could hear the laboured breaths of the suspect, heavy and gasping, and Kjeld knew that he'd be on them by the time he reached the crest of the next hill.

Faster and faster. He couldn't feel his fingers and his face stiffened. Sweat stuck to his chest and back, covering the skin beneath his sweatshirt with a clammy dampness. Just a few more strides. Almost within reach.

The trees began to open up. A light peered through the dense ground cover. Kjeld knew there must be a clearing not too far ahead.

His calves ached. The muscles in his legs cramped. A little further. That's all he needed. He could practically feel the presence of the other person in front of him. He stretched out his arm and his fingertips brushed against fabric.

*I've got you now*, he thought.

They reached the top of the incline and Kjeld leaped forwards.

In his mind the figure was directly in front of him. There was no way he could miss them. His body lengthened like a diver executing a swan dive and he passed through the tree line into an open clearing. But the figure wasn't there. And he didn't hit the ground when he should have. Instead he was in a free fall. Right off the edge of a newly excavated mining pit.

And his last thought before he hit the bottom was that it hadn't been there when he was a boy.

# Chapter 11

Kjeld rounded along the edge of the yard from a separate path that curved out from the forest along the eastern side of the property. The trek back through the woods took three times longer than it had during the chase. Not just because of the build-up of snow, which was slick atop the brambly ground, but because of the shooting pain in his right leg. His hip felt bruised. Nothing appeared to be broken or sprained, but the cold stiffened the injured muscle, making his walk rigid and off balance. His free fall had landed him in a newly dug quarry. Thankfully, however, he'd fallen onto one of the inclined paths carved out on the side of the pit to allow gravel trucks access to the bottom. The distance was little more than his own height. If the dirt road had been built into the other side of the quarry then he would have met a much more permanent end almost fifty metres below.

When he hobbled out of the woods and into the clearing of his father's yard, Kjeld could barely feel his face. The snow lessened to a gentle downfall of flakes, adding to the earlier accumulation on the ground like a half-hearted afterthought. His nose burned from the run-off of hot sweat and snot against the chilly air. His hands, stiff and bruised from bracing his fall, were shoved into the front pocket of his sweatshirt, but they found little warmth there.

Hanna, now dressed in one of Stenar's oversized down parkas and work pants, hitched around her thin waist with a man's belt, rushed out into the yard to meet him.

'My God, Kjeld! We've been so worried!' She wrapped her arms around him. The coat smelled like it had spent years in a stuffy closet full of mothballs.

'Did they come back this way?' Kjeld asked.

Hanna shook her head. 'We haven't seen anyone. I hiked around the edge of the yard to see if I could find out where you went, but the wind was too hard. God, you're freezing. You need to get in the house.'

Kjeld pulled out of her embrace and tried to give a smile, but the sting in his cheeks turned it into more of a grimace. 'Did they take anything?'

'Take anything?'

'From the barn. Did it look like anything was missing?'

'I haven't been in the barn,' Hanna said, pulling off the thick work gloves from her hands. 'Here, put on these gloves before you get frostbite.'

Kjeld glanced around the yard. The slow walk back had lowered his heartbeat. The throbbing in his ears ceased and he was struck by the quietness around them. It was unnerving how silent it was. There was something missing from the air.

'They've stopped crowing,' Kjeld said.

'What?'

'Where's my father?'

Hanna followed Kjeld's gaze around the yard and then back to the house. 'I don't know. I haven't seen him.'

Kjeld turned and headed towards the barn, his pace quickened by a sudden sense of urgency. Hanna followed after him.

The first thing Kjeld noticed when he walked through the barn door was the stillness. Stenar stood beside the rookery in his slippers, bracing himself against one of the wooden beams that Kjeld's great-grandfather had installed. The chicken-wire door was wide open. Empty. Kjeld craned his gaze upwards and saw the ravens perched in the rafters, peering down at the scene with hard unblinking stares.

'Someone was in the barn,' Stenar said. 'I told them I saw someone in the barn.'

Kjeld stepped closer to the rookery until he was standing beside his father. A mound of dirt reaching his knee had been unearthed inside the rookery. Kjeld leaned forward, looking through the chicken-wire grating and down at the hole that someone had hastily dug out beneath the rows of pegs and nests.

Hanna crept up behind Kjeld and followed his gaze.

'What is that?' she asked, fingers clenching at the gloves in her hands.

'I told them,' Stenar repeated.

One of the ravens flapped its wings overhead and Kjeld felt a shiver go up his spine, but not from the cold. At the centre of the hole was a smooth curve of yellowed bone that dipped into a dirt-filled eye socket.

'It's a body,' Kjeld said. 'And someone tried to move it.'

* * *

It was almost noon by the time Gunnar Ek and his lacklustre forensic team showed up at the house. By then the sun was already beginning its descent, welcoming the extra hours of darkness that came with the oncoming winter.

Kjeld sat on the back stoop watching as the police ran tape along the property, cordoning off the barn from the rest of the yard, and began placing numbered evidence markers around the footprints in the snow for the photographer. He had chain-smoked his fourth cigarette and was beginning to feel a numbness at the back of his throat where he'd inhaled too deeply. He thought of that body in the dirt, its face partially excavated. Decomposition had set in a long time ago, but it still had remnants of skin, dried and pulled taut against the skull. Kjeld reasoned it couldn't have been more than a few years old. Then again, the ground this far north was cold practically the entire year round. He could recall digging trenches in the woods with his friends during the height of the summer as a young boy and being amazed by the coolness of the dirt just a few inches from the surface. That might have been enough to preserve a body longer than expected.

The back door creaked open and Kjeld could smell the lingering scent of Hanna's perfume, still as strong as it was the night before. He exhaled a circular puff of smoke and for an instant it froze in the chilly air before dissipating into a thousand invisible particles.

'Your dad's calmed down a bit,' she said. Her voice was quiet, almost apologetic, but she was shaking. Her initial reaction had been to ignore what they'd discovered in the barn, but the shock was starting to kick in. 'He's upstairs trying to sleep.'

Kjeld only half heard her. His expression was taut. And while his focus seemed to be on Gunnar's crew, combing through the yard for evidence, his thoughts were a million miles away.

'My God, Kjeld.' Hanna wrapped her arms around her chest, less against the cold than the realisation of what was out in the frigid air. 'There was a body out there. A *body* buried in your dad's barn.'

But hearing it spoken out loud only made it seem more unreal to Kjeld. Someone had buried a body in his father's barn. His father had witnessed it. He'd said as much from the beginning. But who had he seen? Whose body was that partially decomposed in the icy ground? And, more importantly, was his father involved?

'I didn't believe him,' Kjeld said. Across the lawn, Gunnar was yelling into his mobile phone. His words, muted by the distance, reminded Kjeld of the yapping of a small dog. Ankle-biters as his dad used to call them.

'You should come inside. It's freezing out here. I made some sandwiches. I know it's not much, but—' She hesitated. 'I didn't know what else to do. I do that kind of thing when I get nervous.'

'Make sandwiches?'

'Keep busy.'

Kjeld smudged the cigarette out on the concrete step and stood up. 'You don't have to worry about it. I'm sure this wasn't exactly what you were expecting.'

'Expecting?'

'From a one-night stand,' Kjeld said, immediately regretting his choice of words.

Hanna remained quiet. She was still wearing his father's baggy work pants, but she'd replaced the oversized parka with a sweatshirt that Kjeld recognised as his own. *Varsundpojkarna FF* was printed across the chest in faded letters. Kjeld nodded to it.

'That's from another lifetime.'

Hanna glanced down at the sweatshirt and shrugged. 'Found it in the closet. You weren't that bad back then.'

'I never should have been a keeper.'

'But your arse looked good when you dived for the ball.'

Kjeld snorted.

'They let girls play on the team now,' Hanna said, turning her attention back out to the yard.

Kjeld could sense that she was trying to distract herself from what they'd discovered in the barn. He couldn't blame her. For most people, football was an easier topic of conversation than murder.

Kjeld shook his head, less in disappointment than in not knowing what else to do. 'Women's teams were always better anyway. The women's national team has at least placed in the last decade.'

'You guys just take longer to mature,' Hanna joked.

'Well it's good they put girls on the team. We could have used them back when we were still in school.'

Hanna crossed her arms over her chest. 'It's because there's not enough boys.'

Kjeld frowned his confusion.

'There's been a sharp decline in children at the Varsund

secondary schools. Lots of families are moving south. Or, at least, the wives and kids are. Like I said, the schools are better down there.'

'So is the weather.'

'That, too.'

Another silence fell between them, less awkward than the first. Kjeld was picturing his father's face when they found the body. Reluctant but relieved. Kjeld had recognised a kind of acceptance in his father's face. An expectation that this would eventually come to light, clouded by the confusion of a man who wasn't completely in control of his faculties. On any other person Kjeld would attribute that kind of uncomfortable solace with guilt, but in this case he wasn't so certain. What bothered him more, however, was that he couldn't decide if his uncertainty came from his father's mental deterioration or Kjeld's own complicated history with the man.

'Who was it?' Hanna asked, cutting through Kjeld's thoughts.

Kjeld shook his head. 'I have no idea.'

'Do you think your father—?'

'I didn't believe him. He said he saw something. He called me up for the first time in I don't even know how many years and I thought he was doing it to rile me. I thought he was just trying to stir up all that old shit again. I thought he just wanted to get my attention.'

Hanna paused. 'Well, he did. You came up here, didn't you?'

A camera flash shined through the cracks in the barn panelling, followed by an outburst of agitated cawing.

'Yeah, I guess,' Kjeld said.

He gave one last fleeting glance out towards the woods where he'd chased away the suspect.

Then he turned his attention to Hanna and tried to offer a conciliatory smile. 'What kind of sandwiches did you make?'

* * *

83

The forensic team took the better part of the day combing through the barn and the surrounding woods. One of the technicians who made the trek out to the mining site where Kjeld had fallen found a piece of cloth that had torn on a low-hanging spruce branch. When she asked Kjeld for his clothes to take into evidence for comparison she mentioned that he was damn lucky that he'd fallen where he had. Any further up along the ridge and they would have been dealing with two bodies instead of one. He supposed it was meant to be comforting, but Kjeld didn't feel any more at ease.

Something about the entire situation was wrong. Not the body or the near-death tumble over the mining ledge or his father's sombre disassociation preceding the discovery, but something that Kjeld wasn't seeing. It gnawed at him.

'Can we talk?'

Kjeld looked at Gunnar who had since covered his comb-over with a knit cap pulled down below his ears. Then he followed his old friend into the hallway so their voices wouldn't travel up the stairs and disturb his father.

Gunnar fidgeted, keeping his gaze lowered so he wouldn't have to meet Kjeld's eyes.

Kjeld crossed his arms over his chest and waited for the inevitable. The good old following the course of justice procedure that all police officers learned to say. The kind of phrase that was supposed to insinuate that it had nothing to do with any past history or personal grievances, but more often than not had exactly to do with both of those things. Particularly where Gunnar was concerned.

'I've got to take Stenar in for questioning.' Gunnar shifted his weight from one foot to another.

'The hell you are,' Kjeld said, but it was more a complaint than a threat. He knew the routine. He understood the process. But that didn't change the fact that Gunnar was a shit excuse for a cop with a years' long grudge big enough to match the chip on

84

Kjeld's shoulder. Dead body in his dad's barn or not, it was hard for Kjeld not to take it personally.

'Don't make this hard on me, Kjeld. You know how this is going to go. Everyone is going to get questioned. That doesn't mean anything.'

'And how long will it take before questioning becomes an official arrest?' Kjeld didn't even try to hide his growing temper.

Gunnar's cheek twitched and the thick vein on the side of his face bulged out from beneath his cap.

Gunnar took a deep breath.

Kjeld could see by the sudden stiffness in his posture that Gunnar was doing his utmost to keep calm. It was an expression that Kjeld was used to. He'd seen it on the face of his chief more than once, particularly in those moments when Kjeld was about to do something stupid and irrational. Kjeld didn't think he was being irrational now, however, but his perception might have been biased. He had too much history in Varsund and too much bad blood with its self-appointed chief investigator.

'I understand there are some personal circumstances that might cause some difficulty in—'

'He has dementia,' Kjeld interrupted. He dropped his arms from his chest and took a step forward, forcing Gunnar to lift his gaze and pay attention. Kjeld could tell that Gunnar was doing his best to maintain that "big man" composure like he had in his office, but there wasn't an imposing desk between them for Gunnar to hide behind now and Kjeld had both height and hair on his old friend. 'His mind is confused. There's no way to know if anything he tells you will be truthful. Any statement he gives will be inadmissible in court.'

'We can have a doctor in the room to make sure your father isn't overstressed.'

'You mean coerced?'

Gunnar's mouth pursed into a thin line and Kjeld realised he was on the edge of going too far.

'What are you saying?'

'You know damn well what I'm saying. I don't trust you, Gunnar.'

Gunnar sneered. 'That's quite the predicament, isn't it?'

Kjeld didn't respond.

'You don't trust me because of what happened in the past. I don't trust you because of what I read in the papers last week. I see what you're trying to do out there in the big city. Trying to pretend like you haven't fucked up. Like you're untouchable. Except you did fuck up, Kjeld. And I'd be willing to bet there's some truth to what people are saying.' Gunnar gritted his teeth. 'I could ruin you if I wanted to. I could bring the whole thing toppling down.'

'Not without ruining yourself.'

'You think anyone cares about a crooked cop in Varsund Kommun? No one even knows where that is. No one who matters.'

'*I* know where it is.'

'And yet the first chance you get, you'll be on the road back to Gothenburg. As if this place never existed.' Gunnar poked Kjeld in the shoulder with a gloved finger. 'You've got way more to lose than I do.'

Gunnar was right and Kjeld realised then that the grudge between them was not one-sided. 'I want an impartial psychiatrist. Someone from out of town.'

'Fine.'

'And a lawyer.'

Gunnar scoffed. 'It's just questioning, Nygaard. He's not being charged. *You'll* be questioned, too.'

'Yeah, but I can remember not burying someone in my dad's backyard.' Kjeld took another step forward until he was within a few inches of Gunnar. He knew it was pure bravado. He wasn't going to lose his cool in front of his old college buddy, but Gunnar didn't know that. 'My dad called you and told you he witnessed something. *You* chose not to take it seriously. Don't forget that.'

Gunnar hesitated, the tenseness practically radiating off his body. Then he relaxed and gave a wry smile. 'All right, Nygaard. Get your lawyer and your doctor and whoever else it is you think your dad needs to answer a few harmless questions. But I want both of you down at the station before three o'clock on Monday afternoon, regardless of whether you've managed to get your people together. And I'm sure I don't need to insinuate how this will look if you fail to show up. Your father might be innocent of not recalling the past, but I wouldn't put it past you to tell a few tall tales.'

Gunnar took a step back, bundling up his coat around his neck as he went for the door. Before he left he shot Kjeld a knowing glower. 'Wouldn't be the first time, after all.'

# Chapter 12

'*Hej!* You've reached Sara's voicemail. I'm probably out wrangling kids. Leave me a message!'

Kjeld left an exasperated "call me" after the tone. He checked for any new texts and was surprised to find he had none. Nothing. Not even from Esme. That was a first. But he was more surprised by Sara. He'd called her at least four times since Gunnar left, but as far as Kjeld could tell she was still ignoring him. Albeit rightfully so. He'd been kind of a jerk the last time they spoke.

He crossed the living room to stare out the window into the backyard. The blue and white police tape, lit up by the forensic team's work lamps, zigzagged across the yard, fluttering every time the wind kicked up through the trees. They'd covered half the barn in a large white sheet, most of which seemed to be an attempt to block the hole in the roof. A special animal unit had to be called in to gather the birds, although that had been an easier task than manoeuvring around the decades of junk that Stenar had piled up in the barn.

The forensic team was still working well past dinnertime, trying to excavate the body, but Kjeld found that he wasn't much interested in that process. He was too distracted by the overwhelming darkness. In a few more weeks it would be pitch-black before noon and the entire region would be shrouded in almost six months of perpetual night. Just another reason why he lived in Gothenburg. It was far enough to the south to offer a few extra hours of daylight during the winter.

Kjeld watched the crime-scene specialists as they hurried in and out of the barn in their protective clothing. After a while his thoughts began to drift to that half-uncovered grave. He supposed that any normal person would have been shocked or dismayed to find a body on their property. Kjeld just felt empty. It wasn't that he didn't have sympathy for whatever poor bastard lay buried in the dirt beneath years of bird shit, but it just reinforced how very little he knew his father.

What could have happened?

Kjeld had gotten a good look at his father's face when they discovered the body. Stenar hadn't been surprised, but Kjeld didn't expect that. His father had already admitted that he'd witnessed a murder. But there was something else in his father's eyes. Defeat? Resolution? Kjeld had left the family home as soon as he was old enough so he couldn't be certain that he knew how to interpret his father's expressions. Adding dementia to the matter only made Stenar harder to read. But Kjeld had the nagging sense that there was something more behind his father's vacant eyes. Sadness? Regret?

Maybe he was just clutching at straws.

A hand on his shoulder tore him from his thoughts.

'Your dad's sleeping,' Hanna said.

'Thank you.' Kjeld tried to sound appreciative, but the words fell dead in the air. He pinched the bridge of his nose. He felt a migraine coming on. 'You didn't have to stay, you know.'

Hanna grinned. 'Well, my car is still in the Gruva car park so I kind of did.'

'Shit.' Kjeld shook his head. 'I completely forgot about that.'

'It's all right. You had other things to deal with.'

Kjeld turned away from the window and looked at her. She

wasn't wearing any make-up. The natural look added a few years to her face, but it suited her. Without the blush and foundation she reminded him more of the young girl selling raffle tickets at the spring fair. Hanna hadn't been his first kiss, but when he was a teenager every kiss had been memorable. And Hanna hadn't insisted on it being anything more than what it was, which might have explained why this one memory of her was fonder than those he had with others he'd gone to school with. It made him wonder how things might have turned out if he'd stayed in Varsund. Would they have grown apart? Remained friends? Become something more? Except it was pointless to imagine. Because Kjeld didn't stay in Varsund. And he never would have. Not for anyone.

A sharp cackle of ravens outside broke the silence and interrupted his thoughts.

'I'll drive you back to your car,' he said.

'Are you sure?' she asked. 'I don't have anything going on this weekend. If you want me to stick around and help you with your dad, I can.'

He paused for a moment, staring into her dark eyes and remembering how nice it had been not to wake up alone. He wouldn't have minded spending another night forgetting that he was a single nearly nonexistent dad approaching forty who spent more time with the dead than he did with the living. It would almost be worth the few hours of denial.

Almost.

'I'll get your coat.'

* * *

The drive back from the Gruva took thirty minutes longer than normal after a logging truck pulled out into the road, forcing Kjeld to wait for the loggers to finish loading the eighteen-wheeler's semi-trailer with recently cut pine before veering off to the side street that led up to his father's place.

The backyard was still lit up in sporadic corners from the forensic spotlights. Occasionally one of the lights would flicker out because of the cold and a technician would scurry out to their van and thaw the extension cords with a battery-powered hair dryer.

Kjeld followed the low beams of light until they faded out in the snow, dissipating into the shadows formed by the trees. He caught himself staring for an inordinate amount of time at the bend in the yard, where it curved into forest. And although he couldn't see anything, he had the eerie sense that someone was watching him from behind those trees. He drew the curtains. Out of sight, out of mind.

The inside of the house was uncomfortably quiet.

Kjeld checked on his father who, for the first time since Kjeld had arrived, was resting peacefully. Occasionally he would mumble something in his sleep while the crusty corners of his mouth were wetted with drool. Kjeld imagined that his sister would have wiped that off, but Kjeld was too afraid he would wake his father and send him into a fit that would result in neither of them getting any sleep. After a few minutes he closed the bedroom door, careful not to make too much noise, and turned on a hallway light in case his father decided to wander. The only thing worse than his father falling down the dark stairs in the middle of the night would be Sara screaming at him for his selfish negligence.

He needed to find a lawyer.

Kjeld dialled Sara again. Still no answer.

Kjeld shoved the phone into his back pocket and began the search for his father's old rolodex.

The house wasn't that large. Three bedrooms on the second floor. Kitchen, living room, and parlour on the first floor. No office. The living room had been his father's office back when he was working, but Sara had tidied it up so much that it barely resembled the chaos of Kjeld's youth. If his parents had kept any important documents or a filing system of professional contacts, Kjeld couldn't recall where they might have been. Kjeld did remember that there had been a rolodex at one time because he had a clear memory of playing with it when his father wasn't looking, but his memory didn't include a hint as to where it would be. Assuming, of course, that it even still existed. If there had been anything useful, like the deed to the property or a phone number to a family lawyer, Sara probably had it sequestered in her house. She'd always been rather anal retentive when it came to keeping track of things. Not like Kjeld. He couldn't keep a receipt to save his life.

Then he remembered Sara mentioning the boxes in the cellar.

The house didn't have a full cellar originally, just a small space beneath the kitchen barely large enough for one person to stand, but Kjeld had fragmented memories of his father and grandfather digging it out to make space for storage and his mother's preserves. Kjeld must have been a toddler back then because the images of that time were blurred and incoherent. The sound of a shovel piercing the ground, the feel of the dirt between his small fingers, his mother's tired smile as she looked on.

The new set of stairs, which were at least thirty years old by now, had been built into the old pantry that sat off the side of the kitchen. Kjeld reached up and pulled the drawstring on the dangling lightbulb. He winced as a haze of yellow dust illuminated the path downward and descended into the cool basement one step at a time.

The cellar still wasn't very deep and Kjeld found that he had to hunch over to prevent his head from bumping against the old leaden pipes, added after his parents had a new well installed on the property. The smell of must and damp concrete invaded his nostrils. On one wall sat rows of wooden shelves with neatly stacked boxes, meticulously labelled in Sara's large handwriting – Dad's Equipment, Mum's Needlework, Grandpa's Tools, Family Photos, Excess Kitchen, and so on for the length of the entire wall, from floor to ceiling. On the bottom shelf, saved from the moist floor by little more than an inch and a piece of plywood, were three boxes that had his name written on them. Kjeld, Kjeld, Kjeld. No other description. The one furthest from the stairs looked like it'd been chewed on by mice.

Kjeld shoved the boxes aside, skimming over the various labels. The further back he searched, the older the boxes became and he wondered what relics of the past might be hiding within them. Some of the labels had smudged over time and Kjeld took a quick look inside the cardboard to see if it held what he was looking for. Old cameras from his grandfather's bird-watching hobby, videocassettes of Sara's dance recitals, his father's high school and college diplomas, and his mother's collection of vinyl and 8-tracks including a rare American release of Sweetwater's first album. Kjeld made a mental note to come back later and take that with him.

Behind the box of records, shoved deep into the cellar corner, was a book-sized box marked with his father's writing. *N.M. Miscellaneous*, scribbled across the top. Kjeld racked his mind but couldn't for the life of him think what N.M. might stand for. He pushed aside the box of records and pulled the other box out. The cardboard was soft and warped. The box wasn't heavy, but something inside clanked when it jostled.

Kjeld tore off the packing tape and stared inside. Papers, plasticised documents, folders, his father's rolodex – jackpot! – and a metal tackle box. That was odd. He couldn't recall anyone in his family being keen on fishing. In fact, he had a clear memory of his father giving him a good tongue-lashing after finding out that Kjeld and his grade school friends had gone trout fishing in the river that cut through the northern part of Varsund, separating the town limits from the vast wilderness that stretched towards Norway. His father's anger hadn't come from a place of concern for the boys' safety, however, but out of fear that Kjeld and his friends might have disturbed the natural ecology of the river.

Kjeld could remember it clearly. Those had been his father's exact words. "You might have disturbed the natural ecology of the river." Because nature had always taken precedence over nurture where his father was concerned.

Kjeld pulled out the tackle box. There was a thick layer of grime on the lid, giving the once silver metal a shoddy blackened hue. Kjeld went to open the box, but was stopped by an old combination lock that had begun to corrode from leaning against the dank cardboard.

He set the tackle box on the ground and ripped open the box containing his grandfather's tools. Then he dug through the mess of old screwdrivers and wrenches until he found what he was looking for: a rust-covered bolt cutter.

The lock snapped off with very little force, clinking as it hit the ground. Kjeld set the tackle box back up on the shelf so it was closer to eye level and opened the lid. He stared at the inside, disappointed and confused.

Why would anyone lock *that* up?

# Chapter 13

Kjeld sat on the edge of his childhood bed, the rusty tackle box in his lap. He felt like he was losing his mind.

Inside the box was a stack of old Polaroids tied together by a brittle rubber band that had long since lost its stretch and had begun to fray and peel where it met the corners of the photographs. When Kjeld picked up the stack of photos the rubber band fell away in pieces at the bottom of the tackle box.

He spread the photographs across the duvet.

Kjeld had never seen these images before. There were a few of the family, mostly during what appeared to be an outdoor picnic. Midsommar, perhaps. One that caught his attention showed his parents, sister, and him as an infant, held by his mother, standing in front of the house. It stood out because Kjeld had never seen a picture of himself at that age. He was so small in the photo that it couldn't have been too long after he was born. In fact, it might have been the only photo of him before age two that Kjeld had ever seen.

He continued rifling through the pictures. One of Sara – "age three" was written on the back – in a sandbox. Another depicted his father and grandfather standing side by side in front of the barn. A photo of the rookery before his father built the more elaborate nesting nooks and perches that were still out there now.

The rest of the photos were older and completely unfamiliar to Kjeld. They showed what appeared to be a dinner party at a house that Kjeld didn't recognise. A house that was too nice to be in Varsund. Kjeld's mother featured in most of the pictures. She looked young and vibrant and at an age that must have been around the time his parents got married. His father still had their wedding photo on his nightstand and the way Kjeld's mother's face looked in that photo matched those in the tackle box. It was strange. Like looking at someone through a mirror.

Kjeld paused longer on one of the photographs, yellowed with age. In the picture his mother was sitting at a baby grand piano in a long evening gown. Her hair was done up in a twist and she was looking back over her shoulder at the photographer with a vibrant and playful smile. A wave of nostalgia, warm but conflicted, passed over him as Kjeld recalled a memory from his childhood.

Kjeld sat at the upright Bechstein piano nestled in the narrow corridor between the foyer and the living room, legs dangling. He was tall enough to reach the pedals if he sat on the edge of the bench, but he didn't know how to use them, so he sat further away until the backs of his knees hit the corner of the seat. If he sat in that position long enough, toes brushing at the floor during their idle swings, his legs would start to tingle and go numb. Then he'd scoot forward again until they regained sensation.

His mother was a talented pianist and she'd started teaching Kjeld to play since before he could remember. She tried with Sara, as well, but Sara hadn't taken much interest in it. Truth be told, Kjeld wasn't interested in music either – he'd rather be out in the woods looking for limestone fragments or huggorm snakes – but he enjoyed the time spent with his mother. And because he enjoyed her company and revelled in the pleasure she took when he accomplished something new, he tried his best to learn how to play.

Today, however, he sat alone and that ebbed his desire to practice.

The yelling didn't help either.

'I won't have that man in my house!' Stenar's voice bellowed from the kitchen.

In contrast Eiji's voice was calm and composed. 'Isn't it time you two let bygones be bygones? You're best friends.'

'That man is *not* my friend. He insults me. How dare he after all these years. After what he's done. And not only that, he insults my work. It's no big secret that Norrmalm Industries has been deliberately subverting the national environmental guidelines in order to maximise their production output. They're destroying the Varsund forest.'

Kjeld didn't hear his name in the argument, but for some reason he still felt like it was his fault that his father was upset. He brought a hand to his left ear where it was wrapped in sticking plaster and white bandage after the incident in the barn the day before. The day that stranger came to visit. Kjeld was still shaky from the experience, but mostly he was ashamed. He felt stupid for being so afraid.

Kjeld stared down at the ivory-coloured keys, running the pads of his fingers over them without making a sound. He didn't want to hear his parents fighting, but he didn't want to anger his father by making too much noise. Perhaps if he played something quiet, it would blanket the sounds of their argument. Perhaps if he played well it would even cause them to stop.

He spread the sheet music for his mother's current practice song, Chopin's *Nocturne in C minor, Op. 48, No. 1*, across the music rack. The song was far too advanced for him to play both the upper and lower staffs, so he started with the right hand until he had the tune and slowly added in the dominant chord with the left hand. He was always a little off with the timing, the left hand beginning a split second behind the right, resulting in a jilting discordance.

But the arguing continued.

'It's been years, Stenar. You know how difficult things were back then. He lost his wife, for God's sake. And things weren't easy for us either. You have to let it go. If not for you then for our family. I won't stand for this kind of animosity in the house. Not around the children.'

'He didn't give me a choice.'

'But *I* am.'

Kjeld pressed down harder on the chords, focusing on the sound to drown out the voices. The song was marked *lento*, but he found himself quickening his pace as he reached the twenty-fifth measure and practically pounding the keys when he turned the page to the forty-ninth. He continually missed the A-flat and by the time he reached the final section, which should have increased in intensity, he was so lost in being loud that there was nothing left that even remotely resembled a tune.

A gentle hand was placed on his shoulder, quietly urging him to stop. He did. Then he scooted over to allow his mother room to sit beside him.

Eiji picked up the music and neatly set them aside. Then she placed an intermediate learner's book on the rack.

Kjeld breathed a sigh of relief.

'Let's try something a little more fun,' she said. The rims of her eyes were red and Kjeld knew she'd been crying. But there were no tears on her face and her mouth was drawn in a smile. 'You play the bass clef and I'll play the treble.'

Kjeld clenched his eyes shut, forcing the memory away. When he opened them again he set the photo down and picked up another. It was the smile. The smile was wrong in every image.

Kjeld always remembered his mother as being quiet and tired, her smile sad. The woman in these photos was a far cry from that lonely woman in his memory. This woman was bold. Her hair loose, lips red. She looked like a Stockholm socialite, not the wife of a reclusive backwoods forester. This woman looked like his mother, but Kjeld didn't recognise her. Nor did he recognise the other people in the photos, mostly men in suits with glasses of champagne in their hands.

Kjeld flipped over the back of one of the photos and read the inscription. *N.M. Christmas Party 1978.* A year before he was born. Sara would have been a year old then, but his mother didn't look like a woman with a one-year-old child. Or, at least, didn't look the way she had when Kjeld was that young. He placed the dinner party photo side by side with the photo of his mother holding him as an infant. She had so much life in the first photo. How could little more than a year change so much in a person?

Kjeld sighed and was about to drop the rest of the photos back into the tackle box when he came across an even older photo. This one was of his father during his required military service. Nineteen and awkward. He stood beside another man in their uniforms, arms around each other, posing with wide smiles and their standard-issue rifles. Kjeld homed his attention in on the other man. An older version of him was also present in one of the photos of the Christmas party with his mother, but there was something else about his face that was familiar. Kjeld had the feeling he'd seen it somewhere before, somewhere recent, but he couldn't quite place where. He turned the photo and looked at the back. There was nothing written on it. Kjeld looked at the man with the familiar face. Maybe he just resembled someone he once met. Then he directed his attention to his father. Young, smiling, happy. Like the photo of his mother, an image that didn't match with his memory.

How could he not know these people?

\* \* \*

Ahlgren Plumbing Services. Dahl Roofing. Forsberg Cabin Rentals. The rolodex was like a trip back in time. Kjeld's father, it seemed, had deemed it important to categorise every workman, every motel, and every healthcare professional that the family had ever used. Even Kjeld's childhood dentist, Dr Horn, a German transplant with snaggleteeth and a glass eye who was dead going on twenty years now, was still listed in the collection of phone numbers, albeit the card had taken on a faded yellow hue.

Kjeld flipped through the rolodex, trying not to let his mind wander to the tackle box of unfamiliar photographs. Trying not to wonder why his father would hide them, locked away and forgotten in the musty bowels of the cellar. Or had it been his mother's secret collection? Was she the one who'd concealed those images from view? Images that had since been overlooked or displaced in the years following her death.

She looked so happy and radiant in the party photos. And so despondent holding that infant in her arms. Holding him. As though something in that year had broken her spirit and sucked any joy right out of her.

It was painful for Kjeld to think that it might have been him who'd torn that optimism from her life. That his birth had shattered any future happiness she might have had. But when he saw the photographs and looked at the dates, it wasn't a far stretch of the imagination.

His fingers stopped on a card near the back of the rolodex.

The business card was slightly faded and torn in the upper right-hand corner. It was heavier than normal, printed on a high-quality cardstock. The design was simple, elegant, like one would expect to see for an elite firm for large corporations. Not the kind of attorney for a man who scraped by just enough money a year to live comfortably in the middle of nowhere. Not the kind of attorney the average run-of-the-mill working-class wage earner could afford.

*Erik Norberg, Advokat: Contract & Family Law.*

Why would his father need a contract lawyer?

Kjeld took out his mobile phone and began dialling the number on the card.

'Let's see if Mr Norberg is still practising,' he said aloud to himself.

# Chapter 14

## Söndag | Sunday

The next morning Stenar acted as though the discovery of a body in the barn had never occurred. He woke up, showered, dressed himself – although his shirt was on backwards – and made his own breakfast without any difficulty. Kjeld was almost envious of his ability to forget. There were so many moments in his life he wished he could hide in the back of a drawer and never think about again.

While they ate breakfast, Kjeld tried to bring up the photographs that he'd found the night before, but his father either didn't understand him or was ignoring his questions. Kjeld considered pushing further, but decided it was too early in the day to start arguing. Perhaps he would try again later, if his father was in a stable mood. When they finished and Kjeld had put away the dishes, he told his father that he was going to hike up into the woods behind the barn and see if he could find any trace of the person he'd chased. He wasn't prepared to leave the investigation in Gunnar's hands. Even if Gunnar was capable of finding out the truth of what happened in the barn, Kjeld didn't trust him to be forthright about it. And he didn't want to take any chances.

'I'm going with you,' Stenar said as he grabbed his winter coat from the rack in the hall.

'It could be a long hike.'

'I've hiked Kungsleden from Abisko to Nikkaluokta and that's mostly alpine.'

Kjeld thought about mentioning that it had probably been more than thirty years since his father made that trip, but decided that, like the photographs, it was an argument not worth getting into. Instead he snatched a spare coat from the closet, retrieved his father's hiking stick from the corridor, and went out into the yard.

Much of the snow that had fallen the day before had already melted, but the air was still frigid, nipping at Kjeld's face. He zipped the coat up through the collar to break against the cold. The slope that he'd scrambled up during the chase was too slippery for Stenar to walk on, so they took the long way around following an old trail that he and his father used to hike when he was a boy.

The ground crunched beneath Stenar's boots and Kjeld slowed his pace to make sure his father didn't slip on an unseen patch of ice. But unlike Kjeld, who still had some pain in his hip from the fall, Stenar seemed to have no difficulty navigating the terrain. Not that this should have surprised Kjeld. His father had probably hiked this path hundreds, perhaps thousands, of times over his lifetime. As had his grandfather and great-grandfather before him.

They reached a bend where the well-worn path disintegrated into a deep stretch of forest. Kjeld knew they would have to cut to the right and continue upwards in order to find the cavern he'd fallen into the day before, but Stenar persisted on continuing straight on.

'The cavern is this way, Dad.'

'That's not where we're going,' Stenar said, using the hiking stick as leverage to step over a fallen log.

'We came out here to follow the path of the person who was in your barn. They didn't go this way. I chased them in the other direction.' Kjeld stared off towards the right. He could see where the ground lifted up towards the ridge and the sudden openness peeked through the trees, letting in more light.

The path his father was on led deeper into the forest where, despite the early hour, it was still dark and murky.

But Stenar wasn't letting up and Kjeld didn't know how he'd manage to get his father back to the house if he had one of his Alzheimer's-induced episodes in the middle of the woods. Instead of risking his father becoming violent as he did at the dinner table the day he arrived, Kjeld continued after him off the main path.

'Where are we going?' Kjeld asked.

'It's not far from here,' Stenar replied, slowly weaving through the brush.

Further into the forest there was still a thin layer of snow on the ground, through which the mossy undergrowth occasionally seeped through. The spruce stretched above them like bristled statues. Their trunks were bare nearer to the ground, blocking out the sky with their slim branches of thick green nettles, creating a spiny canopy overhead. Kjeld felt like the trees were closing in on them and his heart pounded in his chest against this unexpected claustrophobia. He stepped on a twig and it snapped. The sound echoed in every direction. He cast his gaze behind them, feeling eyes on the back of his neck, and half expected to see someone following. There was no one there. He'd never feared the forest growing up, but something about it now unnerved him. And he couldn't shake the feeling that they weren't alone.

'I think we should go back.' Allowing his father to go with him had been a foolish idea. Anything could have happened out there and they would be miles away from help.

'Not much further now,' Stenar said.

Where was his father taking them?

Kjeld's thoughts returned to the barn and that gruesome

discovery. He tried not to imagine the worst, but that's what he'd been trained to do. And it wasn't a stretch of the imagination to consider the fact that his father may have been more involved than he'd let on. After all, what reason would anyone else have to bury a body on his property?

They crossed a small creek, after which the ground became marshier. Kjeld could feel his boots sinking into the wet earth, each step more difficult than the last. Just as he was about to insist that they turn back, the boggy ground opened up to a small clearing. Tucked into the corner of that clearing was a hunting cabin with a single window and a moss-covered roof.

Stenar sat down on a bench beside a fire pit to catch his breath. There was no smell of fire, but Kjeld noticed that the ash in the pit was black as though it had been recently used. For all other intents and purposes, however, the place appeared to be abandoned.

'Whose place is this?' Kjeld asked, surprised to find a clearing this deep in the woods.

Stenar leaned his hiking stick against his leg. 'Mm?'

'Does somebody live here?'

'Who?'

'The cabin, Dad. Who does it belong to?'

Stenar craned his neck to look at the cabin. His face showed little recognition. His legs had brought them to this place out of some blip in his memory, but his mind couldn't recall why.

Kjeld made his way closer to the cabin and peered in through the window. The thick layer of dust and grime on the glass made it impossible to see inside. When he went around to the door, however, he stopped, surprised to see his own name carved on a dark piece of wood above the threshold.

No, not his name.

'Is this great-grandfather's cabin?' Kjeld asked.

Stenar didn't reply. He just mumbled to himself, digging his hiking stick into the ash of the fire pit.

Kjeld opened the door and peered inside. It was a cramped single room with a bed built into the wall. There were sheets on the bed, indented from the weight of someone who'd been sleeping there, and blankets piled up at the foot of the mattress. On the floor were dozens of empty inferior-brand Finnish vodka bottles and crushed beer cans. The smell from inside was the ripe and pungent odour of sweat and alcohol that almost made Kjeld gag.

He shut the door and walked around to the back of the cabin where he was surprised to see a narrow dirt road leading through the trees and a car covered in a heavy rain-proof tarp. He lifted the front of the tarp, revealing a silver mid-size Mercedes-Benz CLK-class coupe which, aside from some weathering rust on its lower frame looked to be in perfect condition. Kjeld pulled off the rest of the tarp and peered inside. Clean leather interior. Empty. And no licence plates. A car he knew did not belong to anyone with the last name Nygaard. He snapped a photo with his phone and covered it back up.

When he made his way back to the front of the cabin, his father was gone, the hiking stick lying in the dirt beside the fire pit. His panic was instantaneous. He hurried down the wooden pathway, fearful that his father might have fallen into the marsh, but he wasn't there.

'Dad?' he called out. No reply.

He bounded back up to the cabin. Empty.

'Dad!'

His breath quickened. His heart beating so loudly he thought he could hear it. Where could his father have gone off to? He hadn't left him for more than a few minutes.

A door slammed.

Kjeld turned to see his father stumbling out of a decrepit outhouse, which Kjeld had failed to notice because it was half buried in the overgrowth. Stenar was still zipping up his slacks when Kjeld caught him by the arm.

'You can't walk away from me like that!' Kjeld was unsettled by his own distress. It reminded him of the time he'd misplaced Tove in the H&M at the Nordstan shopping plaza. She'd thought it'd be funny to hide under a rack of sweaters while he madly accused everyone in the store of snatching his daughter.

Stenar stared at Kjeld as though he'd just lost his mind. 'I had to piss.'

'Next time you tell me before you go walking off!'

Stenar tugged away from Kjeld's grip and marched over to the fire pit.

Kjeld took a deep breath and tried to calm himself, but he could feel his temper begin to boil beneath the surface. He pressed his fingers against his temples and reminded himself that everything was under control.

Except it wasn't.

They'd found a body in his father's barn. And now his great-grandfather's near-dilapidated hunting cabin was hiding a car whose cost probably exceeded his yearly salary. Things were verging on being further out of his control than he anticipated.

As he helped his father get back onto the path, a rustling behind the trees caused the hairs to prickle on the back of his neck. He peered into the forest. It was more than likely an elk. Still, Kjeld didn't see anything but a never-ending stretch of naked trees and frost-covered forest floor. There was nothing out there. Nothing but the eerie sensation of being watched and an unexplainable urgency to get out of those woods.

# Chapter 15

## Måndag | Monday

Since the discovery of the body on the Nygaard property Varsund's normally quiet half-hearted excuse for a police station was bustling with people. Gunnar had called in extra forensic technicians from Östersund, which wasn't much of a city on its own – nothing in Jämtland was – but at least had a small unit familiar with uncovering the cadavers of lost hikers who foolishly took to trekking the northern ridge of the Sylan mountain range during the off season. A forest didn't always need a thick labyrinth of trees to cover a person's tracks. Sometimes all it took were miles and miles of desolate stone and a horizon of similar-looking peaks to set a person wandering in circles.

The police station was small and had the awkward appearance of looking like an afterthought. Probably because it was. When Kjeld was a boy, Varsund didn't have its own police station. Ulf Arnö, the former police chief of Varsund, worked out of a tiny converted broom closet in the post office. Varsund never really had any problems except for the occasional fight between drunken miners at Gruva pub or the rare domestic spat that sometimes ended with a husband getting the bad end of a load of buckshot. When that happened, Ulf would just lock the intoxicated miners up in the mail room. There wasn't much a drunk could do to a bunch of envelopes, after all. And if the situation was more than Varsund's two-man police force could handle, like when Kristina Andersson blew off her husband's face with his own shotgun so badly that his body had to be identified by the busty mermaid tattoo on his forearm, Ulf would call the good folks down in Östersund to help out. Or the mountain patrol in Åre if it was winter and the roads were closed.

When Kjeld and his father arrived at the station just after ten o'clock in the morning Gunnar was already there waiting for them.

'Good morning, Stenar,' Gunnar offered by way of forced politeness. No handshake. Then he glanced at Kjeld, lips pursed in a sneer. 'Kjeld.'

Stenar watched absent-mindedly. As though he weren't in the same space as the other two men. They could have been strangers for all his expression suggested.

'Will you be doing the questioning?' Kjeld asked.

'I will,' Gunnar replied.

'Then I want to be present in the room with my father.'

Gunnar scoffed. 'This isn't an interrogation, Kjeld. We've been over that. It's just a formality.'

'Fuck you, Gunnar. I know how you take care of formalities.'

Disdain spread across Gunnar's face like a wildfire. Kjeld could see that he was doing everything in his power to keep his calm. He had to hand it to Gunnar. He may not have changed much over the years, but he had a better grip on his temper than he did when they were schoolmates. Pity Kjeld hadn't learned to do that as well.

'You have a lawyer *and* a psychologist on the way. This isn't the big city. Our rooms get crowded with more than four people.' Gunnar reached out and took Stenar by the elbow. 'Come on, Stenar. Let's go have a chat about your barn.'

Kjeld clenched his teeth at the sight of Gunnar taking his father's arm. He could feel his self-control cracking. It took almost everything in him not to impulsively shove Gunnar away.

'Excuse me, gentlemen,' an unfamiliar voice interrupted.

Everyone turned their attention to the man standing nearby. The tension between them was almost palpable.

'I'm Erik Norberg. Here to provide counsel for Stenar Nygaard.'

Erik Norberg, whose secretary Kjeld had a very brief conversation on the phone with the night before and whom Kjeld wasn't entirely sure would pass on the message, was nothing like Kjeld had been expecting. He was a peculiar-looking man, probably in his early to mid-sixties. He was short, barely reaching Kjeld's shoulder in height, and was bald on the top of his head. He had a thick bristly moustache that covered his top lip, which Kjeld imagined would make it difficult to understand him, but when he spoke it was with a clear, albeit snooty, accent of one of those old-money Stockholm suburbs. Kjeld got the impression that the accent was only half affected. He was also sweating profusely across his forehead and refused to look Kjeld directly in the eyes, but whether that was from self-perceived class differentiation or short stature, Kjeld couldn't say.

'If the two of you are done with your discussion, I'd like to proceed. I have a very busy schedule and I don't want to take up more of Herr Nygaard's time than is absolutely necessary,' Erik said.

Stenar stared at the lawyer and Kjeld thought he saw a flicker of recollection in his gaze.

Gunnar cleared his throat with a cough and motioned to the officer and technician to let go of Kjeld. 'Yes, of course. We'll be in room two down the hall.'

Before Kjeld could say anything to the attorney, Erik turned to him, staring with wide protruding eyes that rarely blinked. 'I think it's best that you wait out here. The fewer distractions, the quicker this will go.'

Then he escorted Stenar into the closed-door conference room and Kjeld was left on his own in the hall. A few minutes later, a psychologist from Region Jämtland Härjedalen, who got lost on one of those "damn winding logging roads" and spent forty-five minutes circling the entire Kommun, came scurrying in; her thin snow-slick heels sticking to the frayed carpet and making an odd rip-clunking sound when she walked. She, too, disappeared into the room with Kjeld's father and the stout lawyer.

Time ticked by slowly.

Kjeld punched the buttons on the vending machine in the hallway attaching the station to the community centre. He was annoyed at himself for allowing Gunnar to rile him up so quickly. Frustrated that he hadn't been able to speak with the lawyer and ask him a few questions. And he worried that the scene in the lobby might have sent his father into a state of disorientation. As much as he didn't want Gunnar to be the one questioning his father, Kjeld wanted to know the answers to those questions. He needed to know.

The vending machine beeped and a Japp chocolate bar fell into the tray.

'Damn,' he said as he bent over to take the chocolate bar out of the machine. He thought he'd hit the button for a Bounty.

Kjeld wandered back to the uncomfortable folding chairs in the reception area and took a seat. The long hallway of beige carpeting, matching beige walls, and closed office doors reminded him of an elementary school without that tell-tale smell of young children. It made Kjeld feel like he was waiting to be called in by the principal.

He took a bite of the Japp bar, disappointed in the lack of coconut but satisfied to have something to stave off the urge to stand outside and smoke half a pack of cigarettes. His phone buzzed and he opened up a message from Esme. It was a picture of his cat lounging on his couch with extra emphasis on his belly, which hung partly over the edge of the cushion. The accompanying

111

message was: *"Your cat is obese. I replaced his food with a diet brand. It's Hill's Science Plan. You owe me 569 kronor."* The app indicated that she was still typing. Another buzz followed by *"Make that 600 kronor. Petrol money."* Kjeld sighed and was about to put his phone back into his pocket when Esme sent another message: *"Giving my statement today. I'll let you know how it goes."*

Fuck. He'd forgotten all about the Aubuchon case. Kjeld knew his suspension meant that he wasn't obligated to complete the work he'd started on it, but dumping it all in Esme's lap after everything she'd done for him had been uncommonly callous. He could probably write up his version of the events and send them off to the chief before the start of the week, but then he'd have to remember what version of the events Esme was sticking to. The actual version, no doubt. The truth. And she could do that, of course, because she wasn't the one who shot Nils. She didn't put her best friend in the hospital. She didn't come close to killing a colleague. Kjeld did.

\* \* \*

The second Sara saw her brother sitting in the lobby of the police station she could feel her blood boil. And while he sat there focused on his mobile phone, she walloped him in the shoulder with her handbag.

He responded by looking at her like she was a lunatic. She was not. As far as she was concerned, she was the only person in their family with any common sense. Let alone any respect for the well-being of other people.

Kjeld was selfish. And clearly he'd only gotten worse with age.

'What the fuck, Kjeld?' Sara said. She hated using profanity and absolutely refused to do so in front of her children, but Kjeld just brought it out in her. Whenever she was around him, she couldn't help herself. He aggravated her beyond belief.

'What?' he asked.

Sara didn't trust his play-acted naivete for a minute.

'I just got your messages. What did you do? Where's Dad?'

There was a pause where Kjeld averted his attention away from her and Sara knew he was hiding the urge to roll his eyes. He was so predictable that way. He never could take a challenge head on. Not from her, at least. He always acted like she was making up reasons to be angry with him. Like she was purposefully trying to provoke him. And then he would shrug his shoulders or roll his eyes like *she* was the one who didn't see what was going on. But that's where her brother misjudged her. Sara saw everything that was going on. And she wouldn't fall for his sly attempts to make it seem otherwise.

Still, if he rolled his eyes she would, without hesitation, whack him with her purse again.

Kjeld turned in the chair so he was facing her. She could see he was about to go on the defensive.

'I tried all night to get ahold of you,' he said. 'Actually, I started calling Saturday afternoon. You didn't pick up. I'm sure your call log will back me up on that.'

'I had to drive Tom to work. He's been on a temporary project in Östersund and the truck wouldn't start yesterday. Then I had to take the kids to sports practice, drive back to Östersund to pick Tom up, and make dinner. I haven't been on vacation, Kjeld. It's not like I've been lying on a beach somewhere purposefully ignoring you. And why didn't you call me yesterday?' Sara sat down on one of the folding chairs beside him, shoving her purse in her lap.

'I did call you yesterday.' He didn't look too certain about that. 'You could have texted.'

'You do not have the right to lecture me about not answering the phone,' she snapped, knowing Kjeld couldn't argue with that. When it came to getting back to people, he was completely unreliable.

Kjeld stretched his legs out in front of him and glanced back to the beige hallway of closed doors. Sara followed his gaze.

'Tell me what's going on.'

'We found a body.'

'Don't fuck with me, Kjeld.' This time she didn't wince when she swore. Kjeld seemed to notice because he raised a brow.

He took a bite of a chocolate bar. 'We found a body in the barn.'

Sara's response caught in her throat. She felt a chill go through her and she clenched her fingers around the handle of her purse like she was wringing out a wet rag.

Kjeld scrutinised her face as though he was searching for the answer to a question he hadn't yet formed. She looked away from him, afraid that if he saw her frustration that it would overpower every other emotion she had and prevent her from speaking to him calmly. But before she could say anything, Kjeld spoke.

'Dad's okay. I don't think it even really registered with him.'

'You mean he was *there*?'

Now she was fuming.

'He's the one who found it.'

Sara punched him in the shoulder. 'What do you mean he was the one who found it? What the hell were you doing while he was in the barn finding a goddamn dead body?'

The more she spoke the shriller her voice became.

The station receptionist looked up from her desk and peered at them through her angular glasses. Sara recognised her as being the daughter of their old primary school librarian. She couldn't remember her name, but she had that same shushing sneer and high-angled brows of the woman who used to wave the "be quiet" ruler at her during study breaks.

Kjeld seemed to recognise that librarian look as well because he lowered his voice to avoid any more unwanted attention. 'I was chasing the person who was trying to dig up the body. *That's* what I was doing. I was trying to find the person who uncovered it in the first place, without whom Dad never would have found the body.'

'Don't be a smartarse,' Sara said, digging into her purse for a bottle of prescription pills. That Kjeld could be so nonchalant about all of this was driving her up a wall. She shook one circular tablet into her palm and tossed it into her mouth.

Kjeld leaned toward her, trying to read the label, but Sara quickly covered it with her palm.

'What's that?' he asked.

'It's for my anxiety,' she said. She clicked the lid back onto the bottle and dumped it back into her bag.

'Since when are you on anxiety pills?'

'Oh for Chrissakes, Kjeld. Since I've become a mother of two with a husband who's been laid off from his full-time job. Since my family has been living hand-to-mouth on government assistance to cover the weeks when Tom can't get any work. And since I've had to quit my own job to take care of my demented father from dawn until dusk because my shithead brother can't get off his fuckin' high horse and pick up the goddamn phone.'

*Breathe*, she told herself. She could feel her heart pounding in her chest. She'd forgotten how difficult her brother could be. How aggravating. It was a wonder to her that he managed to make it this far in his life being as irresponsible as he was. She would never say it out loud, but she thought it was a blessing that Tove was with Kjeld's ex. If Kjeld couldn't be entrusted to take care of an old man then there was no way he was capable of looking after a child.

It broke her heart to think that because she loved her niece. But as much as it pained her to admit it, Tove was better off with Bengt. Sara wondered if Kjeld realised that. If he knew that Bengt was still sending her Christmas cards. Back when they were together he used to scribble Kjeld's name on the cards, no doubt hoping that Sara wouldn't notice the forgery. She assumed it was his way of keeping the wary peace between her and Kjeld. But Sara knew that Kjeld had never signed a Christmas card in his life. And he never would. It would never cross his mind to do so. That wasn't important to him. Bengt had always kept up

115

appearances for him when it came to family things. He never missed a holiday or one of her kids' birthdays. Sara wasn't even certain that Kjeld knew his own daughter's birthday. He was careless and unreliable. He was an infuriating brother, a neglectful son, and probably an absent father.

But it wasn't Sara's place to tell him that. Besides, she suspected that he already knew.

She pitied him, but she didn't feel bad for him.

'I'm sorry,' he said.

'Don't be sorry. Be present. Pay attention. The world doesn't revolve around you and your woe-is-me wall of emotion. You're not the only one who's gone through shit. You're not the only one who has a monopoly on hating their life.'

Kjeld nodded. Then, seemingly out of the blue, he asked, 'Do you know anyone with a Mercedes?'

That took her off-guard.

'What? No?'

'Dad didn't buy one and forget about it?'

'If Dad had a Mercedes do you think I'd be spending my days chauffeuring everyone around in my piece-of-crap station wagon? Which is on its last leg, by the way.' Sara huffed. 'Now where's Dad?'

Kjeld tilted his head towards the first closed door in the hallway catty-corner from the reception area. 'In questioning.'

'Questioning?' Sara's eyes widened. She could feel that fury beginning to stew inside her again.

'With a lawyer and a psychologist,' Kjeld added before she could interject. 'Like I said, I tried to get ahold of you. But they're just trying to get a picture of what happened. It's a formality. They're going to question me too.'

'About this person you say you chased?'

'There was someone. They were trying to cover their tracks.'

'And how would they know to do that?' Sara asked. 'Why now?'

Sara silently chastised herself for leaving their father in her

116

brother's care. She couldn't imagine how horrifying and confusing the situation must have been for their father. Dealing with Kjeld. Finding a body. Talking to the police. She wished she'd picked up her phone earlier. If she had she could have been sitting in the interrogation room with him, making sure he was safe and calm. How could Kjeld allow him to be in there alone with strangers? How could he be so negligent?

'They must have thought there was a chance someone else would find it first,' he said. 'They must have believed it was going to be found.'

'But how could they know that?' Sara asked.

Kjeld didn't respond. He looked like he was in a daze and Sara touched his shoulder to get his attention. 'How could they know someone else might find the body first?'

But Sara thought she already knew the answer to her question. It was because the person knew a detective had come to investigate their deranged father's allegation. A person who was afraid that detective wouldn't give up until he'd exhausted his resources. But the list of potential suspects could have been endless. Varsund was a small town. Sara was certain that everyone knew Kjeld was back. But who knew that their father witnessed something in the barn? And who would they go after next to keep their secret?

# Chapter 16

'Interview commenced at 10.47. Chief Inspector Gunnar Ek of the Varsund Police Department is present with Kjeld Nygaard. Please state your name for the record.'

Kjeld cleared his throat and leaned forward.

'Detective Inspector Kjeld Nygaard,' he said, purposefully enunciating the first two words, which Gunnar had no doubt intentionally left out.

Gunnar pretended not to notice. 'Did you want an attorney present?'

'Do I need an attorney?' Kjeld asked.

'It's your right.'

'Am I under suspicion for something?' Kjeld leaned back in his chair.

'No,' Gunnar said. 'This is just to get a statement of your side of the events.'

'The events?'

'The events preceding the discovery of the cadaver in your father's barn.'

'Oh, those events,' Kjeld mocked. 'No, I don't require an attorney for that.'

Gunnar looked up from the file in front of him and sent Kjeld a cold glare. Then he went back to scribbling in the margins of a piece of loose-leaf paper that sat beside the file.

Kjeld grinned.

'In your own words then, tell us what happened.'

'My dad broke two eggs on the floor,' Kjeld said, matter-of-fact.

'Your dad – what?' Gunnar ceased writing.

'My dad broke two eggs on the floor. I started to clean it up. Hanna. That's Hanna Eklund, who you saw at the house the other day, offered to make my father some eggs. Over easy is what we agreed to, I think. Then my dad said that he needed to feed the birds. I insisted it could wait until after breakfast. That's when my father noticed that someone had been in the barn.'

Gunnar pursed his lips. It was clear to Kjeld that he was refraining from saying what he was really thinking: that Kjeld was jerking him around with inane facts. That was partly true, but Kjeld didn't like the way Gunnar had spoken to him from the get-go. From the minute he'd walked into his office a few days ago and presented him with the human tooth he'd found in the barn. Gunnar deserved as many derivative details as Kjeld could come up with.

'And how did he know that someone had been in the barn?' Gunnar asked.

'The barn door was open.'

'You can see that from the kitchen?'

'Clear as day.'

'And what time was this?'

'Morning. Maybe around seven. It wasn't completely light out, but it was light enough. Also, the birds had been making a lot of noise.'

'Noise?' Gunnar quirked a brow.

Kjeld crossed his arms over his chest. 'Are you asking me to imitate them?'

'No. Just to elaborate.'

'They were cawing and crowing like someone had disturbed

them. They were agitated.' Kjeld didn't add that they always seemed agitated.

'And then what happened?'

'I went out to the barn to see what was going on. Someone shoved the door in my face before I could look inside and then ran off into the forest. I pursued.'

'On foot?'

'No, with a helicopter,' Kjeld said, sounding more irritated than he intended. 'Of course, on foot. You've seen those woods. It's one bramble bush after another. There's no other way to get through the trees.'

'And you got a good look at this person?' Gunnar asked.

Kjeld thought back to the chase. He remembered a dark-coloured jacket. Black. Possibly dark blue. He thought there may have been a stripe on the sleeve. Purple? The hood was up hiding their head. The snow blurred almost everything else. The flakes had hit his eyes like sharp clouds, obstructing his vision like an icy spider's web.

'Not really,' Kjeld admitted.

'Did you notice anything significant about them?'

'I think they were shorter than me.'

'You think?'

'They knew the terrain well. Knew where to step and where not to. They weren't fast, but they were agile. They'd been there before.'

Gunnar continued to write in the notepad. Kjeld tried to get a look at what he was writing, but the man's scrawl was indecipherable from across the table.

'Man or woman?'

Kjeld shook his head. 'Couldn't say with any certainty.'

'At what point did you lose track of the person you were pursuing?'

'The suspect, you mean?'

'Let's just say person of interest.'

'When I fell into the quarry.'

Gunnar sent Kjeld a genuine look of surprise. Didn't he know?

'The one at the top of the hill,' Kjeld clarified. 'Well, the embankment. The ground heaves upward about a kilometre from the house. Maybe more. Maybe less. It was hard to judge the distance with the snow. But it felt like it was really close to my dad's property. They aren't digging on his property, are they?'

Gunnar averted his attention from Kjeld, refusing to make eye contact. He glanced over at the clock on the wall, but Kjeld had the impression he wasn't actually checking the time.

'Gunnar?'

'Most of the land north of Varsund is owned by the mining companies. Has been for decades. You know that. I'm sure they're well within the appropriate property lines,' Gunnar said.

Kjeld wasn't convinced.

'When did you find the body?'

'I didn't. My dad did.'

'About what time was this?'

'When I got back to the barn. Must have been about thirty minutes, maybe forty-five, after I lost track of the *person of interest*.' Kjeld took an audible breath. 'No later than eight.'

'Did you touch it?'

'No.'

'Did anyone touch the body?'

'Not that I saw,' Kjeld said drily.

'And you didn't find anything else of note? Nothing suspicious?'

Kjeld thought about the silver Mercedes under the tarp at his great-grandfather's hunting cabin. He didn't know if he'd call it suspicious, but it was peculiar. There was no doubt in his mind that the vehicle didn't belong to his father and while it was on Stenar's property, he couldn't discount the small access road in the forest. Anyone could have left it there without his father knowing. He decided to keep that to himself for now. At least until he had time to investigate it personally.

'Nothing.'

'And for the record it was just you, Stenar Nygaard, and Hanna Eklund in the barn?'

'No.'

Gunnar blinked.

'There were about a dozen corvids, too.'

'Cor-what?'

'Ravens,' Kjeld said. 'The ravens were there, too.'

# Chapter 17

The large hand of the neoclassical Viennese mantel clock tugged itself into the new hour and released a pleasant chime.

Roland snipped off the end of a Fuente Don Arturo cigar and tossed it into the fireplace. Then he reached his hand into the hearth and lit the cigar against the flickering flames. Once lit he took a puff, exhaled, and took another. Start quick, savour slow. At almost 760 kronor a roll he wanted to be sure it lasted more than an hour.

'You're sweating,' he said. The cigar began producing a thick white smoke and Roland eased off the puffs.

David wiped his palm across his brow, smearing the sweat back into his hair. It was a light shade of blond, almost white, like his mother's. He was an attractive man with a smile not unlike Peter's had been, bright and absorbing. Although on David it was less sincere. He was thinner than Roland, a consequence of his health problems. Having a pacemaker at thirty-six didn't exactly make him a likely candidate for muscle-building sports, but David kept himself in good shape. Mostly by having vigorous sex with Roland's mistress. He didn't think Roland knew, but he did. Roland was aware of everything that went on in the Lindqvist family. It was his business to know. When he looked at David now, he imagined his heart was racing. And he wondered if that's why David looked so nervous.

'It's hotter than hell in here,' David said. He walked over to the cabinet where his father kept the whisky and poured himself a glass of the first bottle he found.

Which was exactly why Roland kept the good whisky in the bottom drawer of his desk. It was wasted on his son.

'Is this about the email?'

David took a swig and then poured himself another half a glass. 'So you did get it?'

Roland pursed his lips and tried to remember at what point in his life he'd allowed his son to become so wasteful.

'I did,' Roland said, sitting down in one of the wingback chairs positioned in front of the fireplace. His body sank into the well-worn leather. He was in good shape for a man his age, no one could argue that, but the familiar imprint of his body in that chair felt good on his lower back.

'It's a scam.' David crossed the room and stood beside the hearth. Another swig and his glass was set down on the mantel beside the Austrian clock.

A premonition of David knocking over the timepiece and causing it to shatter on the floor made Roland wince.

'A scam?'

David took out his mobile phone and read the email verbatim. '"Dear Lindqvist family. Hope all is well with you. My apologies for falling off the grid the last few years. I've been doing a lot of soul-searching in this time and feel like I've finally found some answers. Best wishes to you all. Hope to see you soon. Peter."'

David shoved the phone back into his pocket.

'It's obviously not Uncle Peter. Someone probably hacked into his account. They're probably looking to make some easy cash or stir things up. Maybe even someone from the company. Someone who isn't happy with the merger.' David looked down into the yellow flames. A line of sweat was beginning to form on his forehead again.

Roland took another puff on his cigar. 'Who's to say it isn't Peter?'

David scoffed. 'After all this time? Right at the moment when MineCorp is about to buy out Norrmalm for 250 million euros?'

'I didn't realise you were so interested in the company.'

'I work there,' David insisted.

'Hardly.'

'Well, I'm interested in the investment.'

'In your future inheritance, you mean.'

'Same thing.' David took another swig of whisky.

Roland could tell he wasn't even trying to enjoy it. Such a waste. Certain luxuries were meant to be savoured. Food, drink, cigars, women. These weren't things you chugged or inhaled or devoured. Like a full-bodied single-malt scotch they were meant to be sipped. To allow the aroma to sweep over one's senses. They were things to indulge in, but to indulge steadily over a period of time so that all aspects of their essence could be appreciated.

Roland didn't think David appreciated anything. Least of all the life of leisure that the Lindqvist men before him worked tirelessly hard to achieve so that their descendants could waste it on foolishly lustful extravagances.

'If it is Peter then I will welcome his return. It hasn't been easy running Norrmalm without him.'

'It was my understanding that the board of directors ran Norrmalm,' David said flippantly.

'And as Peter's proxy *I* run the board of directors.'

'Correction. You *did* run the board of directors. Once MineCorp signs the contract then everything belongs to them. Then we'll be rid of it.'

'You mean you'll be rid of any responsibility to ensure its success for future generations,' Roland snapped. He set his cigar down on a tray on the side table and stood up. This conversation was ruining his smoke. He'd already wasted enough time and money on the other man in the room. He didn't see any point in wasting a good cigar on top of that.

'Oh, come on, Dad. You know you'll be glad to be rid of it. Besides it's not like the business is performing like it used to. The competition is too stiff in this market. And Jämtland is dried up anyway. At least where mining is concerned. Everyone knows the only real industry left up here is lumber.'

Roland could feel the anger building up inside of him. As a father he'd always tried to be a patient man. When David and Inger were young he almost always made it to dinner, unless business ran over. He had an agreeable relationship with his wife that both he and she had managed to negotiate over the years, particularly when it came to keeping their family together. He gave his children everything they ever wanted and more. He wasn't perfect. He wasn't the sort of father who attended his children's football matches, but he always donated to the teams. His children had attended the best universities overseas. Vacations to the most exotic places. He ensured that his family was never in want of anything. And that was why he boiled on the inside whenever he looked at his ungrateful son. Because David needn't want for anything and yet nothing was ever enough.

'You should show more respect for this country. For the land that has given you everything and then some. You wouldn't even be here if it weren't for dried-up Jämtland.'

'Well, I'm sick of Jämtland. I'm sick of its dirt and its rocks. I'm sick of the trees and the elk and the toothless backwoods *bondlurkar*. The hell with all of them. As soon as this merger is done I'm out of this hellhole.'

Roland slapped David across the face.

The reaction was so quick even Roland didn't see it coming. Afterwards it left a sting on his palm. David flinched, but didn't look surprised, and for a brief second Roland felt a pang of guilt. Then David finished off the rest of his whisky

126

in a gluttonous gulp and any shame Roland might have had for hitting a man with a heart condition disappeared like black smoke in a night sky.

'It's not Uncle Peter,' David said, wiping the sweat from his forehead again.

'I never said it was,' Roland said, his tone soft but stern.

'Five years, Dad. It's been five years.'

'I know how long it's been since I've seen my brother.'

'Then you can agree it's not him. Uncle Peter is dead. He has to be. No one just drops off the grid completely.'

Roland wasn't surprised that David would think this, but he didn't agree. He remembered how burned out and depressed Peter had been when he left. He could understand the need to walk away from everything. Had circumstances been different, he might have done so himself.

'If you do anything to delay this merger then MineCorp is going to back out. They'll back out and find some other piece-of-shit mining company to invest in. Don't ruin this, Dad. You said it yourself that you never wanted to run this company. That you'd be glad to be rid of it when the right opportunity came along. This is that opportunity.'

Roland turned away from his son and stared into the hearth. The flames flickered between vibrant orange and yellow, casting dancing shadows on the wall. Occasionally the wood popped and crackled. He was trying to imagine what Peter would have done in his situation. How would he have dealt with this predicament? Except the thought was a hollow one. Peter never had a good-for-nothing son to badger him for his wealth and his influence. He didn't have a daughter who wasted her allowance and her degree by lying on expensive beaches hoping to be noticed by someone just as materialistic and insipid as herself. Peter, for better or for worse, had been saved that kind of dogged torment. And even if Peter's wife and unborn child had survived that tragic birth, Roland suspected he still wouldn't have had the same problems. His children wouldn't have been wasteful.

And they wouldn't have been so quick to destroy everything their father had built for them.

# Chapter 18

Sara was helping their father into his winter coat when Kjeld stepped out of the interview room.

Gunnar made it clear that he didn't want to stick around for chit-chat and made a beeline for his office the moment he clicked off the tape recorder. Kjeld was glad for that. He didn't think he could handle any more false pleasantries. Not that he'd ever really been all that pleasant to begin with. Kjeld had a knack for getting on people's nerves. Particularly people he knew well. And whether Gunnar liked to admit it or not, probably not, Kjeld knew more about his past than anyone else in that small mining town. Knew enough to make things difficult for him.

Kjeld walked past the reception desk and into the main entranceway.

Erik Norberg stood off to the side, deep in conversation on his mobile phone while he shoved documents into his briefcase.

'I'm taking Dad home,' Sara said.

Stenar looked over at Kjeld. His eyelids were drooping and his lips turned downward in a heavy frown. He looked like a man asleep on his feet and Kjeld surprised himself by the sudden sense of worry that his father might fall over.

Sara wrapped her own scarf around Stenar's neck and tied it

129

in a knot near his throat so it wouldn't fall off. When she looked away to get her car keys out of her purse, Stenar began to pull at the scarf.

'I'll be along in a bit,' Kjeld said. He wanted to catch the attorney before he left and ask some of his own questions.

'Don't be too long. I have to pick up Tom in a few hours.' She sighed when she realised Stenar had undone the scarf. 'Come on, Dad. It's cold outside.'

'Aren't you coming?' Stenar asked, his tired expression fixed on Kjeld as Sara retied the scarf.

'I'll meet you at the house, Dad.'

Sara walked Stenar to the exit. When she held the door open for their father she glanced back at Kjeld. 'Maybe you can pick up some groceries on your way home. If you're going to stick around, the least you could do is help with the day-to-days.'

Then they left.

A wave of relief washed over him as Kjeld found himself alone with his own thoughts for the first time since he showed up on the front steps of his father's home. He'd forgotten how mentally exhausting Varsund was. Even without his father's illness, the act of juggling family, old friends, and small-town life was enough to drive him crazy. Adding an unexpected crime scene to the mess just tipped it over the edge.

It seemed Kjeld couldn't do anything right. Even the right thing, in this case the decision to help uncover the mystery his dad could no longer remember, turned out to be the wrong thing.

The attorney shuffled past him.

'Excuse me,' Kjeld said, catching the shorter man by the shoulder.

Erik turned and looked up at Kjeld. His eyes were sullen and chronically hyperthyroid. The reflection from the fluorescent ceiling lights beamed off his bald head, reminding Kjeld of a bowling ball after getting a fresh wax. The man didn't say anything. He just stared at Kjeld with his protruding eyes and waited for him to say more.

'My name is Kjeld Nygaard. I'm the one who called your office,' Kjeld said. 'Stenar is my father.'

An uncomfortable pause on Erik's part followed. 'Really?' Erik replied, furrowing his brows and eyeing Kjeld more keenly than before.

That struck Kjeld as an odd reply, but he continued without comment. 'I was hoping you could update me on how the interview went.'

Erik pursed his lips and shifted his weight from one leg to the other. 'Do you have legal power of attorney with regards to your father's health?'

Kjeld hesitated. 'Uhm, I'm not sure. Probably not. My sister does most everything. I don't live around here anymore.'

'Legally I'm not supposed to consult with anyone outside of my client and his healthcare power of attorney,' Erik began. Kjeld could sense an unspoken "but" in there, but the word never fell from the lawyer's lips. His expression did falter, however, and Kjeld could see that the man was struggling with a decision.

'If it helps, I'm a detective inspector from Gothenburg. I was with my father when he found the body. In fact, he called me last week about having witnessed a murder. That's why I came up here. To see if there was any truth to what he said.' Surely that warranted some information. This was his father, after all.

'And did he tell you whose murder he witnessed?' Erik asked.

Kjeld could feel himself growing more and more impatient with the way the attorney was avoiding his questions. He was hitting one dead end after another. First with his father, then with Gunnar, and now some hotshot lawyer who Kjeld knew nothing about. And the fact that Norberg refused to answer even the simplest of his questions was enough to make him lose his cool again. This time, however, he managed to temper himself.

'Not yet.' Kjeld paused. 'But I believe he was there. I believe him when he says he saw something.'

'From what I understand a forensic team is still collecting

evidence from the grave site. The body has been sent temporarily to the local morgue. There's a pathologist working on the preliminary findings as we speak, but I suggested to the interviewer that they might want to have it transferred to a larger facility. Some place more familiar with these kinds of discoveries.' A single tear dripped down Erik's face and he took a handkerchief from his pocket and dabbed at the corner of his left eye. 'My apologies. My eyes swell in this weather.'

'Is there something wrong with having the body analysed locally?'

'As I'm sure you're aware, Herr Nygaard, this is a tight-knit community. Word travels fast. And in an effort to protect your father who, whether directly or indirectly involved in the scene in his barn, may come under police scrutiny, I think it best that the remains are processed by people unfamiliar with the town. Everyone knows everyone here, after all.'

'I don't know you,' Kjeld said.

Erik slipped the handkerchief back into his pocket. 'I don't live in Varsund. Thank God. I only come up here when business demands it.'

'Business?'

'I have other clients in the area.'

'I see,' Kjeld said. 'Well, I appreciate you coming out here. I admit that I was a little surprised to find the name of a lawyer in his records. I didn't think he'd ever needed one.'

Erik smiled. The action was forced and it looked unnatural on his face. 'People rarely like to admit having need of an attorney.'

'That I can understand.' Kjeld despised talking to his own lawyer even more than his ex. Not just because there were so many similarities between the two. 'How can I go about paying you for your time?'

Erik shook his head. 'No need.'

'Don't tell me you work pro bono.'

'I have an agreement with your father that dates back a few years. There won't be a charge for my services.'

Now it was Kjeld's turn to stare. 'An agreement?'

'There's really no cause for concern, Herr Nygaard. Besides, I understand the strain that your father's illness must be having on your family. I wouldn't want to burden you even further by adding an unnecessary expense to your situation. I'm happy to help out free of charge.'

There was something insincere in the man's voice. Kjeld didn't trust anything that was free.

'No, it's all right,' Kjeld said. 'I'm happy to pay. I want to be sure that my father is getting the best advice there is. I'd feel more comfortable paying. If you'll just send me an invoice—'

'There isn't any advice better than what I'm offering you right now,' Erik interrupted.

Something changed in the lawyer's expression. He was clearly annoyed, but there was something else in his look. An uncanny fear in his eyes, not unlike what Kjeld was used to seeing across the table in police interview rooms. The fear that someone might find something else. The fear that forced someone to lie.

'And what advice is that?' Kjeld asked.

'To let me do my job.'

'For nothing in return? Without payment?'

Erik shook his head, but Kjeld suspected it was more in frustration than disagreement.

'You couldn't afford me anyway.'

Kjeld didn't think Erik meant to be callous or disingenuous, but it was hard not to feel like the man was mocking him in some way. 'What can I do then?'

Erik dabbed at his eye again. 'You can find out whose body that was in your dad's barn and who put them there.'

# Chapter 19

The last time Kjeld visited the Varsund Kommun morgue was when his mother died. It had been warmer that day, the snow long since melted into the rainy months of spring, but in his memory it had been chilly. He remembered standing behind the window, alone, while the local doctor who'd been Kjeld's paediatrician growing up tried to convince him to hold off until the funeral home had prepared her. Kjeld couldn't wait. He had to see her.

Some people say the dead look like they're sleeping, but that had never been Kjeld's perception. Every time he'd seen a cadaver, whether it was his mother's in Varsund or an unknown victim of some heinous crime in Gothenburg, he saw death as it actually was. Impermeable. Changeless. Forever. Perhaps his mind lacked the imagination to trick itself into believing the bodies lying on those cold metallic tables were in a temporary state of unconsciousness. Or perhaps he needed to cling to that permanence of death in order to appreciate life. Regardless, he could never convince himself that the dead looked like they were sleeping.

To him that was more of a nightmare than a dream.

It was Erik Norberg who had, unconsciously or not, planted the idea of attending the pathological examination in Kjeld's mind. If he could get a head start on discovering whose body they'd found then perhaps he could use that to jog his father's memory. Kjeld knew it was a long shot getting into the morgue. Varsund was such a small town that most people were keenly aware of who was allowed to do what. But he couldn't rely on Gunnar to keep him in the loop. And Kjeld needed to understand what his father was unable to tell him. Which was why he did the one thing he knew would get him some answers.

He used his police ID to lie to the pathologist on duty.

'I've just finished my initial assessment,' Helen Akerman said, jotting down a few notes on a clipboard before setting it aside and dropping her pen in a stainless-steel kidney dish.

Helen, like many highly educated professionals working in Varsund, wasn't a native of the town and for that Kjeld was grateful. It saved him that cramping sensation of claustrophobia he experienced whenever he was in town, knowing people were watching him and whispering behind his back. *There goes Kjeld Nygaard*, he imagined them saying. *The boy who left his hometown roots for the big-city life. The man who didn't stick around to care for his family. The detective who befriended a serial killer.*

Helen pressed a button on her phone's playlist. It skipped over to a new song. The Yardbirds began their chant-like opening to "Still I'm Sad", but the small speakers emitted a tone that was too top heavy. Without the bass the harmony was tinny. A discordant whine.

'I've been stuck in a oldies-but-goodies phase for the last three months,' she said without encouragement. 'Can't get enough British psychedelia. Much to my family's dismay, of course. But it helps me focus. Keeps me in the moment. And this fellow's not complaining.'

She gave the partly decomposed remains of the body on the slab a tap on the shoulder. Or what was left of it.

'Beatnik?'

Kjeld canted his head to the side. 'Sorry?'

'Are you into classic rock?'

'Oh.' Kjeld shoved his hands in the pockets of his jeans. The room was cool and his fingers felt stiff. 'Sure, but I think my tastes are a little more mainstream.'

'Beatles or Stones?'

'Late Beatles. Early Stones.'

'Lennon or McCartney?'

'Harrison.'

Helen's attention perked. 'Interesting.'

Kjeld stepped closer to the edge of the table. The lack of smell was what struck him first. He was too accustomed to fresh bodies. Recent killings. There was no odour of death here. Only a whiff of earth and dirt. Not unlike the smell of clothes that had been tucked away in the back of a dark closet for too long. 'What can you tell me about the body?'

'Aside from the fact that he looked like he was a real hand jiver back in the day?' She stepped around Kjeld to the top of the table where there was a better view of the skull.

Helen ran down the basics, some of which Kjeld had already reasoned. The body was that of an older male. Somewhere in the range of fifty to seventy years of age. The clothing found among the remains had been removed upon arrival and placed in plastic bags on the counter to be sent back to the police for further analysis. Helen had discovered some blood on the shirt, but little else. Normally a pathological examination would expect to find minimal to no traces of skin, but the temperature of the ground had been cool enough that there were still some patches of leathered dermis along the arms and chest cavity. The organs had long since liquefied into the dirt and the face had been eaten by all manner of insects. Not the normal blowflies one would expect in a body left above ground, but those few six-legged subterranean dwellers who took whatever sort of nutrition nature provided for them. Dead or otherwise, it didn't matter. All in all, a nicely preserved human specimen. Of course, it would have made everyone's job easier if the body came with a wallet.

'How long was he underground?' Kjeld asked.

'Difficult to say without more invasive testing. The conditions of the burial site and the temperature of the ground have preserved him better than if he'd been left out in the open or buried outside of a structure where the weather could have done more damage. But my educated guess would be at least a few years. Maybe longer. I'll have to send in some samples for testing. That will give us a more accurate indication.'

'No indication then of who he was?'

Helen shook her head.

'A driver's licence with the victim's name and birthdate would have been the cherry on the cake. But that would be too much to ask for,' Helen said. 'And it makes your job less exciting, too, I imagine.'

'Discovering a body is exciting enough,' Kjeld replied drily.

'Really? I always thought investigators lived off the thrill of a challenging puzzle.' Helen shrugged. 'Then again I see bodies every day. Guess you could say I'm a little numb to them by this point.'

Kjeld couldn't argue. He was numb to them as well.

'Anything else you can tell me that might help?'

'He has a relatively intact dental set. Aside from one of the molars on the bottom right which is missing he has good-looking teeth. Definitely someone who took pride in their biannual checkup with the dentist. Which reminds me that I need to make an appointment for my kids. My boy's already had two cavities this year. And God knows I could have saved myself some trouble if I'd flossed more. No more *Lördagsgodis* for us.' Helen's face reddened. 'Sorry, I don't get to talk to people very often. Well, not to someone who talks back anyway!'

Helen picked up her pen and made a note in her autopsy report about the missing second molar.

'So … older male who took good care of his teeth?' Kjeld was hoping for something more. 'Do you think we can rule out lower socioeconomic background?'

Helen shook her pen at him. 'I don't like to make those kinds of assumptions. Some people just have really good luck when it comes to genetics. Maybe he won the good teeth lottery. If you're asking if he was fit with an expensive bridge or had veneers, then no. But, like I said, he didn't need them.'

She clicked her tongue against the back of her front teeth. 'I'll be transferring the body to the lab in Östersund. They shouldn't have any trouble finding a dental match. All you have to do is file a subpoena for medical records.'

Which would be simple if Kjeld was in Gothenburg. If he knew who the victim was. And if the body hadn't been found on his father's property.

'There's also an old leg injury.'

'How old?' Kjeld asked, hoping that might be something he could uncover without lying to another doctor.

'Long before whoever did this to him. Early adulthood, I would surmise. You can see the residual fracture in the left tibia where it never fully healed.'

The last song ended and was quickly followed by the fuzzy echo and reverb sounds of Pink Floyd's "See Emily Play". Kjeld knew the song, but only liked the piano bridge and the awkward way Syd Barrett's voice faded out at the end hitting an almost dissonant tone. And it was during that dissonance that he noticed something on the back of the skull.

'What's that?' he asked.

Helen leaned forward, cradling the skull between her gloved hands, and ran a thumb over a long crack near the base of the parietal bone. When she turned the skull completely over Kjeld could clearly see a fragment missing from the occipital plate.

'Hm? Oh, penetrating trauma,' she said. 'Something sharp entered the left side of the skull and dug directly into the brain.'

'Is that the cause of death?' Kjeld peered over her shoulder to get a better look.

Helen gave him a dry stare. 'It was a sharp object jabbed into his brain.'

'Any idea what it could have been?'

'Hard to say. But whatever it was, it hurt.' Helen sighed, her expression more disappointment than sorrow. 'All that money on a set of straight bicuspids. What a waste.'

# Chapter 20

Kjeld thought about calling Hanna after he left the morgue to see how she was doing, but realised after the fact that he didn't have her phone number. His wry and often unkind inner voice told him that was the consequence of following a drunken one-night stand with a rotting cadaver. That was no way to impress a woman.

Before getting on the road that led back to his father's house, Kjeld stopped at the ICA supermarket in Varsund's city centre. He barely made it through the produce department before he realised that people were staring at him and he cursed his decision not to drive to the Coop thirty minutes away just to avoid their accusatory glares. Word travelled fast. Not just about his situation in Gothenburg, but about the discovery in his father's barn. While he was in the dairy aisle trying to remember if his father had any milk at home, he overheard an elderly couple behind him whispering about a murder.

He left without buying anything.

Instead he stopped at an OKQ8 petrol station with an attached kebab shop instead. He ordered two pizzas, one with tuna and shrimp and one with mushrooms, from the boy behind the counter and then walked next door to the service station shop for cigarettes, two bottles of Coca-Cola – which told him to share a Coke with Matthias and Emily – and a bag of salty salmiak liquorice. At the register he added a last-minute pack of spearmint gum and a Bounty chocolate bar to the purchase.

He'd practically inhaled two cigarettes and half the chocolate bar when the boy waved to him from inside the kebab shop that his order was ready. Kjeld stubbed out his cigarette on the sidewalk, threw the second half of the chocolate bar in the trash, picked up his order, and began the bumpy drive home.

When he pulled up in front of the house, Sara was already storming out the front door ready to give him a tongue-lashing for taking so long. She was late picking up her husband from Östersund and both the kids needed rides to the community centre for some kind of school service project. She was speaking so quickly that Kjeld couldn't keep up with what she was saying. And before he could get a word in edgewise she was slamming the door of her Volvo and speeding down the drive.

Kjeld looked to the house and saw his father standing at the window, staring out at him with tired, watchful eyes. By the time Kjeld walked in the house the pizzas were cold.

\* \* \*

When Kjeld entered the living room after reheating the pizzas in the oven he thought he saw his father's eyes light up like a kid on Christmas morning. He even set his book, a collection of northern Scandinavian nature photography, to the side and sat forward in his chair expectantly. Something about that action reminded Kjeld of his cat when he sat in front of the food bowl waiting for him to finish measuring out the kibble into a plastic cup on the kitchen scale. He never used to measure pet food. Not until he moved in with Bengt. He'd been as strict on the cat's diet as he had been on Kjeld's and the habit stuck with him even after the separation. Although, if Esme's text messages were to be believed, it hadn't helped any.

Kjeld set the pizzas on the coffee table and pulled it closer to his dad's chair, an old leather recliner that had stopped reclining before Kjeld left home as a teenager. It was cracked along the armrests where the fabric had begun to thin and peel and the way his father sat in it, half hunched and sinking, made Kjeld suspect that some of the springs beneath the cushion were broken. It was a wonder that Sara hadn't replaced that chair years ago. She'd probably tried and their father probably threw a fit. He'd always been good at that, even before he was diagnosed with dementia.

Kjeld cut the tuna and shrimp pizza into eight manageable slices and held the plate out to Stenar. Stenar took it and placed it in his lap.

'I haven't had a pizza in years,' Stenar said, his voice harsh and gravelly.

'Do you need a napkin?' Kjeld asked.

'I can manage.'

Kjeld screwed the lid off one of the colas – *Share a Coke with Emily* – and set it on the end table beside the photography book. He kept the Matthias bottle for himself, chugging most of the bottle before he started in on the pizza.

'It might not be any good,' Kjeld said with his mouthful. 'I had to reheat it.'

'Frozen?'

'Kebab place on 340.'

'Three-forty?'

'Fiskevägen. Next to the petrol station.'

Stenar nodded his head. 'That used to be a bait and tackle shop.'

'Really?' Kjeld tried to remember that, but nothing came to him. Then again, he hadn't really been out that way much as a boy. When he wasn't at school or on the football field he was out in the woods, trying to discover what his father and grandfather had found so fascinating about the wilderness. For a time he thought he'd found it, but he lost it quickly after.

'Owner was German,' Stenar said. 'Can't recall his name. Came out here in the late Seventies. Left in the Nineties, I think.'

'I think they're Turkish now,' Kjeld said. He finished off a slice of pizza. It was good, but the mushrooms were soggy. 'At least, I think that's what they were speaking behind the counter.'

'Turkish?'

'The people working at the kebab place.'

'Oh, I see,' Stenar said between bites. 'I've never seen a Turkish fisherman.'

They ate in silence for a few minutes, Stenar slouched in his chair and Kjeld hunched over the coffee table so he wouldn't spill any of the gooey cheese on the floor. On the outside it probably looked like a casual scene, a father and son sharing lunch, talking about the olden days. But for Kjeld it was anything but casual. Anything but normal. For him it was uncomfortable, but the longer he spent in the presence of his father, the more difficult it was for him to determine if that discomfort came from the past and the events that had pushed them apart or from the present and Kjeld's reluctance to let go of bad memories.

Memories that he was beginning to believe were coloured by the unforgiving perspective of a confused and lonely child. Memories that may not have been as bad as he'd allowed them to become in his mind.

Kjeld finished off the rest of his cola in a single gulp and forced back the urge to belch.

'That reminds me,' Kjeld said, cutting himself a new slice of pizza. This time he pulled the mushrooms off and set them on the side of the plate. 'I found something in the cellar.'

'You shouldn't go down there,' Stenar said, his voice becoming traditionally paternal, and Kjeld knew what he was going to say before he said it. Because he'd heard it so many times in his youth. 'The stairs aren't solid. You could trip and fall.'

'I was careful.'

'I've been meaning to fix those stairs.'

'The stairs are fine, Dad. You did fix them.'

'I did?'

'Yeah.'

Stenar brought another slice of pizza to his mouth. One of the shrimps fell off and landed in his lap. He didn't notice.

'I found a fishing tackle box in the basement with a bunch of photos inside.'

'Someone should organise the family photos one day. Your mother was working on that. She was putting together a scrapbook. But she's too sick to work on it now. I don't want to bother her with it.'

Kjeld held back a sigh. 'These were different photos, Dad. They were locked up.'

'Locked up?'

'In a tackle box. Old photos of you and Mum and some other people. A couple were from a Christmas party.'

Stenar slowed his chewing. His gaze drifted away from Kjeld and focused on the pizza. It could have been his memory striving to make a connection, but Kjeld had the distinct impression that his dad was trying to avoid the conversation. Or, perhaps, come up with a lie that would appease Kjeld to drop the topic.

Stenar shrugged. 'We used to go to a lot of parties. Eiji is a beautiful dancer.'

'Someone wrote 1978 on the back of the photo. Sara would have already been born,' Kjeld insisted.

Stenar looked down at his pizza. Then he took a sip of cola and set it down shakily beside his nature book. 'That was a long time ago.'

'There were quite a few people in the photo I didn't recognise. Especially the one with Mum. Where was that Christmas party? The house didn't look familiar.'

Stenar stiffened. He set the unfinished slice of pizza back on his plate. 'I'm not hungry anymore.'

'You've barely eaten anything,' Kjeld said.

'You shouldn't be digging around in my old things,' Stenar snapped. His face contorted into one that Kjeld remembered clearly from his childhood. Anger and disappointment. 'Can't you learn to respect another person's privacy? You have no business trifling through my things or your mother's. It's nothing that concerns you.'

It was like a slap to the face. Just when Kjeld was beginning to think he had misjudged his father and his childhood, perhaps even this bizarre situation in the barn, he was reminded of how things had really been. Endless memories of yelling and blaming. A tight grip on his arm when he didn't listen. The hurtful words. His mother's quiet sobbing. Stenar may not have had any memory of it, but Kjeld still did. And when Stenar raised his voice, Kjeld was transported back to his childhood and all those altercations, fleeting in the moment but significant over time, that had led to his sudden departure from Varsund.

It filled him with rage.

'Eat your lunch,' Kjeld said through gritted teeth.

'I won't.'

'Eat your goddamn lunch or I won't make you any dinner.'

Stenar glared at him. There it was. There was the man who never saw anything of worth in his son. The man that Kjeld always knew despised him although he could never figure out why.

'Sara won't stand for this,' Stenar said.

'Sara isn't here!' Kjeld yelled. 'Sara is sick and tired of taking care of you and listening to you talk crazy about your goddamn birds and not even being able to remember what fuckin' day it is. She's not here. And as soon as this bullshit with the barn is settled, I won't be here either.'

Kjeld laughed out of hurt and frustration. He could feel the heat in his face rising. He clenched his fists together just to keep them from shaking and even though he knew he would regret every word he was about to say he didn't stop himself. 'You had a dead body in your yard! For Chrissakes, Dad. A dead body

145

that you say you saw, but you can't remember. It's a fuckin' joke. *You're* a joke.'

Stenar threw his lunch on the floor. The ceramic plate hit the edge of the coffee table and chipped, but didn't completely break. The leftover pizza slices slid and landed cheese-side down on the small circular rug on the centre of the floor.

'I'm not making you anything else,' Kjeld said between agitated breaths.

'I don't want anything from you,' Stenar said. His eyes were watering, but Kjeld thought the tears were more from the frustration of the heightened emotion in the room than any actual regret. 'I've never wanted anything from you. I never wanted you.'

Kjeld's breath caught in his chest.

It was something he'd known unconsciously for a long time. He'd always had the sense that his father preferred his sister. Kjeld rationalised it as a child. He told himself it was because Sara was older than him, smarter than him, more polite. He was the younger child and as much as he tried to be like his older sister, they really had nothing in common with each other. Kjeld was always getting into trouble. In school, outside of school, at home. And while he tried to relate to his father as a young boy and show interest in the things his father cared deeply about, Kjeld never seemed to be able to reach past Stenar's distant exterior. It was as if his father had put up a wall between the two of them from birth and no matter how hard Kjeld tried he could never scale that wall, let alone break it down.

Then his mother died and all hope of ever having a relationship with his father died with her.

He needed a cigarette.

Kjeld pushed his plate closer to Stenar's side of the coffee table and stood up. 'You can eat mine if you get hungry.'

His hands were still trembling when he stepped out on the back porch and shook a cigarette from the pack into his hand. Out in the barn the ravens were rustling, cawing like they had when the stranger broke into their space and disturbed their ground. Except the door was closed this time, sealed off with cordon tape. They were alone. Alone and yet they still made noise.

* * *

'What did you do?' Esme's voice was quiet on the other end of the line.

Kjeld sat at the desk in his old bedroom and exhaled a cloud of smoke out the open window. It was cold in the room, the icy coolness in the air signalling that it would snow again tonight, but old habits died hard. He'd never been allowed to smoke in the house. Not in his parents' house. Not in Bengt's house. Not even his own house, thanks to his insufferable landlord. And like measuring the kibble for the cat, the fear of the unseen consequence stuck with him.

He dangled the cigarette out the crack in the window and watched as his smoky breath disappeared into the grey sky.

'I said some things I shouldn't have.'

'How is that any different than normal?'

Kjeld looked down at the tackle box photos, spread out over the desk. 'These things were cruel.'

'I'm sure you didn't mean it, Kjeld,' Esme said. She was trying to be reassuring, but Kjeld could hear in her voice that she was more worried than anything else.

'I did mean it though. I meant every word.'

'You've been under a lot of stress lately. The Aubuchon case, this thing with your dad, Nils—'

'I don't want to talk about Nils,' Kjeld said.

'You're going to have to talk about it eventually.'

Kjeld picked up the photo with him, Sara, and his parents in it. His mother was holding him, one arm tucked up under him for support, the other wrapped partly around his chubby infant body. His legs were dangling like two pale sausages. He didn't have

147

any hair in the photo. His mother said he was the exact opposite of his sister when he was born. Sara came out easy with a thick head of hair. Kjeld, on the other hand, took almost twenty-seven hours of labour before he decided to enter the world, "bald as a baboon's bottom" his mother used to say. It was one of her favourite stories to tell people. He supposed a story like that would have embarrassed most young boys, but Kjeld had always liked that story. Maybe because he could hear in his mother's voice the unconditional love she had for that moment. For him. She'd always wanted a son, she told him.

'He's alive. He's been arrested. When I get back to Gothenburg the chief will make me see a shrink just to make sure I'm fit for duty. I'll talk then.'

There was a long pause on the other end of the line. Kjeld tried to hear sounds in the background, but wherever Esme was it was quiet. Quiet aside from her slow steady breaths.

'Tell me what's going on, Kjeld.'

'I don't even know anymore,' he said, turning his gaze away from the photographs to exhale another cloud of smoke out the window. 'I'm beginning to think I'm the one going crazy. They haven't identified the body yet, but—'

Esme interrupted him before he could even finish taking a breath. 'The *body*? You didn't tell me anything about a body.'

'I'm sorry, Esme. I've been in a haze.' Kjeld held up the Christmas party photograph. His mother looked so happy. He'd never seen a smile like that on her before. It was so honest. Genuine. Free from the burdens of being a wife and a mother out in the middle of nowhere. 'My dad was right. He did see something. We found a body in the barn. Someone broke in and tried to remove it. I chased them into the woods, but lost them.'

The silence on Esme's end repeated itself except this time Kjeld couldn't even hear her breathing. She did that sometimes when she got frustrated with him. She just clenched her teeth and fumed.

'I'm coming out there,' she finally said.

It didn't surprise Kjeld that she would say that. He appreciated her concern for him, unnecessary as it often was. It was
comforting to know that he at least had one person on his side.
One of these days he would ask Esme why she cared so much.
Why she always went out of her way to be protective of him,
even when he was wrong. Why she was willing to occasionally
bend the rules for his benefit. Then again, maybe he wouldn't
ask. Maybe he didn't want to know. If he knew then he'd have
to be responsible for that knowledge and any consequences that
resulted from it.

And Kjeld had already made it clear that he was a failure when
it came to his responsibilities.

'You don't need to do that.' Kjeld's gaze went over the rest
of the picture. There were at least ten people in total. With the
exception of his mother they were all men. His father was missing
from the photo. Was he the one with the camera? The man
directly beside his mother was the same man from his father's
military photograph. He was tall, broad-shouldered, and had one
of those dangerous smiles that looked like it could charm just
about anyone into doing anything. The man's arm was wrapped
around his mother's shoulder. Not intimately, but in that familiar
way of two people who'd known each other for many years.

'The case has been postponed pending witness testimony.
The defence is considering changing their plea. The chief has
me on desk work anyway. Give me your address. I can be there
in two days.'

Kjeld didn't say anything. He barely even heard Esme over
his own thoughts. His attention was focused on another figure
in the back of the photograph. One he hadn't noticed until that
moment. He was younger in the picture and he had more hair
than he did now, but Kjeld still recognised that short stature and
those wide eyes.

'I have to call you back, Esme.'

'Don't you dare hang up on me, Kjeld Nygaard.'

Kjeld ended the call. Then he smudged his cigarette out on the inside of the window pane and raised the picture to the light to get a better look.

What was Erik Norberg doing at a Christmas party with his mother?

# Chapter 21

Gunnar printed out the preliminary forensic results from Dr Akerman and read them three times before he decided to make the call. He knew it was too early to say anything. Akerman would be handing off the cadaver to a more established team from Östersund and they would be able to do a full analysis, including a search for matching dental records. If they were lucky this would give them an almost one hundred per cent chance of uncovering the identity of the body or, at the very least, narrow the field of investigation. And while Gunnar didn't know with any certainty whose body had been discovered in the Nygaard barn, he had his suspicions. Suspicions that were very nearly affirmed by Akerman's note about an old leg injury. Suspicions he had to share with Roland Lindqvist.

He just didn't want to make the call. That's why he read the report three times before he decided to pick up the phone. He wanted – no, he needed to be certain of the facts even if there weren't many. And he needed the confidence that came with making such a call. Confidence that came with reading those results multiple times and committing the words to memory.

Gunnar cleared his throat and dialled the number. After the fourth ring he thought it might go to voicemail and he felt a weight in his chest lift. Then the phone connected.

'Yes?' Roland's voice was business direct, but Gunnar thought he could hear impatience in his tone.

'I've just been sent the preliminary results from the body on the Nygaard property,' Gunnar said.

'And? Is it him?'

'It's still too early to say.' Gunnar paused. 'But there are a lot of similarities.'

* * *

A quick Google search confirmed everything Kjeld had already assumed about Erik Norberg. He was an attorney who started off his career in family law and then, presumably realising the devastating effects that could have on a person's psyche combined with the menial pay, changed to international business with a focus in contract law. He had his own firm, Norberg & Associates, which was situated in Stockholm, and according to their website most of their connections were in the big business fields – health, engineering, financial services, logistics and transportation, and oil and gas. By law they weren't allowed to list their clients directly, but based on the sleek layout of their homepage and the tailored cut of Norberg's suit in his business profile photo, it wasn't hard for Kjeld to guess.

So why Varsund? And why his father?

Kjeld compared the photo from the tackle box to the one on the law firm website. He had more hair on his upper lip than he did on his head today, but there was no arguing that short stature and those bulging eyes. Kjeld was certain he was the man in the picture, standing off to the side of the group and staring straight on. He looked like the least interesting person at the party. Like the odd kid out during an after-school football match. The kid who was forced to sit on the bench and wait for someone else to get tired or hurt before he could play. Even the way he held that glass of champagne in his hand made him look awkward. The others, Kjeld's mother included, appeared well practised in the art of elegance. Norberg hadn't yet reached their level of well-bred sophistication. He was still learning.

*N.M. Christmas Party 1978.* Kjeld tried to think of any local Varsund residents with those initials, but no one came to mind. Then it occurred to him that it was entirely possible that the party wasn't in Varsund. It wasn't like the Kommun was teeming with wealthy elite. And there were only so many houses that could support the inner decor that he was seeing on the walls behind the group of partygoers. Maybe it was somewhere else. But why would his mother, a simple Norrland girl, be there?

Kjeld shoved the Christmas photo into his back pocket. Maybe it was time to look closer at Erik Norberg.

# Chapter 22

## Tisdag | Tuesday

Nils shouted something at him that Kjeld couldn't understand. Kjeld raised his service weapon, finger close to the trigger. It started to rain. Nils aimed his gun as well, but this time it wasn't directed at Kjeld. It was pointed at his daughter. At Tove.

She stood just a few feet from him, her light red curls matted down by the sudden shower. Tears, like raindrops, streamed down her face. Her eyes pleaded with him to do something. To help her. To save her.

It wasn't real. It was a dream. Kjeld knew that subconsciously, but it didn't stop him from fearing what he saw. It didn't stop him from believing it.

The sound of the rain against the shipping containers filled his head with an overpowering din.

Nils said something that Kjeld couldn't understand and laughed. Kjeld looked back and forth from his friend to his daughter and back to his friend again. He was waiting for Esme to shout. That's when the gun would go off. That's when he would wake up. But Esme wasn't there. Instead Tove reached out to him with a pale arm.

'Daddy?'

The gunshot silenced the sound of the rain.

Kjeld rolled over in bed and stared up at the unfamiliar ceiling. The room was awash in the scent of cigarettes, sweat, and Hanna's perfume, which must have had essence of lavender in it because his nose tickled. Lavender always made his nose tickle.

'What time is it?' he mumbled against her back.

Hanna reached for the mobile phone on the nightstand and pushed the power button. The sudden glow in the pitch-black room was blinding. Kjeld winced.

'Almost seven o'clock,' she said.

'Seven? In the evening?'

'Morning.'

'Shit.' Kjeld sat up and searched through the covers for his shirt. 'I've gotta go.'

'Late for a hot date?' Hanna teased, turning over onto her back so she could watch him fumble around the dark room for his clothes.

'I left Dad alone at home.'

Kjeld cursed himself for being so careless. He'd been so angry with his father that he'd left without thinking. Then he and Hanna started talking and the time simply got away from him.

Kjeld's toes hit his belt buckle on the floor, causing it to clink. He reached down and pulled up his pants. Socks? Shoes? They were probably at the front door. He stumbled into a dresser.

Hanna turned on the bedside lamp, illuminating enough of the room for Kjeld to find his way to the door.

'Sorry I've got to run out on you.'

Hanna sat up and shrugged. 'I'll try not to cry too hard into my pillow after you leave.'

She stretched her arms up above her head and climbed out of bed.

Kjeld paused in the doorway long enough to watch her slip a T-shirt on and step into a pair of lace panties. Her breasts, small but firm, held up the shirt and he could see the hardness of her nipples through the fabric. A nagging voice in the back of his head told him his father could wait another fifteen minutes, but the guilt of their argument drew him out of those thoughts.

'You know, if you wanted to come by later—'

'I have to work late. And I need to get up early the next morning. Trying to get in as many extra hours as possible before it all goes to shit. The word on the street is that we're all going to get sacked when the Norrmalm merger goes through.'

'I'm sorry.'

'It's not your fault.'

'I could promise not to keep you up too late,' Kjeld said. He smiled. It was genuine. He wouldn't argue that she was a distraction from a lot of the stressors he was experiencing then, but he did enjoy her company.

She snorted a laugh. 'I don't trust that promise.'

'Tomorrow then? When you get off work?'

'I'll think about it,' she said.

'I'll try not to think about it,' Kjeld replied.

'You really need to stop being so slick. It's just going to depress me when you leave again.'

Kjeld sensed she was only half joking. As far as options for a good time went, Varsund was considerably limited. It made him wonder what prevented her from moving to Örebro to be closer to her children, but it wasn't his place to ask.

'Well you know where to find me,' he said, turning towards the living room and the front door.

He was zipping up his coat when Hanna hurried out of the bedroom with something in her hand.

'Must have fallen out of your pocket,' she said, holding out the photograph of his mother at the Christmas party.

Kjeld took it from her and nodded. 'Thanks.'

'She's a looker.' Hanna grinned.

'She's my mother.'

'Explains where you got your good looks from.' Hanna leaned closer to his arm to get a better look at the photo. 'God, Erik always looked like a zombie.'

Kjeld blinked. 'Erik Norberg? You know this man?'

'Sometimes I wish I didn't,' Hanna said. 'Nothing against him really, but that guy has the creepiest eyes. I feel like they just follow you around the room. But he's nice. Kind of stuffy, but you know how lawyers are. Roland looks good though. I mean, damn. He's in good shape for a man his age, but in this photo? I'd be eyeing him up, too.'

'Who?'

'Roland Lindqvist. The man your mother is giving the googly eyes to.'

Kjeld brought the photo closer to his face. Sure enough it did look like his mother was smiling at the man on the other side of her. Not the tall one giving her the friendly hug, but the slightly shorter man with the smug grin.

'Wait. How do you know these people?' Kjeld asked.

Hanna tilted her head to the side and looked at him as if to say, "are you serious?" 'Because I've been working for them since I quit college and came back to Varsund.'

She pointed to Roland Lindqvist. 'He's my boss.' Then she pointed to the man with his arm around Kjeld's mother. 'And that's his brother, Peter.'

Kjeld frowned. He felt like there was a piece to the puzzle he still wasn't quite seeing. 'And where is this?'

'Well, that's easy. The Norrmalm company Christmas party. They have it every year. Still do. The speeches are boring as hell but they serve the best champagne. It's when they pass out the employee bonuses. But they definitely scrimped last year. I didn't get as much as I did two years ago.'

157

N.M. Norrmalm Industries. Of course. The largest mining company in the area. Not to mention the place that employed most of Varsund and ensured its continued existence. Without Norrmalm, Varsund would be another deserted mining town, leaving its residents to seek employment in either the timber industry or one of the nearby paper mills. Kjeld couldn't believe he didn't put those initials together sooner. Still, he didn't know why his mother would be at one of their Christmas parties. Then he recalled the photo of his father during his military service with the other man. The man with his arm around his mother's shoulders at the Christmas party. Peter Lindqvist.

'And Peter Lindqvist – he's still in town?' Kjeld asked.

'No, not exactly. He took a break from the company a few years back. I think it was due to stress or his health. I can't really remember all that much about it except that it seemed kind of sudden. Then again, I'm sure his family knew what he was planning. After he left it was his brother, Roland, who took over.'

'When was the last time you saw him?'

Hanna brushed a chunk of curly hair away from her face. 'Years. Probably on his last day when he stopped by the office to say goodbye to Roland.'

'Where did he go?'

Hanna gave a nervous laugh. 'What's with the interrogation, Kjeld? You think the Lindqvists had something to do with what we found in your dad's barn?'

Kjeld didn't know what he thought. He was grasping for straws. But when he thought about that photograph of his father and Peter as young men he felt like he was missing something important. 'I feel like there's a connection I'm not seeing.'

'Look, the Lindqvists are just your typical ridiculously wealthy and slightly overbearing family. Is Roland hard to get along with sometimes? Of course. And everyone knows his kids are selfish twits. But I can't imagine that they'd be involved in a murder.

And I'm certain *someone* knows where Peter is. He's probably enjoying his retirement on a beach somewhere. Greece or maybe one of those islands in the Caribbean where rich people fly to in their private jets.'

'You're probably right. After all, if Peter Lindqvist were missing then someone would be looking for him.'

People didn't just ignore the disappearance of someone important.

'What about this man here in the back?' Kjeld asked. It was a figure that Kjeld hadn't noticed the first time he'd looked at the image. Initially he'd thought Norberg looked the most unrefined, but on closer examination the man on the far right, directly behind Norberg, appeared even more out of place. He wore a shabbier suit coat, which stood out against the smart dinner jackets of the other men.

Hanna frowned. 'You know, this is going to sound really strange, but that looks like the Bear.'

'The Drunken Bear? Valle Dahl?'

'Yes! The man who used to sit outside of the supermarket looking for handouts. It's difficult to say though without the beard. And he looks really young here. But you see that mark on his forehead?'

'I thought that was a smudge in the photograph.'

Hanna shook her head. 'The Bear has a big purple birthmark on his forehead in the shape of a bear. That's how he got his nickname.'

Kjeld brought the picture closer to his face. Sure enough, Hanna was right. It was a mark on his face. He couldn't believe he hadn't seen that earlier.

'Did she work for Norrmalm?' Hanna asked. 'Your mother?'

'No. She didn't.'

'Your dad?'

'He worked for the National Forest Agency. I can't for the life of me figure out what she would be doing with these people.

159

They were exactly the kind of crowd I remember my parents avoiding.'

'Well, she must have been someone special. I've never known the Lindqvists to invite just anyone to their business parties. They must have been close.'

# Chapter 23

Kjeld arrived at home, expecting to find the place in disarray and his father unmanageable. Instead he found him sitting in his reading chair, lucid and calm, incognisant of the fact that Kjeld had been gone at all. His father had even managed to make himself breakfast and was quick to point out that Kjeld had forgotten to pick up the groceries. Kjeld was almost offended. When he tried to ask his father about his relationship to the people in the photograph, however, his father grew irritable and tight-lipped. And when Kjeld mentioned the silver Mercedes behind his great-grandfather's hunting cabin, his father absolutely refused to speak at all. He wasn't going to get any answers this way. He needed to find a more reliable source. He needed to talk to Roland Lindqvist.

From the outside, the offices of Norrmalm Industries weren't much to look at. The front face of the building was made from old limestone and shale that had turned yellow with age and jutted out between the discoloured mortar.

A modern addition was attached on the western side of the building, beyond which Kjeld could catch a glimpse of the retired steel conveyors and ventilation flue from the original mining plant. It had been out of service since the late Nineties when Norrmalm converted the old building to their corporate headquarters and relocated the plant to the northern end of the Kommun. Kjeld vaguely recalled a community uproar from local miners who hadn't been pleased with the fact that they would have to leave their homes earlier to account for the longer travelling time. He supposed, however, that the need for a paycheque outweighed the inconvenience. After all, the further north one went, the fewer options there were for work.

The interior of the building was more streamlined and metropolitan than Kjeld anticipated. In place of that earthy scent of rock and dust, which he'd come to associate with Varsund, was the unnaturally sterile odour of industrial cleaning supplies and modern fixtures. Austere like a financial institution. The sleek rectangular design, inconsistent with the untamed woodland around it, belied Kjeld's perception of what belonged in Varsund. This was too contemporary and fresh for the town he remembered. It gave him the same disquieting sensation of displacement that he had whenever he attended a formal event. This was a company built on the backs of sweaty, dirt-stained labourers, and Kjeld felt underdressed in his jeans and lace-up work boots.

After checking in at the visitors' desk, he was directed to sit in a waiting room decorated with black-and-white photographs detailing Norrmalm's progression from its seemingly low-brow roots in the late 1800s to the operational giant it was today. Almost thirty minutes passed before a young receptionist led him wordlessly to the elevator and then down a long corridor to a corner office.

The name on the office door, however, did not belong to Roland Lindqvist.

The receptionist knocked and slowly pushed the door open. The man on the other side was on the phone and held up a waiting finger to her and Kjeld.

David Lindqvist was a striking man. His hair was a light, almost icy shade of blond that was perfectly parted on the right. His skin had a warm, tanned glow of someone who had just returned from a tropical vacation, but without that red undertone that came with being subjected to direct sunlight. Kjeld assumed the man got his vitamin D from a salon or a bottle, although the evenness of the colouring seemed to discredit the latter. His eyes were a soft shade of green and he had one of those faces common to men's fashion magazines. Square jaw, high cheekbones, and a nose that looked as though it had been carved by a sculptor in the Italian Renaissance. He was tall, close to Kjeld's own height, with the physique of a cyclist. It wasn't difficult to imagine him spending his mornings on a Peloton bike. Overall, he was immaculate. Pristine in appearance from the cut of his suit to the gleam in his shoes.

Kjeld sensed almost immediately that he wasn't going to like this man.

'Do you know what day it is? I don't have time to go over this with you again,' David said to the caller. 'I don't care about fluctuating market returns and quarterly goals. I just want to be notified the minute my father gets out of his meeting with the MineCorp representative.'

He placed his hand over the speaker and shot a glare at both Kjeld and the receptionist. 'What is it?'

'I'm sorry to bother you, Herr Lindqvist,' the receptionist said. 'But this man is here from the police.'

David stared at Kjeld before returning to his call. 'I'll get back to you later. Keep me updated.'

He rang off and dropped his mobile on the desk. 'I assume you have some identification?'

Kjeld took his formal police card and badge out of his back pocket and held it up for the other man.

'Nygaard,' David read off the card, purposefully elongating the second syllable more than was necessary. 'Danish?'

'A few generations back,' Kjeld replied.

'Gothenburg? You're a long way from home, Inspector.'

'I was hoping to speak with Roland or Peter Lindqvist.'

163

'Roland is in a meeting and Peter is indisposed,' David replied. 'But I'm a Lindqvist. Perhaps I can help?'

There was something about the way David referred to himself as a Lindqvist that bothered Kjeld. Still, he kept his cool, as he should have done during his meeting with Gunnar, and held out the old photograph of the Norrmalm Christmas party.

David looked at it, his lips pursing into an agitated grimace. Then he nodded before turning his attention to the receptionist. 'Thank you, Lena. That'll be all.'

The receptionist left, closing the door behind her.

'Good God. I guess Norberg always was an ugly son of a bitch.'

David waved a hand to the leather chair across from the desk and Kjeld sat down. He felt a little guilty using his badge to get into the building. It was a blatant misuse of his power. First of all, he had no jurisdiction in Jämtland. Secondly, he was on suspension and technically should have turned his badge in before he left Gothenburg. But that was the least of his wrongdoings over the last few weeks. He doubted that would be the straw to break the camel's back.

Kjeld looked at the brass-coloured name plate on the man's desk. 'David Lindqvist?'

'Roland is my father,' David said, slumping down in the chair behind the desk. He shook his head at the photograph and laughed. 'Seeing this has made it worth coming into work today. Can you believe people used to actually dress like this? God, sometimes I wish I could go back in time just to see the ridiculous things people thought were cool.'

'Hip,' Kjeld said.

'I beg your pardon?'

'What they thought was hip at the time. You know, groovy.'

David looked at Kjeld's deadpan expression as though he were uncertain if he was making a joke or being serious.

David snorted. 'Proof that my dad always looked like an arsehole.'

164

'Which one is he again?' Kjeld asked.

David set the photograph on the table and pointed to the man to the right of Kjeld's mother. The one with the leering grin.

David's phone jingled, one of his social media apps alerting him that someone in his "Close Friends" network had added a new post. He opened it in full view of Kjeld's gaze. The image was a brightly coloured photo showing a woman's outstretched legs, toenails freshly painted a coral hue, in front of an open ocean. David scoffed, annoyed. 'My sister. Probably the most filtered person on the internet. I wish these damn things gave you the option to dislike a post. What about you?'

'I don't filter,' Kjeld said flatly.

'What did you say this was about again? Gothenburg police? I think you might have taken a wrong turn somewhere.'

Again David's tone irked Kjeld. It was haughty. Flippant. And it reminded Kjeld of his early days as a beat officer in the big city when his colleagues persistently picked on his northern accent and small-town roots.

'I'm helping out the local police on an investigation,' Kjeld lied.

'You know, you look awfully familiar,' David said. 'Are you a local?'

'I grew up in Varsund, but I haven't been back for quite some time.'

'I don't blame you.' David leaned back in his chair and crossed one leg over the other at the knee. 'Place is a shithole.'

'It does leave something to be desired,' Kjeld said. He tapped the centre of the photo. 'Do you recognise this woman?'

David craned his neck and then shook his head. 'Never seen her before.'

'So, as far as you're aware, she didn't work for Norrmalm?'

'When was this picture taken?'

Kjeld flipped the photograph over to display the date.

'In '78? That's way before my time. I couldn't tell you. She might have been a secretary or something. Or somebody's date.'

'This man's date, perhaps?' Kjeld asked, motioning towards the man on his mother's left.

'Uncle Peter?' David laughed. 'Hardly. No way. Absolutely not.'

'How can you be sure? Like you said, it was before your time.'

'Uncle Peter never brought dates to company shindigs. Once his wife died he went on the straight and narrow as far as women were concerned. Everything was about work for him. Norrmalm or nothing.'

'Was?'

'He went on sabbatical a few years back. More like an early retirement though, if you ask me. Haven't really kept in touch.'

Kjeld removed another photo from his pocket. The one of Stenar and Peter from their military days. 'What about this man? Do you recognise him?'

David's face hardened and for a second Kjeld thought he saw something in the man's eyes that looked like recognition, but David shook his head. 'What did you say your name was again?'

'Kjeld Nygaard.'

'Nygaard who used to be a local boy.' David clicked his tongue. 'Are you sure we haven't met?'

Kjeld felt his patience dwindling. 'I think I would remember if we had.'

David shook his head. 'No. Sorry. I don't recognise that man.'

Kjeld slipped the photos into his jacket pocket and stood up. 'I'm sorry to have taken up your time.'

'If you have any more photos of Norberg with hair then you're welcome to as much of my time as you want. Anything to wipe that smug look off his face. The guy is an arse. Thinks he's better than everyone, but he's not. He's from Ödeshög.' David said it like it was a crime. As if Varsund was any better.

'Do you think your father will be available to speak with me today?'

David shrugged. 'Hard to say. He's in the middle of a merger. Contract negotiations. You know how it is.'

166

David, like so many people Kjeld had crossed paths with over the last few days, riled his patience. Even the comments that weren't meant to be glib provoked him. But while Kjeld didn't feel any closer to understanding why his parents were in a photograph with Varsund's most well-established family, David had at least confirmed some of what Hanna had told him. Still, he sensed he would have to speak to Roland to get more information. Or better yet, Peter. 'Perhaps you could let him know that I'd appreciate him making time in his schedule to speak with me.'

'Perhaps.' David smiled, but Kjeld wasn't convinced that there was any sincerity in it.

'Thank you for your time.'

'Anything to help the law. Best of luck on your investigation, Officer.'

'Detective,' Kjeld corrected and left.

# Chapter 24

Stenar was in the front yard pulling frost-covered weeds with his bare hands when Kjeld returned from his impromptu meeting with David Lindqvist.

Kjeld sighed, still mulling over the businessman's peculiar reaction to the photograph, as he climbed out of his car and went up the overgrown walk to his father.

Stenar tossed another handful of weeds into a broken wheelbarrow full of unused tiles, probably from when his father planned to remodel the kitchen almost twenty years ago, and looked up with a grin. 'Good! You're here. You can help.'

'Dad, it's freezing outside. And these weeds are all dead anyway. There's no point in pulling them,' Kjeld said. Then he saw his father's hands, red from the cold and cut up across the palms. 'For God's sake, you're not even wearing any gloves.'

'If you don't get them out, roots and all, then they'll just grow back even stronger.' Stenar stretched down for another prickly stem, but his left knee still wouldn't bend fully and the weed was just out of reach. 'Could you give me a hand here?'

Kjeld stepped around the wheelbarrow, wrapped his hand around the thick weed near the base of the stem, and tugged. A large clump of dirt came up along with the roots, leaving a noticeable hole in the ground. He tossed the weeds in the barrow.

Stenar nodded as though he were pleased with the results. 'That's how you do it. Glad to see you didn't forget everything I taught you.'

'It's a weed, Dad. It's not rocket science.' Kjeld wiped the dirt from his hands on his jeans. 'Come on. Let's go inside and get something to eat.'

'I'm not hungry.'

'Well, I am.'

Kjeld took his father by the arm and helped him around to the front of the house. Once they were inside, where thankfully his father hadn't gotten it into his mind to turn off the heat as a means for conserving electricity as he had been apt to do when Kjeld was a teenager, Kjeld ran a dishrag under the kitchen tap and washed off both of their hands. Then he dumped a few cupfuls of ground coffee into the filter of the coffee pot and set the water to boil.

He pulled back his mother's floral curtains and gazed out into the yard. It was early afternoon, but the sun was already past its zenith and the overcast skies turned the world a dreary shade of ash grey. It tricked Kjeld's mind into thinking it was much later. Again he felt that sensation of being watched. And he narrowed his vision, half expecting to see movement between the trees.

Nothing.

Even the ravens were quiet.

'I feel like there's someone out there,' he said.

'There's no one out there,' Stenar replied, sitting down at the kitchen table in the chair that used to be reserved for his mother.

His father was probably right. He was probably just paranoid. All of the suspicious, gossiping eyes were in town. Out here there was nothing more than miles and miles of wilderness.

Except there had been at least one person out in those woods.

The one Kjeld had chased through the snow. And while he might have imagined the chatter around town, he hadn't imagined that.

Kjeld opened the refrigerator and groaned. 'There's nothing to eat but—'

'Herring.'

Life was a cruel joke.

'I refuse to smell like pickled fish for the rest of the day.' Kjeld pulled out a triangular block of hard cheese and a bag of soft wheat polar bread from the cooling drawer. Someone with better foresight than himself must have put it in there so it wouldn't go bad. 'Besides, you shouldn't eat fish every day. It'll give you mercury poisoning or something.'

'The levels of mercury found in herring are negligible.'

'But they're still there,' Kjeld replied. He grabbed the cheese slicer and set two plates on the table beside the bread and cheese.

'Herring is such a small fish. You'd have to eat an unfathomable amount of herring in order to experience the effects of mercury poisoning.' Stenar took a slice of round bread from the bag and dropped it on his plate. 'Butter?'

Kjeld went back to the fridge and returned with the butter and a wooden spreading knife. 'Everything in moderation, I suppose.'

'Shark, swordfish, and king mackerel are the biggest mercury culprits. Or basically anything out of the Gulf of Mexico,' Stenar said, sweeping the butter knife across the bread in well-practised repetition.

Kjeld was reminded of how the body's muscle memory was always the last to go. He didn't want to think about what everyday motion his body would remember when the rest of his mind was gone.

'I guess we're fortunate enough to get most of our fish from Norway then. But you still shouldn't eat herring every day.'

'It won't kill me.'

'No, but your breath might kill me.'

Stenar stopped spreading the butter to stare at Kjeld. Then his face broke into a smile. A real smile. Perhaps the first one Kjeld had seen since he arrived. 'That's a good joke.'

'I do my best.'

Kjeld sliced off a few strips of cheese for the both of them and they ate their sandwiches in silence. Outside the snow started coming down in thick fluffy flakes, covering the ground in a soft layer of white. It looked like dandelion seedheads. A breeze kicked up through the trees and Kjeld watched as one of the cordon tapes snapped off the barn door and began flapping against the wooden planks.

'I'm sorry about yesterday.'

Stenar looked up from his sandwich. 'What about yesterday?'

'About the things I said.' Kjeld sliced off another piece of cheese and ate it plain. 'I was out of line and angry. I didn't mean it. Not really.'

Except he had. He'd meant it in the moment. Just as he was certain that his father had meant the things he'd said. But had circumstances been different, had they both been in control of their emotions, neither of them would have said anything.

Stenar stared at Kjeld, but didn't say a word.

The coffee pot gurgled that it was finished and Kjeld got up to pour two mugs. 'I just want to understand all of this. And I don't, Dad. I really don't get any of it. Milk?'

'Black.'

Kjeld sat back down. He took one sip from the mug and cringed. He'd overdone it on the coffee grounds. It was strong enough to float an egg.

Stenar drank it like it was water.

'Who was it, Dad?'

'Who was who?'

'In the barn. Who was the body we found?'

As if on cue Stenar turned his attention back to the window, staring off in the distance with vacant eyes.

'You called me,' Kjeld said. 'You called me and said you saw something. I thought you were just rambling. Even after Sara told me what you'd seen I didn't believe you and I apologise for that. You were right. There was a murder. But who was it? You say you saw it. What did you see?'

'They were arguing.' Stenar's voice cracked.

'Who was arguing?'

'I saw them arguing. I can't remember what it was about, but I knew it was something they weren't supposed to know.'

Kjeld frowned. 'Something *who* wasn't supposed to know?'

'I made a promise. I promised I would never talk about it. And I didn't. I didn't talk about it with anyone.'

'But who was it? Who did we find out there?'

Stenar's lower lip quivered and Kjeld noticed he was clenching the butter knife like a dagger. Then a tear fell from Stenar's cheek and plummeted into his coffee.

'My friend,' he said, breathing heavily. 'My best friend.'

* * *

Kjeld handed the old military photograph to Stenar. They'd moved to the living room so Stenar could relax more comfortably in his chair. Sitting at the kitchen table, with a direct view of the barn, kept his father distracted and Kjeld wanted to be certain he had as much of his attention as he could get.

'Was this your friend?'

Kjeld was conflicted by his father's admission. He knew that if the body out in the barn truly was that of Peter Lindqvist then it wouldn't bode well for his father. Not only because of the Lindqvists' power in the community, but because if Peter and his father had been friends then the circumstances looked even more suspicious. It wouldn't take a leap of judgement to consider that his father might be responsible for Peter's death in some way. Friendships did fall apart, after all. Sometimes violently.

Kjeld knew that all too well.

But to entertain the possibility that his father was capable of murder? Kjeld had spent years thinking ill of the man, but his father wasn't a killer. He couldn't be.

Stenar gave the photograph little more than a cursory glance and then handed it back to Kjeld. Looking at the image seemed to cause him physical pain.

'That's Peter,' Stenar said, nestling back into his chair and holding the coffee mug close to his chest.

'Peter Lindqvist?' Kjeld asked.

Stenar nodded. 'This was up in Norrbotten during our conscription service. You don't know what real cold is until you're lying on your stomach in a self-made ice hut during winter training while the wind sweeps over the gulf from Finland. My nose hairs were frozen for six weeks straight.'

'The regiment at Boden?'

'That's where the garrison was, but we had terrain exercises all over the northern regions. Spent a lot of time in Lapland. In that desolate space above Kiruna. But most of the training exercises were in Norrbotten. Especially near the border. Got a taste for Finnish squeaky cheese made from reindeer milk. That's the only thing up there, after all. Reindeer, cloudberries, and cold.'

'Tell me about Peter.'

Stenar sipped his coffee. 'He was excited about serving. It was something of a tradition in his family to stay in and enlist after conscription. Not make a career out of it, mind you, but at least go through the formal training and serve a respectable number of years. Then go home and take on the family business. Peter didn't stay in though. He broke his leg on one of the training exercises just before the end of our service and it never healed properly. He couldn't run anymore. Not for any extended periods of time. Even walking was sometimes a struggle for him.'

'He broke his leg?' Kjeld remembered the injury the pathologist pointed out on the cadaver and the muscles in his shoulders tensed.

173

'He walked with a cane afterwards.'

Kjeld listened to his father and tried to put the pieces together in his mind, but it was still difficult to get past the fact that his father had such sudden moments of clarity. Moments where even Kjeld forgot that he was suffering from irreparable mental deterioration. Stenar spoke of this time, which must have been more than fifty years ago, as though it were yesterday. And yet sometimes he looked at Kjeld, his own son, and didn't recognise him.

'What happened to him?'

Stenar rubbed the side of his face. 'I need a shave. What day is it? Sara always gives me a shave on Sunday.'

'It's Tuesday. She must have forgotten. I'll help you shave later.' Kjeld sat forward on the couch. 'What happened to Peter Lindqvist, Dad?'

'What do you mean what happened to him? He went home. He took over the family business. He made a lot of money.'

'You mean Norrmalm Industries?'

Stenar pulled on the short white hairs that were growing on his chin. 'Peter never had to work hard for anything in his life. Everything just came to him naturally. I used to think it was because he was rich, but he just had one of those personalities that you couldn't ignore. He was elegant and charming. People couldn't say no to him. You didn't want to. You know what I mean?'

Kjeld did. Nils had been like that. Back before Nils went off the deep end and started murdering government officials, that is. Nils was a real sweet talker. Everyone loved him. He was the exact opposite of Kjeld. Kjeld had always been the least alluring of the two of them. Not because Kjeld couldn't be charismatic and friendly, but because Kjeld was rougher around the edges. Nils had always managed to come off as an open book, never mind the fact that it was a book of lies. People were drawn to him because of that openness. If people were drawn to Kjeld it was only because they wanted to understand what it was that made a man so broken and impassable. That's how Bengt had always described him. Broken and impassable. Like he was some kind of unpaved mountain road blocked by fallen trees.

'I know what you mean.'

Stenar shook his head. 'I never could understand what people saw in him. In the beginning I guess I was enthralled by him as well. And it was nice having a buddy who had everything. But that changed after Norrmalm. Peter thought that place made him invincible.'

'Did you ever work there?' Kjeld asked.

'Me?' Stenar scoffed. 'Never. I would never. You know what that place does, don't you? It destroys everything. They cut down the trees. They dig up the earth. They force out the natural fauna. And then they poison the ground with their excavation techniques. Do you know how many indigenous plants are endangered in Sweden because of mining operations like Norrmalm?'

'I don't.'

'Too damn many. And for what purpose? Profit. It's disgusting.'

Kjeld thought about the Norrmalm Christmas party photo that had set his father off the other day. How did that fit into all of this?

'What about Mum?'

Stenar narrowed his eyes. 'What about her?'

'Did she feel the same way?'

Stenar fidgeted in his chair. 'Your mother loves nature. She doesn't approve of Norrmalm any more than I do. Ask her. She'll tell you.'

'But she was friends with the Lindqvists as well, wasn't she?'

'Of course, she was. We were all friends at one time. But friendships change over the years. I don't think I need to tell *you* that. I might be out in the middle of nowhere, but I still get the news. Sara told me about your friend, the one who killed all those people.'

Kjeld winced. *His* friend. As though Nils had somehow become his responsibility. But he had in a way. That's what had led to the stand-off at the APM Terminals port, after all. Kjeld's feelings of guilt for not seeing through Nils's deception earlier. And his subconscious feeling responsible for resolving the situation. For taking care of the Nils situation. Because Nils *had* been Kjeld's friend. And Kjeld should have seen something. He should have noticed something was wrong. That was his job, after all.

'You're right. I missed that. I didn't want to see the truth.'

'Some truths shouldn't be seen. Some truths are best left buried.'

An uncomfortable silence fell between them, but Kjeld couldn't tell if he felt uneasy because of the conflicting thoughts of Nils that the conversation had caused in his mind or because of the more pressing tension – that the body in the barn might have belonged to his father's good friend and the owner of a company that ensured the existence of the entire town.

For the first time since he'd seen his father, Kjeld looked at him with the eyes of an investigator. It was futile to ask himself if this was a man who could kill someone. If there was one thing Kjeld had learned in his time as a detective with the Gothenburg police, it was that everyone was capable of killing someone. Everyone had at least one murder inside of them. It only required the right circumstances – a well-timed argument, an irreconcilable rage, a sudden inability to rationalise – for that murder to occur. For most people that was never. The circumstances and components necessary to fuel within them the kind of action that led to murder were never met. Those people went about their lives content. Angry, perhaps, but content. And free from guilt. But the potential was always there. Kjeld had seen it in so many unsuspecting faces. Which is why when he looked at his father it wasn't with the question of whether Stenar was capable of murder. It was with the question of whether he was capable of murdering a friend and then covering it up from the rest of the world.

Kjeld watched Stenar. Watched how he sipped his coffee and

scratched his face. Watched how he fussed to get comfortable in his chair and lost his attention every time the birds cackled in the distance. Kjeld watched and reasoned, trying to see beyond what he actually knew of his father and what he believed to be true.

In the end he decided he didn't know. He couldn't read his father any better now than when he was a boy. If anything, his father had become more of an enigma to him.

'Was that the body of Peter Lindqvist we found in the barn, Dad?'

Stenar brought the mug to his lips and tried to sip, but it was empty.

'Dad?' Kjeld softened his tone.

Stenar didn't look up. His face went pale. Arm dropped at his side.

'Was that Peter in the barn?'

Stenar groaned. His chest heaved, mouth sucking in breaths of air like a fish out of water. He tried to set the mug on the side table, but it fell to the floor.

'Dad? Are you okay?'

Kjeld was halfway off the couch when Stenar clutched at his chest. His body stiffened, eyes wide and pleading, then he went limp.

# Chapter 25

## Tolv år sedan | Twelve years ago

Kjeld tugged a warped plank of plywood out from behind the stack of junk and unused tools his father had pushed up against the inside wall of the barn. The wood was flimsy, probably from moisture, but it wasn't rotten. It would serve its purpose well enough and seal up the hole in the roof of the barn, at least until his father decided to be less frugal with his money and hire a professional to replace the mouldering beams and broken tiles.

'You're not going to use that, are you?' Stenar grabbed the board out of Kjeld's hands and shook it. The plank wobbled, but didn't crack. 'This isn't any good. The snow will press down on this until it snaps. This will never hold. You need real boards. Something thicker.'

'It's only temporary, Dad. It'll close up the hole until you can get someone else out here to fix the roof. That's the problem.'

'You said you would fix the roof.'

'No, I said I would seal up the hole. I'm not a roofer. Besides, if I go up there and lay down new tiles and it starts leaking again next year, then you're just going to be pissed at me.'

'What's the point of going up there and nailing in a piece of shaky plywood if it's just going to fall apart again?'

'The point is to close up the goddamn hole, Dad.' Kjeld clenched his jaw. He tried not to let his father's nagging get the better of him, but it seemed the longer he was away from Varsund the more difficult it was to come back. And the greater the rift between him and his father grew.

'I don't appreciate you talking to me like that. Your mother would have never stood for you talking like that in the house,' Stenar chastised.

'Well, I guess it's a good fuckin' thing we're not in the house then, isn't it?' The words came out quicker than Kjeld could reel them in.

Stenar glared at him. 'If that's how you feel about it then you can forget about the roof. I'll fix it myself.'

Kjeld laughed out of frustration. It had been like this every day since he'd come home to spend a long weekend with his dad for his birthday. Sixty years old and still as grumpy and exhausting as he'd been when Kjeld was a boy. Sara thought differently, however. She thought sixty was a reason to celebrate and she had begged Kjeld to visit. It was supposed to be an opportunity for everyone to reconnect and put the past – namely Kjeld's decision to move away, his choice in careers, and his mother's death, which still weighed heavily on everyone despite being years ago – behind them. But that's not how it had gone. His dad had been hounding him from the minute he stepped through the front door. And Kjeld was done with it.

'You're not fixing the fuckin' roof on your own. You're too damn old to be climbing up on a ladder by yourself. You could fall and kill yourself and nobody'd even know.'

'If you would just repair the damn thing like you said you would then I wouldn't have to get up there and do it on my own.' It had only been a few years since Kjeld had last been home, but his father's voice had become more gruff since then.

179

'Goddammit, Dad, that's what I'm trying to do!'

Stenar dropped the plywood plank on the ground and stepped on it. The force, while not hard, was enough to crack the board down the centre.

Kjeld threw his arms up in the air. 'Great. Now I can't fix the hole even if I wanted to.'

'You disappoint me.'

'*I* disappoint you? Do you even hear yourself right now? I'm trying to help you. I'm doing what you asked me to do. But instead of thanking me or offering me some constructive assistance, you're belittling me.' Kjeld closed up the toolbox he'd set up on his father's old workbench. 'I'm done. You want to get up on a ladder and break your neck? Fine. But don't expect me to show up for your funeral.'

Stenar flinched and Kjeld could see he'd gone too far. The urge to apologise was instinctual, but he was furious and he refused to allow his father to win this argument. He rarely had his father's attention. And, good or bad, it was still attention.

Across the barn the ravens chittered in their rookery, their cawing chorus increasing in volume to match the heated exchange between Kjeld and his father.

'I don't know how I raised someone so belligerent and disrespectful.' Stenar turned his back on Kjeld and made his way over to the rookery. He took a handful of feed from a pail that sat beside the door and tossed it through the chicken wire. The ravens immediately flew down from their perches and began pecking at the ground.

Kjeld followed after him.

'Really?' Kjeld couldn't believe his father was that oblivious. 'You have been badgering me my entire life. You have been on my back since the day I was born. I've never lived up to your expectations. I've never made you proud. And not for lack of trying. But you've only ever been interested in your damn birds.'

180

'Sara never disappointed me.'

Then it was Kjeld's turn to flinch.

'How could Sara disappoint you? She never did anything with her life!'

Stenar took another handful of seed and tossed it in the rookery. 'She stayed in Varsund. She's found herself a nice man.'

'Is that what you want me to do? Stay in Varsund and find myself a *nice man*?' Kjeld mocked.

'Don't be impudent. Your sister is responsible.'

'She's boring.' Kjeld crossed his arms over his chest. 'And she doesn't like it here any more than I do. She's just too afraid to stand up to you. She feels guilty that you're alone. Well, I don't feel guilty. This place was suffocating me. I couldn't stay here.'

'You've always been so aggressive.' Stenar wiped his hands on his pants. 'You've never appreciated this place. The grass is always greener somewhere else. But I've got news for you, son. You take yourself with you. If you don't like yourself, it doesn't matter where you are. Then you might as well be here.'

'I like myself just fine.'

Stenar opened the door to the rookery and reached inside. A large black raven flew down onto his arm from a higher perch and Stenar took him out, closing up the door behind him. The bird hopped up onto his shoulder and peered at Kjeld with its dark gleaming eyes.

Kjeld took a step backward.

The raven craned its neck unnaturally from one side to the other, nearly one hundred and eighty degrees. Then it dug its sharp beak into the space beneath its left wing, cleaning between the feathers.

'Could you put that back, please?' Kjeld's voice faltered.

Stenar reached into his pocket for a piece of dried fruit and held it up. The raven snatched it out from between his fingertips quicker than Kjeld could blink. 'Why? He's not doing anything.'

'Seriously, Dad, I really don't like those things,' Kjeld said.

'I have to exercise them. They're intelligent creatures. They can't be locked up all day. They need to get out and stretch their wings.'

'Can you at least wait until I'm somewhere else before you do that? You know how I feel about them.'

The raven crawled down Stenar's arm and he pet it like one might a cat. The raven responded by letting out a high-pitched chirp. 'There's nothing to be afraid of.'

'I didn't say I was afraid. I said I don't like them.' But Kjeld could feel a cold sweat beginning to form on the back of his neck.

Stenar stepped closer. 'If you just held one for a moment, you'd realise they're harmless.'

'Harmless? Do you remember what they did to me?'

'You're over-reacting.'

'Over-reacting? Those things could have killed me! And where were you when I needed you? I was out here forever before anyone came for me.'

'It wasn't that long.'

The raven craned its head and pecked at Stenar's shirt sleeve.

'It was long enough.'

Stenar challenged Kjeld's stare. 'If you don't like it here then leave.'

'What the hell, Dad? How many times are we going to have this same argument? It doesn't matter if I like it here. I came out here for you. To spend time with you and Sara. To wish you a happy birthday. To help you with the damn roof. And just because I'm uncomfortable around your stupid birds, you want me to leave?'

Of course, Kjeld knew that wasn't what the argument was about at all. It didn't have anything to do with the roof or the birds, and everything to do with some unknown resentment his father harboured for him. Because Kjeld had never been the son his father wanted. And without his mother to brace the bullhead-edness of the two of them, there was nothing to keep them from tearing each other apart.

'I want you to leave because I don't need you. If you can't respect this place and these creatures, then you can get out.'

The raven flapped its wings before shooting Kjeld a threatening stare. It might have been Kjeld's imagination, but he thought the bird was protecting his father. Taking his side.

'Now you're just being ridiculous. Let's go back to the house. We'll drive down to the hardware store and buy a better piece of wood.'

Kjeld reached out to try and give his father a pat on the arm – a meagre attempt at an apology – but the raven dashed forward and pecked its beak into the back of his hand. Kjeld ripped his hand away, tearing skin. Blood dripped down to his wrist.

'That fuckin' thing just bit me!'

'He didn't mean to,' Stenar said, petting the bird.

'Didn't mean to? That thing is a nightmare! They all are!'

Stenar turned away, back towards the rookery.

Kjeld pressed his palm down on the wound to stifle the bleeding. 'You know you're right. I can't respect this place or you. Not with those things around. Not knowing what you let them do to me as a boy. You want to change that? Then get rid of those monsters and let's start over.'

Stenar didn't respond right away. He kept his back turned to him, hiding his face from Kjeld's view. But Kjeld knew from the moment he said the words how his father would answer. He just hoped that for once he might be wrong.

'Get out and don't you dare think about coming back.'

Kjeld froze, certain that he'd misheard his father. But when Stenar turned to face him there was no mistaking the cold look in his eyes.

'Get out!'

# Chapter 26

## Nutid | Present Day

The doctors had taken his father in for surgery and Kjeld hadn't heard anything since. Every time he tried to ask a passing nurse or medical assistant what was going on, they just told him to take a seat. They'd let him know when they knew more. But he'd been sitting there for almost two hours, watching as patients limped past him down the hall, and still hadn't heard a word from anyone.

And the ugly mid-century decor of the waiting-room interior was beginning to enrage him.

The Varsund Kommun hospital was built in the late 1960s to accommodate the sudden influx of labourers for the logging and mining industries and hadn't been updated since. The waiting room was row after row of plastic chairs, held together by a metal rail like something out of a train station. They were also small, as though they were made for children, and the blunt curve of the seat pressed into his lower back, forcing him to lean forward in a hunch. Another nurse walked by with no word. He supposed that was a good sign. If it had been bad, then someone would have told him something. Someone would have come out, grave-faced

184

and solemn-spoken, and delivered the inevitable bad news. But no one did. Receptionists continued to answer the phones behind their concrete barricade, painted in alternating orange and brown triangles, which Kjeld assumed was all the rage fifty years ago, orderlies pushed empty beds, nurses shuffled along to their duty stations in no particular hurry, and no one told Kjeld what was going on.

He looked down at his phone. No new messages. Not even from Sara, who was the first person he called while he followed the ambulance through the winding forest turns before reaching the main road. He thought about calling her husband, Tom, but realised he didn't know his number. Was there someone else he should call? Esme came to mind, but Kjeld didn't know if he could handle the brutal wave of questions she would no doubt throw his way. Bengt? Stenar was Tove's grandfather, after all, even if she'd never met him. Kjeld supposed she had the right to know. But talking to Tove meant first talking to Bengt and Kjeld didn't think he could handle the patronising tone he knew he'd hear in the man's voice. Not after their last conversation. Kjeld couldn't listen to any more condescension disguised behind false friendliness.

He skimmed through his list of contacts and stopped on Hanna's. Hanna would pick up. She might even listen with a degree of compassion. Kjeld had the impression that she actually liked him. Liked his father, too. Yes, he could call her. Would that be considered taking advantage of her feelings? Was it selfish knowing that she'd pick up because she was interested in him even though he knew full well that what they had wasn't meant to last beyond the time it took Kjeld to resolve the situation with his dad? Probably. But Kjeld suspected she knew he wasn't serious about relationships. He never was. That was his problem.

'Herr Nygaard?'

Kjeld moved his thumb away from the call button and looked up at the doctor. He was a good-looking man. He stood a few inches shorter than Kjeld, his dark hair swept to the side by way of a thick layer of gel, and he wore a white coat that had been freshly starched. Kjeld's first thought was that he was just one of many Indian doctors who came to Sweden to take on the work in the rural clinics that the Swedish doctors didn't want, but when he spoke his Swedish was perfect. Probably even better than Kjeld's. He had one of those reassuring physician smiles that irked him. A smile that reminded Kjeld of Bengt's doctor. The one who managed his treatments. The one who filed a restraining order against Kjeld after Kjeld broke his nose upon discovering Bengt's medical treatments also included Michelin-star dinners at the Upper House restaurant overlooking the city from the Gothia Towers.

'That's me,' Kjeld said.

'I'm Doctor Goswami. I've been attending your father.'

'Is he all right?' Kjeld sat up. His back cracked at the sudden change in posture.

'He suffered a mild heart attack, but he's going to be fine. I'd like to keep him overnight for observation, however. We'll do some more tests in the morning to make sure he doesn't have any partial blockage of the major arteries.'

Kjeld sighed and rubbed his palms over his face, wiping away the tension headache that had begun to throb behind his eyes. A cigarette would have done wonders for his nerves. 'Will I be able to see him?'

'They're transferring him to a room on the second floor. Visiting hours are until nine.'

'Thank you. I appreciate it.'

The doctor nodded and walked back to the nurses' station.

Kjeld stepped outside for a cigarette and sent a quick text to Sara. A few seconds later his phone pinged, but it wasn't from his sister. It was multiple texts from Hanna.

*There's a rumour in town that the body belongs to Peter Lindqvist. Is that true??*

186

*Can't be. Got a work email from him on Friday. Sent to all of the executive staff. Is someone playing a prank?*

In her next message she sent a screenshot of the email. Kjeld turned his phone to enlarge the image. He didn't know Peter Lindqvist, but the timing was unsettling. And rather than alleviate Kjeld's concern that the body might have belonged to Norrmalm's CEO, as his father suggested, it magnified it.

The flashing lights of an oncoming ambulance lit up the drive to the emergency room's side entrance. Kjeld took out a cigarette from his pocket, but his lighter was empty. He cursed to himself and threw the lighter in the trash. Then he went back inside and made his way to the stairwell.

# Chapter 27

It was another hour before Kjeld received a call from Sara that she was on her way to the hospital. When she arrived, Stenar was still asleep, but the on-duty nurse assured them both it was normal. It could be hours before he woke up and when he did he might be disorientated from the surgery.

Kjeld stood at the end of the hospital bed while Sara sat in the chair, leaning over the edge of the mattress and holding their father's hand in her own. She had a firm expression on her face, but Kjeld could see that she was distraught. He expected her to rain hellfire upon him, but she didn't. Perhaps she recognised that their father having a heart attack was a result of old age and bad health. That it could have happened regardless of Kjeld being there. That it hadn't been Kjeld's fault. He hoped that's what she was thinking. Maybe that would help convince him.

Sara wiped a tear from her face. 'What did the doctor say?'

'That it was a mild heart attack. He said Dad would be okay. They repaired a blockage or something. I'm not really sure. It was hard to pay attention. He said he wanted to keep him under observation for the night and do a few tests in the morning before determining when he could go home.'

'I'm such an idiot,' Sara muttered. 'I should have been there. I promised to take care of him.'

'You couldn't have done anything differently. These things happen.'

'It doesn't change the fact that I feel guilty.' Sara smoothed down the blanket over Stenar's chest. 'I feel like I'm losing my mind. First the thing with the barn. Now this. I'm literally at my wits' end.'

'Anything I can do?'

'Give me the last few years of my life back?'

'Preaching to the choir, sis.'

Sara tried to smile, but the effort never made it to her eyes. Kjeld didn't really know what to say so he didn't say anything. Instead they shared the silence for a few minutes, the lull broken up by the occasional beep on the heart monitor and their father's shallow breathing. After a while, Sara looked back at him. She had a measure of composure in her face that surprised Kjeld. He remembered her being much more histrionic when they were children. Even when they were young adults she was prone to being a little hysterical. It was just proof that she'd been through the proverbial trenches with her family. With *their* family. The first family that Kjeld had abandoned.

'You hungry?' she asked.

'Not really.'

'You want to come over for dinner anyway?' Before he could decline she added, 'Tom and the kids would love to see you. It's been such a long time.'

'What are you making?'

'Spaghetti?'

'The way Mum used to make it?'

'That's the only way I know.'

'Sounds good.' Kjeld smiled, but it felt forced. And he imagined it was just as flaky as hers had been.

189

Sara nodded. 'I have to pick up the kids from school and stop by the store on the way home. How does six o'clock sound?'

'That's fine.'

'You going to head back to Dad's before then?'

Kjeld looked over at his father, watching his chest rise and fall, wondering if he'd pushed him too far on the event he witnessed in the barn. It wasn't his fault. He didn't block his father's arteries. He didn't cause the heart attack. He didn't believe a bit of his own thoughts.

'No,' he said, uncertain if it was for his own sake or his father's that he decided to remain. 'I think I'll stay here. He shouldn't wake up alone.'

# Chapter 28

Tom's handshake was firm but soft. He had the smooth touch of an office worker. The hands of a man whose most tactile confrontation was the persistent typing of fingers against a keyboard. A far contrast to Kjeld's hands which were rough, coarse around the palms, and covered in cat scratches.

'Kjeld!' Tom exclaimed, holding on to Kjeld's hand a little longer than Kjeld would have liked. 'Good to see you! How long has it been?'

'A while,' Kjeld replied with a crooked grin, pulling his hand out of Tom's squishy grip.

'Three years!' Sara called out from the kitchen.

'That's right!' Tom said. 'When we went to Gothenburg for the Tall Ships Regatta Festival. That was great, wasn't it?'

'Sure, I guess. If you like ships.' Kjeld preferred to keep his feet on dry land. The last time he was on a boat was for Bengt's thirty-eighth birthday party. Kjeld ended up spending half of the trip spewing his guts over the bow and the other half sleeping on a bench in the cabin. Needless to say, he wasn't the seafaring sort.

Tom opened his mouth to reply, but was cut off by the screeching wails of two children racing down the steps from the second floor. The boy, who was the older of the two, reached Kjeld first and held up his hand for a high five, but before Kjeld could respond he was tackled around the waist by the girl.

'Uncle Kjeld!' the girl shouted, tightening her hug. Then she picked her legs off the ground and dangled by the strength of her own embrace. She felt like an anchor.

Kjeld struggled to remember their names.

'Stop being such an attention queen, Lykke!' the boy yelled.

'I am not!' Lykke replied.

Kjeld gently lifted her underneath her armpits and set her back down on the ground. Then he adjusted his jeans back on his hips.

'Don't yell at your sister, Alexander,' Tom said. 'How about the two of you go help your mum set the table?'

Lykke dashed off to the kitchen, play-acting the role of the dutiful daughter, and Alexander followed, rolling his eyes.

'They're getting big,' Kjeld said, vaguely recalling the time he strolled the docks with them during the ship festival. What he remembered more clearly, however, was how Tove was supposed to be with them. But that had been right after their separation and Bengt had been extra spiteful in those months. He did everything he could to keep Tove from Kjeld. Kjeld tried to fight that for a while, but he eventually gave up. Emotions gradually cooled down between them and they managed to find common ground. But Kjeld never did try to gain full custodial rights as Tove's biological father. Now when he saw his daughter it was during weekends that were convenient for Bengt. Or on the odd occasion when Bengt had to go out of town for work.

Tom nodded. 'Eight and ten. Hard to believe, right? They grow up so fast.'

'That they do.'

The house was dark because it didn't have many windows, built back before architects realised that people needed sunlight to maintain a healthy level of optimism, but the furnishings were light-coloured oak and pine. Sara had attempted to brighten the

192

living and dining room with a coat of sterile white paint, but it just made the shadows from the hanging lamps all the more visible. The walls were mostly bare aside from a few school photographs of Lykke and Alexander and a framed needlepoint of Van Gogh's "Sunflowers", which Kjeld recognised as once hanging in the living room of their parents' house. He thought perhaps that his mother had made it, but he could have been wrong. He didn't have any memories of her doing needlepoint, but it felt like something she might have done when he was very young.

Kjeld recognised the dining-room table as also having been from their parents' house. It was a sturdy rectangular block of wood with thick rounded legs that could easily fit six people. Eight if the space it was occupying hadn't been so small. As it was, it practically took up the entire room.

Lykke set the plates in front of the chairs and Alexander followed her with the cutlery.

'You want a beer?' Tom asked, passing Sara in the tight kitchen to get to the fridge.

'Yeah, that'd be great,' Kjeld said, hovering near the doorframe. He felt awkward around Tom, but he couldn't tell if it was because Tom's politeness was so overbearing that it almost seemed fake or because of his irritating deference to Sara.

Tom walked back out into the dining area and handed Kjeld a can of beer. Kjeld accepted it with a polite nod, popped the tab, and took a sip. The taste was weak and watery. He glanced down at the label. Two point eight per cent. Supermarket beer.

Tom sat at the table, took a long swig from the can, and gave a satisfied sigh. It was probably his first taste of alcohol in years.

Kjeld went to pull out one of the chairs when Lykke hurried over and tugged him at the elbow.

'Sit here, Uncle Kjeld! This is where I always sit! You can sit next to me!'

'Are you sure I can sit there?' Kjeld asked, his tone unconsciously adjusting to the sort that was expected when speaking to children. Lykke's enthusiasm reminded him of Tove.

Lykke laughed, pulling the chair out for Kjeld. 'Of course, silly. Mum won't care.'

'Well in that case I would love to sit next to you. You are my favourite niece, after all.' Kjeld helped her pull the chair the rest of the way out from under the table and took a seat.

'I'm your only niece!'

'Really? Are you sure? I could have sworn there was another around here somewhere.'

'You're crazy, Uncle Kjeld.' Lykke giggled and ran back into the kitchen.

Tom set his beer on the table. 'You're good with kids.'

Kjeld shook his head, leaning back into the chair. The flowery cushion that was supposed to be tied to the seat slid out from under him and he fidgeted to adjust it. He hated chairs with detachable cushions. They seemed so impractical.

'Not really,' Kjeld said. 'To be honest I usually scare them.'

'Could be that they just scare you and you're deflecting your feelings about them.'

Kjeld raised a brow. 'Shit, Tom. Did you get a psychology degree since the last time I saw you?'

Tom chuckled. 'I've been doing a lot of reading on self-awareness. Trying to get in touch with my base self. You know, my cores and ideals. Help me get a better understanding of who I am in the world and what I need from the environment and people around me.'

Kjeld didn't really know how to respond to that. 'Sounds deep.'

'He's supposed to be researching how to find a job,' Sara said, walking out from the kitchen with a pot of spaghetti.

Lykke chased Alexander into the living room, screaming like a banshee.

'You, two, knock it off!' Sara yelled after them.

194

'When I discover who I am and what my inner values are then I'll be able to apply them to my career prospects,' Tom said without missing a beat.

'I asked him to update his résumé and this is what he goes out and does.' Sara rolled her eyes on her way back to the kitchen. 'We need money, not existentialism.'

Tom waved a hand at Sara and focused his attention on Kjeld. 'The book I'm reading now guarantees that you'll either receive a promotion at work or find a better job if you follow their steps towards personal empowerment and self-understanding. It's only a matter of patience and reflection.'

'And finishing the book,' Kjeld said.

'Don't encourage him.' Sara placed a pot of sauce and bowl of salad on the table. Then she shouted for the kids that dinner was ready.

Lykke and Alexander came running from the other room, pushing and shoving to be the first at the table. Lykke gave Kjeld a big grin as she climbed up into the chair beside him. She was missing one of her front teeth.

Kjeld motioned to her mouth. 'You've got a hole.'

'I can slurp spaghetti through it. Wanna see?'

'Sure.'

'No,' Sara interrupted. 'There will be no slurping at the table.'

Alexander belched.

'No burping either.'

Alexander made a goofy face. 'Slurping and burping.'

Lykke giggled.

'Sounds like a good name for a band,' Kjeld said.

'Or a carnival game.' Tom finished his beer and got up to get another.

'Did you really shoot someone, Uncle Kjeld?' Alexander asked.

'Alexander!' Sara glared from across the table. 'Where did you hear such a thing?'

'The internet.'

195

'Not everything you see on the internet is true,' Sara said.

'But did Uncle Kjeld really shoot a guy?'

'Was it a bad guy?' Lykke asked, eyes wide.

Kjeld tried to think of an appropriate way to answer their questions, but was thankfully spared by Sara who, being the model of overworked maternity, interrupted him. She was probably afraid he would answer truthfully. She was probably right.

'All right, that's enough of that kind of talk,' Sara said, placing a napkin in her lap. 'Who's going to say grace?'

Never having been a particularly religious household growing up, Kjeld wasn't prepared for the act of prayer before eating. Sara shot him a pressing stare from across the table, one meant to insist that he follow suit, but he just stared back at her with equal defiance.

When he didn't respond, either in word or action, Sara resorted to using that reserved tone of voice that was anything but innocuous. 'Kjeld?'

Kjeld gave his sister an irritated look. 'Jesus Christ, Sara. It's not Christmas.'

Lykke stared at Kjeld with her mouth wide open in shock. 'You said Jesus Christ.'

'It's not a bad word, Lykke.' Alexander reached across the table for a bottle of cola. 'It's just a name.'

Sara sent Kjeld one of those admonishing glares from across the table and then folded her hands in front of her. 'Just because you're going to hell doesn't mean the rest of us have to join you.'

Sara cleared her throat and the rest of the table followed her in bowing their heads while she said a short prayer about being grateful for food and family.

Kjeld watched the scene as he would a group of macaques grooming each other at the zoo. With an awkward sense of foreign familiarity. When the prayer was over Lykke looked up at him expectantly and he pretended like he had just raised his head. Then he finished the watered-down beer in a single gulp and

196

tuned Tom out as he continued his diatribe on the merits of self-discovery.

* * *

'Sorry I was kind of snippy with you at dinner,' Sara said, slumping down on the overstuffed sofa.

Kjeld scooted over to give her some space. After dinner Tom took the kids upstairs to get them ready for bed and read the next Chapter on his path to self-enlightenment. Kjeld had stayed downstairs to help Sara clean up.

'I know you didn't mean it.' He really wanted a cigarette.

'I didn't. I don't. I really don't. I just haven't been dealing well with everything.' She placed one of the flower-print throw pillows in her lap and wrapped her arms around it.

'You've done an amazing job.'

Sara scoffed.

'No, seriously. Taking care of Dad and your own family? I can't even take care of myself.'

'Well, you're a man. That doesn't exactly qualify you for being able to multitask.'

Kjeld reached over and gave her a playful nudge in the arm. 'You can be such a bitch sometimes.'

'I know.' Sara ran her fingers over the seam in the pillowcase. 'I just hope he's going to be all right.'

'The doctor seemed optimistic,' Kjeld said, stretching his legs out in front of him and crossing them at the ankles.

'It's a horrible thing. There are days when I'm so overwhelmed I can't help but think that things would be easier, better even, if he weren't around anymore. I mean, it must be so painful for him, too, you know? Knowing that he can't remember. Getting frustrated all of the time. It must be hell. But then I think this is my dad. I can't lose him. I can't live without him.'

'Can't live with him either.'

Sara sighed. 'When Mum died I felt so alone. And then you and Dad had that fight and you stopped coming up here and I really was alone. Except for Tom, of course. But I felt so abandoned. And when Dad got sick I just started feeling like everything was falling apart around me.'

'Mum's death was hard for everyone,' Kjeld said, pulling on his earlobe.

'She always liked you better.'

'She didn't like me better. Just differently.'

'She babied you.'

Kjeld shrugged. He'd never seen it that way. He had the impression that his mother just felt sorry for him. Kjeld always imagined it was because he challenged their father. The two of them were consistently butting heads about one thing or another, all the way up to adulthood. Kjeld just assumed his mother was trying to ease the tension between them. He never felt coddled or overprotected. She made sure he fought his own battles, both at home and at school. But he did feel that she tried to allay the confrontations she seemed to know he would face growing up. She understood that for all of his self-professed hardness on the outside, he was soft on the inside. Sensitive, although she would never have used that word. Kjeld was grateful that she hadn't.

'I just failed to live up to Dad's expectations of me. Mum didn't have any. She just wanted the both of us to be happy. She didn't care where we were or what we did as long as we were happy.'

Sara flattened the pillow in her lap. 'And are you? Happy?'

Kjeld wasn't sure. 'I think I was. For a little while.'

'With Bengt?'

'I fucked it up. I know I did. But things just got so complicated. So serious.'

'Mum would have liked him.'

'Doesn't really matter now.' Kjeld looked down at his shirt and noticed a small spaghetti sauce stain. He tried to scratch it off, but that didn't do anything.

Upstairs Alexander and Lykke chased each other down the hall in a typical pre-bed preadolescent ritual. It shook the lamp above their heads and Kjeld watched it begin to swing, wondering if the ceiling was strong enough to withstand two kids who'd had too much caffeine at dinner. The muffled tone of Tom urging them to go to bed sounded more like a cry for help than a demand. Did Tove do that, too? Did she argue against her bedtime and cause chaos through the house in a last-ditch effort to stay up for fifteen more minutes? Kjeld didn't think so. Tove was uncommonly well behaved for a child of six. Clearly the result of Bengt's meticulous nurturing, because there was nothing but chaos in Kjeld's genes.

'Do you think Gunnar will figure out what happened in the barn?' Sara asked. Her voice was strained and the word "barn" came out choked. Her fingers clenched at the seams in the throw pillow.

'I think he has to at least make an effort to try,' Kjeld said, holding back the urge to scoff. He still didn't know if Gunnar was more help or hindrance when it came to the discovery in his father's barn. He wanted to believe that Gunnar would look into the situation fairly, unbiased, but he didn't know the man anymore. 'Do you know anything about a Peter Lindqvist?'

'Who?'

'Peter Lindqvist. Dad said he was an old friend of his.'

Sara shook her head. 'I know the Lindqvists own Norrmalm Industries. Everyone knows that. I vaguely remember hearing that there was a son and a daughter, but they must not have gone to school in Varsund. They were probably sent off to a boarding school. Otherwise I would know them.'

'You're probably thinking of David Lindqvist. He's the son of Roland Lindqvist.'

'Then who's Peter?'

'Roland's brother,' Kjeld said. 'According to Dad they were both stationed up in Boden during their military service. I think he might be the body we found in the barn.'

Sara laughed in disbelief. 'That's ridiculous. Don't you think that if one of the owners of the largest mining companies in northern Sweden was missing that we would have heard about it? Besides, why would anyone bury one of the Lindqvists in Dad's barn? He had nothing to do with that company. It must be someone else.'

'How do we know Dad didn't have anything to do with Norrmalm?' Kjeld asked.

'Because he didn't.'

'But he knew him.'

'Kjeld, stop.' Sara sighed. 'You're making it sound like it's possible that Dad was involved in something. He wasn't. And I don't even believe he really saw what he thinks he saw. He's not well. He hasn't been well for a long time. And, sure, maybe he was friends with the Lindqvists when he was younger, but that doesn't mean anything.'

'What if Gunnar finds evidence that Dad was to blame?' Kjeld pulled idly on his beard, which had grown too long.

'Dad can't remember. He can't stand up for himself. And even if he did—' She shook her head. 'You can't blame someone for a crime they can't remember, can you?'

Kjeld thought about it before replying. 'No, I wouldn't think so.'

Sara nodded. She looked a tad more relieved but not entirely satisfied with his answer. Then again, neither was Kjeld.

'Is it true what they said in the papers?' Sara asked.

'About what?'

'The Kattegat Killer. Did you really know him?'

Kjeld leaned his elbow on the armrest, resting his face in the palm of his hand. 'Yeah.'

'Were you close?'

*Not close enough apparently*, Kjeld thought. Not as close as he'd wanted to be. But that had been years ago, back when Kjeld was new on the force. Green in all the ways a young police officer could be and should be. And Nils wasn't in his league. Not professionally and least of all personally. Still, they'd become friends. Nils had been a mentor to him. Nils got him over that hurdle from parking fines and parade routes to honest-to-goodness police work. And then to detective.

'He was my partner for six years before he transferred into administration. We saw each other almost every day in that time.'

Did that make them close? Kjeld had been racking his brain for weeks on that account. How could he have spent years as Nils's partner, sat with him for hours on stakeouts eating drive-through takeaway, celebrated birthdays and holidays with him, and not realised that he was a cold-blooded killer? How was it possible to be close to someone and not know anything about them?

'Are you all right?' Sara turned to him, her expression softened to one of concern. She looked like their mother in that moment. Not in stature or appearance. She definitely took after their father in that respect. But something in her eyes. Maybe it was just that maternal look. Something that said she was really worried about him and that her worry was unconditional.

'I'm fine,' Kjeld said, offering a half-hearted smile.

'Really?'

'As fine as anyone who found out their best friend was a murderer and shot him in cold blood could be.'

Sara paused. 'Is he dead?'

Kjeld shook his head. 'No. That's the one thing I did do right.'

Not that Kjeld hadn't wanted to kill him in that moment. He had. He'd wanted to watch him die for all the reasons a person wanted to see someone suffer, not the least of which was the betrayal he felt. Betrayal to the police force. Betrayal to the truth. Betrayal to their friendship and to everything he'd ever taught Kjeld, which amounted to nothing more than a pile of lies.

Thankfully Kjeld had restrained himself against his own selfish desires. Now Nils could stand trial for his crimes and rot in a cell for the rest of his natural life.

Sara nodded. It was clear from her silence and her tight-lipped expression that she didn't know what to say. Kjeld saved her from having to come up with any comforting pleasantries by standing up and stretching his arms above his head.

'I should get going,' he said.

'You sure you don't want to stay?' Sara asked. Kjeld could hear in her voice that she was just being polite.

'No, but thanks anyway,' he said, making his way to the front door. 'I'll see you around. Thanks for the pasta.'

'Kjeld?'

'Mm?'

'Thanks for getting Dad to the hospital.'

# Chapter 29

The drive back to his father's house was quiet aside from the elk that jumped out into the road, causing Kjeld to wear his brake pads down to almost nothing in order to avoid it. He drove the rest of the way home at half his original speed, high beams glaring into the black nothingness that was the deep forest roads around Varsund Kommun. These were the things he'd forgotten since he'd moved to the western coast. The wild animals, the small-town people, the perpetual night.

When he pulled up in front of the house, the living-room light still lit from when the ambulance arrived, Kjeld noticed a small car parked a little way up the road. His headlights illuminated the vehicle's side panel and Kjeld got a good look at that familiar shade of serpentine green.

'Fuck.' He groaned and turned off the ignition.

He was barely out of the car when the shadowy figure rushed at him. Kjeld wasn't sure if he should expect a hug or a punch. What he got was a semi-serious shove in the shoulder.

'I've been calling you for five hours!' Esme yelled.

'You're *always* calling, Esme. You make it impossible to tell if it's really urgent.' Kjeld's tone was intentionally flippant. 'You didn't have to come. I can't believe you drove all the way out here. *Is* there an emergency I don't know about?'

'Get over yourself. I just spent half a tank of fuel driving around these scary back roads. Did you know GPS doesn't work out here? There aren't even any street signs. I had to ask some kid at a kebab shop how to find this place.' Esme's southern accent thickened with her level of frustration.

'Could he understand you?'

Esme huffed. 'That's not funny. I've been sitting out here for almost two hours freezing my arse off.'

Kjeld gave a half-hearted smile and then nodded to her car. It was a Volvo 66 DL that Esme had inherited from her uncle a few years ago. She loved it, which was all the more reason why Kjeld mocked it, but it was in good shape for its age, despite looking like pea-green baby vomit. 'It's a miracle you were even able to make it up the hill with that piece of shit.'

'Oh, fuck you, Kjeld.'

'Well, my parents aren't home,' he joked.

Esme shoved him again and then rolled her eyes before walking back to the car. She was what some people might consider elfish in appearance. She was petite, not quite a foot shorter than Kjeld but close, and had a slim physique that was hidden beneath a puffy winter coat. Her hair was dark brown, almost black, chopped unevenly just below the shoulders like a punk rocker, with a fringe that covered her eyebrows. On the left side of her face, just below the corner of her lips, was a small mole that was so dark against her pale skin it almost looked drawn on. Her ears were pierced, but she never wore earrings, and around her thumb was a broad silver band. She'd once told Kjeld it was her grandfather's wedding ring, but he never did believe that story.

Kjeld exhaled a frosty breath against the cold, still air. Seeing Esme filled him with an unexpected sense of comfort. He was glad she was there. Glad that he wasn't the only one willing to drop everything and make the drive up to Varsund on little more than a notion that something wasn't right. Esme was a good friend. A better friend than he was to her. And whatever the reasons for her concern, he didn't deserve it. Not that he would ever tell her that.

Kjeld took out his keys and started for the house when Esme shouted at him.

'You could give me a hand, you know!'

'*The Discrimination Act of 2009* protects the right of gender equality among all Swedish citizens, particularly co-workers in a shared workplace. If I help you, I might inadvertently demean your ability to do things on your own. Don't blame me. I'm a feminist.'

It was a joke, but Esme didn't look amused. She rolled her eyes and tugged a pet carrier out from the back seat of the Volvo. A shrill hiss cut through the air.

'Shut up and get your fuckin' cat.'

\* \* \*

Kjeld measured out the new Science Diet kibble and poured it into a small bowl while Esme made a fresh pot of coffee.

Oskar lay on the kitchen floor like a dog, his thick ginger-furred belly blobbing out to one side. Maybe it was Kjeld's imagination, but he actually thought his cat looked slimmer since the last time he saw him. Then again if this week had proved anything to him it was that his memory wasn't entirely reliable. Not when it came to people who were close to him. He set the bowl on the ground. Oskar reached out with one paw and tried to scoop the dried food out of the dish without getting up. He managed to get one piece of kibble out of the bowl, which he ate lying down.

Pathetic.

'Is your dad going to be all right?' Esme asked.

Kjeld had already forgotten their short exchange between the front door and the kitchen, where Kjeld told her in as few words as possible about the body in the barn, the photographs, the unfamiliar car hidden behind the family hunting cabin, the missing town drunk, the CEO on sabbatical, the untimely email sent to the Norrmalm employees, and his father's heart attack. He slumped down in the chair his father usually sat in. The springs were definitely broken.

'Yeah. The doctor said it was just a mild attack. He should be able to come home in the morning.'

Esme took a bottle of milk out of the fridge, eyed the date with a heavy dose of suspicion, took a sniff, and then put it back. 'Do you have any sugar?'

'Check the cupboard above the bread box.'

After a minute of shuffling through various tins and easy-make boxed dinners, Esme found the sugar, tucked away in a corner but sealed. She poured two spoonfuls into the mug for herself and then joined Kjeld at the table.

Kjeld sipped his coffee, black like it had been that morning, but not quite as strong.

'Tastes good,' he said between slow sips.

'That's why I've been trying to get you to switch from that instant shit. That stuff's not real coffee anyway. And it's worse than that sludge they serve at the station.' Esme swiped the thick fringe from her face and tucked some of the loose strands behind her ear.

The ravens, seemingly aware that someone had returned home, began cawing in the barn.

'What was that?' Esme asked.

'The birds.'

'Birds?'

Kjeld blew across the top of his coffee to cool it down. 'My dad keeps ravens. It's kind of a family tradition passed down from my great-grandfather. They're out in the barn.'

'You come from a family of ornithologists?' Esme looked sceptical.

'More like nature enthusiasts.'

'I always knew you were a little weird, but ... birdkeeping?'

'They're not mine,' Kjeld insisted.

'Not yet,' Esme said playfully. She was trying to lighten the mood. It wasn't working, but it was a welcome distraction. 'Do I need to be concerned that you might have a midlife crisis next year and decide to give up the murder squad in exchange for a career in poultry?'

Kjeld sipped his coffee. 'Poultry only includes domesticated fowl. It doesn't include ravens. There's a distinction.'

'Distinctions are for the birds.' Esme grinned.

Kjeld gave her a blank stare.

'It's a joke. You know. It's *for the birds*.'

'That was terrible.'

'Yeah, it was.'

Kjeld didn't laugh at Esme's tired joke, but he couldn't stop the small quirk of a smile from tugging at his lips. He appreciated her efforts. As annoyed as he could be with her at times, Kjeld could never stay frustrated with her for long. Esme knew better than anyone, except for perhaps Bengt, how to coax him out of his mood.

Still, the sound of the ravens cawing reminded him of the responsibility he had to them now that his father wasn't home. He tried to recall the last time someone went out to feed them, but couldn't remember. He'd have to go out there soon. If there was one thing his father was sure to remember when he came home it was those damn birds. And Kjeld had a suspicion that if anything happened to them, his father would lose all ability to communicate on any meaningful level.

They were all he had, after all.

'I should probably go out and feed them soon.'

Esme frowned. Kjeld didn't look at her, but he could sense she was giving him that dreaded look of concern she was so good at. It had taken a few years of working together before they'd come to understand each other. Before they learned to work as a team. Kjeld hadn't treated her well in the beginning. He was always running off after his own leads and forgetting to keep her in the loop. Whether that had been on purpose or out of habit from having worked on his own for so many years he couldn't say, but eventually she stood up to him. She asserted herself as his equal. She proved to be a more than competent investigator and an even better friend. Despite Kjeld's standoffish and sometimes difficult personality, she supported him. He felt she knew him. Or, at least, knew him as much as any one person could really know another person. Recent circumstances were beginning to make Kjeld question whether he knew anyone at all.

'Are you okay, Kjeld?'

He canted his head to the side and looked across the table at her. He felt this sudden urge to cry, but he didn't. It was as though a pit of untouched emotion finally decided to crawl up his throat and attempt to break his resolve. He swallowed it back down to his stomach with a sip of the coffee. Hot, heavy liquid to quash the cold threat of despair.

'I don't know,' he said. 'I really can't say. I don't even know what to think right now. And I'm not exactly unbiased here.'

'What do you know so far?'

'It hasn't been confirmed officially, or at least no one's told us yet, but after talking to my father I suspect the body is that of Peter Lindqvist. He was the head of a mining company just north of here. Been in the area for generations. I found a photograph of him and my father as young men. Dad says they were friends. They were stationed together during their conscription service period. According to Dad he broke his leg during a training exercise. And the pathologist said the body we found had an old leg injury as well.' Kjeld rubbed his chin. He needed a shave. 'But there's another man who's missing. Valle Dahl. He was something of a town drunk. He was also in one of the photographs.'

'Are all small towns full of suspicious disappearances or just the one you're from?'

'I did meet one man from the photographs. A lawyer named Erik Norberg. Some hotshot with an office in Stockholm. I found his number in my dad's things. I suspect he might also work for the Lindqvist family. Or at least for their company.'

'He's a corporate attorney?' Esme asked.

'Contract law.' Kjeld shook his head. 'There's some kind of connection between my father and this company, but whatever it is I can't see it. All I know is that he was close enough with the owner that he and my mother used to attend their Christmas parties. But I think it stopped shortly after my sister was born.'

'Did they ever talk about them when you were growing up?'

'Not that I remember. And I don't remember anyone ever coming by the house. My dad kept us pretty isolated. He didn't like people so much. Nature was always more important to him. Still is. Those damn birds are practically his legacy.'

'And the car?'

Kjeld pulled up the photo on his phone. Esme studied it with a grim stare.

'Have you told the local police about it?'

'Not yet.'

'Kjeld …' She refrained from scolding him, but Kjeld could practically hear what she was thinking.

'I know. And I will tell them about it. Just as soon as I know how it got there.'

'As soon as you have control of it, you mean.'

Kjeld knew what she was getting at. She was suggesting that he was withholding information from Gunnar because he was afraid of the consequences. That vehicle, if it had anything to do with the man buried in his father's barn, could implicate his father in the man's death. It could be proof that his father had murdered a man. And whatever feud Kjeld had with his father, he didn't want that to be true.

'When I have more information, I'll tell the police,' Kjeld said.

'I promise. But first I have to see how all of the pieces fit together. And right now I can't see the forest for the trees.'

Esme held her mug in front of her with both hands. That was her thinking pose. Kjeld had seen it often enough in their office. So many cups of coffee had gone cold while Esme Jansson worked through the thoughts in her mind. It was like a self-induced trance. She had an uncanny ability to visualise things in her mind. Not quite an eidetic memory, but something she referred to as *puzzling* or, as she sometimes liked to clarify it to others, the ability to put together the picture of something in her mind before ever seeing the pieces. It had gained her the reputation among their colleagues of being a little bit odd, but that might have explained why Kjeld had eventually taken a liking to her. They were both outcasts among outcasts in a way.

She brought the mug to her lips, took a sip, and seemed surprised that the coffee wasn't scalding. The trance was over. 'So as far as I can tell you have two major questions that need answering. The first, did your father do it? And the second, regardless of who murdered this man, whether it's Lindqvist or not, why? I'm including all the whys in one for the sake of simplicity, but most importantly, why him? Why here? Why dig him up now?'

It wasn't until Esme went into full investigation mode that Kjeld realised how relieved he was to have someone else – someone he trusted – involved in the case. And while he struggled with the fact that Esme might learn more about his life before becoming *that* detective in Gothenburg, the one who was known for being as reckless as he was determined when it came to his cases, he was pleased to have her by his side. With any luck she would help him to see the situation from a more impartial perspective. Perhaps she could even help him to ignore his prejudice, which had spilled over to everything this investigation touched – his father, Varsund, Gunnar, his memories of the past.

Kjeld tried to treat it like any other case in his mind. What were the major motives for murder? Kjeld remembered sitting in a lecture at the police college when a guest speaker from the University of Copenhagen gave a talk on the five basic reasons why a person committed murder. Listed from least to most common these motives were: war, hate, politics, revenge, and jealousy. Kjeld remembered the lecture so well because afterwards there had been a heated debate about the difference between revenge and jealousy. More than half of the students in attendance felt that revenge and jealousy went hand in hand. That a person couldn't possess the desire to seek revenge without first expressing some form of jealousy and vice versa, that murders based on envy were at the core a kind of revenge. Most of the students were thinking about cheating spouses, of course.

But Kjeld remembered sitting there in the curved seats of the auditorium and thinking that a child who was beaten his entire life could want revenge against the parent who hurt him. Or that a woman who was raped could kill her rapist in revenge. He also thought he remembered stories about American soldiers returning home only to receive poor integration counselling from their government-sponsored healthcare providers and murdering their doctors as revenge for their wives and families leaving them. Kjeld agreed with the lecturer. He didn't think revenge had to have a basis of jealousy for someone to use it as a motive. Likewise, he could see how someone might kill solely as an act of envy, completely isolated from an act of retaliation. Wasn't that a basic human condition, after all? Wanting what somebody else had?

The image of Nils on the docks popped into his mind and Kjeld shook it away. 'Whether my father was involved or not, I think it has to have something to do with the Lindqvists' mining company. That's the only thing that makes sense right now.'

Oskar scooped another pawful of kibble onto the floor and crunched them between his teeth one at a time.

Esme reached across the table and placed a hand on Kjeld's. She gave his fingers a gentle squeeze. 'Then that's where we'll start.'

# Chapter 30

Kjeld sat on his father's bed, deleting Esme's missed-call messages from his phone. The house was eerily still. Even the birds had settled down for the night, leaving Kjeld with the uncomfortable feeling of being completely alone in the universe. And were it not for the fact that he knew his partner was asleep in the room across the hall, he might have even believed it.

Knowing that Esme was there to help was like a breath of fresh air to Kjeld's restless mind. It was crazy, of course. Driving all of that way just because he refused to answer his calls, but Kjeld appreciated it. It was a reminder that he didn't exist in a vacuum. That even though he sometimes was alone or felt alone, he wasn't. Not completely. There was always someone whose life was affected by his absence. And even though he would probably spend the next few years joking with her about the time she drove halfway across the country just to deliver his cat and berate him about ignoring her messages, he knew he would do the same for her. Esme had been there for him during some of his darker moments. She knew better than anyone how easily he could slip into that terrifying bleakness that followed an episode of tragedy. And he suspected that she believed he was more affected by the situation with Nils than he was letting on.

His thoughts drifted back to the nightmares he'd been having. He could still picture them clearly in his mind – Nils raising his weapon, Esme shouting in the background, Tove staring up at him with fearful eyes, the rain matting down her curls and tearing over her freckled face. Tove hadn't been there when the shootout actually occurred, but for some reason his subconscious persisted on inserting her into the moment. Kjeld's heart raced just thinking about it.

It could have been worse. It could have been so much worse.

He suddenly had the need to hear her voice.

Kjeld scrolled through his contacts until he came to Bengt's name. He hesitated, just long enough to take a deep breath and slow his heart rate, then pressed the call button.

The phone rang four times before Bengt answered.

'Do you know what time it is?' Bengt's voice was groggy, half asleep.

Kjeld glanced at his father's alarm clock. It was almost midnight.

'I'm sorry,' Kjeld said. 'Can I talk to Tove?'

There was another voice in the background. It was muffled, but Kjeld could hear the complaining whine in its tone. After a pause, which Kjeld interpreted as Bengt moving to another room, his ex gave an exhausted sigh. 'She's in bed, Kjeld. Can't this wait until the morning?'

'Not really.'

The line went quiet. Kjeld, all too accustomed to Bengt's silences, frowned. And when he couldn't wait any longer, knowing that Bengt could easily hang up on him, he begged. 'Please, Bengt? I just need to hear her voice. I just need to make sure she's okay.'

'Are *you* okay?'

'I'm fine. I'm—' Kjeld took a deep breath. 'It's been a trying week.'

'Give me a minute.'

Kjeld took the phone away from his ear and pressed the speaker button. He could hear the sound of Bengt's voice, quiet and calm, waking Tove up. Kjeld imagined her curled up against her stuffed animals and her polka-dot bedsheets. Was she still sucking her thumb at night? He felt guilty that he didn't know.

'Daddy?'

Kjeld breathed a sigh of relief when he heard her voice. An unconscious smile crossed his lips. 'Hey, sweetheart. How are you?'

'I'm sleepy,' she said with a yawn.

'I know. I'm sorry I called so late. I just missed you.'

'I miss you, too, Daddy. Are you coming to visit soon?'

'I hope so. I'm going to try to. Would you like that?'

'I'd like to go to the zoo.'

'Maybe we can do that the next time I come over.'

'Okay.' Tove yawned again.

'I'm going to say goodnight now, sweetheart. You can give the phone back to Papa. I love you.'

'Love you, too.'

Kjeld turned off the speakerphone and brought the mobile to his ear. On the other end of the line was the faint sound of Bengt tucking Tove back into bed. A minute later he was back. It was impossible for Kjeld to ignore the worry in Bengt's voice and he didn't know if he should feel angry, relieved, elated or sad.

'What's going on, Kjeld?'

'I've made so many mistakes. I don't know where or how to begin to fix them.'

'Well I wouldn't recommend starting in the middle of the night.'

Kjeld laughed. 'Yeah. Fair point.'

'Look, I have to be up early for work,' Bengt said.

Kjeld thought he heard him hesitate, but he may have just imagined it. 'I know. I'm sorry I woke you.'

'Are you at home?'

The question should have been innocuous, but Kjeld knew what it really meant. He'd never been the kind of person who

214

drowned his sorrows and depression in a bottle of vodka until he blacked out, but he'd had his benders in the past. Although his had usually been prefaced with an indulgence of prescription medications and the occasional dose of E. But it had been years since he'd fallen that low. Long before the situation with Nils or his father.

'I'm at my dad's place.' As an afterthought Kjeld added, 'Esme's with me.'

'Good. All right, well, I suppose I'll see you in a few weeks for your weekend. You won't forget this time, will you?'

'No,' Kjeld said. 'I won't forget.'

'I hope not. She's looking forward to it,' Bengt said. 'Goodnight, Kjeld.'

'Goodnight, Bengt.' Kjeld held on to the line, waiting to see if Bengt would say something more. What he was hoping to hear, however, Kjeld wasn't sure. Or, perhaps he simply wasn't willing to admit.

The phone beeped. The call had been ended.

Kjeld dropped the phone on the empty side of the bed and lay down. He stared up at the ceiling for what felt like hours before he finally closed his eyes. Then he waited for the nightmares to come, but they didn't.

# Chapter 31

## Onsdag | Wednesday

The persistent pressing of claws into his cheek and the high-pitched wail of a cat who thought he was hungry woke Kjeld from another restless sleep. He focused his eyes in the darkness to the digital alarm clock on his father's nightstand. The red numbers glared back at him: 4.57.

'Couldn't you have at least waited three more minutes?' Kjeld grumbled.

Oskar responded by lifting his back leg in a ballerina pose and licking the soft fur on his neutered balls.

'Arsehole cat.'

Kjeld pulled on a sweatshirt, which quickly reminded him that he needed to do laundry, and crept down the stairs as quietly as possible so as not to disturb Esme in the other room.

When Esme came down an hour later, showered, dressed, and looking like the chipper early bird that she was, Kjeld was sitting on the back-porch steps smoking a cigarette and eating a hardboiled egg. He didn't really start functioning until after lunch and that was on a good day. In contrast, Esme was always ready to hit the ground running.

She sat down beside him and immediately turned up her nose. 'Chrissakes, Kjeld. You're rank.'

'I haven't had time to do laundry,' he said, exhaling a cloud of smoke away from her.

'Do the world a favour and at least shower. Or brush your teeth.'

Kjeld ran his tongue over his front teeth as though expecting to find some kind of greasy film that could account for the smell. He just assumed it was a combination of the cold egg and the cigarette smoke that bothered her. His hygiene wasn't that bad. Esme was just unnecessarily tuned in to the odours of other people.

'What, are you pregnant or something?'

She jabbed an elbow into his arm.

'Watch it now! Fuck, Esme. It was a joke.'

'You can't joke about that kind of shit, arsehole. That's what gets people written up for sexual harassment.'

Kjeld flicked the ash from the cigarette onto the step beside his boot. 'Are you feeling sexually harassed?'

'No, I have hyperosmia, but that's beside the point.' She crossed her arms over her chest and clenched her fingers into her wool sweater. 'It's fuckin' freezing out here.'

'It's warmer than yesterday.' Kjeld tossed the rest of the egg in his mouth. When he asked his next question he did so with his mouth full. 'Hyper-what?'

'Hyperosmia. It means I have an increased olfactory acuity.'

Kjeld stared blankly at her.

'A heightened sense of smell,' she clarified.

'Yeah, I know what olfactory acuity means. How is it you've never told me that before? I didn't know people could just get that.'

'Because it's none of your business and normally you don't smell like a wet dog who's been digging his nose in the garbage.' She tugged her sweater up around her neck. 'And you don't just

217

*get* it. It's genetic. Well, in my case it's genetic. So trust me, you need to take a fuckin' shower.'

'Yes, ma'am,' Kjeld said, but his tone was only half-mocking. He might give Esme a hard time on occasion, but in almost all matters she was right. And he already knew from the moment he slipped on his unwashed sweatshirt that he smelled.

'You got anything to eat other than eggs?'

Kjeld stubbed out the cigarette on the porch. 'Bread and cheese, I think.'

'Vegan,' Esme said, looking at him with a "come on, I know you know this" gaze.

'Don't you usually put creamer in your coffee?'

'Nobody's perfect.'

'Shit, Esme. Before you know it you'll be wallowing with the rest of us carnivores.'

She rolled her eyes and stood up. 'I'm going to put on the coffee. It's too damn cold out here.'

'You're such a southerner,' Kjeld said, inwardly cringing at how much that comment made him sound like his father.

'Better that than hypothermic,' she replied. 'Go take a shower. I'll see if I can't find anything healthy for breakfast.'

Kjeld used the railing to pull himself up to a stand. He scratched at the hairs along the side of his jaw. They were long enough to tug on now. 'Guess I should probably shave.'

Esme stopped in the doorway and looked back at him. 'I wouldn't. It looks good on you.'

'Really?'

Esme stared at him and for a moment Kjeld thought she was doing that thing she did with her mind. He thought she was *puzzling* him. Then she shrugged. 'Makes you look like less of an arsehole.'

She went inside, the rickety screen door slamming shut behind her.

\* \* \*

After a quick shower, change of clothes into something he hadn't worn for three days in a row, and a breakfast consisting of a cup of coffee and a slice of bread with lingonberry jam, Kjeld took Esme out to the barn so she could see the scene for herself.

Esme walked around the inside of the barn, careful not to disturb too much more than had already been disturbed by Kjeld and his father continually going out to feed the ravens. She crouched down beside the empty grave. The birds watched her with wary eyes, shining in the shadows of the rookery.

'It's not very deep,' she said.

'I think the assumption is that the killer didn't have time to dig a deeper hole.'

'Or didn't have the energy.'

She stood up and scanned the barn.

Kjeld assumed she was looking for anything out of the ordinary, but to a city girl from the southern tip of the country just about everything in that barn was probably out of the ordinary.

'What are the police saying?'

'Not much. I'm not exactly on the best of terms with the local inspector,' Kjeld admitted.

'What'd you do? Piss in his garden when you were a kid?'

Kjeld thought about Gunnar. Thought about the moment that their friendship was replaced by an unspoken promise never to tell the truth about what happened during their early training years. That had been a mistake. A rookie mistake, but a mistake nonetheless. Kjeld had learned from it. Gunnar, on the other hand, well, the jury was still out where he was concerned.

He shrugged. 'Something like that.'

Esme shook her head disapprovingly. 'You're unbelievable, you know that? Do you have any friends? Is there anyone you haven't pissed off?'

Kjeld glanced over at the large raven with the crooked beak. What had his father called him? Hermod? 'Probably not.'

'It's not a wonder you're still single.'

'I'm single by choice,' Kjeld insisted. 'There's a difference.'

'No one is single by choice, Kjeld.'

'What about you?'

'I turned down a hot Tinder date to come up here and check on your pain-in-the-arse self.'

'Well if it's meant to be, I'm sure he'll swipe right on you again.'

'She might not.'

Kjeld raised his brows. He couldn't tell from her deadpan reply if she was serious or pulling his leg. 'Why, Detective Jansson, I had no idea you were playing the field.'

'I'm keeping my options open.'

'I prefer my options to leave before I wake up.'

'Which explains why you can't keep anyone around for more than a week.'

'You've stuck around.'

'Unfortunately that's my job.'

Esme turned around and headed back to the door.

Kjeld couldn't see her face, but he had the impression that she was frowning. Whether that was from something he said or something else he couldn't say. As well as he knew Esme, he oftentimes found her difficult to read. They were friends. Good friends. They trusted each other in a way that only partners could trust each other. With their lives, their safety, their truths. But despite their closeness Kjeld rarely ever opened up to her and, whether of her own preference or because it felt too awkward to be too serious with him, she didn't either. There were times, however, like when Kjeld was on the verge of ending things with Bengt, a period in his life that was overshadowed by heavy emotion and too many prescription medications, when he thought there might be something more between them. Kjeld would have been lying if he didn't think he'd seen the potential for something between Esme and himself, but Esme, as supportive and sympathetic as she was, always kept a careful distance from him. Either she didn't feel that way about him or she knew what everyone eventually found out – a relationship with him was a recipe for disaster.

Kjeld followed her out in the yard, hands shoved into the pockets of his jeans.

As they approached the back door a figure trekked around from the side of the house. That swooping blond hair unmistakable even from a distance. Kjeld held back a groan as Gunnar waved his hand like a coach on the sidelines of a football match trying to get a player's attention.

'Nygaard!' he called out. 'There you are. I've been knocking for almost ten minutes.'

'I wasn't in,' Kjeld replied, his expression straight-faced.

Esme sent him a sidelong glance. She knew her partner well enough to know when he was mocking someone under the guise of pseudo politeness.

'Where's your father?' Gunnar asked.

'He's not home,' Kjeld said.

'Is he at Sara's place?'

'He's in the hospital.'

Gunnar flinched, but the reaction was fleeting, quickly recovered after a slow blink and a throat-clearing cough. 'Is he all right?'

'He had a heart attack.'

'Was it serious?'

'It was a heart attack.'

'I see,' Gunnar said. He smoothed his hair back with a gloved hand. 'I'll go speak with him there then.'

'What is this about?' Kjeld asked.

Gunnar pursed his lips as though he couldn't quite decide how to respond to Kjeld's question. It made him look constipated. Like a man who was trying hard not to strain.

'Gunnar? Why do you need to see my dad?'

Gunnar took a deep breath and exhaled. There was a slight wheeze in the back of his throat when he finally answered. 'I have a warrant for his arrest.'

'What?' Kjeld's focus broke. He stared at Gunnar, searching the man's face for something that would give this information credibility. Something that would make sense. 'What for?'

'For the murder of Peter Lindqvist.'

# Chapter 32

The hallway outside of Stenar's hospital room was chaos by the time Erik hurried in, sweat pouring from his bald head after having accidentally turned up the heated seats in his hire car. He wiped a handkerchief across his forehead and approached the arguing group that crowded around the room.

The two Nygaard siblings had practically barricaded themselves in front of the door, Kjeld yelling in the face of the local police inspector while the doctor and an unfamiliar woman in a wool cardigan and with a thick fringe that covered her eyebrows stood off to the side trying to ease the situation by insisting unceremoniously that everyone calm down.

This was exactly why he'd gotten out of family law.

Erik took a deep breath, straightened his tie, and gave his best attempt at looking taller than he actually was.

Then he walked down the hall while nurses watched on like vultures from their station, salivating for something to gossip about with their friends after their shifts. Nothing exciting ever happened in Varsund, after all.

One glance in Erik's direction sent Gunnar into an exasperated groan. 'You called a lawyer?'

223

'My father has the right to understand what he's being charged with,' Kjeld said.

'Understand?' Sara interrupted. 'How can you expect him to understand? He's sick. You're all insane. This is entirely unacceptable. I can't believe you would stoop this low, Gunnar.'

'I'm just doing my job, Sara,' Gunnar said.

Erik stepped into the fray.

'If I could interrupt for a moment,' Erik began, holding up his hands in a gesture of impartiality. 'I think it would be best if I speak to the doctor and Inspector Ek about this in private so we can discuss the legality of the situation and determine what's best not only for the police investigation but for Stenar's health as well.'

Doctor Goswami breathed a sigh of relief. 'Yes, I think that would be wise.'

Gunnar nodded, but Erik could see he wasn't exactly pleased with having to agree. He looked like the kind of man who only agreed to things when it was politically advantageous to do so. Whether this was one of those occasions was yet to be seen.

'Do you have an office where we can talk, doctor?' Erik asked.

'Yes, of course. This way.'

Doctor Goswami led Erik and Gunnar down the hall, but before they turned into another corridor Erik glanced back at Kjeld and his sister who stood fuming in the doorway to Stenar's room. This was why he hated getting involved with families. They were all the same.

* * *

It took thirty minutes for both Erik and the doctor to convince Gunnar to agree to allow Stenar to remain in the hospital until an impartial psychiatrist from outside of Varsund could give their opinion on the state of Stenar's mental health and whether he had the cognitive ability to understand the charges against him. When he relayed this information to Kjeld, the son seemed satisfied that his father was receiving appropriate protection. Erik noticed that there was a considerable amount of suspicion on the younger Nygaard's part with respect to the local police inspector, but he didn't ask. To be honest, he didn't want to know. Sara, on the other hand, seemed less pleased with the circumstances, insisting that there be another option wherein she could take their father home. The unfamiliar woman with the fringe just looked on quizzically like she was mentally solving a sudoku puzzle.

'The doctor said he would be able to go home today,' Sara insisted.

Her tone was even more demanding than her brother's and Erik briefly wondered if this was something she inherited from one of her parents or just something she'd picked up from having lived in the unforgiving backwoods of Jämtland county for her entire life. Both, he imagined.

'Doctor Goswami said there were still some concerns with Stenar's tests this morning. They want to do another ECG later this afternoon and keep him under observation. I know this may seem unfair to you, but this actually works in Stenar's favour.'

'How's that?' Kjeld asked.

The woman with the fringe perked up and stared at him like she could see right through to his bones. It made Erik uncomfortable.

'Your father's Alzheimer's, provided the psychiatrist declares it to be in the later stages, protects him from undergoing police questioning. If he's physically ill then even if they do have compelling evidence against him, they won't be able to force him to trial. Even if they determine he is responsible for the death of Peter Lindqvist—'

'He's not,' Sara interrupted.

Erik paused before continuing. 'Even if they determine he is responsible for Lindqvist's death, the state won't require him to serve time. They can't punish a man for doing something that he can't remember doing.'

'He'd be able to go home?' Sara asked.

225

'Or remanded to a care facility,' Erik said. 'I don't specialise in criminal law, but I'll get in contact with someone who does. Don't worry. We'll settle this quickly. In the meantime, try to keep him calm. And don't talk to him about the case. God forbid he actually admit to something. Truthful or not, that would make things more difficult.'

* * *

Erik adjusted the heat level on the seats of his hire car while he waited for his hands-free calling to connect. From his spot in the car park he had a direct view of Kjeld, who stood outside the hospital entrance blowing clouds of cigarette smoke into the air while talking to the woman with the fringe in the fuzzy cardigan.

The call connected and Roland's voice boomed out of the speakers.

'Norberg! Wasn't expecting to hear from you so soon. Did you get the final documents from the MineCorp agreement?'

Erik lowered the volume. 'Yes, I did, but that's not why I'm calling. I'm in Varsund.'

'Varsund? I thought you were going to finish everything up from Stockholm.'

'I was called back for something else,' Erik said. He watched as Kjeld finished his cigarette and lit up another. 'We need to have a chat about Nygaard.'

There was a pause on the other end of the line, interrupted by static crackles from the car speaker. When Roland responded it was with confused uncertainty in his voice. 'Nygaard? You mean Stenar? The old bird-watcher?'

Erik watched as Kjeld dropped the cigarette to the pavement and stubbed it out with his boot before following the woman to an ugly green Volvo.

'No,' Erik said. 'Not Stenar. The other Nygaard.'

226

# Chapter 33

While the doctors took his father away for his afternoon testing, Kjeld drove back to Norrmalm Industries and tried to get a meeting with Roland Lindqvist while Esme went into town to get the groceries he'd been putting off and to see if she could find any information on the disappearance of Valle Dahl. Not for the first time he found himself questioning how he'd managed to keep Esme as a friend after all the grief he gave her. When this was all over, he would have to remember to be more appreciative.

'You just missed him,' said the young intern behind the desk, pushing his thick-framed glasses back onto the bridge of his nose.

Bengt had glasses like that.

'Do you know when he'll be back?'

'I think he took the rest of the day off.'

Kjeld cursed under his breath.

'You could possibly catch him at home,' the intern said, voice waffling. Normally it would be inappropriate to give out the personal information of a colleague, but they were all about to lose their jobs anyway. Well, he would, at least. And he'd have to find another company to finish his internship at. A task that wouldn't be too easy in the middle of the year.

227

'Where's that?' Kjeld asked.

'Älgvägen. Across the river.'

'Number?'

The intern laughed. 'Seriously? It's the only house on the street. And trust me, you can't miss it.'

* * *

The intern wasn't wrong. Even if there had been other houses on the street, and there wasn't one for miles in either direction, Kjeld never would have mistaken which was the Lindqvist house.

It was a two-storey building with a singularly peaked roof and three dormered windows on the upper floor, architecturally uncommon for the region. The wood was painted traditional Falun red, like most houses in the country, except the tone appeared slightly darker and less coppery than the colour on his father's home. Kjeld wondered if that was a trick of the light – a few minutes after three and the sun was already disappearing beneath the tree line – or if the paint had been specifically chosen to stand out. The trim around the windows was bright white and the front door – blue, sheltered by an upstairs balcony accented by curled moulding – sat back on a rectangular veranda.

He was met at the door by a cleaning woman who led him into a parlour. The walls were covered in an intricate design of textured wallpaper, not unlike what could be found in the royal palace in Stockholm, that was probably original to the house. The furniture was ornate and antique. Dark wood. Gold-leaf. Not what Kjeld expected when he met the younger Lindqvist, who exuded nothing but modern style and ego. This was the room of a wealthy family. Old money. The kind that someone, generations before, had worked hard to obtain. And this room was the last remaining shrine to that past.

But Kjeld knew this room although he'd never set foot in it before.

This was the room with the piano.

The one his mother played before he was born.

The room from the photograph.

He thought of that image of her. Glancing over her shoulder. Smiling. Exuding a vibrance that Kjeld had never known.

He gently lifted the piano fallboard and looked down at the keyboard. Pristine. Seemingly untouched. And he caught himself wondering if his mother's fingers had been the last ones to touch those keys.

'Jesus Christ!'

Kjeld turned to see a woman standing in the doorway.

She was probably in her early sixties. She wore a long dress, mauve-grey in colour with pintucks and floral appliqués, that while slightly loose still flattered her figure. Her hand was clutched to her chest and around her wrist was a gold bracelet shaped like interwoven leaves. Her hair was blonde. That same icy shade as David's. And she looked as though she'd just seen a ghost.

'I apologise if I startled you,' Kjeld said, placing the fallboard back down on the piano and covering the keys.

'It's not that,' the woman said. 'It's just that for a moment I thought you were someone else.'

Kjeld was about to ask who when the woman stepped through the doorway to approach him. He held out his hand to her by way of introduction, but she didn't accept it. She merely held her hands clasped in front of her like a surly schoolmarm and stared at him straight in the eyes. It was unnerving not because of the directness but because Kjeld had a sense that she saw something in his face that he did not.

'Sylvia Lindqvist,' she said.

'Kjeld Nygaard.'

'Nygaard?'

'Yes, my father lives in—'

229

'I don't mingle with the townspeople,' she said a tad too curtly. Then she relaxed her shoulders. 'That must sound incredibly vain. And it's true, I won't pretend that I don't have a measure of narcissism in me. Cynicism, too, which is why I haven't asked you yet why you're here.'

'I was hoping to meet with Roland.'

'Of course, you were.' Sylvia made her way over to an antique bar cabinet that stood in the corner behind the piano. 'Drink?'

'No, thank you,' Kjeld replied. And then as an afterthought added, 'I'm driving.'

'That's very law-abiding of you,' she said, fixing herself a glass of brandy.

'I'm a police inspector.'

'Aren't you all supposed to be incorrigible drunks? Or is that simply a Hollywood stereotype?'

'There's an element of truth to most fiction, isn't there?'

'And an element of fiction to all truths.' Sylvia smirked. 'I like you, Inspector Nygaard. You're not boring. Even if you are only here to see my husband.'

'Is he in?'

'He is not.' She drank the entire glass in one gulp and poured herself another.

'Will he be back s—'

'He's with his mistress. Trying to get over the news of his brother, no doubt.' Sylvia closed the cabinet and made her way back towards Kjeld. She looked at the piano as though suddenly remembering that he had shown interest in it. 'Do you play?'

'Not well and not recently.'

'Nobody in this house plays either, but it is customary to have a piano, is it not? It gives a room a certain kind of warmth and weight. Stature. And there's inevitably someone at the dinner party who can play something that isn't "Chopsticks".'

Kjeld reached into his pocket and took out the photograph

from the Christmas party. 'I wanted to ask your husband if he could tell me more about this photo.'

Sylvia took the photo and held it up to eye level. Then she flipped it over, reading the date. She shook her head.

'I didn't meet Roland until 1980.' She turned the photograph over again, her expression tightening. 'Look at him. Leering. He never could keep his hands to himself.'

'Do you recognise any of the others?'

'Naturally that's Peter there. And Erik, of course. Always trailing behind Peter and Roland like a lost puppy.' She licked her lower lip. 'This man is familiar. Yes, yes I remember him.'

Kjeld leaned in to see which man she was pointing to.

'Valle Dahl.'

'Is that his name?' Sylvia shrugged and handed the photograph back to Kjeld. 'He had a grudge against Roland for something. Can't remember what. They quarrelled a few years after we were married and then I didn't see him again. I assume he quit or was let go. If you're no longer at the Christmas parties then you aren't part of the family anymore.'

'Family?' That struck Kjeld as an odd choice of word.

'You know. The *Norrmalm* family. The company family.'

Kjeld slipped the photograph back into his pocket. He was disappointed. Although the information about Roland and Valle having an argument was interesting, he'd been hoping for more about his parents. More about their relationship to the Lindqvists and how that may connect to the body buried in his father's barn.

'Are you sure you won't have a drink?' She peered at him again with that invasive stare, but as before Kjeld had the feeling that it wasn't him she was really seeing. Like she was imagining someone else.

Then again, that might not have been her second drink of the day.

'I ought to be going.'

'Do you have a card?'

'I beg your pardon?'

'So my husband can get in touch.' She took a sip of her drink.

Kjeld retrieved a card from his wallet. Sylvia tucked it between her index and middle fingers as one might a cigarette.

'I'll tell him you stopped by. Can't promise he'll call back. He's a busy man. Or, at least, that's what he's been telling me for the last thirty years.' She winked, intentionally provocative. Definitely not her first drinks of the day. 'But I might call.'

Once outside, Kjeld took a deep breath. That house had been suffocating. Not just Sylvia Lindqvist's haughty affluent damsel routine, but the entire feel of the house had been tight and claustrophobic. Like the house's history was desperately pushing from within the walls, forever trapped between wooden planks and timeworn insulation.

It was stifling. Almost worse than the town itself.

The sun was nearly buried beneath the horizon, that slender layer of light blue quickly dispersing into the purple-black of night. Not yet four in the afternoon and it felt like ten. In Gothenburg it would still be light for at least another hour.

His phone vibrated in his pocket. A message from Esme.

*Did you get in touch with Roland? Checked out the local library. Found old news articles on Valle Dahl. Cave-in led to the death of three miners in 1983. Dahl was supervising. Drinking on the job. Gonna look online and see if I can find anything else. Call me.*

A few seconds later she sent another. *Also tried to contact the municipality about getting a list of Mercedes sedans registered in the area. No-go without a warrant.*

Kjeld sent a quick reply. *Spoke with Sylvia Lindqvist. Roland's wife. Confirmed bad blood between Roland and Valle. Heading back to hospital.*

Kjeld glanced back at the house. Sylvia Lindqvist stood in the parlour window, a dark shadow against the light in the room, watching him. Her earlier words echoed in his thoughts. Valle Dahl had a grudge against Roland. They'd quarrelled. Kjeld had no doubt that this argument directly related to the event at the mine Esme had just texted him about. But did that relate back to Peter or his father? Had they been involved somehow as well? Was the animosity between Roland and Valle enough to lead to murder? And if so, why Peter?

Why not his brother?

# Chapter 34

The heart monitor beeped in regular intervals until the sound blurred in with the background and added to the white noise of the room. Kjeld sat beside the hospital bed, his father's aviary atlas on Northern European birds on his lap, and tried to read the Chapter on ravens. His eyes kept getting distracted from the words and after having read the first paragraph on their worldly distribution he settled on skimming over the pictures instead.

Stenar rolled over onto his back, his eyes partially open, stuck together by the crusty discharge that came with sleep. He wiped his fingers over his face, spreading the hardened residue "eye goobers", as Kjeld's daughter would call them, onto his cheeks.

'Kjeld?'

'Yeah, Dad. It's me,' Kjeld said. He leaned over and scratched off the crust from Stenar's face. Then he wiped it on the starched hospital bedsheet.

'Where am I?' Stenar's voice was slow and lethargic like a man who still wasn't fully awake.

'You're in the hospital.'

'Are you okay?'

'Yeah, Dad. I'm fine. You had a mild heart attack, but the doctors say you're going to be all right. Nothing to worry about.'

Stenar raised a hand to his chest and noticed the IV tube stuck in his arm. He pulled at it.

Kjeld reached forward and took his father's hand so he would leave the tube alone.

'Just calm down. It's going to be all right. I know you're confused,' Kjeld said. 'Sara was here earlier. She said she's going to bring her kids up tomorrow to visit.'

'I don't want to see them,' Stenar grumbled.

'I think they'd like to see you. They would have been here today, but the doctors thought you needed more rest.'

'I don't need any rest. I need to go home. I have to feed the birds. Hermod will be waiting for me.'

Stenar tried to sit himself up, but the angle of the bed prevented him from getting more than a few inches off the mattress.

Kjeld placed his hands on his father's shoulders and gently eased him back down. Then he adjusted the bed so his father could sit up more naturally. 'I've been feeding the birds. You don't have to worry about them.'

'You?'

Kjeld understood his father's disbelief. Even he found it hard to accept that he'd gone out into that barn alone to feed the ravens. The last time he'd done that was when he was a child and it hadn't gone overly well. Kjeld ran a finger over the tip of his ear where a piece of cartilage was missing.

'I can't say they enjoy what I've been feeding them, but they're not going to starve. They'll be there when you return.' Kjeld held up the aviary atlas and handed it to Stenar. 'I've been reading up. I couldn't remember what their usual diet was.'

Stenar coughed. It was a thick gurgling sound. 'They're opportunistic omnivores.'

'That means they'll eat anything, right?'

'Grains, berries, fruit. Meat, of course.'

'Yeah, I remember meat,' Kjeld said, pushing back a memory from his childhood.

'Serendipity.'

'What's that now?'

'It's how they feed. Ravens will take what they can get.' Stenar coughed again. His eyes almost glazed over as he recalled the one thing dementia could never take from him. His birds. 'Most people think they're just scavengers, but that's not true. They'll eat carrion if they have to, but they'll hunt and they'll steal. They'll do anything to survive, but not at the expense of their family. They'll share with other ravens if they find more than they can eat on their own.'

Kjeld leaned back into the plastic hospital chair. It was uncomfortable like the ones in the reception area and it caused his lumbar region to ache. After an hour of sitting there it was beginning to throb. The back ache combined with his father's sudden lucidity on a topic that Kjeld had never enjoyed made him restless and uneasy. 'I don't want to talk about the birds.'

'Why not?'

'I just don't. I don't like the birds, Dad.'

'You used to when you were a boy.'

'Yeah, well, that was a long time ago,' Kjeld said.

A nurse walked by and peeked her head in. She scribbled something on the whiteboard near the door and then moved on to the next room.

'What changed?' Stenar asked.

'You know what changed, Dad.'

Stenar didn't respond. Instead he turned the page in the atlas. Raven conservation and management.

'You left me in that barn for hours,' Kjeld finally said, teeth gritted together. 'You left me in there while they attacked me. While they bit at me and made me bleed.'

'That's absurd. Ravens don't bite.'

'Fine. Pecked. Tore. Whatever. That's not the point. Why didn't you do anything? Why did you just leave me there? Why didn't you help?'

'I was …' Stenar wavered. His eyes took on a glossy sheen as though he remembered something, but he either couldn't or wouldn't form the words to explain himself.

Kjeld suspected it was a little bit of both. He waved a hand in the air as though to brush the conversation away. 'Forget about it. It doesn't matter.'

But Stenar didn't look relieved to have the topic changed. He held on to the aviary atlas as though it were keeping him grounded. As if he letting go of the book might disrupt the laws of gravity and send him floating up to the ceiling, out an open window, and into the vast nothingness of space. And when Kjeld saw that look on his face, that pained teeth-clenching strain of a man who had a secret, he knew his father remembered. He remembered a lot more than he was saying. In that brief inter-lude between Kjeld's childish outburst and those shiny images of scavenging birds, Stenar might have remembered everything.

'When is my granddaughter coming?' Stenar asked, shaky fingers struggling to turn the page. He licked his index finger in a feeble attempt to give himself more grip. It didn't help.

Kjeld reached over and turned the page for him. 'I told you. Sara is going to try and bring the kids up tomorrow. The doctors were afraid you would overdo it today if you had too many visitors.'

Stenar shook his head. 'My other granddaughter. When is Tove coming to see me?'

Kjeld winced. 'She's not coming, Dad.'

'Why not?'

'Because she's in Gothenburg.'

'Why?'

'Because that's where she lives.'

'But why isn't she with you?'

'Because she's with her father, okay? She doesn't live with me.'

The words came out louder than Kjeld had expected and he was immediately embarrassed, concerned that one of the nurses would tell him to keep it down. Or worse, leave. He stood up and crossed the room to the small sink. The room was cool, but he felt hot around his neck. He ran his palms under the sink and splashed a handful of water on his face to ease the sudden heat as well as his anger. No, not anger. Frustration.

He cupped his palms under the tap and took two quick gulps of water before turning it off. Then he walked over to the window, which gave a rather unceremonious view of the car park, sporadically illuminated by commercial LED lighting that took on a murky yellowish haze against the falling snow. An ambulance turned on its emergency lights and pulled soundlessly out of the garage along the side of the hospital and peeled out into the road. Kjeld pulled down the shade, blocking the outside world from view.

'But you're her father,' Stenar said, closing the atlas.

'Biology doesn't mean anything,' Kjeld replied and he believed it. He may have provided the seed necessary for his daughter's birth, but that didn't make him her father. Not her real father, anyway. That title was reserved for the person who took care of her. For the man who made her breakfast in the morning, drove her to dance class, read her stories before she went to bed. Not for Kjeld. Not for the man who popped in when it was convenient or when he felt guilty. Real fathers didn't do that.

'No, I suppose not, but that doesn't change the fact that you're her father, too.'

Kjeld pressed his fingers into his lower back. Then he twisted from side to side in a failed attempt to get a crack out of his spine. 'Sure. If you say so.'

'I never begrudged your choices, you know,' Stenar said, fussing with the top blanket on the bed. 'I never cared about any of that. Did you know that among birds it's fairly common for—'

'Stop,' Kjeld interrupted. 'Just don't. I don't want to hear it. I don't want to hear any of it.'

Stenar frowned. 'Why did you never bring her to see me?'

'Why? *This* is why. Because you and I don't have a relationship,

238

Dad. We haven't since I was a boy. If Mum were alive then maybe things would be different. She was the only reason I kept in touch as long as I did, but after she died—' Kjeld took a deep breath. 'I'm tired of pretending like you and I ever had a good relationship. You've never seen me as anything more than a failure. And you know what? I don't care anymore. I don't even know why I came up here. I don't know what I thought it would achieve. We can't even have a normal conversation without fighting with each other. That's why I never brought Tove up here to meet you. Because she's got enough disappointment in her life with me. She doesn't need it from her grandfather, too.'

Stenar ran his eyes over the cover of the atlas. It was an old edition. Outdated by probably twenty years, but still in readable condition. All of his books were well cared for. His books, his research documents that he rarely looked at anymore, his collections. They were all timeworn, cherished, and intact. It was a pity the people in his life couldn't be the same way.

'She has the right to meet her grandparents,' Stenar said. His voice was soft, uncertain. 'Your mother would like to meet her. I know she would. Eiji has always been very fond of children.'

Kjeld frowned. Anger suddenly replaced with surrender. He'd been fooled again. Fooled into believing that his father knew what he was saying. How much of the conversation had been a farce? How much was just his father's mind picking up on details of the past and correlating them to the present? How much of it was just lies provoked by cognitive glitches?

'I'm going to go out for a bit.' Kjeld grabbed his jacket, still inappropriately insulated for the unpredictable northern weather, and made for the door.

'Could you tell Sara I'd like herring and pancakes for dinner?'

'Sure, Dad,' Kjeld said as he was halfway out the door.

He slipped his jacket on as he headed for the stairwell. He tried not to think about how bitter he was. How he wanted to get outside and scream at the night. He tried to push the thoughts

239

of Tove from his mind and the awareness that his father, despite his addled brain, was right. Kjeld was her father even if he didn't feel like it. Even if he didn't act like it. But he couldn't shake an even harsher realisation – that he'd become his own father. Absent, obsessed with his work, unable to reconcile the misjudgements of his past with the faults of his present.

Except Stenar had one thing over Kjeld. Stenar, despite everything, never ruined things with Kjeld's mother. They were together until the end. Twenty-three years of marriage. And it would have been longer had that slow-growing glial tumour not taken his mother before her time. Kjeld's longest relationship had been little more than five years and it only lasted that long because a baby came into the picture. Twenty-three consistent years to Kjeld's on-and-off five. In that respect his father was the better man. But that didn't stop Kjeld from wishing that his mother had been the one to live.

\* \* \*

The blazing glare of his headlights against the blackness of night was the only sign of life on the road outside of Varsund. Snow pelted the windshield in a wash of white and the wipers worked overtime to keep the glass clear. But even when the flakes were swept away Kjeld could barely see more than fifty metres in front of him.

He drove without heed or intention other than to get as far away from Varsund as possible. No destination in mind. No thoughts other than those of anger, spite and regret.

On the radio a local late-night talk programme was discussing the current police investigation. No names were mentioned, but Kjeld was certain all of Varsund knew about the body found on the Nygaard property. Word travelled fast in a small town. He changed the channel. The lilting sound of a Sami woman singing *joik* wailed through the speakers. It was a sad song, the a cappella undulations of her voice ebbing and flowing at unexpected intervals, evoking the disquieting improvisation of pain. There weren't any lyrics. Just sounds. Aching tonal expressions that reflected Kjeld's own turbulent state of mind.

He drove until there wasn't anywhere left in Varsund Kommun to drive. Right up to the Norwegian border where a medium-sized stone pillar off the side of the road announced the boundary of the two countries in carved letters, as if Kjeld couldn't already feel the change in the pavement. Bumpy and pothole-filled on the Swedish end suddenly turning into a smooth black surface on the Norwegian side. A small but fitting reminder that even the great social democracies of Scandinavia had varying qualities of life. It made Kjeld wonder if his own life would have been any different had he been born twenty miles to the west.

The snow came down harder. Unforgiving. And the singer's voice turned mournful like the endless dark that stretched out on either side of the road.

It took minutes before Kjeld realised he was crying. Not the kind of weeping that congested the nose and made it difficult to breathe, but an unceasing flood of tears. Soundless and without reprieve.

# Chapter 35

Aside from the occasional beeping of the monitor beside his bed, the hospital room was eerily quiet. But not quiet like home. Stenar clutched the aviary atlas between his fingers. He wasn't agitated, but he did feel restless. His arms were tired, heavy, and his thoughts were dulled by whatever medication they'd given him to relax. Why didn't he feel relaxed? Why did he feel like he had to be active? To get up and do something?

Except there wasn't anything to do. Kjeld was taking care of the ravens, which meant there was nothing for Stenar. And even though that nagging voice in his head had difficulty accepting the idea that his son was minding the birds in his absence, he believed him. Kjeld had always been a stubborn boy. Reckless and unruly, not to mention obstinate, but he wasn't a liar. Eiji used to say that it was impossible for Kjeld to lie. The few times he had lied as a child he gave himself away with an awkward glance or a pout or by breaking down in tears because he felt guilty for trying to deceive his parents. Lying wasn't in his nature. If he said he was taking care of the birds then Stenar had no reason to believe that wasn't the truth. Even if he knew Kjeld hated the ravens more than anything. Stenar himself being the only possible exception.

He sighed and glanced over to where his nightstand should

242

have been. Where was his photograph of Eiji? Had someone moved it?

Stenar tried to turn, but he had an ache in his torso that prevented him from too much rotary motion. What had he done with his wife's photo? Had she moved it while she was cleaning? Did Kjeld take it?

A nurse walked into the room. She was short, shorter than Eiji, but she had the same shoulder-length blonde hair and honest smile. Her teeth were a little crooked in the front. Eiji's teeth had been crooked too. Not glaringly so, but just enough to be endearing.

'How are you feeling, Herr Nygaard? Do you need any more water?'

Stenar shook his head. His thoughts became more rapid and confused. Where had Kjeld run off to? Hadn't he just been here? Where did he say he was going? It had been something about the barn, Stenar was almost certain of it. Something about the birds. But Kjeld shouldn't go out to the barn. The barn wasn't safe. That's where it had happened. And if Kjeld went out there then he could get hurt. He could get hurt like the last time.

'It's not safe, Eiji,' Stenar said, again trying to change his position in the bed.

'You're perfectly safe here, Herr Nygaard,' the nurse comforted. 'I'm just going to change your fluids.'

Stenar heard the nurse's words, but he didn't understand them. He didn't understand what Eiji was talking about. Eiji shouldn't have even been there. She had left for the Christmas party hours ago. Left him alone with Sara after their argument. The argument that was his fault. He'd been so stupid and foolish to accuse her of taking Peter's side. She'd only been trying to support their old friend after the loss of his wife and child. She was right. Peter was only doing what he knew best. Running that mine was all he was capable of controlling and it was the only thing that took his mind off his grief. And what had Stenar done? Ruined their friendship because he'd been too upset about the conservation of the local wildlife to help him. And now Eiji was angry with him. And Kjeld was angry, too.

'I have to go.' Stenar pulled at the peripheral intravenous line on his hand. 'I have to stop Kjeld from going into the barn. He's going to get hurt.'

The nurse placed a consoling hand on Stenar's arm. 'It's going to be all right, Herr Nygaard. Do you know where you are?'

Stenar grabbed the nurse's wrist. 'Why did you do it, Eiji? Why?'

'Please, let go. You're hurting me.'

'Why did you go to the party? We agreed we weren't going to go. Not after what he did. He's a criminal. He's destroying the forest. He understood the harmful effects of his operation and he didn't care! How could you take his side? Why would you do that?'

The nurse tugged her arm, but Stenar's grip tightened. She reached over to the side of the bed and pressed the emergency call button.

'I'm sorry, Eiji. I'm sorry I didn't listen to you. But he was going to destroy everything I worked to protect. That damn company was ruining everything beautiful and pristine about this country-side. How could I forgive him for that? How could I let that go?'

Another nurse and a broad-shouldered orderly entered the room. Stenar was gripping the blonde nurse's arm so tightly that her hand turned red, her wrist already beginning to bruise. The orderly held Stenar down by the shoulders, distracting him while the other nurse injected a sedative into his line. Within seconds Stenar's grip loosened.

His head throbbed and his eyelids began to droop. The book in his lap slid off the side of the bed and hit the floor, but Stenar's senses had already started to dull and he didn't hear the sound of the old binding snapping along its well-worn crease. He thought of the birds and hoped that they wouldn't be angry with him. Then he thought of Eiji. She would forgive him eventually. Their love for each other was enough to get them over this hurdle. They just needed time. Before his eyes closed fully, he saw a glimpse of his boy, of Kjeld lying in the dirt, crying, face covered in blood. Stenar never should have let him go out to the barn on his own. He should have been there with him. And if it hadn't been for Peter, he would have been.

If it hadn't been for Peter none of this would have ever happened.

# Chapter 36

## Torsdag | Thursday

Kjeld woke up to a knock on the glass near his head. He was freezing. His breath was visible, hovering above the steering wheel like a cloud before forming a small circular damp spot on the windshield in front of him. Along the edges where the window met the steel frame of the car were frozen blossoms spreading out to the centre, giving the impression of broken crystal.

Kjeld turned his head to the side and saw Hanna, bundled up in a faux fur-lined coat, staring back at him with that concerned look mothers often gave their children. He tried to start the car so he could roll down the window, but the battery was dead. It didn't even try to roll over. It just puttered, whirred, and then died. He opened the door and swivelled his legs out onto the street. His back groaned from sitting in the same position for hours.

He leaned forward and spat a yellow glob of morning phlegm on the ground.

'Lovely.' Hanna turned up her nose.

'What time is it?'

'Almost six.'

Kjeld looked at the sky. It was dark and the lamplights were lit. It distorted his perception of time. 'In the morning?'

'Of course, in the morning.' Hanna scoffed. 'How long have you been out here?'

'All night, I suppose.' He climbed out of the car and slammed the door shut behind him.

'All night?' The wind pushed at her hood and Hanna tugged it back over her head. 'Why didn't you come inside?'

Kjeld didn't have an answer to that. It was a simple question. Why didn't he go inside? Why did he spend the night risking hypothermia by sleeping in a car in freezing temperatures? Why didn't he go home? Why did he have to be such an arsehole? They were all simple questions, none of which had simple answers.

'Guess I fell asleep,' he said. 'Can I come in now?'

There was a moment then when Kjeld thought she might turn him down. It wasn't a hesitation on her part so much as a fleeting lull in the space between them. Not long, but long enough for Kjeld to question whether he'd overstepped his boundaries. It wouldn't have been the first time that week.

She gave an exasperated sigh in the way one would after discovering that a puppy had just accidentally pissed on the carpet. Then she smiled.

'Of course. Come on, ya old charmer. Let's warm you up.'

* * *

Hanna's house, albeit 1970s style on the outside, was completely remodelled on the inside to look like a swanky apartment one might expect to find on an Airbnb advertisement for Old Town in Stockholm. Everything was, in the IKEA fashion, white and rectangular and clean, accented with pastel blues and pinks. Hanna herself stood out in stark contrast. Not just because her skin was at least four shades darker than her Liatorp-model coffee table, but because she struck Kjeld as being more adventurous than do-it-yourself furniture pieces, thick-weave throws, and magazine-styled sofa pillows.

He sat in the corner of her couch, a low-backed retro model with attached cushions and short wooden legs that forced him to slouch so as not to aggravate his lumbar region any more than he already had, and cradled the coffee mug she'd given him. Like the throw pillows, which he'd carefully pushed to the side, the mug was a soft rose shade. On the forward face of the mug was the phrase "all I need is coffee and mascara" in gold cursive font. Kjeld agreed with the first half, but thought he'd do better to save the world the horror of seeing him with thick black lashes. Besides, that would clash with his ruddy hair.

Hanna sat down on the couch beside him, close enough for their knees to touch.

'All right, handsome. Spill it.'

'What?' Kjeld's thoughts were in a haze and his fingers were still stiff from the cold.

'What's going on with you?' Hanna asked.

'What do you mean?'

She tucked her legs up beneath her in a pose that, while it looked extremely photogenic due to the slender length of her calves, Kjeld couldn't imagine was comfortable.

'I know two nights together might not qualify me as having a professional opinion on your state of mind, but I've seen enough vacant eyes in my time to know that something's not right. And I'm not talking about the obvious. God knows I drank an entire bottle of Riesling on my own after we found that body. But you don't strike me as the sort who gets his panties in a twist over corpses.' She brought her own mug, baby blue with "everything's gonna be all right" wrapped around the cup, to her lips in a short sip. 'Spit it out. What happened?'

'I had a row with my dad.'

'Come to blows did it?'

Kjeld snorted. 'Not exactly. Might have been easier if it had.'

Hanna nodded. 'Dementia is a bitch. My grandmother had it bad. She practically raised me, you know, because my mum was always working to pay the bills. One time I was over at her house. We'd just had the most marvellous day. You couldn't even tell that anything was wrong. She was going on and on about these stories from her childhood and when I was a little girl. It was beautiful. We must have been going on like that for four or five hours and then she just stopped, stared straight at me, and asked me what my name was. We'd just spent hours talking about things we'd done with each other when I was growing up and she didn't have any idea who I was. It just about broke me.'

'I'm sorry,' Kjeld said. He brought the mug to his face and let the steam waft over his nose and lips.

Hanna shrugged. 'Life is shitty sometimes. I remember thinking there were all these things I wished I could say to her. And I did say them eventually, but I don't know if she understood any of it. Guess it was more for my own well-being than anything else.'

There were a lot of things that Kjeld wanted to say to his father, but none of them were good. Certainly not for anyone's well-being. Some of the things he had managed to say. Instead of feeling better, however, he just felt worse. Worse because he knew his father wouldn't understand or would forget five minutes later. Things he should have said twelve years ago, perhaps even earlier. Then maybe he wouldn't be carrying around his guilt like a suitcase with a broken wheel.

Hanna understood. And not just because she'd watched her grandmother fade into a stranger. She understood because, like Kjeld, she was from Varsund. She was familiar with the struggle of growing up in a place where nothing was private. A town where everyone knew the locations of the closets each family used to hide their proverbial skeletons. She understood the challenge of trying to leave. Of knowing the likelihood that she and everyone she grew up with would eventually take on the roles of their parents and grandparents. She saw the cycle. She was part of it. Maybe that was why Kjeld felt like he could open up with her about his father and his past in a way he couldn't with Esme. There was a kind of safety net with Hanna he didn't have with his partner. Because when this was all over she wouldn't be a part of his life in Gothenburg. When this was over he could finally put it all behind him.

'I always told myself I would never be like my father. It was the one thing I promised myself growing up. That no matter what I did or who I ended up with, I wouldn't be like him. Especially if I ever had my own children. I would be different. Better.' Kjeld took a sip. 'I didn't even really want kids. I didn't plan for that. I think part of me always knew I was too selfish to be a parent. Too fearful that I'd fail to do it right. Don't get me wrong. I love my daughter, but I'm not a good father.'

'I think most parents feel like that at some point.'

'Maybe, but I became everything I promised I wouldn't. I used to think that it was because she was young. That maybe it wasn't in me to get along with small children, but I think it's just me. And now I've passed down this derelict parent gene to her and I'm afraid the circle will never stop.'

Hanna reached over, placed a hand on his thigh and gave it a gentle squeeze. 'You're not your father, Kjeld. Whatever happened in the past, it's in the past. Don't be so hard on yourself. Raising kids is a rollercoaster that never ends. Sometimes you're at the top of the hill heading down at breakneck speeds and sometimes you're on the loop. No one does it right. Everyone fails. It's just a matter of doing your best.'

Kjeld cracked a smile. 'Where'd you hear that? Off the back of a cereal box?'

'Just something my therapist used to say when I was going through my divorce,' she said, grinning. 'Kinda stuck with me.'

'I like that.'

'Just remember, you can leave whenever you want. You've

already done a lot by coming up here. I'm sure your family would understand if it's too much for you.'

'I think you give my family too much credit.'

'You gotta take care of *numero uno*, handsome.'

'Something else your therapist said?'

'Nah. Heard that on *RuPaul's Drag Race*.'

Kjeld laughed. It felt good. It was a pity that Hanna was so entrenched in Varsund. Kjeld thought she might be someone he could spend more time with. Maybe someone he could come to feel serious about. But not in Varsund. Varsund was a pit of despair. And as soon as he was able he would be on the road and back to the busy streets of Gothenburg.

'I have to see this through. I'll have too many questions if I don't. It's just a matter of putting together the pieces. Unfortunately, right now they don't fit.'

'The pieces about your dad?' Hanna asked between sips.

'Oddly enough I think it's more about my mum.'

'The lady from the photograph?'

Kjeld nodded. He didn't know why, but he had a nagging feeling that his mother's relationship to the Lindqvists had more to do with the corpse in his father's barn than anything else. Jealousy was the number-one cause for murder, after all. Jealousy followed by revenge. Could something have happened that pushed his father over his breaking point? A crime of passion gone dreadfully wrong and then forgotten about?

Kjeld didn't know, but he felt he owed it to himself, and to his father who sounded so desperate on the phone when he called him, to find out. Even if it didn't heal the wounds between them. Even if his father didn't remember that he'd helped.

As if sensing his thoughts, Hanna shook her head. 'But your dad is so—'

Kjeld quirked a brow.

'I don't know. I just … He seemed nice. Granted, I'm a stranger,

251

but he didn't strike me as the kind of person who would be responsible for a murder.'

'They never do.' That was one of the first tenets of good police work. Never underestimate the ones you least suspect. Kjeld had ignored that rule once before to disastrous results. Never again.

'So how do you find out?'

'Find out?' Kjeld asked.

'How do you find out about the connection between your mother and the Lindqvists? Have you spoken with Roland?'

'I tried. I got waylaid by his son.'

Hanna let out an irritated groan. 'That man is so disgusting. What a creep.'

'Like Norberg?' Kjeld remembered she also referred to Norrmalm's lawyer as creepy.

'Hardly. I'd take Norberg over David Lindqvist any day. That man is ... guh!' She shivered. 'Every time he looks at you it's like he's imagining what you look like naked.'

'Isn't that a self-confidence booster? To help you speak in public or something?'

'Not where David is concerned. There have been more than a few receptionists who've seen him off the clock, so to speak. Needless to say, they aren't working at Norrmalm anymore.'

'He's into weird stuff, you mean?' Kjeld leaned forward to the coffee table and set his mug on a glass coaster.

'I mean he's not exactly in the running for feminist of the year.' Hanna looked at the rim of her mug where she'd smeared her lipstick. 'He's the sort who thinks he's God's gift to womankind. I hear things sometimes. Nothing good.'

'Yeah I got the impression he likes to be in control.'

'Deep pockets, small package. At least that's the word around the water cooler. He might be good-looking, but I wouldn't touch that with a ten-foot pole.'

Hanna glanced at her wristwatch and then stood up to gather her purse. She searched through the large pouch, items rattling against each other, until she found a lipstick tube. She used a mirror beside the front door to touch up the areas she'd smeared. It was dark red. Like blood under a dim lamplight.

'What else do they say around the water cooler?'

'That David will do anything to make a buck. And he hates Norrmalm Industries. He can't wait for this merger to go through so he can take his profits and get the hell out of Dodge, as the Americans say.'

'You mentioned the merger earlier. Is Norrmalm restructuring?'

'Roland is selling to some other mining company. Of course, all of us lower tier people will probably lose our jobs in the downsizing, but the Lindqvists will be sitting pretty on their newfound fortune.'

Kjeld thought about those bins in his father's basement, remembering the wording on the outside of the cardboard that he'd found the tackle box in. *N.M. Miscellaneous.* What else could have been in those boxes? What else didn't he know about his parents and their relationship to Norrmalm Industries?

'Anything for money, you say?'

Hanna grabbed a scarf from the coat rack near the door and wrapped it around her neck. 'Anything.'

'Sounds like a motive.'

'For selling the company?'

'For murder.'

# Chapter 37

The cellar steps creaked beneath his footsteps. Kjeld ducked his head to avoid hitting the lightbulb that dangled above the stairs and made his way down to the cold dank room below.

He immediately went back to the box labelled *N.M. Miscellaneous*, which still sat partially opened on the shelf beside his mother's vinyl collection. Inside the box Kjeld found much of what he remembered seeing a few days prior. Invoices, half-faded documents that were barely legible, empty folders. It was as though someone had reused the box without changing the writing on the side. There was nothing in the box's contents that gave Kjeld any indication that either of his parents had a connection to the mining company. Perhaps they had just been friends with the Lindqvists. Nothing more. His father knew Peter from the service, after all. It was possible that they'd stayed in touch afterwards. It wasn't like Varsund was that big a town. Everyone knew everyone.

And everyone was supposed to know everyone's business, too. So why didn't Kjeld know? Why didn't Sara? What was his father keeping from him? What didn't he see?

He felt stuck. He'd hit a wall as far as this investigation was concerned. If only he could have managed to speak with

Roland Lindqvist or gotten more information out of his trip to Norrmalm. If only his father could remember what had happened. If only he'd never decided to drive out to Varsund and dig up a past that had caused him nothing but misery.

Kjeld tossed the box back on the shelf and shoved it up against the wall. Damn his father. Damn his dementia. And damn himself for ever thinking that he could ever find a reason to explain why his father despised him or why his mother had to die before her time or why someone had buried the body of Peter Lindqvist in his family's barn.

He clenched his fist and punched the side of the box in the space between the *M* and *Miscellaneous*. The clinking sound of something metal falling out from the worn edges of the box and hitting the concrete floor subsided his anger.

Kjeld crouched down and peered underneath the shelves. Against the wall was a shiny gleam. He reached under the shelf, decades-old cobwebs tickling at his fingers, until he felt the object.

A key.

The key was small, too flimsy for a door, not unlike the kind used for bicycle locks. Attached to the key was a looped piece of thin braided leather as though it had once been worn like a necklace. The number 026 was engraved on a circular piece of metal, like a tag, clipped to the braid. Kjeld had seen one of those before, but not for years. It was a safety deposit box key.

The key itself Kjeld didn't recognise, but the braid conjured a memory he had of his mother. His mother had a bracelet that looked similar. It, too, had been braided from thin strips of leather. It stuck out clearly in his mind because Sara had wanted one as well and that was when his mother taught her how to make friendship bracelets. Sara must have made dozens over the course of that week, leaving them all over the house. His father hadn't been happy about the mess.

Did this key belong to his mother? As much as Kjeld felt like she wouldn't have need for one, he couldn't help but feel like this key, like the photographs in the tackle box, was hers. But if so, why were they hidden, stuffed away in a box left to moulder and rust in the damp cellar? Why would she need a safety deposit box in the first place? His father had a safe in his bedroom where all of the important family documents were kept. If this box belonged to his mother, then what was she keeping in it?

What could she possibly have to hide?

There was only one bank in Varsund and it had been there since the town's conception. Norrmalm aside, the bank was the only business that had never gone out of business. And if this key matched one of the deposit boxes at the bank, it wouldn't be difficult to find out.

And if Kjeld got lucky with this discovery, perhaps he'd never have to go into town again.

# Chapter 38

'Technically I shouldn't be sharing any of this information. But since we've received confirmation from the dental analysis, it's in our best interests to work together to find out what happened to your brother,' Gunnar said, pouring himself another glass from the whisky decanter in Roland's office.

As far as he was concerned, that was the best thing about being Varsund's only police inspector. Wining and dining with his so-called betters. Not that Gunnar thought Roland Lindqvist was better than him. Richer than him, sure. But better? Gunnar had earned the respect of the community in the years since he'd taken over from his predecessor. Hell, Varsund actually had a police station now, thanks to him. Well, mostly thanks to the Lindqvists who'd paid for the remodelling of the community centre that allowed for the opportunity to convert some of the unused office space into a police station, but also thanks to Gunnar who did all of the promoting and secured enough votes from local residents to pass the initiative.

Richer, not better.

Gunnar took a swig from the glass and smacked his lips together. 'That'll do it. That'll put hair on a man's chest.'

He set the glass down and leaned back into the leather chair.

Roland sat at the large mahogany desk across from him, not drinking. 'I wouldn't want you to impede the course of justice. Not by any means. But you have to understand how this news has affected my family. Knowing that someone murdered my brother has caused quite a stir. Not to mention the emotional impact. We'd all feel a lot better if we knew whether we should be worried about anyone coming after the rest of the family.'

Gunnar nodded, his comb-over bouncing atop his head. 'Naturally. I can't imagine how you must be feeling.'

'That's why I had some of my own IT specialists look into the email we received. I'll share the findings with you, of course. The results were concerning.'

Gunnar pursed his lips. He didn't like his competency as an investigator called into question. He'd turned in that information about the emails to forensics days ago, but Varsund didn't have any technical specialists so the request had been forwarded on to Östersund where it took a back seat to their cases. It wasn't Gunnar's fault they were slow to respond.

'Concerning?'

Roland pushed a piece of paper across the desk. 'According to the specialist, the email was sent from my brother's phone, but it was connected to a cell tower in Varsund Kommun at the time.'

Gunnar scanned the document, but didn't actually read it. He was thinking about what Roland said, slowly putting the pieces together.

'Well, we already knew that Peter wasn't the one to send the message. The coroner's dating of the—' Gunnar stopped himself before saying "corpse". Oftentimes the showy process of sounding professional made him forget the personal aspect of who he was talking to. He cleared his throat. 'The coroner's results indicate that the deceased had been in the ground since around the time he went missing. Or, in this case, since he presumably went on his sabbatical.'

It had been a persistent question on Gunnar's mind. Why

had the Lindqvist family not responded earlier to Peter's disappearance? Why did they seem so content to believe that the man needed time away from the company? And so much time? Even Gunnar could see that didn't follow a logical pattern of behaviour. Then again, the Lindqvists weren't exactly "of the people". Perhaps in the world of the wealthy and extravagant a person's desire to disappear and cease all contact was considered a normal routine.

But he doubted it. He imagined that, like everything, it all came down to money.

'Were they able to track the communication to an IP address? Anything to narrow the location?'

Roland shook his head. 'It appears that the messages were delivered and then the mobile was turned off. It hasn't received or transmitted anything since the day the emails were sent. My specialists explained to me that the window of time was too small to get a more accurate idea of where the phone was during transmission. Varsund Kommun was the best they could do.'

'Which means the likelihood that the killer is a local just increased.'

'My thoughts exactly.'

Gunnar held up the slip of paper. 'May I keep this?'

'Of course,' Roland replied.

Gunnar folded the document in half lengthwise and slipped it into the inside pocket of his suit jacket. He made it a habit of dressing above his station whenever he called on the Lindqvists. When he called on Roland, mostly. Although there had been a time when he used to exchange handshakes with Peter as well. As Varsund's number-one public servant, Gunnar inherited the invitation to their annual Christmas parties by default, but he liked to believe it was because the Lindqvists also saw something of merit in him. Perhaps even someone who could one day make the profitable leap to the private sector.

Gunnar didn't mind playing the long game.

'There's something else I'd like to discuss with you before you leave,' Roland said, interrupting Gunnar's fantasies.

Gunnar picked up the whisky glass and took a sip. 'Of course.'

'It's concerning the Nygaards.'

'The Nygaards?' Gunnar wasn't surprised by the mention of his old academy friend's family name. It was natural that they might come up in conversation as a result of where Peter's body had been discovered, but there was something in Roland's voice, strained and perpetually serious, that gave Gunnar the impression that a request was about to follow. A request that may not have been entirely above board with respect to the law.

'Tell me about this Kjeld Nygaard. You know him, don't you?'

Gunnar heaved an irritated sigh. 'Yeah. We knew each other growing up. Did our police training together. He thinks he's a hotshot. Works in Gothenburg these days.'

'Is he an honourable sort?' Roland asked.

'That's a loaded question where Kjeld is concerned. He can be counted on. Dependable. But he's also something of a loose cannon. You've heard about the Kattegat Killer?'

Roland gave a slow nod, his interest in the conversation piquing.

'Well,' Gunnar continued, 'that was Kjeld. Not the killer, obviously. But he was the one who caught him.'

'Sounds like he's a capable investigator.'

'Except that it was his best friend. A colleague he's worked with for more than a decade. And he didn't notice. Didn't put the pieces together until four people were murdered. Hell, maybe even more. From what I read in *Aftonbladet* they're still negotiating to find more bodies.'

'Sometimes it's the people closest to us that fool us best,' Roland said, clasping his fingers together near his chin.

'There's a rumour that he didn't follow protocol when he caught him either. He shot the guy. Almost killed him.'

'Revenge?'

'Or Kjeld was trying to cover up his own involvement.'

A silence fell between them. Gunnar didn't actually believe that Kjeld was involved in the Kattegat murders, but he didn't mind fanning the flames of suspicion. Especially if it made him look better.

'What about his relationship with his father. Good?'

'Rocky, if I recall correctly. Conflicted.'

'I've heard that Stenar Nygaard has dementia. Is that correct?'

'The doctor I spoke with did say he was in a later stage of Alzheimer's. He still has periods of lucidity, but from what I understand it's progressive.'

'So in the event of a conviction, he wouldn't serve out a prison sentence?'

The question took Gunnar off-guard. He hesitated in answering, his mind racing to put together the unspoken pieces of the puzzle while Roland stared him down from across the broad desk. A desk that was probably worth more than a month of his salary. A salary that was a pittance for what he really did for the Varsund community: ensured its safety and longevity.

He sat forward, adjusting his position on the hard leather cushion of the chair. His sense of discomfort was sudden and difficult to hide.

'If the evidence points to Stenar as the person responsible for Peter's death, and if the doctors declare that he is incapable of remembering the crime, then no. He wouldn't serve out a prison sentence. In all likelihood he would be remanded to a state medical facility.' Gunnar paused. 'But that's only if it can be proved beyond a reasonable doubt that he was the culprit.'

'From what I understand, you've filed for his arrest,' Roland said.

'Yes, because there was enough evidence to continue questioning him, if possible. And to further the investigation into other areas of the house and property. But we don't have enough evidence to charge at this point. There may still be other lines of inquiry.'

'What if there was enough evidence?'

Gunnar felt his grip on the whisky glass slipping and he quickly finished off the rest of the drink before setting it down with a clink on Roland's desk. 'What are you saying?'

'I'm saying that it might be beneficial to everyone if Stenar were to be found guilty. He won't go to prison. His memory is fading so there wouldn't be any humiliation on his part. And my family could put all of this behind them, quickly and quietly. Without causing any unnecessary stir.'

Without interrupting the flow of business, Gunnar translated.

'What you're suggesting isn't lawful.'

'But you have experience in that.'

Gunnar frowned, a sour taste building in the back of his throat. 'I beg your pardon?'

'In breaking the law,' Roland said. 'From what I hear, you do it very well.'

# Chapter 39

Varsund Regional Bank was an old wooden building with a stone foundation. When Kjeld was a young boy it had been painted a dark shade of blue, almost grey, and added a quaint appearance to the tired downtown thoroughfare. Now it was a yellow eyesore and looked more like a kebab shop from the outside than a place one would go to enquire about a loan.

Hanna had offered to drive Kjeld into town, but he chose to walk. As she was one of the few people who lived close to the town and not out in the hinterlands, like Kjeld's father, it wasn't much of a distance to travel on foot. Once she'd driven away, however, he realised his mistake. The temperature had dropped below freezing and he was still wearing the thin autumn jacket he'd brought with him from Gothenburg. But Kjeld didn't call her to come back. He was too stubborn and she was already late for work.

The bank didn't open until ten so Kjeld sat in a small café across the street, drank two cups of mediocre-brewed coffee, ate a pistachio cinnamon roll that he immediately regretted ordering after the first bite, and sent Esme a text to meet him in town as soon as she was up. He'd need her to take him to a garage so he could get a replacement battery for his car. He considered adding a "pretty please" to the text to soften the frustration she was no doubt experiencing after he'd inadvertently left her alone at his father's house without warning, but knew she wouldn't fall for it. Instead he sent a second text that consisted of nothing more than an emoji of a cat blowing a kiss.

Sweet, but shameless.

Kjeld watched from the window as a bank employee emerged from inside the building and unlocked the main entrance. Then Kjeld finished the rest of his coffee, ignored his urge to pee, and headed back out into the cold.

A bell jingled over his head as Kjeld entered the bank.

'Good morning,' the blue-suited man at one of two desks greeted. He stood up and held his hand out to Kjeld. His handshake was firm, but friendly, much like his appearance. He was typical of what Kjeld considered the "young professional". Clean cut and well groomed. His hair was dark blond, trimmed shorter on the sides than on top, and his suit was tailored to taper towards the waist in order to accentuate what Kjeld imagined to be a well-defined chest beneath his starched shirt. Thin. Probably a runner. Maybe a cyclist. The bank employee smiled, showing off his unnaturally white teeth, and Kjeld knew immediately that he was in the presence of the kind of man who could charm an old lady into an adjustable rate mortgage.

'Morning,' Kjeld said. 'I'm here about a safety deposit box.'

'Sure. What size are you looking to rent?'

Kjeld reached into the pocket of his jeans and removed the key with the thin leather strap. 'No, I'd like to open one.'

'Of course,' the bank employee said, smile ever present. 'What's the number?'

Kjeld flipped the key over to look at the faded masking tape. 'Zero-two-six.'

'And the name?'

Kjeld faltered in his answer. The bank employee raised a brow expectantly. Kjeld tried to cover his hesitation with a feigned laugh.

'I'm sorry,' Kjeld said, dissimulating more awkwardness than he actually possessed. It was a routine that Esme encouraged him to use more often. Better to charm than repel, she would say. 'This is kind of embarrassing. To tell you the truth, I've never opened one of these before. I inherited the key from my parents.'

The smile slowly began to dissipate from the bank employee's face. 'We're not really authorised to open safety deposit boxes for people who don't know the name on file.'

'Even with the key?' Kjeld did his best impression of a pout. He imagined it might have been more successful without his untrimmed beard.

'I'm sorry.'

Kjeld sighed, his gaze darting over the man's desk. Neat. Tidy. Too tidy, really. The only memorable items on the desk were a blue coffee mug with the bank's insignia on the side, a silver nameplate with the name Sven Larsson, and a framed photo of a Yorkshire terrier.

People loved to talk about their pets.

'Cute dog,' Kjeld said.

Sven's smile returned, cheeks flushing a shade lighter than his skin before taking on an embarrassed rosy hue. 'Thanks. She's a rescue.'

'So is my cat, but he's not quite as adorable. Even with a low-carb diet and a personal trainer he'd still manage to look grumpy in pictures.'

Sven laughed.

'What's her name?' Kjeld nodded to the photograph.

'Blix.'

'My cat is Oskar. Named for the *Sesame Street* character.'

'Is he a grouch?'

Kjeld grinned. 'You have no idea.'

There was a lull in the conversation and Kjeld looked down at the key in his hand. He ran his fingers back through his hair, tucking a dishevelled strand behind his ear. 'I'm sorry. I've been impolite. It's been one of those weeks, if that wasn't already painfully obvious. You don't look like you're from around here. Nobody around here knows how to wear a proper suit, for one. For another it's almost impossible to find someone with a sense of humour. My name is Kjeld Nygaard.'

'You're right! No one in this town knows how to take a joke,' Sven said with a laugh. 'Sven Larsson. It's nice to meet you. Are you Danish?'

'My great-grandfather was. It's a family name, but I grew up in Varsund. A tragedy, I know. I managed to get out, but just barely. You've got a little fluff.' Kjeld reached forward to remove a small piece of thread from the other man's shoulder. 'Where are you from?'

Sven blushed. 'Västerås.'

Kjeld raised a brow. 'Wow. Big city.'

'This is a temporary posting, but it lets me put "manager" on my résumé. After a year I'll be able to transfer to a larger financial institution.'

Kjeld feigned surprise. 'Well now that would be something. I'm sure you'll be a shoo-in for any position you apply for. Actually I just so happen to know someone at Nordea Bank in Västerås. I'll be driving back that direction on my way home. I could stop by and drop your name. Tell them about the excellent customer service the residents up in Varsund have been getting from their local credit union.'

There it was. That glimmer in the other man's eyes that told Kjeld he'd hooked him. Everyone wanted out of Varsund. It was the perfect lure.

Still, Sven hesitated.

'Look, I don't expect there to be much in there,' Kjeld continued, 'but my sister and I are thinking about selling the house and we haven't found the deed yet. And if it were in this deposit box it would really help us out.'

'Well.' Sven bit at his lower lip and canted his hips to one side.

266

'If you give me your parents' surname and if it matches then I suppose it would be okay.'

'I would be so grateful.'

Sven pulled up the database on his computer. 'Name?'

'Nygaard. That's with two A's. You know, from the Danish side.'

Sven typed it in and frowned. 'Nothing.'

Kjeld pursed his lips.

'Mother's maiden name, perhaps?'

'Rosell.'

Sven shook his head. 'Sorry. There's no one by either of those names in the system.'

Kjeld twirled the key between his fingers. Neither of his parents had a safety deposit box. Then why have a key? Whose key was it?

'I wish I could have been more help,' Sven said. His face was sympathetic, but whether that was because it was the first time anyone in Varsund paid him any heed or because he really was hoping Kjeld would put in a good word for him at Nordea was difficult to say.

'Could you try one more for me?'

'All right.'

'Lindqvist.'

Sven typed in the name. He stared at the screen for a moment and then turned to Kjeld, face brimming. 'Looks like third time's the charm.'

\* \* \*

The safety deposit box wasn't much larger than a shoebox and the stiffness with which the key fit into the lock told Kjeld that it hadn't been opened very often, if at all. He pulled back the curtain on the corner office, which Sven explained doubled as their private area since so few people used safety deposit boxes these days, blocking the window view of the bank's lobby, and focused his attention on the box. The Lindqvist box.

Kjeld began to lift the lid when he hesitated. A thought crossed his mind that this was one of those end-of-the-line moments. The point of no return, as it were. Of course there was always the chance that there was nothing in the box, or nothing of relevance. Nothing that might explain to him why the CEO of Norrmalm Industries and his father's supposed best friend lay buried beneath dirt and bird shit in his family's barn for so many years. Nothing that might prove his father's innocence or dispel the anxious fear that his mother wasn't the woman he'd believed her to be. Kjeld honestly thought that would have been worse than uncovering proof that his father was a killer. Learning that his mother was somehow involved.

He took a deep breath and exhaled, cursing the 2005 smoking ban that prohibited the use of cigarettes in public buildings. Then he opened the box.

Kjeld didn't know what he'd expected to find so when he opened the box and only found a few slips of paper attached with a paperclip he couldn't say he was surprised. He removed the documents from the box, unclipped them, and spread them out over the table. Four pages typed on what was probably an old Facit typewriter judging by the distinguishing marks at the sides of the paper where it had caught on the release lever before being pulled through. The date at the top of the first page was 1978.

He read through the document three times before he realised what he had in his possession. It was a contract between his father and Peter Lindqvist, signed by them both and witnessed by Erik Norberg, rectifying a dispute – the nature of which was unexplained within the pages of legalese – by an agreement that Norrmalm Industries would never attempt to purchase or mine on the Nygaard property so long as the Nygaards refrained from sharing information related to the Lindqvists or their public assets. The document was, at least from Kjeld's perspective, vague. But that might have been a result of the missing pages. Kjeld checked the pagination at the top and saw that at least three pages had been removed from the document.

And whatever information they referenced was removed with them. It was, however, from what Kjeld could determine, essentially a gag order. One family's silence in exchange for another family's promise not to profit off their land.

Except they were profiting.

Kjeld pictured himself chasing that figure from the barn through the woods, recalling his shock at slipping over the edge of the unfamiliar ravine and into the mining pit. It was so clear in his mind because he remembered not only being surprised that the pit was there, as it hadn't been when he was a young man, but also because it was so close to his father's property. Perhaps even on his property. And yet here he had a notarised contract between his father and the Lindqvists that Norrmalm would never extend to the Nygaards' land. Not so long as Stenar, and presumably Kjeld's mother, abided by the dubious terms of the agreement, which essentially boiled down to one thing – don't talk.

Don't talk about what? What information could his father have that would affect the marketability of a business worth billions of kronor? And how did that relate to Peter Lindqvist's death? Or did it?

Kjeld folded the contract and slipped it inside his jacket pocket. Then he closed up the safety deposit box and left it on the table. As he passed through the bank lobby he gave Sven an acknowledging nod, the kind that would have gone hand in hand with a tip of the hat if he had one, and made his way to the exit.

Sven, who looked to be laying out some kind of financial plan for a young woman with a crying baby in a stroller, excused himself from the desk and caught Kjeld at the door. He slipped his business card in the front pocket of Kjeld's jeans and gave him an eager but authentic smile.

'I get off at six every day. In case you want to get a drink before you head back home,' Sven said with a wink before returning to the woman with the stroller.

Kjeld watched the bank manager walk away, not bothering to hide his admiration for how the man's slacks fit, professionally snug. It really was a well-tailored suit. Then he remembered the picture of the terrier on the desk. It was a pity. Kjeld was definitely more of a cat person.

\* \* \*

'Hey, Kjeld!'

Kjeld looked up in time to see Tom running across the street. Well, it wasn't so much running as it was a kind of half-hearted jog. Unlike Kjeld, the man was bundled up in a ski jacket and thick gloves, giving him the impression of being much wider than he actually was. Kjeld immediately thought of those cartoon penguins Tove watched on Saturday mornings.

Tom wobbled to a stop when he reached the sidewalk and nodded to the bank. 'Setting up an account?'

'Closing one, you could say.'

'When one door closes, another one opens?' Tom grinned and Kjeld noticed that he had a yellowish stain on his front teeth. Probably from too much coffee. Kjeld didn't think he was a smoker.

'Something like that.' Kjeld reached into his pocket and took out a pack of smokes.

'Those things'll kill you, you know.'

'So people keep telling me.' Kjeld turned his head to the side and lit a cigarette.

'I convinced Sara to quit five years ago. It's done wonders for her stamina. She doesn't get out of breath as much as she used to.'

Kjeld quirked a brow, uncertain of whether his brother-in-law was making a reference to their bedroom activities or was simply unconscious of the double meaning of his words.

Tom rubbed his gloves together. 'Aren't you freezing?'

Kjeld held up the cigarette. 'Portable heating device.'

Tom laughed. It was a high-pitched and grating sound.

'Aren't you supposed to be in Östersund?' Kjeld asked. 'I thought Sara said you were doing part-time work there nowadays.'

'I've got the day off. I'm just in town running errands.'

Or trying to run, Kjeld thought to himself. He took a drag on the cigarette and exhaled the smoke away from Tom's face.

'What account were you closing? Stenar's?'

Kjeld licked his lips and looked at Tom carefully. The man had always struck him as weird, even before he'd married Sara, but for some reason he seemed even stranger now. Then again, it could have just been Kjeld's prejudice towards Varsund and everyone in it. Lately he'd been wondering if his bias towards his old hometown wasn't a little unfounded.

'A safety deposit box of my mother's,' Kjeld finally relented to say.

'Really?' Tom raised both brows high into his forehead, completing the cartoon penguin look.

'Yeah, I found a key in some of Dad's old things.'

'Anything interesting inside?'

Kjeld shrugged. 'Just an old document.'

'Of what?'

'A contract between Dad and the mining company. I don't know what it is exactly. It was missing some pages.'

'Norrmalm? Huh. That's odd. I thought he hated that place,' Tom said, but the tone in his voice suggested that he didn't think it was odd at all. 'Well, hey, it was nice seeing you again, but I gotta dash. Gotta get these errands done before Sara calls.'

Tom reached out and gave Kjeld a friendly slap on the shoulder. It made Kjeld feel uncomfortable.

'Yeah, sure.'

'You should come by for dinner again soon. I could let you borrow one of my self-empowerment books. Gotta make peace with your inner self, you know. That's important. Could help you quit smoking, too.'

'Wouldn't want to interrupt your own progress by taking your source material off your hands.'

Tom laughed again, his pitch higher the second time around. Maybe it was an effect of the cold air. 'You're a funny guy, Kjeld. You should lend Sara some of that humour of yours. She's so serious all of the time.'

Kjeld flicked the cigarette ash on the ground. He thought he'd been obvious in his intonation, but Tom had somehow mistaken his sarcasm for wit. Peculiar man.

Tom didn't seem to notice Kjeld's lack of response, however. He was already crossing the street again, his soft figure waddling beneath his thick ski jacket.

Kjeld took out his phone. He had a text from Esme. She'd replied to his flirty cat emoji with an angry cat one and an anagram that indicated she was on her way to pick him up. Kjeld breathed a sigh of relief, glad to know that she wasn't angry with him. He would make it up to her somehow but, knowing Esme as he did, she'd probably draw it out for weeks just to teach him a lesson.

He finished his cigarette and tossed it on the ground. Then he lit another and dialled his sister.

# Chapter 40

'Is Norrmalm Industries mining on Dad's property?'

There was a pause on the other end of the line and Kjeld thought that he heard the sound of a car engine shutting off. He turned up the collar on his thin jacket to block some of the wind from chilling the back of his neck and took another drag on his cigarette. Then Sara's voice interrupted the silence.

'What did you say?'

'That day I was chasing the stranger from the barn – the day that Dad and I found the body – I fell into an excavation pit. At the time I thought it was really close to Dad's property, but now that I think about it I'm fairly certain that it was actually on his property. Did you know anything about this?'

'What? No,' Sara replied, more miffed than Kjeld expected. There was a short delay before she continued and the initial annoyance in her voice was gone, replaced with worry. 'I mean, I know that they've been mining closer to town and I know it was close to Dad's place, but I didn't realise they were digging *on* it. Are you sure?'

'Well I can't be certain until I find the property survey for Dad's place, but I remember running all over those woods when we were kids. I'd be willing to bet almost anything that they're digging on his side of the boundary.'

'Maybe he sold it?' Sara asked.

'Dad would never sell. That land has been in the family for generations. There's nothing on this earth that would convince him to sell, least of all to a company that was planning to dig it up. No, he wouldn't do that.'

'You don't know that, Kjeld. You haven't been around for a long time. Dad isn't the same man he was. Hell, he wasn't the same man ten years ago. He's been through a lot. You know how it was for everyone after Mum died. It's possible he would have sold off a parcel or two.'

Kjeld tugged the sleeve of his jacket down to cover the fingers holding his phone. The wind changed direction and he turned, inadvertently exhaling a cloud of smoke into the face of an old woman tugging a shopping trolley. She swore at him with a mouth only a miner could love, sent him a sneer, and rolled her large-wheeled grocery trolley over his foot.

'Same to you, lady,' Kjeld muttered.

'What was that?' Sara asked.

'Not you,' Kjeld said, grateful that he'd had the foresight to wear boots. His city shoes weren't meant to withstand Varsund's early winters. Or its shoppers. 'Some lady just—Forget about it. I think you're wrong. I don't think Dad sold anything to anyone. I think they might be digging on his property illegally.'

Sara paused again and this time Kjeld thought he heard the sound of a voice on a speaker.

'Where are you?' he asked.

'I'm at the hospital pharmacy picking up Dad's medications. They're letting him go home today. I left you a message on your voicemail. Didn't you get it?'

Kjeld couldn't recall receiving any calls from his sister or the hospital.

'My phone might have been out of range when you called. Are you bringing him back to the house?'

'No, I'm bringing him to my house. I think you've proven well enough that you can't be trusted to keep Dad safe.'

'What are you talking about? It's not like I gave him a heart attack. I mean, come on, sis. He's old. That wasn't my fault.'

'You stress him out, Kjeld. Increasing his anxiety is not helping him get better.'

'He has Alzheimer's. He's not going to get better. He's only going to get worse. I'm trying to help.'

'How? By riling him up and making him remember things? That's not helpful. If anything that's just speeding up his confusion.'

Kjeld dropped his cigarette and stubbed it out on the ground with his toe.

'Listen to me. I'm doing the best I can. Dad wanted me to help so I'm here helping. Sure, we've had a few arguments along the way, but I'm on to something here. And that something has to do with Norrmalm Industries. I know it.'

Sara sighed. On the other side of the line it sounded like a wind tunnel blowing directly into Kjeld's ear and he pulled the phone away from his face until he heard her begin to speak again.

'I don't know where the property survey is. It might be with my stuff or it might be in the cellar. Hell, I don't know if we even have one. I've never looked for it. But you can't just go around accusing Norrmalm of illegally mining on Dad's land.'

'I won't.'

'Do I have to remind you that Varsund is a mining town? Practically every family here depends on Norrmalm to put food on the table. It's not a joke to say that they're the pillar of this community. They are. Quite literally, in fact.'

A bell dinged in the background. Kjeld assumed it was the pharmacy calling up a new number.

'I'm not going to say anything without proof, Sara. I'm not an idiot. I just thought I should let you know that there's more going on here than just Dad claiming to have witnessed a murder.'

'*Supposedly* witnessed a murder. Just because they found a body doesn't mean he was actually there.'

'He was there,' Kjeld insisted. 'And I think that mining quarry I fell into is the link connecting all of this.'

'Like I said, if they're on his property then he probably sold it. It's possible. There was a period of a few years where Dad was doing all sorts of crazy things. Would it surprise me? Sure. But I wouldn't put it past him.'

'I found something that may prove otherwise.'

'What do you mean?'

'I found a contract between Dad and Peter Lindqvist. In it Lindqvist agrees never to try and purchase let alone dig on Dad's land.'

'Peter Lindqvist the dead guy?'

'The same. How'd you hear about that?'

'Word travels fast. It's impossible to keep a secret in Varsund. Not one like that anyway.'

There was a mumbling of unintelligible voices on the speaker, probably muffled by Sara covering the phone with her hand. Kjeld tried to listen, but he couldn't understand anything. It was almost a minute later before Sara's voice returned.

'I'll look for that survey when I get home.'

'Thanks, sis.'

'But you need to keep this to yourself until we can prove any of it. You don't have to live in this town, but I do. And I do not want to be known as the woman who tried to sue the only reputable business in town only to find out there was absolutely no basis to my claims. Do you get that?'

Esme's olive-green Volvo pulled up in the temporary parking across the street.

'Kjeld? Do you understand me?'

'Yeah, sure. I get it. Look, I gotta go. My ride just got here. Call me if you find that survey.'

Kjeld rang off and stepped out into the street. A four-door

sedan swerved past, practically clipping him from the kerb. He shouted at the driver, but received a wrinkled middle finger in return, held up beside a hand-pull shopping trolley in the passenger seat.

# Chapter 41

'I need to talk to you.'

Roland closed up the laptop on his desk and turned his attention to the man across from him. All those years of knowing him and he still couldn't get used to those bulging eyes.

'The deed is done, Erik. I don't know what you want me to say at this point.' Roland leaned back into his chair, half turned to face the glass window overlooking the cavern. The orange hue of bedrock was lightened by the snow, giving it an almost crater-like appearance. From first glance it could have been the surface of Mars. 'By the end of the year these offices will be packed up and we'll be replaced by Holm and the rest of the MineCorp group. The deal is made. I couldn't go back on it now even if I wanted to.'

Erik wiped a handkerchief over his sweating brow and dabbed it at the corner of his eye where it had begun to tear. This weather was a bear on his condition. His eyes had been swelling more than usual with the early winter chill. He didn't normally have this problem back in Stockholm where the weather at least had the decency to wait until December to turn frigid. January if it was feeling particularly gracious.

'That's not what I mean,' Erik said, his voice low and apologetic. 'It has to do with Peter.'

Roland turned his chair back towards his desk and stared across the dark mahogany finish at the lawyer.

'What about Peter?'

'I know something about him.'

Roland's expression drew into a hard scowl. He was trying to decipher the meaning behind Erik's words without jumping to any conclusions. His body, however, betrayed him. His heart was already galloping in his chest in preparation for the words that would follow.

'Don't tell me you know who killed him,' Roland said. Terse.

'What?' The comment took Erik off-guard. 'No, of course not.'

'And you didn't kill him, did you?'

'God, no. Roland, that's not what I meant at all.'

'Then what did you mean?' Roland stared at him, his patience worn thin.

'I know why he left,' Erik admitted. The confession came out of him in a heavy gasp of breath like he'd been carrying it around for years instead of days. 'I know why he really went on sabbatical.'

That wasn't what Roland was expecting to hear and he frowned. 'We all know why he left, Erik. He was burned out.'

Erik reached into his pocket and removed a letter. The envelope was sealed with a signature across the back. Erik had been holding on to it for years. He'd tucked it away in his safe at home, never thinking that he'd have to deliver it. Thinking about the consequences it could have now made his palms sweat.

'The last time I saw Peter he left this in my office.' Erik sighed, realising how ludicrous that must have sounded aloud without any context. He dabbed the handkerchief at his eye. The conjunctiva was red from irritation. 'It was after he announced his sabbatical. He came by and we had a drink. A few drinks. Nothing out of the ordinary. Just talking about the good old days. About how things were different when we were younger. How Norrmalm was different. You know.'

'Peter never had any trouble talking about the company. It was all he had,' Roland said, eyeing the envelope with distrust.

'He spent a lot of time talking about how the pressures had finally gotten to him and his regrets over the years. I won't get into those. You know what I'm talking about.'

'Yvonne.'

Erik nodded. 'I can't imagine how that must have been for him. Even now when I think back, I have trouble making sense of it. It's not right for someone so young and full of life to be taken from this world.'

Roland considered saying something on that matter and then didn't. In the great scheme of things, there really wasn't anything to say about it. The death of Peter's wife and child had been tragic, but it was something they all mustered through eventually. And as sore a subject as it had been at the time, it was decades in the past. Roland could hardly even remember what she looked like now. 'What's in the envelope, Erik?'

Erik took a deep breath. 'At first I thought he would come back after a few months. A year, at most. But he didn't. I guess a part of me was concerned at the time, but I rationalised it. Peter valued his privacy, after all. He told me to keep this letter for you until he returned. And I was only to give it to you should he … well, should something happen to him. I didn't get the impression that he was worried about anything. He was just tying up loose ends. Being safe. You always hear stories about healthy people suddenly becoming ill or passing without warning. That's what he said, anyway. That was his reasoning. But when I heard that the police had verified his death … I don't think Peter had this in mind when he wrote whatever is in this letter.'

Roland listened, his gaze unwavering from its stare. He was searching Erik's face for some fault in the story. Some glimmer of a lie. But he didn't see anything. Then again, it was hard to see anything beyond those protruding peepers.

Roland reached forward and tried to tug the letter out of Erik's grip, but Erik tugged it back.

'Let me say one more thing. You know what this company means to me,' Erik continued. 'My career is built on Norrmalm and its success. Peter made that happen. Without him I would still be practising family law in some suburban village, living alone in a one-bedroom apartment without a balcony, and wishing I'd had the gumption to pursue corporate law. Peter is the one who gave me that confidence. I know it was none of my business disagreeing with your choice to sell, but I hated to see that era end. Especially without him.'

Roland turned back to the window, the tension in his face lessening. As much as he hated to admit it, he believed Erik. He believed his pitiful story about feeling he owed a debt to Norrmalm and to Peter. On anyone else it might have seemed too pathetic, but Erik had never been the kind of man who stood comfortably on his own two feet. And when he did gain some semblance of self-assurance it was on the backbone of more confident men. Men like Peter.

'Peter leaving was a sore topic for me at the time,' Roland said after a pause. 'I didn't want this for myself. I wasn't expecting it or prepared for it. I know I shared in the ownership, but Norrmalm was always supposed to be Peter's company. When he told me he was leaving I didn't take it well. We argued.'

'He may have mentioned that.'

'We're all just stubborn old men, aren't we? When I signed that declaration of death in absentia I thought I was doing the right thing by my family. I really did. And then they found that body and I just knew. I knew it was my brother before the police even told me. It was a feeling in my gut. And it felt like my fault. Like I had murdered him. That somehow by signing that document I'd made it real.' Roland pinched the bridge of his nose. 'What's in the letter?'

'I don't know. I never read it. But I think it might be—' Erik cut himself off. There was something else on his mind, but he hesitated sharing it.

Roland raised an eyebrow. 'What is it?'

Erik cleared his throat. He was ashamed by his own indecision to come forward with the truth, but he'd once made a promise to Peter that he would never break his confidence. Except Peter was dead now and that meant Erik was the only one holding on to the guilt of a secret that wasn't even his own.

'Peter had a secret,' Erik admitted. 'And I think he meant to tell you with this letter.'

# Chapter 42

'Find anything yet?'

The floor was a mess. Stacks of mouldy, cobweb-covered boxes and papers pulled up from the cellar lined the living room. Kjeld had looked through so many documents – everything from old auto mechanic receipts to some of his dad's work invoices – that his eyes were beginning to cross.

Stenar, who'd been reluctantly dropped off by Sara after he'd thrown a fit at her house and frightened her children by breaking a lamp because he wanted to be taken to his own home, hovered over the old record player at the far side of the room. He flipped through the stack of vinyls that Kjeld had brought up along with the boxes. Every time he pulled out an album he sent handfuls of dust falling to the floor.

Esme held up a sheet of paper, yellowed and frail. 'Geographical property survey from 1979.'

'From 1979? Are you sure?' Kjeld stepped over the boxes and crouched down beside Esme to get a better look.

'From the looks of it your father had the dimensions of the entire plot, from the logging road all the way up to the national park, measured and confirmed by the local planning board. It's notarised at the bottom.' Esme handed the survey to Kjeld.

Kjeld stood up, pacing around the piles of papers as he studied the map of his father's property. 'Does it include a geological estimate as well?'

'I don't remember this one,' Stenar said, slipping the Sweetwater record out of the album sleeve and setting it on the turntable. Within seconds the reverberating vocals of Nancy Nevins singing "My Crystal Spider" resounded discontinuously from the fuzzy stereo speakers of the old record cabinet. The needle skipped at regular intervals.

Kjeld winced at the loudness and made his way over to the cabinet to turn down the volume on the speakers. 'It's going to scratch the record, Dad.'

'It's just a little dusty,' Stenar said, picking up the pressure arm and blowing off the dust and fluff that had collected on the needle over the years. Then he ran his unsteady finger under the needle. A sharp scratching sound emitted from the speakers.

'Just let it be, Dad.'

'Here it is!' Esme pulled out a document from the bottom of one of the boxes. 'According to this, the northern tract that borders the park on one side and a parcel labelled N.M.— Is that ...?'

'Norrmalm Industries.'

'Well, the portion of your father's land that borders the park and Norrmalm's south-western tract is estimated to contain a large concentration of uranium with high deposits of silver, lead, iron and copper.' Esme's forehead pinched in thought.

The needle skipped and "Rondeau" began playing in the background.

'Your mother used to listen to this kind of hippy music,' Stenar said.

'This *is* Mum's hippy music,' Kjeld replied.

Kjeld set the survey on the coffee table. He unfolded the map that displayed the almost thirty acres that encompassed the Nygaard property, including nearby geological landmarks used by the surveyor to point out the boundaries. He was trying to determine how close that pit had been to his father's property. He couldn't have made it as far as the Norrmalm border before he came upon the pit. Could he?

When he realised that Esme hadn't said anything in a while Kjeld looked up. 'I'm sorry. What are you thinking?'

'Eiji always had eclectic taste,' Stenar said, carrying the album cover back over to his armchair.

Esme blinked, breaking her stare to turn her attention towards Kjeld. 'The day you found the body you said you chased someone into the woods.'

'Yeah, and nearly broke my neck in the process.'

'How far did you get before you fell into the pit?'

Kjeld racked his mind to remember. It had been an uphill trek and the weather made manoeuvrability slower than normal. But he could distinctly recall feeling like he hadn't gone far enough to reach the park, let alone one of the Varsund mines.

The record scratched and skipped to the next song.

Kjeld used his pinkie finger to measure the distance between the house and the border drawn by the surveyor. 'It's not possible for me to have made it as far as the property line. There's no way. That mine has got to be on my dad's property.'

'I prefer jazz,' Stenar said out loud to himself. 'Monica Zetterlund was the best jazz singer who ever lived. Her performance with Louis Armstrong was second to none.'

'Kjeld likes jazz, too.' Esme offered Stenar an encouraging smile so he didn't feel ignored.

'No, I don't,' Kjeld replied.

'But you always have that album playing in your car.'

'It's not mine. It's stuck in the CD player. I can't get it out.' The album had belonged to Bengt and got jammed in the CD player back when they were sharing a single car between the two of them. Kjeld hated the album because it reminded him of their last argument. And he would have had it removed, but the vehicle was already on its last leg and rather than replace

285

the entire audio system he was just saving up to buy a new car.

'I find it relaxing,' Stenar continued. 'Helps you think. Like classical music. It's good for the memory, they say.'

Clearly not good enough.

Kjeld sighed and tried to ignore his father's disrupting comments so he could focus on making the connection between the documents and the body in the barn.

'If the mine is on your dad's property,' Esme started, 'then that means Peter Lindqvist breached the contract with your father.'

'Except that mine was new,' Kjeld argued. 'And Peter Lindqvist has been dead for at least five years.'

'Who owns the company now?'

'His brother.'

'I never trusted that man,' Stenar said, seemingly out of nowhere.

Kjeld fixed his gaze on his father. 'Who, Dad? Roland Lindqvist?'

'I don't like the way he looks at your mother.' Stenar turned the album cover over in his hands. 'Or the way he looks at any woman. Like he's entitled to something simply because he's got money.'

Kjeld waited for his father to expound upon what he was saying, but Stenar just slouched in his chair and stared at the writing on the back of the album. He looked like he was asleep with his eyes open.

'We should go out and find the property line,' Esme said.

'I'll go.' Kjeld folded up the property survey and stuffed it in his back pocket beside the redacted contract he'd found at the bank. Then he crossed the room to get his father's winter coat from the rack near the door.

'Don't forget a hat,' Stenar said nonchalantly. He'd only been half there all evening. Sara said that the doctors explained how recent events might cause him to be more muddled than usual. Kjeld knew from the fact that he hadn't mentioned the birds since he'd gotten home that muddled was an understatement. But at least he wasn't throwing a fit.

'I'll go with you,' Esme said.

'No, that's okay. I'll be fine on my own.' Kjeld grabbed a knit cap and pulled it over his head until it covered his ears. Then he took a torch from the drawer in the hall. 'Besides, someone's gotta stay here with Dad.'

'I can take care of myself,' Stenar grumbled.

Kjeld was halfway to the door when Esme called back to him, a joking smile across her face that he knew was meant to alleviate some of his gloominess. 'Try not to fall off a cliff this time.'

# Chapter 43

It was just after six o'clock in the evening, but the opaque blanket of night, interrupted by a waxing gibbous moon and the early twinkling of stars, made it feel like it was much later.

The hard snow crunched beneath Kjeld's boots as he made his way through the birch and spruce trees that covered the stretch of land north of the barn. He tried to follow the same route he had during the chase, but discovered it was just as difficult to keep his bearings without the heavy snowfall as it had been with it.

Halfway up the hill, which warned him days earlier that he needed to improve his level of fitness, he turned and looked back towards the house. It was barely visible through the thin-stretched trees that broke up his perspective like bars on a prison window. The only sign that he was gazing in the right direction was the dim yellow light on the back porch. A few more paces and even that would be engulfed in darkness.

He continued upwards.

He was careful to step in areas where his boots could gain traction in the snow. Off to the west came a howl. Wolves weren't uncommon in the forests of Jämtland, but for the most part they steered clear of humans. Kjeld stopped in his tracks, listened for proof that the howling was getting further away from him, and then went on. Eventually the subtle sounds of the forest, unconscionably loud when focused on and barely noticeable when not, became part of the drone in his head as his mind recycled the events of the day.

Sara was annoyed with him when she came by to drop Stenar off, but Kjeld couldn't tell if it was because he was digging through their father's old paperwork trying to find proof that the Lindqvists had broken a legal agreement not to mine on their property or because Esme was there. Sara had looked at her with a fair measure of scepticism, showing that she didn't fully believe that the woman with the mile-long legs and the thick black eyeliner was just a friend. She wasn't entirely wrong. Kjeld didn't have to exert much thought to know what his sister was thinking. It was clear she thought that he'd found himself another excuse for avoiding his responsibilities to their family. Maybe she was right.

Part of the hill levelled out and Kjeld stopped to take the surveyor's map out of his pocket, nearly dropping the folded pages of the contract he'd found at the bank onto the snow-covered ground. He held the torch near the paper, estimating the distance he'd already travelled from the house. Still within the boundaries of his father's land. He stuffed the map back into his pocket, used a nearby spruce trunk to brace himself as he climbed over a large rock, and continued along the slope.

The moon's glow from the oncoming clearing of trees covered the untouched snow in a glaze of bluish-grey. Kjeld stepped through the final line of forest and onto the small ridge of naked ground that separated the woods from the vast mining cavern he'd fallen into days before. Even with the light of the moon stretching over the distance, the bottom of the pit was hidden from sight, obscured by the shadow of night.

Damn. That was deep.

Kjeld took out the map and used a gloved pinkie finger to judge the distance from the house to where he was now. He counted it three times and compared it to the distance scale at the bottom of the map, but the result was the same. According to the border survey the boundary of his father's property must have been somewhere in the middle of that cavern.

It was true. Norrmalm – no, the Lindqvists – were digging on Nygaard land.

A dull gleam flickered in the corner of his eye and Kjeld turned just as a knife penetrated the thick corduroy of his father's coat. Kjeld reached out instinctively and grabbed onto the sleeve of the lunging arm, but the forward rush of the attacker set him off balance. He lost his footing and fell to the ground, head dangling over the edge of the ridge. The attacker fell with him, landing atop Kjeld in a full-weighted collapse against his diaphragm.

The wind was knocked out of him. Kjeld choked out that last breath of air before his lungs emptied. He looked up at the face of the man atop him, but it was shielded by a dark-coloured balaclava. The man's eyes looked like two black stones in the darkness. Kjeld struggled to catch his breath. Then the attacker shifted his weight and Kjeld's chest heaved.

The attacker scrambled to get to his feet, knee jabbing into Kjeld's hip. Bone to bone. It sent a sharp pain up Kjeld's side and he tugged on the sleeve his fingers were still clenched around to keep the other man on the ground. The knife glimmered in the moonlight and Kjeld threw up his free arm to block the blade from being plunged into his chest. The knife cut through the jacket and slashed his forearm. Kjeld didn't feel anything at first. Then a sharp searing pain rushed through his arm. The wound wasn't deep, but Kjeld could feel a wetness begin to pool between his skin and the fabric.

The attacker jerked his arm out of Kjeld's grip. Kjeld kicked at the man's shin – hard – sending him stumbling into the snow.

Kjeld rolled over onto his side away from the edge of the cavern and crawled to his feet. His attacker limped toward the tree line. Kjeld rushed him, bearing all of his weight against the man's back until they were both on the ground again, grappling between birch trunks. The knife swung at him again just barely missing Kjeld's face. He caught the attacker's knife hand by the wrist and shoved it into the snow. Kjeld thought he heard a crack.

The attacker groaned and clawed at Kjeld's face with his free hand. He was wild but unsteady. Kjeld had the sudden impression that the man wasn't accustomed to close-contact fighting. He was strong, but his breathing was erratic. And not just from the brawl.

A knee jabbed between Kjeld's legs and he immediately felt a rush of stomach contents threaten to surge upwards. He lost his grip on the attacker's knife hand and the blade sliced across his cheek. The attacker squirmed beneath him, trying to loosen himself beneath Kjeld's weight. Kjeld struggled to maintain his position, legs locking around the other man's in a mount. The knife came at him again. Kjeld caught the attacker's wrist and twisted it. The knife fell into the snow.

It was a flurry of arms and fists as they hit and pulled at each other. When the other man opened up enough to give Kjeld free range of his torso, Kjeld threw a punch. He was on top. Gravity was on his side. But when his fist collided with the man's chest it was like hitting a brick. His arm stiffened as the pain against his knuckles reverberated up to his shoulder. The attacker didn't hesitate to take advantage of Kjeld's confusion. He jolted upward and knocked his head against the bridge of Kjeld's nose.

Kjeld fell against the trunk of a nearby birch tree, tried to catch his balance, and stumbled face first into the snow. The attacker clamoured to his feet, panting heavily as he regained his balance. Kjeld flattened his palms out on the ground to push himself up, but a blunt blow to the back of the head sent him sprawling into the snow. Then everything went black.

# Chapter 44

Despite two scarves bundled around her neck, a double-layered down coat and a knit cap, Esme felt the stinging chill of the night as easily as if she were in the nude. The cold saturated everything. And even when she crossed into the woodlands, where the spruce bridled the wind, the freezing air permeated her jeans and stuck to her skin in thin icy tiers. Within minutes she could barely feel her legs. And this was still considered autumn for Jämtland.

She wouldn't be caught dead out here in the real winter.

Damn Kjeld and his bullheadedness.

Five minutes after her partner stormed off into the dark, torch and obstinacy in hand, Esme threw on her coat, grateful she at least had the good sense to check the forecast before making the long drive to the middle of nowhere, and went out after him. Four years ago when she first met Kjeld she never would have risked hypothermia for his sake, but things changed. If it hadn't been for Kjeld she would have died three weeks ago at the hands of the Kattegat Killer. She lit the way with the light function on her phone and was careful to step into Kjeld's footprints to avoid sinking down to her ankles where the snow was fresh.

Kjeld struggled to ask people for help. Which was why when Esme made the decision to get in her car and drive across the country, she hadn't been thinking about whether her presence would actually alleviate the situation. She only thought it was her obligation as his friend and his colleague to be there. To help. But she didn't feel like much help. Kjeld had been different since the shooting at the APM Terminals port. He was more distant. More agitated. And Esme was concerned that the addition of unresolved family troubles, compounded by the recent drama in Gothenburg, would be too much for him.

She worried about him because she cared about him. More than she ought to have. More than he would ever realise.

For a man so adept at getting into the minds of criminals and killers, he was astonishingly dense when it came to reading the people closest to him. But that was probably for the best.

Esme tucked her chin and mouth into her scarf. A distant howl halted her approach. Shit. She hadn't been thinking about wild animals. That wasn't an instinct she'd acquired growing up in the suburbs of Malmö. She quickened her pace. Her legs dragged heavier as she breached the crest of the hill.

The beam of Kjeld's torch, partially entombed in the snow, spread out a mellow gleam against the two wrestling figures.

Esme shoved her phone into her pocket and reached inside her coat for the service pistol she kept holstered against her side. The gloves were too thin and her fingers were tense. Rigid from the cold.

One of the figures got the upper hand, bashing a rock against the skull of the other. Esme caught a glimpse of Kjeld's ruddy hair, darkened by blood, before he fell limp against the ground.

'Stop! Police!' she called out. She raised her weapon.

Kjeld's attacker barrelled at her. She aimed for his left thigh and pulled the trigger.

Click.

Misfire.

The man charged her, knocking her hard in the shoulder. She stumbled backward, sliding on the snow. A pointed tingling shot up through her arm and the gun fell from her hand. The attacker scrambled towards the weapon. The heavy pant of his breath startled her. It was wheezing. Uneven. She kicked out her leg and caught the toe of her boot in his knee. He twisted off-kilter on his ankle and cried out in pain. Then she dived for the gun.

Her fingers, still wooden and senseless from the cold, fumbled to get a good grasp on the grip, which was now slick with snow. And by the time she raised her arms to take aim, the man was rushing her again. Like a freight train careening brakeless downhill.

She pulled the trigger.

Jammed again.

Fuck.

He rammed her head on, propelling them over the crest of the hill she'd just climbed. Esme grabbed on to the attacker's jacket as they rolled, using him to brace against the jagged rocks and shrubs that lay hidden beneath the snow, until her boot caught in between a fallen log, jolting them apart. The man continued to slide downward a few feet before regaining his footing. Esme searched the ground for something she could use to defend herself, but when she glanced in the direction of the attacker she saw him running off into the darkness.

Esme rolled onto her side. Her ankle was wedged within a rotted crevice of the log, twisted at an acute angle. It wasn't broken or sprained, but it hurt. She knew it would be bruised in the morning.

She had to get up in case the man came back to finish what he'd started on the ridge. She had to get back to Kjeld.

She tugged her foot out of its hold and crawled to her knees.

The gunky sound of a wad of chew being spat in the snow stopped her in her tracks. Esme turned her gaze upwards and saw the hefty shadow of someone else standing above her. She caught a glimpse of the animal pelt over his shoulders and imagined it was a bear. Then her eyes focused and she saw the camouflage hunting gear. Only a man. A man brandishing her pistol.

# Chapter 45

The cold burned his face, numbing it of all feeling aside from the sharp tingling where the nerve endings near the top layer of his skin began to freeze. Someone called his name, but they sounded far away. Like they were yelling at him from underwater. He thought of the Doppler effect. Was the sound coming towards him or away from him? He couldn't tell. The back of his head throbbed, pounded. The din in his head made it impossible to focus on anything else.

Someone placed their hands on his shoulder and he remembered his attacker. He tried to shake them away, but ended up rolling into the base of a spruce tree. He mumbled something. It sounded more coherent in his mind than it did when it came out of his mouth. Someone tugged at him. The sound of his name on the air was closer now. It was coming towards him, he presumed, and he lay there with his face in the snow, waiting to hear if the wave echoed away. It didn't.

Another tug. Kjeld thought about fighting against them, but he didn't move. His limbs were stiff and his head ached. He opened his eyes for a second and thought he saw the person he chased away from the barn standing over him. Then he felt his upper body being lifted into the air. He heard his name again. It was a question this time. He tried to reach out towards the figure, but his arms clung to his torso. It was cold. So damn cold.

Then he closed his eyes and everything went dark again.

* * *

The pungent odour of raw fermented fish caused the hair in his nostrils to stand on end. Kjeld rolled over onto his side and vomited on the hardwood floor, just barely missing the carpet. Then he gagged up the acidic taste, which couldn't compare with the smell of putrefied fish, and spat up the rest of the stomach contents that caught in his oesophagus. When he looked up he saw an unfamiliar man kneeling beside him. His skin was thick and leathery as though it had seen too many high summers and just as many hard winters. Thick furrows indented his face along his eyes, disappearing into a grizzled beard that stretched halfway down his chest, curling at the end. What caught Kjeld's attention most, however, was the large port-wine stain on the right side of his forehead in the shape of a bear.

Valle Dahl. The Drunken Bear.

'What the hell?' Kjeld wiped his mouth on his sleeve.

'Surströmming,' Valle replied. His tone was gravelly and his words spoken as though he had a mouth full of potatoes. He held out a can towards Kjeld.

The odour made him wince.

'What?' Kjeld's head was still hurting and his thoughts confused. He must have misheard the man, but it was difficult to think over the odour of rotten fish and body odour coming from the man before him.

'Nature's smelling salts, they are. If surströmming ain't strong enough to wake a man then nothing is.'

Esme hurried in from the kitchen. 'Kjeld! Thank God, you're awake!'

She knelt down beside him and Valle moved away to the sofa where Stenar sat, watching on with quiet concern.

'I was about to drag you into the car and take you to the hospital. You should probably still go. You've been out for almost an hour.' She shoved him gently in the shoulder. 'You scared me to death.'

'I don't need to go to the hospital,' he insisted. The last thing he wanted was to be poked and prodded at by doctors.

Kjeld sat up on the floor, using the record cabinet to support his back. He placed a hand on his head and flinched. He could feel a gash surrounded by a crusty layer of dried blood. Then he remembered the slice to his hand. He glanced down at his palm. It was bandaged up. The tips of his fingers were pale, but not frozen.

'I don't remember walking back to the house.'

'You didn't. Valle and I carried you. You're lucky you don't have frostbite,' Esme said. 'I'm going to get a bucket and clean this up.'

She stood, disappearing around the corner into the kitchen.

An electric heater blared enthusiastically at his face and Kjeld scooted a few inches away from it.

Oskar sniffed at the vomit and then followed Esme into the kitchen, hoping for food.

Kjeld turned his focus on Valle. The man looked like he'd been living rough. Not homeless, but wild. He was bundled up in at least three layers of clothing and had what looked to be a fox pelt wrapped around his neck like a scarf. He wasn't the town drunk Kjeld remembered. Kjeld remembered a man afraid to look people in the eye. A man who sat crouched beside the entrance to the supermarket, holding out a used coffee cup for loose change. This man stood straight, aside from that natural hunch in his shoulders from labouring in the mines as a young man, and his eyes were clear. Sober. Or, at least, temporarily sober. There was still a lingering scent of booze that wafted from his breath. He reminded Kjeld of the frontier men in American westerns. The kind who went up into the mountains for gold and never came out.

297

'A lot of people have been looking for you,' Kjeld said.

'That so?'

'They thought you were dead. Or worse.'

Valle took off his knit cap and scratched the top of his head. His hair was a matted mess of yellow-grey, thin and unwashed. 'What's worse than dead?'

'Did you kill a man and bury him in my father's barn?' Kjeld watched him for some kind of guilty reaction. He didn't get one.

'What?'

'Did you kill Peter Lindqvist?'

Valle laughed, stopping only when the laugh turned into a thick wet cough. 'Son, if I was going to kill Peter Lindqvist, I would have done it decades ago. And I would have started with that bastard brother of his.'

'Roland?'

'He's the son of a bitch who ratted me out to the foreman. Said I was drunk on the job. Drinking on the job? Sure. Everyone had a little bit of something in their coffee to get them through those morning shifts in the winter. But *drunk*? I ain't never worked a day drunk in my life.'

'What about the accident?'

Valle rested his hands on his belt. Kjeld couldn't tell how big he was under the multiple layers of clothing, but he thought the man might have a bit of a gut. Compliments of the same malady that gave him that red nose.

'Do you know who was supervising that day?' Valle asked, but Kjeld had the impression it wasn't really a question.

'The records say you were.'

'O'course they do. Because Roland changed them. Roland was the one working as shift supervisor the day that section of the mine caved in. He's the reason those three men died. But a Lindqvist can't be responsible for anything like that because that wouldn't look good on the company, now would it?' Valle reached into his pocket and took out a can of snus, sticking a piece up

298

under his top lip near the gums, making his speech even more difficult to understand. 'So they laid that on the feet of the only other guy who was there.'

'You?'

'I'm saying that if I was gonna kill a Lindqvist, I wouldn't have started with Peter. I never had no problem with him. He was a good guy. Poor fool probably didn't even know what his brother did. I'm sure he got his father to cover for him. Probably part of what led him to an early grave, too. Old man Lindqvist, that is. I don't know nothing about what happened to Peter.'

'And the drinking?'

'That started after I lost my position at Norrmalm. And I've paid the price for that, too, mind you. Wife upped and took the kids not long after.' Valle glanced at Stenar. 'Your dad was the only one who tried to help me. Gave me some money to start up my own roofing business. Went well for a few years, but ...'

He trailed off and Kjeld didn't need to hear the rest of the sentence to know what Valle meant. It wasn't hard to imagine that Valle wouldn't have been able to keep it together after losing everything. From the moment Roland placed the blame for those deaths on him Valle was doomed to become the laughing stock of teenagers around Varsund. The Drunken Bear who spent his days digging through the bins behind restaurants for scraps and spending what little cash he had on spirits. It was a harsh reminder of how quickly a person's life could turn upside down.

'Never did pay your old man back,' Valle said, truly apologetic. 'But it looks as though he doesn't remember.'

Kjeld thought about mentioning that Stenar wouldn't have expected his friends to reimburse him for his help. There was a lot about his father that Kjeld didn't like, but he wasn't vindictive or ungenerous. When he offered someone his help it was always out of the goodness of his heart, not because he expected something in return.

Esme returned from the kitchen with a bucket and mop, but

her attention was on Valle. She'd been listening in from the other room. 'But where have you been? According to the police, no one has seen you in years.'

'I've been living out of a hunting cabin about two miles west of here.'

'The one on my dad's land?' Kjeld asked, thinking of the bottles he'd found scattered on the cabin floor.

'He said I could stay there until I got back on my feet.'

'Hold up,' Kjeld interrupted. 'Have you been following me?'

Valle turned his head and coughed again. 'I keep an eye on the goings-on in these woods.'

Kjeld should have been more relieved to discover that his paranoia had not been unwarranted, but he wasn't.

'When did you move into the cabin?' Esme asked.

'Going on about three years now, I imagine. I think he might've forgotten about me over the years. He doesn't get out there much. Saw you two the other day though.' The snus slipped down to his teeth and Valle pushed it back up into his gums. 'I expect most people would have thrown me out by now. But not Stenar. He and I are of the same mind when it comes to this land. I learned my lesson after working for the Lindqvists. The land is best left for the critters. I only take what I need to survive and I don't leave a trace.'

*Except when it came to leaving empty beer cans on the floor,* Kjeld thought.

'What about the car?'

Valle shook his head. 'That ain't mine. That was already there when I moved in. Figured it was Stenar's.'

Esme gave Kjeld a solid look.

'Sounds like you know the land pretty well. Maybe you even know what's been going on out here with the mining,' Kjeld said.

'Like I said, I've seen some things,' Valle admitted, using his tongue to move the snus further up against his gums.

The room went silent as Kjeld thought about what else Valle

might have seen. But surely if he'd witnessed the situation in the barn then he would have mentioned it.

Stenar fidgeted nervously on the edge of the sofa, watching Kjeld with frightened eyes. 'I thought you were dead.'

Kjeld pulled a quilt over his shoulders, leaning in closer to the heater. He couldn't decide if he was too hot or too cold. 'Not yet it would seem.'

'You can't die,' Stenar said.

'Don't worry, Dad. I don't intend to.'

It was then that Kjeld remembered his reasoning for going out in the woods in the first place. He dug his fingers into his pockets. Empty. 'Where's the contract?'

'It's not on you?' Esme wiped a rag across the floor.

'Shit. He must have taken it.'

'I don't want you to die, Kjeld.'

'All right, Dad.' But Kjeld wasn't really listening to his father. He was mentally cursing himself for not being able to hold his own out in the snow. Granted his attacker did have a knife on him, but just like the chase through the forest, Kjeld thought he should have been able to get an upper hand on the man. If his chest hadn't been hard as metal that is. He looked down at his knuckles. They were already bruised.

'Did you get a look at the man in the woods?' Kjeld asked Valle.

Valle shook his head.

Dammit.

'Do you have a copy of the contract?' Esme asked.

'No, that was the only one.' Kjeld cursed beneath his breath.

'You looked like you were dead,' Stenar said, fingers fidgeting in his lap.

Kjeld felt like he was in a dream, but he was too hurt to argue. Stenar's worried commentary was impeding his ability to think clearly. Kjeld tried to remind himself that dementia could cause people to say things that were misplaced or to become fixated on a single topic, but the way his father spoke was strange. Or, at

301

least, to Kjeld it was strange. His words sounded like they were scripted. Not what he would expect his father to say to him. Not ever. Not even after almost getting himself killed.

'Maybe there's one at Norrmalm Industries.' Esme dropped the vomit-covered rag into the bucket.

'What do you mean?'

'I mean let's assume Norrmalm has been illegally mining on your father's property. They must have some kind of documentation of it. If your father sold over the land then they would have a bill of sale. If he didn't then they would have to have some kind of proof that they have permission to mine on the land they're on. To have that they'd need to know where the boundaries were so they could come up with a reliable argument as to why they were digging there in the event that anyone discovered what they were doing. They'd have to have original documents so they would know what they were covering up. Including the contract that proves they're not allowed to dig there in the first place.'

'Sounds like a long shot.' Kjeld pinched the bridge of his nose, hoping it might relieve some of his headache. 'But assuming that's true, that's not something they would keep out in the open. That's something you'd lock up.'

'Or stuff in the back of the old paper filing system that they've probably had on site since the company first opened.' Esme carried the bucket towards the kitchen, her voice calling out from the other room. 'A lot of companies don't bother throwing out the old stuff unless they've had everything digitally transferred. And even then, there's always something remaining from the old days.'

Kjeld shook his head. 'No. They wouldn't be that naive. It would be kept someplace where it couldn't get out easily. Where it would be limited to as few people as possible. Probably to the people who were involved.'

Esme walked back into the living room, wiping her hands on the sides of her jeans. 'Your father, Peter Lindqvist—'

'And the attorney who witnessed the document.'

'Norberg.'

'Bingo.'

Kjeld cursed himself for not realising it sooner. Norberg was the link between everyone. His father, the Lindqvists, Norrmalm Industries. His name was on everything. If he didn't have the documents in his possession, he at the very least knew how they were connected and how they might fit into the mystery of Peter Lindqvist's death.

'Dead. Dead.' Stenar scratched at a damp spot on his slacks where a few tears had fallen. 'You looked dead. Kjeld. My son.'

Kjeld slowly stood up and made his way over to the couch, plopping down beside his father. 'I was just unconscious. No big deal. Don't worry yourself about it. It's okay. I'm fine.'

But when Kjeld looked into his father's face he saw something more than worry. It was the look of a man who was terrified. Terrified that he might lose something precious to him. Seeing his father that way shook Kjeld to the bone. He'd never seen such affection in his father's eyes before. Not directed towards him.

'I saw you on the floor. You looked just like him. Cold. Lifeless. I didn't do anything to help him. I wanted to, but I couldn't. I couldn't help him. And then you—' Stenar reached over and pulled Kjeld into a frail embrace. 'I can't lose you, too, son. I can't.'

\* \* \*

Kjeld stood on the back porch, watching as Valle disappeared into the trees. The man promised to make his way into town the next day to give Gunnar a statement and while it was reckless to believe Valle on his word, Kjeld accepted the risk. As much as Valle despised the Varsund community for how it had treated him over the years, he hated the Lindqvists more. And that alone convinced Kjeld that he would keep his word.

He brought a cigarette to his lips and took a drag. Each inhalation increased the dull throbbing sensation at the back of his head. Each exhalation relieved it. The thick expanse of spruce and birch that engulfed everything beyond the barn cast heavy black shadows on the dark snow. The moonlight barely reached through the crowded cluster of trees. The snow looked like an oil slick. Sleek and polished, occasionally iridescent when the moon was at its height directly above the house.

Kjeld missed the rainy days in Gothenburg.

Esme leaned into the open doorway between the porch and the kitchen, arms crossed to hold in the heat from the house.

'Are you going to call the police?' she asked. Her voice was quiet. Concerned.

'And tell them what? That someone, perhaps that same person I chased from the barn, attacked me and ran off with half of a vague contract and a property survey?' Kjeld shook his head. 'I don't know. I'm not sure if Gunnar would even look into it.'

'Someone came at you with a knife, Kjeld. He has to take that seriously.'

'I wouldn't be so sure.'

'What is it between the two of you?'

'I've known him since school. He wasn't my best friend, but we were close. We had all these plans of going to police college together, getting assigned as partners, solving crimes. But we had a falling-out during our traineeship period,' Kjeld said. He dropped his arm to the side and flicked the ash to the ground.

'Let me guess. You both fell for the same person? He looks like someone who fancies himself a Casanova.' Esme offered a smile as though it were meant to be a joke, but her eyes told him she was serious.

'Not exactly. There was a drug case we were both assigned to and it went wrong. Really wrong.' Kjeld took another drag on his cigarette. 'It should have been a simple open-and-shut case, but we thought we were something back then and we got complacent about tailing our suspect. There was a girl. Our informant. She had a connection to the dealer that was going to help us put him away for a long time and end this epidemic of drug-related deaths among teens in the area. The dealer caught her wearing a wire. It was a shit-stupid idea. We had no business thinking we were in control. She died because of our negligence. Gunnar didn't want to get kicked out of the programme so he falsified evidence to place blame on the guy we suspected. The guy's serving a life sentence for homicide.'

'Did he do it?'

'Probably.' Kjeld paused. 'I think so.'

'Then wasn't justice served?'

'Maybe.' Kjeld smudged the cigarette out on the side of the house. 'But we didn't follow protocol. We subverted the law. He might have done it, but we didn't have enough evidence on our own to convince a judge.'

'If you thought it was wrong, why didn't you say anything?'

'I was afraid.'

It would have been a cop-out to blame the situation on peer pressure, although Gunnar had laid the guilt on him pretty hard back then. The truth was that Kjeld was afraid of what would happen if he didn't become a police officer. What would he do? Where would he go? At the time the only thing that he could think of was that he'd have to return to Varsund. That he would live and die in that isolated house in the woods, spending his days feeding the mangy ravens that had been passed down through generations of crazy Nygaard bird fanatics, probably get involved with a local who'd tie him down to the middle of nowhere with a second mortgage and a dog, and spend the rest of his life regretting every minute of it. It scared him then and it scared him now.

Esme placed a hand on the side of his arm. 'You have to stop beating yourself up for something you can't change. Does it suck? Yes, but it's in the past. All you can do is be better in the future.'

'That's what Bengt used to say.'

'Yeah, I know.'

Esme pulled her hand away, tucking it underneath her sweater for warmth. 'I'm worried about you.'

'Don't be.'

'You've just walked out of one stressful situation and into another. I know you think you're up to this, but maybe you're not. Maybe you should consider dropping your personal investigation into this situation with your father.'

Kjeld looked at her in disbelief. 'You're the last person I expected to hear that from.'

'I don't want you to hurt yourself.'

'Hurt myself?' He scoffed.

'You know what I mean. Emotionally. That's not exactly your strong suit.'

Kjeld shook his head. 'You don't understand. I need to know the truth. That's what this is all about. Finding answers.'

'Are you sure this isn't about something else?' Esme asked.

'Like what?'

'Like you trying to prove yourself to your dad? Or trying to come to terms with the fact that he has dementia and can't give you closure?'

Kjeld turned away from her, turning his focus out towards the empty yard.

'I don't know what you're going through because you won't tell me,' Esme continued. There was a hint of sadness in her voice. 'But I understand loss and not having the opportunity to say the important things while it's possible. If you want to make peace with your father, make peace with your father. And if you want to push forward with this, then I'll help. But if you keep digging, you might not like what you find.'

Kjeld nodded, but he didn't say anything. He wanted to thank her, but the words were stuck in his throat.

'You should go inside. Lie down. Get some rest. I'll check in on your dad and make myself comfortable on the couch,' Esme said.

'I will in a few minutes.' He fumbled through his pockets

for another cigarette, but didn't find one. 'I'm glad you're here, Esme.'

'Who wouldn't be?' She smiled, but Kjeld suspected she was hiding her true feelings. 'Don't be long. And get some sleep. Tomorrow we'll figure out how to get into Norberg's office.'

When the door shut behind her, Kjeld turned his gaze towards the barn. A faint glimmer of moonlight peeked through the trees. He listened carefully, but there were no sounds. The ravens must have been sleeping.

*Or waiting*, that timid voice from his childhood thought and Kjeld felt a shiver crawl up his spine. If only those birds could speak. What stories could they tell? What secrets would they share? And would Kjeld be prepared to hear them? He feared that he wasn't.

A whining mewl cut through the silence, pulling Kjeld out of his thoughts. It was Oskar begging for food. Seconds later he was scratching at the door to get Kjeld's attention.

Kjeld inhaled deeply, filling his lungs with the icy air. It might have been refreshing were it anywhere else in the world. He gave one last glance to the barn and made his way into the house.

# Chapter 46

'Who were you talking to?'

Sara finished brushing her teeth, spat in the sink, rinsed, and then stepped out of the cramped bathroom that only qualified as a master bath because it was attached to the largest bedroom. The room was actually a hallway closet that had been converted to a bathroom as an afterthought when they first moved in. But Tom had done much of the work himself to save on the cost of hiring a professional contractor and there was nothing masterful about it.

'What do you mean?' she asked, removing her bathrobe and hanging it on the back of the door. Underneath she wore the same grey nightgown she'd had for the last three years. The fabric was so thin it was a miracle it survived the wash.

Tom watched her from the bed. In his lap was his new self-help book, *Unlocking Your True Potential*, which he had been reading for the last hour, but whenever Sara glanced over at him she could have sworn he was on the same page. Tom had always been an anxious man, but he'd been even more jittery over the last few days. She wondered if she should count the pills in his prescription bottles.

Tom closed the book and set it on the nightstand beside a glass of water and his mouth guard. The mouth guard was supposed to help him stop grinding his teeth at night, but he'd worn a hole right through the rubber and woke up every morning complaining of a tension headache. Clearly it wasn't helping.

'I heard you on the phone earlier. Who were you talking to?'

Sara hesitated, but only for a second. She doubted Tom would notice.

'I wasn't talking to anyone. You probably overheard one of the kids.' Sara pulled back the covers and climbed into her side of the bed. 'Or maybe that was when Kjeld called.'

Tom frowned. Sara imagined she could see the wheels turning in his head like he was trying to solve some complicated puzzle. But it wasn't all that complicated.

Recently she'd felt like they weren't husband and wife anymore. Granted, she took a lot of responsibility for that. She'd become cold and distant since her father's disease had progressed. Adding to that the stress of the kids and Tom's unemployment, she just felt empty and unfulfilled. And while she and Tom slept in the same bed, they hadn't made love in almost a year. She knew that because she could remember the last time clear as day. It was after the Saint Lucia concert at the children's school. Alexander had been one of the star boys in the procession. Lykke's class had baked saffron buns with raisins. One of the raisins in the bun Tom ate had been uncommonly hard and when he took a bite he thought he'd broken a tooth. Sara, overwhelmed by the stress of the holiday season and Tom's unemployment, drank an entire bottle of dessert wine and managed to forget for an evening that her life wasn't her own. Her life belonged to the people around her who she had to take care of. She'd woken up the next day with this sobering realisation and was back to her standoffish self.

It wasn't that she wanted their relationship to be this way, but she didn't know how else to handle the responsibilities of being a parent to her father, her children, and her husband.

'Is it another man?' he asked.

Sara stared at him, mute with surprise. Tom looked at her with an expression she could only describe as frightened. Was she so detached? Was she so unreadable? What did he see when she looked at him? Did he imagine he was staring into the eyes of a stranger?

Sara made an effort to purposefully soften her expression and gave an exasperated sigh. 'Are you asking me if I'm having an affair? Really, Tom? Do I look like I have the time to have an affair? I barely have time to brush my teeth or go to the bathroom. An affair?'

She laughed because she didn't know how else to respond.

'I know I'm not the man you hoped I would be when we got married,' he said. Sara opened her mouth to say something, but Tom cut her off before she could speak. 'I know I've been a disappointment this last year. But I've been trying. I recognise everything you've done for this family. I really do. You're a miracle worker, Sara. I don't know how any of us would be able to get by without you. But I want you to know that I'm here to support you. I'm here to help in any way that I can. When we got married I promised to love, honour and protect you. And that's what I'm doing. I'm protecting you.'

There was something odd about the way Tom was speaking and Sara could feel a pang of doubt and fear creep into her mind. It wasn't what Tom was saying exactly, but what he wasn't saying. And she could feel the hairs on the back of her neck stand on end.

'What do you mean protect me?' she asked.

Tom turned in bed to face her. He wasn't an attractive man with his protruding ears and his overbite, but then she'd never really considered herself an attractive woman. She'd been drawn to him because of his light-heartedness and his desire to have a family. Family had always been very important to Sara and she'd known from a very young age that she wanted one of her own. So when she met Tom that had been the most attractive quality about him.

Now she had her family and she couldn't have been more overwhelmed by it. Or, in the case of her brother and his laissez-faire attitude towards his own familial responsibilities, more aggravated by it.

'In one of the books I've been reading, the author talks about making sacrifices to help the important aspects of your life maintain their balance. By maintaining a balance for what's important a person can then move forward with their own self-discovery. There was an entire questionnaire to determine what those important factors were, but I already knew that you were at the top of the list for me.' He smiled. Sara supposed it was meant to be encouraging, but it only unnerved her more. 'There was a part that talked about how if your partner is too stressed or overwhelmed or unbalanced then you'll never be able to find yourself. There was a term for it, but I can't remember what it was.'

'What did you do, Tom?'

Tom cleared his throat. 'Do you remember last spring when you asked me to watch your dad because you and the kids had dentist appointments?'

Sara nodded. It had been one of the few times she'd asked Tom to look after her father. It wasn't that she didn't trust Tom, but she knew how absent-minded he could be sometimes. Once he accidentally left Lykke at the ICA supermarket because he was too busy thinking about how he planned to fix the garden shed when he got home. She remembered she hadn't left Tom with her father for more than a few hours, albeit longer than she expected because the dentist was running late on seeing patients.

'Well, your dad told me. He told me everything.'

Sara's face paled and she felt like she had a knot in her stomach. 'What do you mean?'

'He told me that he buried the body of a man in the barn.' Tom scoffed. 'I mean, I laughed at first, of course. I thought he was just talking crazy. But the more he talked the more I began to realise that it could be true. That your father may have actually murdered someone and then forgotten about it!'

Sara stared at him in disbelief. 'He told you this last spring? And you're just *now* telling me?'

'I didn't want to put another thing on your plate. I thought, okay, if it wasn't true then it wasn't worth mentioning. And if it was true, well, telling you about it would upset our balance. We wouldn't be able to get back to the way things used to be.'

'What are you saying, Tom?'

Tom took a deep breath and exhaled. 'I'm saying I'm the one who started digging up the body in the barn.'

Sara imagined that the world had just stopped rotating on its axis. Her heart was pounding. The sound echoed in her ears. Tom had dug up the body in the barn. Tom was the suspect Kjeld had chased through the woods. Her Tom. The Tom who once drove the kids to school on a Saturday and didn't realise his error until he passed the park and saw it full of children. The Tom who enjoyed watching home cooking shows, but could burn a microwave dinner meal. And he'd somehow convinced himself that this was good for their family.

'Why?' She didn't mean to yell, but the words came out instinctually loud, exasperated. 'Why on earth would you do something like that?'

'Because your brother showed up!' Tom replied. 'I know how he is. You always say he's like a dog with a bone. He won't let things go. I knew that once Stenar told him there was a body buried in the barn that he would dig up the entire place himself just to prove it was or wasn't true. And if he found out what Stenar did then you would be upset. You'd never be able to forgive Kjeld or your father. And I didn't want that for you. I want you to be happy. I don't want the memories of your family to be tarnished any more than they already are.'

Sara didn't know what to say. She felt like she was in shock. She felt sick. Her heart was racing and her thoughts were in overdrive. How was she supposed to resolve this? Tom had just implicated himself in a crime. And now she was an accessory.

She reached out and took her husband's hand. When she finally spoke, her tone was gentle but firm. She didn't want Tom to mistake anything she was about to say.

'Promise me you'll never talk about this again.' Sara gripped his hand tighter. 'Promise me you'll never tell anyone what you just told me.'

# Chapter 47

The words hit Roland like a freight train and even though he believed them, he'd suspected as much all along, he couldn't get over the initial shock that he'd actually heard them spoken aloud. When he finally came to from his thirty-second lapse of consciousness, wherein he saw his entire world and all his hard work shatter before his eyes, he turned his gaze on his son as though he hadn't quite heard him correctly.

'You did what?'

David sat on the edge of the sofa in the living room of the Lindqvist estate. He was huffing and puffing as though he'd just finished a half-marathon. And he was sopping wet. The melted snow dripped off his clothes and onto the floor, pooling a soggy stain on an antique burgundy-coloured Persian rug that had been in the home since his grandfather built it. His teeth chattered and he looked up at his father like he was in a dream. Perhaps a nightmare.

'I killed a man.'

The phrase repeated itself in Roland's mind, but all he could think of was *I know*. Because he did. He was unwaveringly certain that David was behind his brother's death. And while he had very little evidence to support this belief, while it was mostly a gut feeling, he knew that David killed his brother. Perhaps not directly. Perhaps he'd hired someone else to do it for him, being that David was a coward and a sickly coward at that. But somehow he was still responsible.

Roland couldn't pinpoint the exact moment he knew, but when the realisation came to him it seemed so clear. It was as if everything had finally fallen into place. He'd been livid, of course. Devastated. He may not have ever wanted to fill his brother's shoes – such a feat was near impossible – but he had loved Peter. Some siblings didn't get along, but that had never been the case with the Lindqvist boys. Sure, they'd bickered on occasion. Had their jealous spats from time to time. But in the end they'd had a deep love for each other. The kind of love that only two young men born into extravagance and expected to excel despite the fear that it would be impossible to outdo the successes of their forefathers could have for each other. And realising his own son would be the one to come between them hurt Roland deeper than the knowledge that he would never see Peter again.

But David was still his son. And if there was one thing the Lindqvists had always prided themselves on it was an unwavering allegiance to family. Line of succession was still important to Roland. Of course, Inger would inherit part of Norrmalm Industries as well, but Roland had never had hopes that she would actually do something with her share of the profits besides improve her tan on some exotic beach somewhere. In a way David was equally as incompetent, but there was still a longstanding belief in their family, severely outdated in its misogyny, that the Lindqvist sons would make something of themselves. As much as Roland loathed to admit that David would probably amount to nothing other than a rich philanderer who pissed his money away, he was still a male heir. Roland had to hope that would one day mean something.

'Did you hear me?' David grimaced. His face was pale and his cheek scratched. Dried blood marked where someone's nails had dug into his skin.

If Roland hadn't known better, he would have assumed it was another rough night for David and one of his many whores. The contorted look on David's face, however, torn between fear and frenzy, told him otherwise.

'I heard you,' Roland said, pacing the room in languid steps. He had to think.

'Fuck, fuck, fuck.' David pressed his face into his hands. 'I'm going to go to prison.'

'You're not going to go to prison.' Roland wasn't naive enough to think that money could buy loyalty, but there was a lot that went on in Varsund that never reached official channels. This came from the combination of being isolated from the larger cities and the general willingness of people to do just about anything in the north in order to survive. Living in the middle of nowhere was convenient on occasion. Convenient for business, pleasure, and the occasional wrongdoing.

'I can't go to prison. I just can't.'

'Quit your moaning. I have to think.'

Roland stopped in front of the mantel above the fireplace and glanced up at the oil portrait of his grandfather. He was a lithe but rugged-looking man with a bushy red beard that stretched well below his chin; a reminder of the days when hard work and manual labour actually produced results. Of a time when children accepted their obligation to continue on the family business without complaint and didn't beg their parents for help when circumstances didn't go their way. It wasn't perfect. Everything seemed ideal in retrospect. Roland remembered his father telling him a story of how his grandfather once allowed a mine to cave in on nine men in order to save the lives of fifty. Production was halted for four hours in a feeble attempt to dig beneath the rubble to those who were trapped inside. When those four hours resulted in nothing, the mine reopened.

The business must continue to profit, his father would say. We profit or we die.

But carry the burden of an idiot son whose actions threatened to undermine everything the Lindqvists had strived to achieve over the last four generations? Even Peter would tell him it was his obligation to their legacy to protect the family and its future. It was his duty as a Lindqvist.

David began to sob into his hands.

'I need you to tell me everything,' Roland said. 'Then I'm calling Gunnar Ek.'

David groaned in protest. 'But he's the police!'

Roland looked away from his grandfather's portrait and turned that same steely-eyed stare on his son. 'He's also the only one who can make this disappear.'

# Chapter 48

## Fredag | Friday

Kjeld hadn't slept for more than an hour over the course of the night. When the throbbing at the back of his head, which he was fairly certain was a small concussion, didn't keep him awake the thoughts of the week's events did. He lay in bed, listening to the sounds of the house, and tried to focus his thoughts on the previous night's discoveries. The more he thought about it, however, the more restless he became. Eventually he snuck downstairs for a cigarette and sat on the back porch, wrapped in dusty old quilts that his grandmother had made, waiting for the sun to come up. It was eerily quiet in that last hour before dawn broke through the trees, illuminating the freshly fallen snow in a dull glimmer. Even the ravens were at rest.

When he went back into the house, cold and groggy, Esme was gone. She'd left a note on the kitchen table saying that she was going to drive down to the local planning office and make sure no new surveys had been done on his father's property since the one in 1979. It was a smart idea and Kjeld cursed himself for not having thought of that sooner. Along with a register of local property surveys, Varsund Kommun would also have permits on file for any industrial projects that involved changes to the regional landscape. Which meant that if the mining pit on his father's land was legal there would be a record of it.

Stenar shuffled into the kitchen wearing one slipper. He didn't seem to notice that the other was missing. Nor did he notice that his robe was untied and he was exposing himself. He was thin and the skin around his sides and chest hung in loose wrinkled flaps.

Kjeld gave an inward sigh.

'Let me help you with that,' Kjeld said, crossing the kitchen to pull the robe around his father's torso and tie the belt in a double knot so it wouldn't come undone. Just like he would do with Tove's shoelaces when she spent the weekend with him.

Stenar looked down at the belt and immediately began untying it.

'Don't, Dad. Leave it alone. No one needs to see that.'

'I have to get dressed. I have to go to work.'

'You're retired. Sit down. I'll make some coffee. You can get dressed later.'

Stenar dragged his feet over to the refrigerator. 'Where's Sara?'

'She's at home with her kids. It's just me.'

Kjeld poured a few scoopfuls of coffee grounds into the pot and turned it on. His stomach growled, but he wasn't hungry. In fact, the thought of eating made him sick to his stomach. Hopefully he'd be able to keep a cup of coffee down. Maybe that would be enough.

Stenar sniffed Kjeld's shirt sleeve. 'Have you been smoking in the house?'

'No, Dad. I have not been smoking in the house.'

'I know you try to hide it from me, but you're no good at it. I'm not an idiot. I know you think you're clever, but you're not.' Stenar closed the refrigerator door and shuffled to the kitchen table, nearly losing his slipper as he sat down.

319

'How are you feeling?' Kjeld took two mugs out of the cabinet. 'Did you take your medicine?'

'What medicine? What are you talking about?' Stenar fidgeted with the knot on his belt, arthritic fingers struggling to untie it. 'Where's Sara? She should be here by now.'

The coffee pot rattled on the countertop and Kjeld wondered if he'd accidentally used too much water. He missed instant coffee.

'Sara isn't coming today. It's just you and me.'

Stenar gave a scornful laugh. 'You and me.'

A sore twinge travelled from the back of Kjeld's skull to his forehead. He clenched his eyes shut until the pressure around his sinuses made him forget about the pounding ache just above his neck.

The coffee maker began to leak onto the countertop and Kjeld removed the pot. The machine steamed and hissed as excess vapour released before it was ready. The liquid in the pot didn't look quite done, but it was good enough. He filled both mugs and set them on the table.

Stenar took a sip and spat it back out in the cup. 'This tastes like shit.'

'It can't be that bad.' Kjeld took a sip. His dad was right. He spat it in the kitchen sink and washed his mouth out with water from the tap.

'Valle was here. Did he fix the roof?'

'No, Dad. He didn't fix the roof.'

'Are you going to fix it?'

Kjeld watched him unsteadily, searching for any sign that his father was purposefully bringing the roof up in order to start an argument. But he didn't see any recollection in his father's eyes. Had he forgotten? Or was this an attempt at pretending their argument twelve years ago had never happened?

The doorbell rang. The chime echoed through the house and turned that dull ache in Kjeld's head into a digging pang.

Stenar perked up. 'It's Sara.'

'Don't hold your breath.'

Kjeld made his way to the front of the house and pulled open the door without peeking through the curtains. He felt light-headed as he stared through the screen to the man on the other side, but his expression must have lacked recognition because the caller sent him an equally perplexed look back. No, not perplexed. Surprised. Like he'd just seen a ghost.

'Kjeld?' Gunnar asked.

'Were you expecting someone else?'

'I— No, but I thought. That is, I heard—' Gunnar stopped his stuttering and blinked. Slow and consciously. It made him look dim-witted. It reminded Kjeld of those old black-and-white police comedies where the simple-minded deputy was always the last to figure out the mystery that everyone else had already solved. The wheels in Gunnar's head were turning. Kjeld wondered if it hurt the man to think so hard. Gunnar held back a question and replaced it with another. 'Is your father home?'

'Why?'

Gunnar took another step forward and pulled open the screen door. Kjeld placed his arm between Gunnar and the house, blocking his path.

'I need to talk to him about the Lindqvists.'

'What about the Lindqvists?'

Kjeld's vision blurred. He thought that Gunnar had given his hair an extra side part, but then realised he was seeing double. Kjeld pressed his weight against the doorframe.

Gunnar frowned. 'Are you all right? You don't look good.'

'I'm fine,' Kjeld insisted. He wrapped his fingers around the doorknob for balance, gaze darting between the two sets of eyes in front of him. 'Tell me about the Lindqvists.'

'Can I come in?'

'Not until you tell me what this is about.'

Gunnar hesitated. His expression was wary and he watched Kjeld as though he half expected him to lash out. And if those were

321

indeed his thoughts then he wasn't entirely wrong in his assumption. Kjeld did want to hit him. He wanted to knock him upside the head for causing his father more grief than necessary. Kjeld gave him enough grief. Stenar didn't need an inept police officer piling on more trouble and adding to his confusion. He wanted to thrash Gunnar for being a worthless investigator. Worthless because if he had just listened to Stenar in the first place then all of this would be over. It would be solved or shelved and Kjeld would still be in Gothenburg, none the wiser.

'Kjeld, I think you should sit down,' Gunnar said. His voice was smooth. Slow. It was missing that coarse edge of a man who wanted to impose his ego on others. What was that tone in his voice? Concern?

'I don't need to fuckin' sit down. I need to know what you know about the Lindqvists.' Those were the words Kjeld thought he said, but what came out of his mouth was something else entirely. Something that didn't make any sense at all.

'I can't understand what you're saying, Kjeld. You're speaking gibberish.'

Kjeld laughed. Gibberish? He didn't know what Gunnar was talking about. Gunnar was the one who wasn't coherent. He was the one who wasn't making any sense.

The drumming started again. Hard, pounding clanks against the inside of his skull. He saw Gunnar swaying in front of him like a flag in a breeze. His stomach churned and a metallic taste filled his mouth. And the last thing he remembered was Gunnar's arms reaching for him before he blacked out.

\* \* \*

A bright light flashed over his eyes and Kjeld blinked awake. His vision was slow to return, but when it did he saw himself staring up into a pair of dark brown eyes. Then Doctor Goswami flicked the pen light to the side.

'Welcome back, Detective.'

Kjeld rolled his head. He was lying on a bed in the emergency room, a green curtain half closed to block out the other patients in the room. Gunnar stood in the corner with his arms crossed. He looked irked. Maybe constipated. Possibly both.

'What happened?' Kjeld tried to sit up, but his head felt heavy and he slumped back down.

'Take it easy,' Goswami said. He reached underneath the bed and pressed a button that allowed it to tilt upward. Then he pushed a pillow behind Kjeld's upper back to give him more support. 'You've suffered a serious blow to the head.'

'I know,' Kjeld grumbled. 'Why am I here?'

'You blacked out, dumbass,' Gunnar said. He stepped over to the side of the bed and looked down at Kjeld, his lips pursed so tightly that his mouth practically disappeared.

Definitely constipated.

'Do you remember when you were injured?' Goswami pulled up Kjeld's shirt and placed a stethoscope to his chest.

'Last night.'

'You're such a goddamn idiot.' Gunnar sneered.

'You're lucky someone was there to catch you,' Goswami said. 'You have a concussion. It could have caused brain damage if you didn't get it looked at.'

'He's already brain-damaged,' Gunnar said.

Kjeld tried to glare at his old friend, but the effort required too much energy. And it hurt. Instead he focused his attention on the doctor. 'I thought you were a cardiologist.'

'It's a small town. We all wear multiple hats.' Goswami tucked the stethoscope into the pocket of his white coat.

'I have to get out of here,' Kjeld said.

Goswami placed a palm on Kjeld's chest, preventing him from trying to get up. 'You need to rest. Don't exert yourself. I'm going to write you a prescription for some pain relievers. I want you to stay here for another hour or two until the headache begins to dissipate. Then Inspector Ek can drive you home.'

'My dad can't be home alone.'

'I called your sister,' Gunnar said. 'She's over there with him.'

Kjeld groaned and leaned back against the pillow. Just another thing for Sara to hold against him with regards to their father.

'Try to take it easy,' Goswami said. 'I'll have a nurse write up the discharge papers.'

The doctor pulled back the curtain the rest of the way and headed off to the nurses' station.

Kjeld looked over at Gunnar and offered a pathetic excuse for an apologetic glance. Technically it was more of a scowl, but he would blame that on the bongo drums beating in his brain. 'Thanks.'

Gunnar pulled up a chair and sat down beside the bed. 'Do you remember how you got that injury?'

'Pretty sure someone hit me with a rock. Fuckin' big one too by the way it feels.'

'Who?'

'I don't know. It was dark. A man. Few inches shorter than me. I think he was wearing some kind of metal shield on his chest.'

'Why do you say that?'

Kjeld held up his right hand, dark with bruises over the knuckles. 'Because when I punched him it was like hitting a brick wall.'

'Where did you punch him? Left side? Right side?'

'For Chrissakes, Gunnar. What is this, the third degree? In the chest. I can't remember. My right, his left I suppose.' It didn't make sense for Kjeld to punch diagonally across a chest. Then again it had been dark and it had been a scuffle. He could have been wrong.

Gunnar nodded his head. He leaned forward and rested his elbows on his knees. The look of contemplative constipation was back. From his position on the bed Kjeld could see the bald patch that Gunnar tried to cover up with his ridiculous comb-over and volumising hair-care products. If Kjeld ever started going bald he would just shave it all off.

'What is this about, Gunnar?'

Gunnar glanced out into the room beyond the open curtain, watching as nurses and orderlies made their way from one bed to the next. Replacing IVs, checking stats, refilling water bottles. When he finally turned his attention back to Kjeld the unconscious strain on his face was gone, replaced by weary ease. Like a man who was relieved to get something off his chest.

'I think it was David Lindqvist who you punched.'

Kjeld grabbed on to the side rails and pulled himself up to a sitting position. 'David Lindqvist?'

'I got a call from Roland Lindqvist last night. He told me that David admitted to killing a man. Until I saw you standing at the front door I assumed it was you he'd killed.'

'Let me guess,' Kjeld said, his scowl still present. 'You were coming by to ensure that my untimely death didn't incriminate the pinnacles-of-Varsund-society Lindqvists?'

Gunnar gave a deliberate exhalation, shame written all over his face. 'That's what they wanted me to do.'

'And I'm sure you always do what they tell you to do, don't you? You're such a good dog.'

'It's not that simple, Kjeld.'

'Woof, woof, good dog.'

'Jesus, give me a break. Somehow he found out about what happened during our traineeship. I don't know how. I don't even want to know how. But the threat was more than implied that if I didn't keep David's name out of Peter's death, he would bring that incident to light.'

The fact that Gunnar referred to their informant's untimely murder as an incident grated on Kjeld, but he held his tongue. That was in the past. There wasn't anything he could do about that now. But this situation with his father and the Lindqvists?

That was something Kjeld was determined to see through and set right. Whatever right ended up being.

'Why are you telling me this?' Kjeld asked. It didn't fit his perception of Gunnar. Gunnar wasn't the type to confess to a wrongdoing, especially if keeping a secret would serve his own agenda.

'I'm not proud of some of the decisions I've made over the years. I thought that if I ignored them, they would go away. But one thing led to another and another. Eventually I realised there was no going back. This was who I was. I'd made my choice. Just as I'm sure you've made yours over the years.' Gunnar looked down at the floor. 'But when I thought you were dead I was angry. You worked hard to get out of here only to come back and get killed by some arsehole? That's not right. And then when you answered that door I was so shocked. I said to myself, "This isn't worth it." The Lindqvists aren't worth it.'

Kjeld's usual knack for coming up with a snarky retort failed him. Instead he settled for blunt honesty. 'That doesn't make up for anything.'

'I know.'

But maybe it was a start to resolving some of the conflicts between them.

'So, Roland was blackmailing you to cover up any implication that David might have been involved in Peter's death. Including, apparently, my own unintentional murder, I'm assuming,' Kjeld said.

'Unintentional?'

'I've been in enough scraps to know when someone is trying to kill me and when they're just scrambling.'

'Roland thought that since your father would never serve prison time as a result of his mental condition, it wouldn't do any harm to only document the evidence that correlated with the theory that your father was involved. That way everyone would be protected in the end.' The more he spoke the less convinced Gunnar sounded of his own words.

'No harm?' Kjeld gave a cruel laugh. Then he paused. He forced his mind to push through the pressure in his skull and think. 'And was there any evidence? Was there anything that suggested David was responsible?'

'None that I could find so far.'

'And my father?'

'Nothing that could warrant a conviction. Almost everything we found was circumstantial.'

Everything except the car, Kjeld thought. The car could topple everything. Fingerprints aside, there was no telling what kind of evidence might be hidden under that tarp.

'Then what makes Roland so convinced that his son is responsible for his brother's death?'

It didn't make sense to Kjeld. Kjeld couldn't see a motive. And if his brawl with David was any clue to the type of person he was, then Kjeld was almost positive that David didn't possess the intelligence to pull off murdering a man, leaving almost no trace that he'd done it, and keeping it secret for five years.

'I don't know,' Gunnar said with a shrug. 'He didn't tell me. But he did tell me that David admitted to killing a man in the woods.'

'Very unsuccessfully killing a man in the woods, thankfully.'

'Regardless, I can bring him in for assault if you want to press charges.'

'Won't that put you at odds with Roland?'

'Probably.' Gunnar looked down at his hands before leaning back into the chair. 'But we've been down this road before and I can't do it again.'

'Is that supposed to make me feel better?'

'I know we haven't been friends for a long time, but I'm trying to be straight with you. You didn't talk back then. You didn't give us up. You could have, but you didn't. I appreciate that. I do. I've made something of myself here in Varsund. It's not what I thought I wanted when I was younger, but I like it. And I owe you for that.'

327

Kjeld searched Gunnar's expression for some sign that he, too, had suffered sleepless nights over their decision to plant evidence against the man who killed their informant. A man who was guilty on many counts, and almost assuredly of the young woman's death as well, but who by all rights of law should have walked free. That act had eaten away at Kjeld for years. He still sometimes caught himself trying to make up for it in his other cases. Doing his utmost to accumulate all the actual evidence he could on a suspect before bringing them in. He didn't like loose ends. But when Kjeld looked at Gunnar he couldn't tell if it was guilt over covering up someone's involvement in a murder that bothered him or the fact that the supposed someone was in a class above him. As though wealth and elitism somehow entitled a person to a different set of laws. Kjeld suspected it was the latter that irked Gunnar more than the act of breaking the law. And that the nod to Kjeld's own involvement in Gunnar's current status was more of an afterthought.

But maybe Gunnar deserved the benefit of the doubt.

'There's one thing I don't understand.'

Gunnar canted his head to the side.

'Why would David come after me in the first place? If there's no evidence against him in the murder of his uncle then there's no reason to get rid of me.'

Even if it was true that Norrmalm Industries was illegally mining on his father's property, it didn't make sense for David to try and kill him. What was the worst that could happen? He'd be served a fine for violation of property borders? That would have been a pittance in money compared to what Norrmalm was worth.

Gunnar didn't answer.

'Unless it's not his uncle's death that he believes is worth killing for.' Kjeld thought of the contract that had been taken from him during the fight.

Gunnar pulled a face. 'What then?'

'I'm not entirely certain,' Kjeld said, scratching at the fresh bandage on his palm. 'But I'd be willing to bet that money has something to do with it.'

Gunnar stood up. 'Well, whatever the reason, it'll come out during the interrogation.'

Kjeld noted a different kind of confidence in Gunnar then. Less pompous, more resolute. The way he'd been before the scandal that almost pre-emptively ruined their careers. And Kjeld knew that if he was ever going to be honest with him, now was the time.

'There's something else I have to tell you,' Kjeld said, hoping he wouldn't regret his decision. 'I found a vehicle hidden on my father's property.'

'You *what*?'

'I can't say for certain who it belongs to, but I suspect it might be Peter Lindqvist's.'

'Fuck, Kjeld.' Gunnar took out his phone, scrolling his contacts for the number of the crime-scene technicians. 'What model of car is it?'

'Silver Mercedes. I have a photo on my phone. I can send it to you.'

Gunnar stopped himself before dialling. 'You know what it'll look like if we find your father's prints on that car.'

'I know,' Kjeld said, his heart heavy with grief. 'I know.'

# Chapter 49

Kjeld was standing in line at the pharmacy, ripping off the hospital name band from his wrist, when Esme came rushing through the electronic doors. She'd called him thirty minutes prior to tell him about what she discovered at the planning office but, after Kjeld's interruption explaining that he was in the hospital, she said she'd be there right away and hung up on him before he could say more. When she hurried up to him at the pharmacy counter, her face was peaked and her cheeks flushed. She leaned onto the counter to catch her breath. The pharmacist gave her a stern look and motioned to the red privacy line on the floor.

'It's all right,' Kjeld said to the pharmacist who continued to scan his medications. He didn't care who in Varsund knew that he was receiving extra-strength Ibuprofen for the bump on the back of his head. There were far worse secrets that the people of his former hometown could uncover. Hell, they probably already had.

The pharmacist packaged up the medications in a bag and passed them over the counter.

Kjeld stuffed the bag under his arm and led Esme to the row of seats in the hospital lobby.

'Are you okay?' Esme asked, nodding to the medical tape on his forehead. 'Is it safe for you to be leaving the hospital.'

Kjeld shook his prescription bag, the pills clattering against the inside of the bottle. 'A going-away present.'

'I'm serious, Kjeld.'

'So am I. I'm sick and tired of coming up with nothing but the vague inkling that the Lindqvists and Norrmalm Industries are somehow more involved in the body of Peter Lindqvist being buried in my father's barn and no evidence to support it. It's time to go directly to the source. I need to know what happened and I need to know how it involves my father.' Kjeld unclasped the prescription bottle, popped two tablets in his mouth, and swallowed them dry. The tablets slid down his throat uncomfortably, leaving behind a powdery layer on the top of his tongue that tasted like chalk.

Esme reached over and took the bottle and the prescription bag out of his hands, stuffing them in her purse.

'It's just Ibuprofen,' Kjeld said. His tone was curt, terser than he'd intended.

'I know.' Esme removed a large envelope from her purse. Inside was a duplicate copy of the geographical survey done on the Nygaard property as well as one for the land owned by Norrmalm. 'Did you know that land surveys are available for public access? I didn't. So, I not only requested the most recent one conducted on your father's land, but for Norrmalm Industries as well.'

Kjeld nodded.

'The last time Norrmalm Industries had their property surveyed was going on fifteen years ago when they purchased some undeveloped land around the eastern edges of Varsund's town limits.'

'Sara did mention that they'd increased mining activities around the area. But that's on the other side of town. That's nowhere near my dad's place.'

'Right, and even if it had been, it's a much deeper quarry. I drove by it after I stopped at the planning office. You definitely wouldn't have been walking out of that one after taking a tumble.'

'Guess I got lucky.'

'You have no idea.' Esme sat forward on the chair and shuffled through the papers until she came to one that looked like an invoice spreadsheet. 'These are all of Norrmalm's land purchases in the last fifty years. Also a matter of public record thanks to their corporate status.'

Kjeld leaned over to read the print. 'My dad's place isn't on there.'

'Exactly! That's why I looked at the survey for your dad's property again and this is where it gets a little bit weird.' Esme handed him a thick document he hadn't seen before.

Kjeld skimmed over the first page and then flipped through the multiple pages of detailed scientific information. 'I don't understand. Concentrations of aluminium, iron, nickel, gold? What is this? A mineralogical report?'

'Metallurgical, actually. Look at the date.'

Kjeld turned back to the first page. 'Five years ago.'

'Around the time that Peter Lindqvist went on his sabbatical.'

'Let me get this straight. Five years ago someone performed a geological survey on my father's property specifically looking to prove that the estimates in the geographical survey from 1979 were correct. That it did contain mineable amounts of ore in the ground. And then Norrmalm Industries starts mining on the property without purchasing the land?'

Esme nodded. 'That's what it looks like.'

'And Peter Lindqvist?'

'That's the part that doesn't make sense,' Esme said. 'If Peter was looking to break the contract with your father in order to mine on his land, then his death should have prevented any mining at all. If Peter was trying to stop someone else from illegally mining on your dad's property, say his brother for example, then that might explain why he was buried in the barn.'

'Because it would implicate my father in his death,' Kjeld said. 'And allow that person to continue mining.'

'It fits your father's version of the events.'

'Except that none of this proves anything except that Norrmalm is illegally mining on land that doesn't belong to them.'

'Which is why we need to see the redacted pages from the contract. That could explain the killer's motivation. It could lead us right to them.'

Kjeld pinched the bridge of his nose, willing the medication to work faster on alleviating the dull throb at the forefront of his head. There was something he wasn't seeing. Some important piece of information was missing from the puzzle and he had the nagging feeling that it was more than just land rights. What had the contract said? In exchange for agreeing not to purchase or mine on his father's land, his father promised not to share information about the Lindqvists. But what information could be so dangerous that it would lead to murder?

'Can you have a survey done on someone else's land?' Kjeld asked.

'I suppose so,' Esme said. 'If you pay for it.'

'Then whoever requested the geological survey of my father's property could be responsible for the death of Peter Lindqvist.'

'If the land is the reason for his death then, yes, it would be a plausible conclusion.'

Kjeld flipped through the pages of the metallurgical report. 'Then we just need to find a signature of the person who had this survey conducted.'

'Kjeld,' Esme said, her tone sombre. She held out a page. It was a copy of the invoice signed by the local planning commissioner and the individual who purchased the report.

At the bottom someone had scrawled *S. Nygaard*.

Stenar Nygaard.

# Chapter 50

The news of Peter Lindqvist's death had officially been released to the Norrmalm staff. As a result, the executive board decided to suspend business hours until the following week, closing the company just after the lunch hour.

Esme and Kjeld waited until the last vehicle left the car park before pulling into a space near the side of the building. It wasn't dark yet, but the sky was murky and drab. The inability to intuitively determine the hour messed with Esme's biological clock and she knew now why she preferred the south. Time flowed more naturally down there. The clouds hung low overhead here and although it wasn't snowing, Esme felt like it would sooner rather than later. She couldn't wait to get back home.

'You stay here and I'll search the office,' Kjeld said. It had been his decision to go to Norrmalm Industries first in order to search for the document. He'd called a woman in town – Hanna – who apparently worked as Roland Lindqvist's personal secretary and was all too happy to assist after she, and most of the administrative staff, had received their walking papers that morning. As his secretary, she had access to the master key for the executive floor and promised him that she would leave Norberg's office unlocked before she left for the day.

Esme sensed that Kjeld felt ashamed about asking for Hanna's help, but she didn't bring it up. Even though the conversation occurred over the phone, Esme could tell there was something between them and, quite frankly, she didn't want to know.

'The hell you're going in there,' Esme said. 'You can barely even walk straight and your face is whiter than that snowdrift out there. You'll pass out before you even get halfway across the car park.'

'Esme, I am not letting you go in there by yourself.'

'Why? Afraid a night custodian might come at me with a broom?' She undid her seatbelt. 'You're the dumbass who got himself a head injury. You can play lookout. If you see someone coming, call me.'

'But—'

'The last thing I want to do is drag your deadweight back to the hospital if you fall unconscious again. Yesterday was enough for me.' She climbed out of the car. 'And keep the heat on. It's freezing as balls out here.'

She slammed the door and headed out across the lot.

The service door on the far side of the building was unlocked for the after-hours janitorial staff, just as Hanna had said, and Esme easily made her way through the back entrance and up the stairs to the top floor without being seen.

But when Esme turned the knob on Norberg's door it didn't budge. She tried again. Locked. Esme glanced down the empty hallway and cursed beneath her breath. Kjeld should have asked Hanna to leave the key. That would have covered all their bases. Somewhere in the background she could hear the sound of a vacuum cleaner. She had to think fast.

She removed her wallet from her back pocket and took out an IKEA Family card. She wedged the card into the space between the door and the frame until she could feel the pushback from the locking mechanism. Then she carefully bent the card away from the door handle until it slid between the lock and the frame. The door pushed open with little resistance. Esme stepped inside quickly and shut the door behind her.

Easy as a pancake, as her mother would say.

Norberg's office was plain and outdated, as though he hadn't used it on a regular basis in over a decade. Presumably this was because he spent the majority of his time in Stockholm where he managed most of his clients. There were a few photographs on the wall and a framed certificate declaring him a graduate of law, probably a photocopy of the original, but other than that there were no signs of a personality. Not that he had given Esme the impression of being a man with much of a personality. He seemed like the kind of man who made it through life by determination and a formidable list of influential clients, not by his ability to make idle conversation or impress a group with a well-timed joke. Then again, she'd only seen him briefly at the hospital. Perhaps she was judging him too harshly.

Esme walked around Norberg's desk and looked through the drawers. No documents. On the far wall stood a medium-sized, four-drawer filing cabinet that looked like it had been there since the early Eighties. The top three drawers were unlocked. Esme didn't know exactly where he expected to find a copy of the contract that was in Kjeld's possession before it was stolen, so she tabbed through every file, periodically checking over her shoulder every time she heard the approaching sound of one of the cleaners.

By the time she reached the third drawer, the vacuum cleaner was right outside the door. It was nothing to worry about. The offices were supposed to be locked. No one would try to come inside. Still her pulse quickened. She picked up the pace and skimmed through the folders faster.

Bottom drawer. Locked.

Esme grumbled. She tugged harder on the drawer handle. The entire cabinet rattled in response. She ran her finger over the small key lock. Had she seen a key in the desk? She couldn't remember. She scrambled over to the desk and searched through it. Pens, pencils, notepads, a bottle of Rémy Martin cognac that was more than half empty.

Her phone buzzed in her pocket. It was probably Kjeld telling her to hurry up. She ignored it. All she needed was a few more minutes.

The soft tapping of shoes on carpet.

She looked up at the door, expecting it to open. The shoes moved on. She breathed a sigh of relief. Then she found a sharp silver letter opener pushed back behind the stationery.

That might do the trick.

She crouched down in front of the filing cabinet and jabbed the letter opener into the key slot, wiggling it around to try and get it to turn. There was resistance at first, but when she angled the point she felt the lock begin to give. All that money on fancy windows and the offices were filled with cheap do-it-yourself cabinetry and bargain locks. If she hadn't been so concerned that someone might walk in on her committing what probably looked like some form of corporate espionage, she might have found some irony in that.

Another hard jiggle and something on the inside of the drawer snapped. Success! She dropped the letter opener on the floor and pulled on the drawer handle in one harsh tug. It slid out crooked on its hinges.

Esme licked her index finger and began paging through the files, her focus so intent that she failed to hear the man behind her until he spoke.

'Looking for something?'

Esme felt her stomach drop. Then she turned her gaze upward to meet Erik Norberg. Erik closed the door behind him and while it couldn't be locked from the inside, Esme had the feeling of being cornered. Her eyes darted to the letter opener, but she didn't reach for it. Instead she slowly drew herself to a stand and searched the lawyer's expression for any sign of a reaction, but all she was met with was a grave stare. A stare that was made all the more unnerving by those swollen protruding eyeballs that seemed to peer directly through her.

# Chapter 51

'Please have a seat, Fru—?'

Esme stepped around the desk and sat on the edge of one of the two client chairs in Erik Norberg's office. She didn't know what to expect, but she kept her eyes on him. He seemed calm. Almost too calm. As though he were tired from multiple nights in a row of restless sleep.

'Jansson,' she said. 'Esme Jansson.'

'You're a friend of Kjeld Nygaard's, isn't that correct?' Erik leaned against his desk, arms crossed over his chest. Somehow it made him look even smaller than he already was.

'We're colleagues.' Esme removed her identification badge from her pocket.

'I assumed as much,' Erik said, waving a dismissive hand at her. 'Now tell me why your partner has you rummaging through my filing cabinet. Don't tell me he was too afraid to do it himself. Or did he think that I might be kinder to a soft face if you got caught?'

Esme placed her hands in her lap, anxiously twisting the silver ring she wore on her thumb.

'Well he's shit at picking locks, for one.'

Erik stifled a chuckle. He only looked half amused. 'Where is he?'

'In the car park.'

'And what does he have you searching for while he sits in the car park?'

Esme narrowed her gaze and scrutinised the lawyer. She found she was having difficulty reading his expression. His body language was off-kilter from his words. She had expected a different reaction. Anger. A raised voice. A call to the downstairs security room. But Erik did none of those things. If anything he was the exact opposite. He was relaxed and soft-spoken, seemingly unruffled by the fact that not two minutes earlier she was breaking into his locked cabinet with a letter opener.

A letter opener that still lay on the floor.

She glanced over at it and Erik followed her gaze. Then he bent down and picked up the letter opener, shoving it in the top drawer of his desk.

'I'm not going to hurt you, Detective Jansson. And I'm not going to call security. What would be the point? I'm sure the police will side with you and your partner. I'm just perturbed by the fact that neither of you considered asking me for whatever it is you want to see. Or whatever it is you want to know.' He sighed. Then he slumped down in the chair behind the desk. It was too big for him and the resulting image reminded Esme of a child sitting in the giant chair in front of Ripley's Believe It or Not. He leaned over the desk. 'So I suggest we both save ourselves the trouble of play-acting this charade where we wait for one or the other to break. What were you looking for?'

'A contract.' Esme tucked a strand of hair behind her ear.

'What contract?'

'A contract from 1979 concerning an agreement not to build on a specific property adjacent to the borders of Norrmalm's mining plot.'

Erik raised his brows, giving his already bulging eyeballs the impression of being much larger. Then his left eye began to weep and he took out a handkerchief to dab at it. 'And the parties involved in this contract?'

'Peter Lindqvist and Stenar Nygaard.'

Erik held his breath.

'With yourself as witness.'

'Yes, I remember.' Brusque.

Esme sensed that Erik was weighing two heavy options. She assumed that those options were telling her about the contract or denying that it even existed. She wasn't correct in her assumptions, but neither was she entirely wrong.

'He found the other contract then. Kjeld, am I right?'

Esme gave a suspicious nod. 'Not all of it. Pages were missing.'

Erik folded the handkerchief into a neat square and slipped it into the breast pocket of his suit coat. 'And I presume he's looking to recover the rest of the contract because of the construction on his father's property?'

'So the Lindqvists have been knowingly digging on Stenar's land?'

'It wasn't something I was aware of until after it had already begun. The contract you're looking for is of course legal and binding, but it wasn't made entirely available to all members of the board.'

'Are you saying that Roland and David weren't aware of this agreement between Peter and the Nygaards?'

'I'm saying that they were aware of the agreement Peter made not to involve the Nygaards or their property in Norrmalm business. They weren't aware of the reciprocating arrangement on the part of Stenar.'

'What arrangement is that?'

Erik pulled open the lower drawer of his desk and reached up underneath the bottom of the upper drawer. Esme heard the ripping sound of breaking tape just before Erik placed an old discoloured file on the desk.

'I always had the feeling this would one day come back to haunt us. All of us. Peter, Stenar, myself. You know, Varsund hasn't changed much since its construction, but it was still a different time back then. It was easier to keep a secret. Easier to

340

lie. I believe it was made with the best of intentions, but I always felt a bit ashamed. People deserve to know who they are, after all, without having to suffer the sins of their parents.' Erik ran his hand over the front of the file. The edges were worn and the areas where the tape had held it up over the years were torn. He pushed it across the desk.

Esme accepted the folder with trepidation. She could tell that Erik was being purposefully cautious with his words, as though he might inadvertently implicate himself further in something unseemly. But she also sensed that he was telling her the truth. That he was relieved it would be out in the open. Out of his hands. And while she was surprised that he was giving her the document so freely, she suspected that its contents would reveal why he didn't feel the need to be more protective of it. He looked like a man who'd reached the end of a long road and was glad to be done with it.

Still, she was nervous. Afraid that whatever was inside that document would make matters worse for Kjeld and his father. But there was only one way to know for certain.

She opened the folder and took out the contract. It was exactly the same as the one Kjeld had found in the safety deposit box at the bank except that it contained the missing pages. Missing pages that outlined the exact nature of the agreement between Stenar and Peter. Esme read through it quickly, her eyes widening as she reached the previously unseen pages. It didn't hit her right away what it was she was reading, but when it did she looked up at Erik, shocked and confused.

'But I don't understand,' she said. 'This doesn't have anything to do with Norrmalm or the mining on the Nygaard property.'

Erik pursed his lips and for a brief moment it looked as though the tension in his eyes had loosened, making his gaze slack downwards in unspoken bereavement. 'That's where you're wrong. It has everything to with Norrmalm. And everything to do with the Nygaards.'

# Chapter 52

'Is this it?' Kjeld asked as he slid the pages out of the envelope.

Esme nodded. 'It's a copy of the original, but he said he'd stay around in his office a bit longer if you have any questions. Or if you just wanted to talk.'

'Is there something to talk about?'

'It's a lot to take in.' Esme adjusted the heat in the car, but the vents continued to blow out cold air. She hit the centre of the dash with the palm of her hand. The vents made a wheezing groan and slowly started to warm up. 'You should probably prepare yourself.'

'You read it?' Kjeld asked, searching her expression for a hint as to what he might find written in that document. But Esme was being uncharacteristically stoic. That was more unsettling to him than the fact that Erik Norberg was waiting in case he wanted to talk. Why did that sound more like an offer of therapy than legal advice?

Esme nodded and Kjeld could see in her face that whatever was in those redacted pages explaining the agreement between his father and Peter Lindqvist was more than what they had presumed. Her lips tightened into a line so thin that her mouth almost entirely disappeared. She looked like she was holding her breath.

So much for that hint.

Kjeld opened up the file and read through the document from start to finish without looking up. With every turn of the page he found his body instinctively tensing. His limbs clenched until the muscles strained to their maximum. Back rigid. Brows drew together into a tight constriction of the face. By the time he reached the final page he was leaning so far forward in the passenger seat that he looked like he might hit his head against the glove compartment.

He looked up and stared off straight in front of him.

'Kjeld?' Esme's soft voice broke through his thoughts.

'Mm?'

'Are you all right?'

It was a simple question, but there was no simple answer. Was he all right? No, he probably hadn't been all right for a very long time. In fact, when he tried to recall a moment when he knew that he was all right, when everything in his life was good and he was content with the direction things had gone, he couldn't think of anything. Except for maybe the day his daughter was born. He hadn't wanted children. That had never been something he imagined for his life. But when he held her in his arms for the first time and looked down at her, knowing she was a part of him, he felt what he imagined must have been real happiness. Only he wasn't sure that's what it had been at the time because it was something he'd never experienced before. Everything prior to and after that fleeting moment, however, was proof that Kjeld was very much not all right. And when he looked down at that contract between his father and a man whom he'd never met, who he never would meet, Kjeld didn't think that he would ever be all right again.

Kjeld didn't realise he was crying until the salty taste of silent tears hit his lips. He wiped his fingers over his eyes to dry them.

'No, I'm not,' he said, shaking his head from side to side. He felt like he was moving in slow motion.

Esme reached out and placed a hand on his, tightening her fingers around his palm. The touch made the tears return.

How could he ever be all right now that he knew the truth? How could he be all right when his father was dead?

# Chapter 53

Peter Lindqvist was his father.

Peter Lindqvist was dead.

Dead and buried in the barn where Kjeld had spent much of his childhood.

And now he was spread out on a slab in the morgue, the skeletal remains of a stranger to whom he owed his life.

Five minutes into the drive back to Varsund proper, Kjeld asked Esme to take a turn off down an old logging road. The pea-green Volvo rocked and rattled against every bump on the trail, kicking up less dirt than it would have in the summertime due to the stiffened surface, intermittently patched in snow. The high-stretching birch trees loomed over the vehicle, closing in the further they travelled. The sky above was heavily overcast. Snow clouds. And the eerie lack of shadows on the way added to the tense silence in the car.

Three miles down the road, nestled on the right, was a turna-round. Esme veered off into the curve and parked, staring blankly at the steering wheel while Kjeld climbed wordlessly out of the car. She knew him well enough to realise when he needed to be alone and she let him go without question.

Through the woods along the bend of the road was a thin

path, almost unnoticeable through the snow, formed by decades of hikers, hunters, and fishermen shortcutting to the river. Kjeld pushed through the crooked spruce, stepping over fallen branches, and avoiding the flat stones, slick with ice. He had the urge to get as far away from civilisation as possible. To be somewhere open and free. Somewhere that wasn't suffocated by the choices of mankind. By his family's choices.

Closer to the water's edge the birch trees that still clung to their leaves, rejecting the early brush with winter, stood stoic in shades of warm yellow and orange against the grey and green backdrop. Kjeld took a deep breath and gazed out over the vast, untouched beauty of Jämtland's wilderness, willing it to fill him with something other than the grief that tugged at his chest. The silver water flowed smoothly, kicking up over large dark stones that jutted upward from the riverbed.

When Kjeld thought about the contract his stomach twisted. He crouched down, cupped a handful of cold water, and swallowed it quickly, pushing down the urge to be sick. Why? Why hadn't his parents told him? Why keep it a secret? What was there to gain? The questions rolled through his mind like a boulder tumbling downhill, but every time he tried to reason an answer all he could think of was how angry he was. Worst of all, it wasn't his father or Peter Lindqvist he was angry with. For the first time in his life, Kjeld felt real resentment towards his mother. How could she, of all people, not tell him? That hurt Kjeld more than anything. He'd always been truthful with his mother and she'd always been open with him. Honest, it seemed, in everything except for the one aspect of his life that had formed the basis for who he was – the certainty of his history.

But there was a hollow futility at being angry with her. Like the dead man in his father's barn or the demented forester who barely recognised him anymore, Kjeld's mother couldn't give him any answers. And she could no longer defend herself.

A frigid wind caught up in the trees and passed over him, sending a shiver through his body.

Kjeld's phone vibrated in his pocket. It was a message from Gunnar. David Lindqvist had been brought in for questioning in connection to the death of Peter Lindqvist.

*I'll keep him on ice until you get here*, the message ended and Kjeld couldn't help but laugh at Gunnar's over-the-top phrasing. Some things never changed while others were never the same.

Kjeld's stomach knotted again, more in determination than restlessness. He swallowed down another breath, suppressing that queasy distress from surging up through his chest and throat. There wasn't time to think about the contract now. Later, when everything was resolved, when he had time to process what he'd learned and accept the emotional fallout of his parents' choices, then he could think about it. Then he could decide what it meant for his past and for his future. If it meant anything at all. But for now he had to focus and see this situation through. It was the only way he'd be able to move forward.

Kjeld took one last glance over the river. The clouds were darker in the distance, concealing the northern mountain peaks that ranged near the Norwegian border. A golden eagle soared overhead, its dark wings spread out in a dihedral glide until it disappeared behind an outcropping of pine. That crisp scent of approaching snow, so foreign from the damp industrial smell he'd grown accustomed to in Gothenburg, filled his nostrils. It was peaceful. Serene. On its own, separate from his thoughts and memories, this untamed piece of Varsund was the most beautiful place he'd ever seen. And it struck him then that perhaps his own recollection wasn't what he thought it was.

But that, too, was something to save for later.

One step at a time, he told himself as he made his way back through the forest to the road where Esme was waiting for him.

# Chapter 54

## Trettio år sedan | Thirty years ago

Kjeld didn't know who the man with the hard features was when he opened the door, but his father did. Normally he wouldn't be interested in adult talk, but the strange man was unlike anyone he'd seen before. He was tall and well groomed, ruddy hair slicked to the side with a severe part on the left in a style that reminded Kjeld of black-and-white photographs from the Forties. His posture was incredibly straight, aside from his slight lean to the left where he held himself up by a cane, a parting gift from his military days, making him look like a giant to a boy of eight – nine in a few months – and his clothes were new. Kjeld could tell they were new because his dress shirt looked starched, directly out of the packaging, and no one in Varsund starched their shirts. Not unless it was Christmas.

The man looked down at him and smiled. It was a nice smile. He held out his hand to Kjeld, but before Kjeld could shake it his father pushed him aside and told him to go out to the barn and feed the birds. Kjeld thought about protesting, but he saw that sharp glare in his father's eyes and knew not to press the matter.

Instead he went to the kitchen to gather the pre-mixed meat and seed meal that his father had put together in the fridge for the ravens that morning, grabbed a pail by the back door, and hiked across the lawn to the barn.

Kjeld didn't like the birds.

It wasn't that he didn't like birds in general, but the ravens in the barn frightened him. They were always watching him with their black beady eyes, and he felt like they knew something he didn't. Like they were hiding secrets. Secrets that he didn't want to know.

He stepped inside the barn and closed the heavy wooden door behind him. Once he'd accidentally left it open while he was feeding the birds and they all flew out. They came back a few hours later, of course. They always did. That's what they were trained to do. But Kjeld still spent those two hours frantically chasing them down in the forest, worrying that they might not return. His father would never forgive him if he lost the birds. The birds were his life.

Kjeld lifted the latch on the rookery and stepped inside, the chicken-wire door snapping back behind him.

The ravens sat on their perches, eyeing him with mute curiosity. They were intelligent enough to know that Kjeld wasn't as high on the social hierarchy as his father. The same rules didn't apply.

Kjeld clenched his small fingers around the pail's handle and tried to ignore their stares. They unnerved him with their waiting and their watching. Their knowing. To a young boy they were scary. Scary and smart. Possibly smarter than him.

The ground in the rookery was uneven. Kjeld tripped over his shoelaces and the pail of decaying meat tendrils flew up in the air like rice at a wedding.

A rushed flapping of wings drowned out the clatter of the pail hitting the dirt floor and before Kjeld could scramble out of the enclosed space the hungry ravens were upon him, racing against each other for the scraps that covered him.

349

He curled up onto his knees, arms over his head like he'd prac-tised at school during the civil defence siren tests, and screamed. The birds flocked around him, snatching at the strewn pieces of meat with their sharp claws and dagger beaks. They scratched at his arms until he bled, poking at his scalp and his shirt to get at the raw flesh and carrion. He yelled until his voice cracked, but all he could hear was the cawing and cackling of the ravens as they fought each other for food.

He cried. The birds swarmed.

One of the larger ravens perched on his head and dug its beak into his upper ear. Kjeld screamed and swiped at the bird with his hand and the raven ripped its beak away, taking a large chunk of tissue with it. Blood streamed into his ear, pooling at the opening of the canal, and turned the noise of flapping and cawing into a whooshing din, heightened by the throbbing in his head.

A warm wetness seeped through the front of his jeans and Kjeld cried harder. He opened his mouth to scream again, but he didn't hear his own voice. All he could hear was the raucous screeching of birds. He tried to move, but he couldn't. He was paralysed, frozen in place by the fear that they would finish dining on the meat and move on to him. He sucked in quick uneven breaths. His heart pounded in his chest, beating in rhythm to the pulsing ache in his ear. Feathers flailed against his face and he pushed his forehead to the ground to protect himself. The acrid scent of urine accosted his nose and he began breathing against the dirt floor to block the smell.

The ravens covered his back like the wings of a fallen seraph. Dozens of sable bodies beat against him. Crowing. Clawing. He peeked one weeping eye open and saw the largest of the flock pecking at a piece of meat on the ground near his face. Its red-stained beak was crooked, curved like a scythe. It caught Kjeld's stare and blinked back. Then it picked up the torn flesh of his ear and swallowed it whole.

# Chapter 55

## Nutid | Present Day

Gunnar sat down at the interrogation table across from David Lindqvist. He placed a closed folder on the table in front of him, cleared his throat, and explained that he was going to start the recording. On the other side of the table he could see David begin to sweat. The bright fluorescent bulbs on the ceiling cast a sickly sheen on David's forehead and Gunnar knew this interrogation was going to be quick. He could practically smell the other man's fear of prosecution. Gunnar liked that. It gave him control. And Gunnar couldn't help but feel a surge of ego in the fact that, despite the extra zeros in the Lindqvist bank account and their reputation in Varsund, in this confined space Gunnar was the one in charge.

Gunnar's ego was invigorated even more by the fact that David declined an attorney.

This would be over in no time at all.

'Let's not beat around the bush,' Gunnar said. He sent a glance to the two-way mirror on the side wall, knowing Kjeld was watching from the other side. He had a moment of nostalgia, remembering how they used to practise interrogations in college. They had dreams of one day pulling a "good cop, bad cop" routine on a suspect like in the movies. Had circumstances been a little different this might have been the perfect opportunity and the thought brought a smirk to his lips.

Gunnar folded his hands atop the folder.

David's leg twitched under the table, his shoe squeaking along with the repetitive shaking.

'Did you attack Kjeld Nygaard last night in the woods north of Varsund? For the record I'm presenting Herr Lindqvist with a map of the area.' Gunnar removed a small map from the folder with an area along the Nygaard property edge circled. He slid it across the table.

David didn't look at the map. He swallowed. Gunnar watched as the knot at the front of David's throat undulated up and down like a yo-yo.

'This is all just a formality, right?' David's voice cracked. He leaned forward. 'You're not actually going to charge me with anything.'

'Aren't I?'

'You wouldn't even be here if it weren't for my family,' David whispered. 'My father would see you ruined.'

Gunnar shrugged. 'Maybe your father thinks you're a liability.'

David's brow creased in concern.

'The best thing you can do for yourself is tell me the truth. I can't help you if I don't know what happened. And neither can your father.'

David wiped the sweat from his forehead with his sleeve. 'I didn't mean to attack him. Not really. I was just trying to get something from him.'

'But you did come at him with a knife.'

'I didn't mean to do it!' David pressed his face into his hands.

'You didn't mean to do what?'

'I didn't mean to kill him.'

'Kill who?'

'Kjeld Nygaard. The guy from Gothenburg.'

Gunnar took the map back and slipped it into the folder.

'What was it that you took from him?'

'A document. A property contract explaining the agreement not to mine on Nygaard land. I didn't think he would come at me. I just thought he'd see the knife and give it up. I didn't mean to kill him.'

'And why were you trying to get this document?'

David clenched his teeth. He leaned over the table and replied in a paranoid whisper. 'You know why.'

'Because Norrmalm Industries has been digging illegally on Nygaard property?'

'I didn't know it was illegal. I thought we had the right to mine on that tract of land. Legally, mind you. I have a contract giving Norrmalm permission to work that land in exchange for company stocks. How was I to know that there were extenuating circumstances?' David drew his fingers back through his hair. 'And I certainly didn't mean to kill anyone. We had a fight. It was an accident.'

'You didn't kill Kjeld Nygaard, David.'

David's breath caught in his chest. He stared at Gunnar, searching for a sign that it was a trick. Then he looked to the two-way glass, his own reflection returning his shock. 'He's not dead?'

'No,' Gunnar said. 'Luckily for you he's still alive.'

And if what Gunnar had read about his old college friend in the recent newspapers was true, then killing Kjeld Nygaard would require nothing short of an act of God. Or the devil. Whichever got to him first.

David hung his head and breathed a deep sigh of relief.

Gunnar pushed a stray strand of hair back into his blond quiff. He gave David a minute and then he replied. 'Your uncle, however, was not so fortunate.'

David picked up his gaze. He was confused by the turn in the conversation. And Gunnar recognised it as honest confusion. David wasn't that good an actor. If Gunnar had to place his money on whether David murdered his uncle or not in that moment, he would have gone with not.

'Did you kill Peter Lindqvist?'

'What? No.'

'Did you bury his body in the barn and conceal the fact that he was dead from Norrmalm Industries and the rest of the Lindqvists?'

The twitching in David's leg stopped. His face went white but his body stiffened like a corpse. 'No. I didn't kill my uncle. I had nothing to do with that. I didn't even know he was dead until you told my dad. I suspected something had happened to him, but no. I didn't have anything to do with his death or his disappearance.'

Gunnar cursed to himself. He avoided looking at the mirrored window. He didn't want to give Kjeld the satisfaction of knowing that while he'd solved one mystery, he hadn't solved the other. 'Do you know who did have something to do with your uncle's death?'

David shook his head. 'No. I don't know anything about any of that.'

A tapping on the window broke Gunnar's line of thought. He tried to ignore it at first, but the tapping continued.

He walked over to the interrogation-room door and opened it. 'I'm kind of in the middle of something here.'

Kjeld put his leg in the door so Gunnar couldn't close it and leaned halfway into the room. David looked up at him, his expression startled and confused.

'Why did you think Norrmalm had a right to that land in the first place?' Kjeld asked.

David frowned. 'Because I bought it.'

'Who from?'

'Nygaard.'

354

'Kjeld, seriously,' Gunnar said. 'I can't have you in here during an official interrogation.'

Kjeld ignored Gunnar. 'And who was the recipient of these Norrmalm stocks you sold it for?'

'Nygaard,' David repeated.

Kjeld shoved past Gunnar until he was standing directly beside the table, staring down at David. David avoided his gaze.

'Let me get this straight. Stenar Nygaard sold you a tract of land on his property in exchange for Norrmalm stocks?' It was clear from the look on Kjeld's face that he didn't believe it.

'No.' David pressed a finger against his temple. 'The other Nygaard. His daughter. She's the one who sold it to me.'

\* \* \*

Kjeld leaned against the window on the two-way side of the glass. The room was dimly lit, brightened by the fluorescent gleam from the lights in the interrogation room, and Kjeld caught himself staring at the odd shadow on his palm that stretched across the bandage where David had cut him. Gunnar, only marginally annoyed at Kjeld for interrupting his session, retreated back into the interrogation room to finish the questioning.

David was spilling everything he knew, but it still wasn't enough. It still didn't answer the big question. Who killed Peter Lindqvist? Who murdered his real father? And more importantly, why?

Esme, who had also been watching from behind the glass, took a step towards Kjeld. There was a split second where it looked like she might reach out and touch him, but she must have seen something in his posture that warned her against it because she didn't. Instead she crossed her arms over her chest, her oversized sweater bunching around her neck, and put all of her weight on her right leg.

Kjeld turned off the intercom on the wall and the sounds from inside the interrogation room ceased. Replaced by total silence.

'It doesn't make sense,' Esme said. 'Why would Sara sell your dad's property? What does that have to do with anything?'

Kjeld pulled anxiously at his beard. He'd been asking himself the same question for the last few minutes.

'I know she's been struggling for money, but I can't imagine that on its own would be enough to convince her to go against our father.' Kjeld paused. He suddenly realised the inaccuracy in what he said. Not *our* father. *Her* father. Because Stenar wasn't his father. Not biologically anyway. 'He's always been adamant about the conservation of the Varsund forest. And she's always been close with him.'

'How bad is your sister's situation?'

'What do you mean?'

'Financial instability can be a big motivator. People make crazy decisions when they can't afford to pay their bills or put food on the table. If she truly was having difficulty making ends meet then maybe she thought this was the only viable solution to keeping her head above water. Didn't you say her husband has been having trouble keeping a job?'

Kjeld frowned. It occurred to him then that he'd never really asked Sara how difficult things were at home. He was too focused on himself and his father. He hadn't thought about her at all. 'I don't know.'

'All right. So, she sells off some of the land to cover some bills. Free up some debt. What does that have to do with the murder of Peter Lindqvist?'

Kjeld didn't know. He wanted to believe that it didn't have anything to do with Peter Lindqvist or his murder or his subsequent burial beneath the rookery in his dad's barn. Kjeld, however, didn't believe in coincidences and there were far too many coincidences about this entire situation.

'It's too bad you didn't already know.'

'Didn't already know what?'

'That Peter was your father.' Esme watched the silent

conversation between Gunnar and David through the glass. 'You could have covered all her debts.'

Kjeld pushed himself away from the glass and followed her gaze to the other room. 'What?'

'I mean look at him,' she said, nodding to David. 'He's an idiot. He's never had to do anything in his life and he never will. When Norrmalm sells, he'll make millions. And when Roland dies, he'll inherit millions more.'

There was a moment when Esme's expression became apologetic, but before Kjeld could say something she continued. 'If you'd known Peter was your father then you'd be like David, too. Well, maybe not as much of a pompous arse. But you'd be wealthy. You could have given your sister the money.'

The thought of inheritance hadn't even occurred to Kjeld. He'd been so busy trying to accept the details of his heritage in the missing pages of the contract between his father and Peter Lindqvist that he hadn't actually considered the repercussions of it. The idea that Kjeld had a legal right to all of Peter's possessions, both physical and financial, hadn't crossed his mind. And as he wrestled with that information, another thought, based on little more than a nagging intuition that built up in his gut, came over him.

She knew.

Kjeld didn't know how Sara knew and he didn't know when she'd found out, but in that moment he found himself overwhelmed with the knowledge that she was somehow aware that Peter was his father.

It was the only thing that fitted.

'We have to go,' he said.

'What? Where?'

'Back to the house. Give me your car keys.'

Esme took out her keys, but held them back. 'You're crazy if you think I'm letting you drive my car without me. Tell me what you're thinking.'

Kjeld was halfway through the door when he answered. He didn't know exactly what it was that told him to go home. It was just a feeling. An instinct warning him that something bad was happening. 'I'm thinking that it might be better if my father doesn't remember what happened.'

# Chapter 56

## Trettio år sedan | Thirty years ago

Sara watched from her bedroom window as her brother stormed out to the barn with their father's feed pail. The window was cracked open because it was so hot and humid and she could hear the sound of Kjeld kicking the pail across the yard.

Sara was disappointed. She was supposed to go with friends to the lake, but the forecast was calling for rain. She hated rain. Rain ruined everything. To make matters worse their mother was still in bed with a summer cold and there was no one else nearby to play with except Kjeld. She didn't like playing with her brother. He never wanted to do the things she wanted to do. He just wanted to go outside and explore the woods. She hated the woods. The woods bored her. She wished they lived closer to town. Then maybe she could go with her friends to the ice-cream parlour or the bowling alley or sit on the benches outside of the school and talk about their plans for the new term that would start in a month. Except her parents would never let her go into town alone. Not even with friends. They'd make her take Kjeld with her and there was nothing more embarrassing than having her younger brother tag along with her friends. Especially when their parents let them leave the house on their own. Her parents didn't let her do anything fun.

She let out an exasperated sigh and rolled onto her bed, looking at photographs of horses in the pony magazine she'd borrowed from her friend, Jessika. She'd begged her parents to get her a subscription, but they said it was too expensive. Jessika always let her borrow her magazines, which was nice, but Jessika always took out the stickers and put them on her school notebooks first. That was what all of the popular girls were doing nowadays. Sara wished she had stickers for her notebooks. But the stickers came with the magazines and the magazines came with an annual subscription price that they couldn't afford.

The sound of her father's voice coming from downstairs distracted her from her thoughts. He sounded angry and frustrated. What had Kjeld done this time?

Sara tossed the magazine onto her nightstand and crept out into the hall. The door to her parents' room, where her mother was resting, was closed. She tiptoed down the hall until she reached the staircase. Then she sat on the top step and peered down through the balusters to the living room below.

Her father was arguing with another man. Sara didn't recognise him, but she thought he looked very elegant. He reminded her of the professional equestrians in Jessika's magazine. The sort that always wore knee-high riding boots, threw elaborate dinner parties, and owned an entire stable of prize-winning thoroughbreds. Of course, all of that was just in her imagination. The man wasn't wearing riding boots and while he looked classy, like the charming debonair types in American films, she didn't know if he had stables lit up by crystal chandeliers. She didn't even know if he had horses. The only thing she knew was that he was handsome and tall and had the reddest hair she'd ever seen.

'Absolutely unacceptable,' Stenar said, making a gesture with his hand to show that he was adamant in his opinions. 'You're years too late for that, Peter.'

'You don't have the right, Stenar.'

Sara watched as the stranger – Peter, her father called him – stood his ground in the living room. Open but defensive. It made her think of the guards who stood in front of the royal palace in Stockholm that she saw on a school trip last year.

'*I* don't have the right?' Stenar laughed. Then he cut himself off and lowered his tone. He didn't want anyone to hear him, which just made Sara want to hear more. 'You're years too late for this conversation. I won't allow you to come in here after all this time and break up my family.'

'You misunderstand me, Stenar,' Peter said. 'I don't want to break up anything. I want to be a part of my child's life.'

'Not your child. Mine. You gave up your right to be a father when you decided you didn't want a family.'

Peter sighed.

Sara thought he looked sad. Like someone who had lost something very important to them, but hadn't realised it until much later. She scooted closer to the balusters and tried to listen more intently.

'I did want a family. I just wasn't ready at the time. After I lost Yvonne and the baby I wasn't thinking straight. I was confused. I didn't know what to do. I didn't know who to turn to.'

'You didn't seem to have any trouble turning to my wife.'

Peter ran a finger along the bridge of his nose. 'That was a mistake. But you and Eiji were separated at the time.'

'Not entirely separated,' Stenar insisted.

'You know what I mean.'

'You slept with my wife!'

*Mum?*

'We all made mistakes back then.'

'Except you decided not to live up to your mistakes. You forewent your responsibilities. And who stepped in when you determined that your business was more important than your own child? Me.'

'I know. I also know that I can never repay you for what you've done. But things are different now. I've come to realise that I was foolish in the past. I took advantage of you. Both of you. All of you. I want to make amends. I want to be a father.'

'It's too late for that.'

'But think of the opportunity this would be. What sort of inheritance can either of your children expect from you? Let me take back my obligations as a father and I will ensure that both of your children will be provided for.'

Peter was desperate, but Stenar was resolute. And at the mention of money Sara saw her father's cheeks flush red, hot with anger.

'It's always about money with you, isn't it?' Stenar scoffed. 'Never about anyone's well-being. Never about what it might do to a child to realise that the man they live with isn't their father. Always about you. You're so goddamn selfish, Peter. You've always been selfish. Well, I didn't raise my children to be selfish, and I'll be damned if I see them turn out that way.'

'You're not being reasonable. You can't hide the truth forever.'

'I don't need to hide it forever. I only need to hide it for as long as I live.'

'You're a stubborn ass.'

'I am. But my stubbornness will protect my family from turning out like yours. My kids won't grow up to be entitled or complacent. They'll never be rich, but they'll understand the meaning of hard work. They'll appreciate what they have, even if it's not much.'

Stenar shoved past the elegant man in the direction of the front door. Sara hurried back to her bedroom so he wouldn't see her eavesdropping. She slumped down on her bed and tried to make sense of what she'd heard. This man had been with her mother. What did that mean? Was their father not their father?

She heard a scream. She pushed up the window and listened.

The air was still outside aside from the gentle rumbling of thunder in the distance.

Another scream. Followed by what might have been crying. It was coming from the barn. It was Kjeld. Probably just playing one of his stupid games again. Or maybe he got his fingers too close to the rookery and one of the birds bit him. He would deserve it for being so annoying. For embarrassing her in front of her friends.

Sara shut the window and flopped down on her bed. She stared up at the ceiling, where the paint on the old wooden planks was beginning to chip from moisture, and thought more about the things she'd heard the stranger say.

What did it all mean?

She picked up the magazine she was reading earlier and began skimming through the pages, only half paying attention. A few minutes later it began to storm and her brother's cries were dampened beneath the pouring rain.

# Chapter 57

## Nutid | Present Day

The green Volvo tugged the corners around the winding road that cut through the spruce and birch on the way to the Nygaard house. Kjeld had more than exceeded the speed limit on the main street from Varsund, but the snow-slicked forest road forced him to ease up on the accelerator. A sense of urgency, however, pushed his foot hard on the pedal during the straight sections. Esme gripped the handrail until her knuckles went white, yelling at him to watch the turns. It was nothing short of a miracle that they didn't end up in a ditch.

He parked the car behind his sister's station wagon and slammed the door shut before jumping the front steps to the house.

Empty.

'I'll search upstairs,' Esme said behind him.

'There's also a shed on the side of the house near the well,' Kjeld added.

'On it!'

Kjeld ran from room to room, calling out for his father, but no one answered.

In the kitchen a plate with a bread and cheese sandwich and a tin of pickled herring sat unfinished. Oskar was on the table, nose deep in the herring tin. Kjeld picked the chubby ginger cat off the table and set him and the can of herring on the floor. Then he peered out the window into the backyard where two tracks of footprints, lightly covered by the soft fall of snow, led to the barn. He felt his heart begin to beat faster in his chest and knew he was afraid. Not afraid of what may be happening, but of what would happen. Of what would happen when they were all alone together with the truth.

Kjeld headed out the back door and jogged across the yard; a lone dark figure moving across a sea of pristine white; murky grey clouds in the distance anticipating a coming storm.

Stenar was feeding the ravens in the rookery when Kjeld walked in and Kjeld felt a weight fall from his shoulders. Sara paced back and forth in front of the heavy tarp that draped over the engine of Kjeld's first car. She stopped when she saw him, her face white and rigid.

'Are you okay, Dad?' Kjeld asked. He closed the barn door behind him, hinges squeaking from the cold, and took two slow steps deeper into the barn.

Stenar looked up from behind the wall of chicken wire. There was a rosy colour to his cheeks that he'd been missing since he was released from the hospital, but Kjeld couldn't tell if it was from an improvement in his condition or the cold.

'Just trying to get these chores done before your mum wakes up. Do you see what someone did? Dug a damn hole right in the middle of the rookery. What kind of nonsense is that? Who would do such a thing?' Stenar coughed, scaring some of the birds into the corner perches.

'I don't know,' Kjeld said, turning to face his sister.

Sara ceased her pacing.

'Kjeld, it's not what you think,' she said.

'What do I think?'

365

Stenar crouched down and used his hands to try and push the excess dirt, which had hardened some since it had last been touched, into the hole that had once hidden Peter Lindqvist's body.

Sara fidgeted with her scarf, tightening it against a chill that only she seemed to notice. 'I can explain.'

'David Lindqvist is down at the police station right now telling Gunnar how you gave him permission to mine on Dad's property.'

Stenar paused and peered at them through the chicken wire. 'What?'

Kjeld took another step towards his sister. 'He says he didn't know that Norrmalm Industries had a prior agreement with Dad never to mine on his land. And yet, somehow, he found out about that agreement and nearly killed me for it.'

'Kjeld ...'

'I told you about that. And then you told David, didn't you?'

'I didn't think he would hurt you.'

'Hurt me? He almost *killed* me.'

Stenar dragged himself to his feet and stepped out of the rookery, leaving the door slightly ajar. Wrapped up in a proper winter coat and gloves he looked like the big man Kjeld remembered as a boy, but he could tell from the rickety way his father walked that he was frail and sick.

'Who's mining on my land?' Stenar asked. The pink colour in his cheeks flushed to a pale white.

'Calm down, Dad,' Sara said. 'You have to take it easy. Your heart isn't strong enough.'

'The Lindqvists are mining on your land.' Kjeld shoved his hands into the pockets of his jeans. 'Above the ridge.'

Stenar leaned his weight on a stack of old milk crates. 'But Peter promised me.'

'Peter is dead,' Kjeld said, his glare focused on Sara.

'No, no,' Stenar stammered. 'He promised me. He promised me he wouldn't. I kept my promise.'

'I know you did, Dad.'

Stenar grimaced. He had the look of a man who was both confused and relieved. Tired but finally awake.

'I needed the money, Kjeld. You've got to believe me. I never would have let them touch the property, but I didn't have any choice.' Sara begged. There was truth in her eyes. She wasn't lying. 'I couldn't keep up with everything. The kids, Tom, Dad. I couldn't do it all on my own. I was drowning in debt. This was supposed to pull us out.'

'But you didn't sell it for cash. You sold it for stocks.'

'Yes! Because I knew that the Lindqvists would sell Norrmalm and when they did their stocks would be worth more than any cash payout they could offer.'

'It could have been years until they sold the company.'

'I knew it wouldn't be. I knew that the younger Lindqvists didn't want anything to do with running the company. I knew that as soon as Roland was old enough to retire, they would sell. I just had to hold on until then.'

'How could you know that?'

Sara rolled her eyes. 'Oh, come on, Kjeld. This is Varsund. Everybody knows everything. It was no secret that David only worked there to maintain the image that it was still a family business. And you don't have to look far on the internet to see that his sister is a tabloid drama queen. Someone like that wasn't likely to rush in at the last minute and decide to take a commanding role. Besides, David told me he planned to sell it. That was part of our agreement. He needed Dad's land to boost production and raise interest. He knew that opening a new dig site and proving that there was still a rich amount of ore in the area was essential to getting a good offer.'

Stenar sat down on a milk crate and shook his head. 'Peter would never sell.'

'Is that why you killed Peter Lindqvist?' Kjeld asked his sister. Sara blinked. 'What?'

'To get him out of the way so Roland would inherit his share and David could sell the company?'

'No!'

'Did you kill Peter Lindqvist?' A quiet rage began to build up inside of him. Kjeld could feel it trilling through his body. Because as much as he'd tried to ignore it, the truth was that Peter Lindqvist wasn't just some old friend of his father's. Peter Lindqvist *was* his father. A father whom Kjeld would never get to know, never get to meet, never get to ask the ultimate question – why? 'Did you?'

The snowfall must have increased because the plastic flap the forensic team had placed over the hole in the barn's roof had blown away and thick white flakes began to fall through. Sara wrapped her arms around her chest and bit her lip, trying to avoid the confrontation in the room.

It was Stenar who eventually cut through the heavy air between them.

'It wasn't her fault. It was an accident.'

'Dad. Don't,' Sara pleaded.

'I just wanted to protect you both.' Stenar pulled off one of his gloves and scratched the side of his face. 'I couldn't let anything happen to either of you.'

Kjeld's brows knitted together at the centre of his forehead. 'What did you do, Dad?'

'Nothing,' Sara interrupted. 'He didn't do anything, Kjeld. Don't confuse him.'

'I'm not confused.' Stenar slapped the glove on his knee. 'I'm not confused! Stop treating me like I don't know what happened!'

The ravens rustled in the rookery.

Kjeld crouched down in front of Stenar. 'What happened, Dad? Tell me.'

Stenar heaved a sigh and coughed into his gloveless hand. 'It's all my fault. I'm the one to blame.'

# Chapter 58

## Fem år sedan | Five years ago

Stenar peered through the frost-covered barn window. He could see the ravens flapping their wings in the corner. They were agitated. The rookery was awash with frenzied *prruk-prruk-prruks*, but Stenar strained to hear the voices.

When the two figures came into view, dimly illuminated by the yellow light of the hanging industrial lamps, Stenar narrowed his eyes. His vision was good. It was just about the only part of him that hadn't gone bad in the last few years. Still, he found it difficult to believe his eyes. And in that brief moment of silence before the taller figure released a hearty, mocking laugh, Stenar thought he might have been imagining it all. But there was no disguising that laugh. He used to hear it on an almost daily basis during practice patrols in Lapland. Just as there was no disguising the frustrated voice of his daughter who, despite becoming a responsible adult and mother, still had a nagging whine in her tone when she didn't get her way.

'Is *that* what you think?' Peter chuckled. Despite his age he had a commanding presence. Tall and slender just as he'd always been. Still sporting that bright red hair, although it had thinned out considerably over the years.

'It's what I *know*,' Sara replied. Hands on her heavy hips which, three years later, still hadn't lost the weight she'd gained from being pregnant with her daughter.

Peter shook his head like he was talking to a child. 'You don't know anything.'

'I know you're my real father. I know you tried to take me back when I was little. Well, I need you now.'

'You need my money, you mean.' Peter didn't hide his discontent.

'You owe it to me.'

'I don't owe you anything. You're not my daughter.'

'Yes, I am. And all I'm asking for is a little help. Help for my family. For your grandchildren.'

'I don't know where you got this ridiculous notion and I hate to disappoint you because you really do seem to believe this nonsense, but I am not your father.'

'You are. I know you are. I overheard you when I was a child. You came to the house and tried to take me back.'

Peter paused, narrowing his eyes. The flickering yellow lamp-light cast a dark shadow across his face. Stenar's breath fogged up the window and he wiped it clean with his sleeve.

'Then you heard incorrectly. I didn't visit your father to take back my daughter,' Peter said defiantly. 'I went to your father to take back my son.'

Sara's eyes widened, like two saucers just before they hit the floor and broke into a hundred pieces.

'I'm sorry, but I'm not obligated to you. There was a time when I might have been persuaded to help, but Stenar chose to turn me away. I'm sorry you've wasted your time calling me out here.'

'But that can't be true.' Sara's voice cracked, grief-stricken.

'I don't know what to tell you. I almost had a daughter once, but she died with my wife. I do, however, have a son. Kjeld.'

Peter tried to offer an apologetic glance, but it was standoffish and grim. When Sara didn't immediately reply he turned and made his way to the door, glancing back just long enough to offer what he probably imagined sounded like a courteous end to the conversation. It wasn't. 'I hope you're able to turn things around for yourself and your family. I really do.'

Stenar ached for his daughter. He wanted to rush in there, hold her in his arms, and apologise for keeping secrets. But he didn't have the knees for running and he didn't have the strength to face his old friend. He would wait until he was gone.

Then it happened.

Sara grabbed a shovel that was propped up against the rookery's chicken-wire mesh and, without thinking, slammed it against Peter's back.

The ravens screeched.

Peter tumbled hard against the barn wall, head slamming into a long rusty nail that protruded from the wooden planks. His head stuck, pierced by the sharp end of the nail. His eyes widened in shock. A rasping gasp of air expelled unconsciously from his lungs and then the weight of his body pulled him off the nail to the floor. He hit the dirt in a heavy clump, like a laundry basket of wet washing. His fingers twitched once and then he didn't move again.

The silence that followed was deafening. The ravens sat stringent on their perches, gazing on the scene in a kind of solemn bereavement. After a while, the sound of sobbing broke the stillness. At first Stenar thought it was Sara, weeping for what she'd done in a moment of uncontrollable rashness. Then he realised that he was the one who was sobbing. And the ravens were mourning for him.

# Chapter 59

## Nutid | Present Day

Kjeld was at a loss for words. When he opened his mouth to say something, nothing came out. Not even air. He couldn't focus his thoughts. Normally he was quick to respond. A detective's instinct for survival, preservation of life, kept him on his toes. But he didn't feel that now. He felt like he was in another person's body, powerless to control. He was furious and he was heartbroken, but nothing he could say would change any of that. Instead he found himself staring at a point on the wall across from him where the wood had begun to rot and warp from lack of care, letting in a sliver of grey light from outside. He hadn't even noticed that Esme had made her way to the barn and was standing in the doorway, equally shocked after catching the tail end of Sara's confession.

'Dad helped me bury him. I didn't think anyone would find him here.' Sara's voice trembled.

'And Peter's car?' Esme asked.

'I hid it behind great-grandfather's old hunting cabin. Tossed the licence plates in the marsh.' Sara took a heavy breath before turning back to Kjeld, pleading. 'What else could we have done?'

'You could have gone to the police,' Kjeld said.

'What about my family? Who would take care of them if I went to prison? Tom? He can barely take care of himself. And Dad? Dad can't go to prison.'

'It was an accident, Sara.' Kjeld's irritation overcame his sorrow. He crossed his arms over his chest, unconscious of the cold despite his lack of winter coat. 'If you'd told the truth then you may not have had to serve any time. Either of you.'

'It was my fault,' Stenar said between tears. 'I never should have kept that secret. Your mother never wanted to hide it from you, Kjeld. I'm so sorry. I should have been honest with you kids when you were old enough to know. I was selfish. And now Eiji is dead and Peter is dead and for what? A son who hates me and a daughter who's going to prison?'

Stenar sucked in deep breaths. His chest heaved.

Sara hurried to his side and placed a comforting arm around his shoulders. 'Don't worry about any of that, Dad. It's going to be fine. Everything is going to be fine.'

She looked up at Kjeld, uncertain. 'Isn't it?'

Kjeld pursed his lips. Their options were limited at this point and Kjeld found himself in a dangerous predicament. Not dangerous to his life, perhaps, but for lack of a less hallowed phrase, dangerous to his soul. It was the situation with Nils on the docks all over again. Having to make a choice about his friend – partner, companion, mentor – who while clearly in the wrong still meant something to Kjeld. Only now his friend was replaced by his sister. She'd broken the law. She'd killed a man. But it was an accident. And what good would turning her in do now? Whose pain would her incarceration ease? Roland's? Kjeld's?

He caught Esme's gaze, saw her staunch concern, and knew there was only one way to proceed. 'You have to tell the truth, Sara.'

'I can't, Kjeld. I have a family to take care of. They need me!'

'Stop,' Stenar rasped. 'Tell them I did it. I don't have anything left anymore. I just want to protect you both. You're all I have.'

The cold air made his nose run and Kjeld sniffed. He tried to block out his father's weeping, but it echoed in the rafters. The ravens joined in shortly after with sorrowful caws.

'We can't keep this a secret. I won't. I'm done with not telling the truth. Where has that ever gotten any of us?' Kjeld pulled at his earlobe. 'If you don't tell Gunnar then I will.'

Sara stood up. 'I could leave.'

She looked over at Esme, her face half-pleading, as though convincing her might somehow convince Kjeld. 'Let me go. If you promise to watch out for Dad then I'll take my kids and leave Varsund. You can tell Gunnar what you want, but I won't come back.'

Esme remained silent and Kjeld knew she was letting him choose. This wasn't like the situation with the Kattegat Killer. It couldn't be easily separated into black or white, right or wrong. This was his family. And it had been an accident.

'You know I can't do that, Sara. You're not thinking rationally. The only thing you did wrong was cover up a crime. An accidental crime. And there's hardly any evidence against you. Even if you do get a prison sentence, it won't be for long. A few years is nothing. Your children will still be young when you get out.'

Sara laughed. It was a cruel sound. Derisive. Disbelieving. 'You would think a few years away from your children doesn't matter, wouldn't you? You didn't even fight to keep your own daughter.'

'That's different.'

'Is it? You're an embarrassment, Kjeld. You always have been. And you're a shit excuse for a father. You're selfish. Just like the Lindqvists. You've had all the opportunities in the world and you still don't change. You're a disappointment to everyone around you,' Sara scorned. Her face was red as she approached him. Each fervid step reinforcing her argument. 'I refuse to be like you. I refuse to abandon my children. I'll not let them be raised by another idiot man who puts himself above his family.'

Stenar stood up on shaky legs and followed Sara to the centre of the barn where Kjeld held his position between them and the exit. A gust of wind rushed through the hole in the roof, sending a flurry of golf-ball-sized snowflakes into their faces and blew open the rookery door.

'Come on, Sara,' Kjeld said. 'It's over. We'll go together. All of us. We'll tell them everything. About the contract, the property, Peter. It's the best thing for everyone.'

'The best thing for you, you mean,' Sara snapped. 'Then you can go back to Gothenburg and never have anything to do with us. You'll be absolved of your responsibility to your messed-up family. Then you truly can be the lone wolf you've always imagined yourself to be.'

'That's not fair. You know that's not fair.' Kjeld reached into his pocket and took out his phone.

Sara jumped forward and grabbed at Kjeld's hand. She had a wildness in her eyes that Kjeld hadn't seen since they were younger. That same angry look she used to give him when he beat her in foot races across the yard or when their mother insisted that she take him with her when she was spending time with her friends. A look that he recognised now as jealousy. Pure and unadulterated.

Kjeld tugged his hand away from her. Sara was robust. She'd inherited that stocky toughness from their father. From Stenar. But Kjeld had the advantage of height and physical strength. Lungs notwithstanding.

The barn filled with the frantic tune of ill-tempered crows. The older birds uttered grating *kraas* while the younger ones wailed high-pitched *prruks*.

From behind, Stenar reached forward to place a hand on Sara's elbow. The action was meant to be calming, but Sara reacted like a caged animal. She flung her arm backward and hit Stenar in the face just below the eye. Stenar staggered backward.

And then came the attack.

Stenar had forgotten to close the chicken-wire door on the rookery. The ravens whooshed out of the rookery in a single black mass of feathers and claws. They swarmed around Sara's head. Pecking. Flapping. Scratching. She waved her arms above her head to fend them off, but that only antagonised them further.

Stenar yelled, but his voice was drowned out beneath the clamour of caws and the beating of wings.

Kjeld raised his arms to protect against the assault, moving around the frenzy of feathers to get to his father. Esme hurried inside as well, helping Stenar catch his balance. Once the two of them were safely outside, Kjeld turned back to help his sister, but was seized by a wave of panic. The ravens covered Sara like a teeming mob, screeching and squawking. Looking at her all he could see was himself as a boy. And before he knew it, he was outside the barn shutting the door on the screams of his sister, which had joined the ravens' caws like a discordant choir.

# Chapter 60

Kjeld stood in front of the house beside the broken picket fence and watched as Gunnar's police car pulled out onto the road, tyres crunching over snow and gravel as it disappeared between the naked trees with his sister in the back seat.

Esme, bundled up in a puffy winter jacket and scarf, crossed her arms over her chest. A gust of wind blew her fringe into her face and she swept it to the side, tucking the longer strands behind her ear. When she finally spoke her breath froze in the air like little clouds. It made Kjeld crave a cigarette.

'There's one thing I still don't understand. Why would Sara dig up the body?' she asked, tilting her gaze towards his face.

'I don't think she did.'

'Then who?'

That was something Kjeld hadn't had time to ask his sister, but he suspected that even if he had she would have avoided answering the question. He knew his sister well enough to know that she would protect the people close to her no matter what. And their father aside there was only one other family member she would need to protect. The person who would be in charge of caring for her children if she went to prison.

'I don't know, but I have the suspicion that might have been

377

her husband's doing. Maybe he found out and was afraid I would find it. I can't imagine why he would do that, but I know I didn't chase my sister out into the woods.' Kjeld reached into his back pocket and removed his cigarette pack. Only one left.

'But how could you have possibly found the body if no one had started digging it up in the first place?'

'He must have known I wouldn't be satisfied until I'd done a better job at looking into Dad's story than Gunnar. Maybe he was afraid that Dad might slip up and say something and that I'd end up digging up the entire barn myself just to prove him wrong.' Kjeld used his hand to block the wind while he lit the cigarette. He took a deep drag and exhaled.

'At least I'm not the only one who thinks you're a stubborn mule.' Esme shook her head. She tried to keep a straight face, but Kjeld could see the beginnings of a grin tugging at the corner of her lips.

'You're definitely not the only one.'

Esme nodded to the cigarette. 'Well that explains why you couldn't catch him. Or her. Whoever it was.'

'Hm?'

'In the woods,' Esme clarified. She took the cigarette out of Kjeld's mouth and dropped it in the snow. 'If you're going to be chasing people in the woods then you should stop smoking.'

Kjeld laughed. 'Just one of the many bad habits I ought to change.'

Esme nodded. Kjeld expected her to say something, but she didn't. After a pause he broke the silence. 'When are you heading back to Gothenburg?'

'Tomorrow morning. I've been ignoring the chief's calls for days. I can't put him off any longer. Besides, one of us has to do their jobs.' She tucked her hands into her armpits for warmth. 'When will you come back?'

'As soon as I get things settled here with my father. I just have to make sure he's in a safe place.'

'Are you going to be okay on your own?'

'I'm not on my own. Not really.'

'No, I guess you're not.' Esme brought her hands to her face and breathed hot air against them. 'God, it's fuckin' freezing out here.'

Kjeld laughed. 'And it's not even winter yet.'

'I'm going inside.' Esme turned and headed up the steps to the front of the house. When she realised Kjeld wasn't following her, she glanced back. 'You coming?'

Kjeld stared off down the empty road. A light flurry of snow fell between the trees, sticking to the barren branches until the darker shades of bark were camouflaged in white. Kjeld looked back at Esme with a tired smile.

'Soon,' he said. 'After I check on the ravens.'

# Chapter 61

## Lördag | Saturday

After waving Esme off the next morning, Kjeld called Hanna and asked if he could come around and see her. She agreed and Kjeld stopped by the local supermarket to pick up some fika pastries on his way over.

He'd barely finished recounting the events leading up to the confrontation in the barn when Hanna lit up one of the thinly rolled smokes from a pack of Marlboro Golds.

'*Sara?*' Hanna turned on the exhaust above the stove to dispel the smoke from her cigarette. 'I don't believe it.'

'It was a shock,' Kjeld admitted. 'I know it's not my fault, but I can't help but feel responsible in a way.'

'There's nothing you could have done.' Hanna flicked the ash from the cigarette into a small tapas bowl on the stove.

'No, but I could have been more involved in her life. And in my dad's life. I didn't have to be so estranged from them.'

'But that wouldn't have changed the fact that Peter was your father. It was your parents' decision to keep that a secret from the both of you. You weren't the cause of your sister's jealousy. The lies were.'

In his heart Kjeld knew that. The rational portion of his mind understood that he couldn't have done anything to change what had happened. It had been an accident, after all.

'Is she going to be all right?' Hanna asked.

Kjeld nodded. The ravens had clawed up Sara's face pretty badly, but they hadn't done any serious damage. The paramedics cleaned her up before Gunnar took her into custody and while she looked visibly shaken, Kjeld thought it was more from the fear of telling the truth than of what the birds had done. 'Physically, at least.'

'Will she go to prison?'

Kjeld shrugged. 'Depends on what she says and what kind of evidence they're able to find. But I doubt it. She might be fined for the deal she made with David over Dad's land, but I don't think Norrmalm would risk a lawsuit right now. Not when they're finalising their merger. That wouldn't be good for the company's image. It's already going to be a field day for them now that news is out that Peter was killed.'

'You did the right thing.'

Kjeld wasn't so sure. He'd done the right thing legally and morally, but emotionally? Kjeld knew his sister would never forgive him. Not even if the court threw her case out on lack of evidence, which it probably would. He thought his father might forgive him though, and for some reason that seemed to carry more weight with him now. Assuming he remembered any of it.

'What about you? Looking forward to Varsund returning to its sleepy ways?'

'I'm thinking about making some changes actually.'

'Leaving Varsund?'

'Norberg said he's looking for a new personal assistant at his office in Stockholm.'

'I thought he was creepy.'

Hanna laughed. 'I can handle creepy.'

Kjeld smiled. 'I don't doubt it.'

'So, what's next?'

'Once I get things arranged here with my father I'll be heading back to Gothenburg. I've got some things at work that need settling. And some apologies to make.'

'Don't forget to take care of yourself, too.'

'I'll try.'

Hanna held the cigarette out to him. 'One for the road?'

Kjeld thought about it. He could practically taste the slow burn at the back of his throat and the temporary ease to the tension headache it would provide. But like all addictions it would eventually leave him empty, craving more. In the end, he shook his head.

'Keep it. I think it's about time I quit.'

# Chapter 62

## Måndag | Monday

Kjeld stared up at the portrait of the man above the fireplace. He may not have noticed it upon first glance, but after closer scrutiny he began to see the similarities. Ears that pinched back at the top and hung a tad lower than expected, giving the face a peculiar dissymmetry. Nose not large, but prominent. A jaw that cut a sharp turn down towards the chin. Kjeld even recognised the lines at the corner of the man's eyes as the same ones he saw in the bathroom mirror, creasing into his brows. And, like Kjeld, he looked like a man who could use a good night's sleep. And then of course there was the hair. There was no mistaking that resemblance.

'My grandfather, Mikael,' Roland said. He passed Kjeld a dram of whisky. 'Your great-grandfather.'

'Looks like a hard man.' A trait that Kjeld thought might run throughout the entire Lindqvist family. From what he'd learned of Roland in the days following Sara's arrest, he had a shrewd and manipulative aspect to him. And while that should have made Kjeld uncomfortable, knowing that he'd plotted to place the

383

blame of Peter's death on his father, Kjeld found himself uncommonly forgiving towards Roland. Not because he was family, but because Kjeld knew something about being in the shadow of a favourite child.

Kjeld brought the glass to his face and took a deep whiff before taking a sip. It burned the back of his throat and he coughed.

'He was, but he was also a good man. It wasn't easy running a mining operation back in those days. The dangers were greater, the risks were higher, and he had to make a lot of sacrifices, which we take for granted now. But he always did what he thought was right. And he wasn't afraid to dig in the dirt beside his men.' Roland looked as though he might say more, but didn't. Instead he turned away from the fireplace and took a seat on the sofa.

Kjeld watched Roland with a strange sense of ease. There was no discomfort between them. From the moment they first met, Kjeld felt like he was in the company of someone he'd known for a long time. He didn't feel like he was home, because he wasn't. Home would always be his father's house on the outskirts of Varsund, a cramped three-bedroom cabin stuffed with nature books and his mother's Mora clock. Home would always be the house with the barn and the ravens cawing through the night. But while he didn't feel like he was home at the Lindqvist estate, he did feel like he was in the presence of someone familiar.

He was, after all.

'And Peter?' Kjeld asked.

'Peter was the same. He was a decent man. Not perfect. He definitely stumbled along the way, but he tried to follow his heart as much as possible. You know, for all their differences, Peter and your father had a lot in common.' Roland rolled the whisky glass in his hand. 'I remember when they had their falling-out, Peter was devastated. They were close friends. He took it really hard.'

Kjeld sat in one of the leather chairs beside the sofa. 'I wish I could have known him.'

Roland nodded. He wiped away the start of a tear from his

eye and took another sip. 'I never really knew Stenar well, but I remember Peter once saying that the best thing to come out of freezing his balls off in Lapland was the fact that he got to do so with his best friend by his side.'

Kjeld chuckled. 'Yeah, my dad used to say something similar.'

'From what I can tell you're a lot like him, you know.'

Kjeld raised a questioning brow.

'A lot like Peter, I mean. He wasn't closed off, but he was careful not to let people get too close to him. After his wife, Yvonne, passed away he maintained a cautious distance with everyone. I assume he was afraid to get hurt again.'

'Am I so obvious?'

Roland grinned, shaking his head. 'I admit I'm getting some of this information second-hand. What I couldn't glean from your recent notice by the press I got from Gunnar Ek.'

'Ah, all reliable sources then,' Kjeld said. Normally he might have been offended, but in this case he couldn't argue. The comparison was true. 'I've always considered myself a difficult man to get along with, let alone like.'

And he could count on one hand the people who saw through his difficulty to a man worth getting to know.

'There's only one thing that bothers me,' Kjeld said.

Roland leaned forward by way of a question.

'The emails. The ones that were supposedly sent by Peter. I know my sister wasn't behind that.'

Roland nodded. 'Erik.'

'Norberg?' Kjeld couldn't reason that in his mind.

'He felt indebted to Peter for helping him obtain the career he has. Apparently, he and Peter had a heart-to-heart during their last meeting. And a tad too much to drink. Peter accidentally left his mobile phone behind. Erik found it.' Roland turned his attention to the fire. 'He tried to stall my selling of the company. He thought if he could sow enough doubt that I would wait and he could use that time to determine what really happened to Peter.

And, I'm assuming, to make certain that you wouldn't be cut out of the inheritance if it did go through.'

'I never would have pegged him as being so—'

'Loyal?'

'I was going to say ballsy.'

Roland laughed. 'He's an odd man, but a decent one.'

A silence fell between them and Kjeld caught himself staring up into the piercing gaze of the man who was his great-grandfather and wondering if he was very different from the great-grandfather he'd always heard about at home. And he wondered if Peter had been much different from the man who'd raised him. Would he have stayed in Varsund if he'd been raised a Lindqvist? Would he have followed a career with the police? Or would the events in his life still have led him to where he was now? In the end he decided it was superfluous to consider the what-ifs of his life. Besides, he was fairly certain that he knew the answers.

'Will you be facing prosecution back in Gothenburg?' Roland asked, cutting through the stillness.

The Aubuchon case. The Kattegat Killer. Kjeld had almost forgotten. It had been little more than two weeks since he was put on temporary suspension pending the court's investigation into the handling of the case, but it felt like months.

Kjeld shrugged. 'Probably just a slap on the wrist. I made some mistakes, but the biggest one they can't prosecute me for.'

'What's that?'

'Naivete.'

Roland nodded as if he understood and Kjeld believed that he did.

'If there's anything I can do to help.'

'I appreciate it,' Kjeld said. 'But it's one of those things I have to do on my own. The mistakes are mine and the least I can do is take responsibility for them.'

It occurred to Kjeld after the fact that his words could have been interpreted as twofold, for both his actions as well as Peter's.

But Roland didn't seem dismayed by the suggestion that so much heartache could have been avoided if Peter had told the truth. Or Stenar, for that matter.

'Just know that, regardless of everything, you still have family here. I know we're not exactly admirable. God knows that if my children weren't my children, I wouldn't have anything to do with them. But they're family. And so are you. I know that can't make up for the past or anything you might have missed out on had Peter been in your life, but you're not alone. I can't say for sure what Peter would have wanted, but I think he would have liked you to know that you're one of us.'

Kjeld welcomed the sentiment, but while he knew Roland meant what he said, the truth of the matter was that it didn't ring entirely true for Kjeld. It was too soon. Perhaps in time he might feel like he was a Lindqvist. But for now he felt as he always had. Like the son of a forester. Like a boy who spent his summers searching for rare plants and animals instead of learning how to inherit a corporate legacy. Like a child who, despite the bad memories, had enjoyed picking chanterelles with his father and travelling north of Kiruna to watch the reindeer migrate across the taiga forest. Like a Nygaard.

Kjeld took one last lingering glance at the portrait above the fireplace and raised his glass to Roland. 'To family then. With all its faults.'

Roland smiled. 'To family.'

# Chapter 63

## Torsdag | Thursday

The room at Granngården Retirement Community in Östersund had a window that overlooked Lake Storsjön with a backdrop of the piste on Gustavsbergsbacken where the city hosted the Biathlon World Championship in 1970. It was too early for ski season, but Kjeld could see pinpricks of colour on the slope that indicated a few winter enthusiasts who couldn't wait for the official opening. It was beautiful, but Kjeld would be glad to get back to Gothenburg and the rain.

'These pictures are crooked,' Stenar said.

Kjeld turned away from the window. 'Let me help you with that.'

There wasn't a lot of space in the room, but Kjeld had brought as many of his father's favourite pictures from home as he thought the walls could handle. Most of them were landscape paintings of northern Swedish forests. But Kjeld had also taken down some of Stenar's framed specimen collections. Butterflies, flowers, plants. They made the walls look crowded, but that's how his father had always liked it.

Kjeld straightened the framed black orchid that had previously hung in the kitchen. 'Better?'

Stenar nodded. Then he shuffled over to his armchair, the same one from the living room, and fell into the cushions. Beside him on a small bookshelf was a collection of books on local flora and fauna and, of course, his aviary atlas.

Kjeld sat on the edge of the bed. His father hadn't said anything about the barn since Sara's arrest. He hadn't said much about anything. The first few days away from the house had been difficult. He'd fought against Kjeld and the staff at the retirement community with that confused belligerence most Alzheimer's patients developed. The nurses told Kjeld it was a normal progression of the disease, but Kjeld knew he would have done the same thing if someone tried to remove him from his home. He would have gone down kicking and screaming, as well. Once the room began to take on a better resemblance of the old farmhouse in Varsund, however, Stenar seemed to calm down.

'I'm going to have to leave soon, Dad.'

Stenar reached over and took the aviary atlas off the shelf, setting it in his lap.

'Yes, yes,' Stenar said, opening the book to a centre page. 'You're busy.'

'I have to finish up a case at work, but I'll come back and visit as soon as it's all settled. Then maybe we can talk some more.'

'What do you want to talk about?'

'Anything. It doesn't matter. Whatever you want.'

'Will you feed the birds before you go? I've got a pain in my knee. Don't think I can make the walk across the yard.'

Kjeld held in a sigh.

Three days prior, Kjeld had gotten in contact with a local wildlife sanctuary who agreed to take on the ravens. They would train the younger birds to be reintroduced into the wild while the older ones would remain at the sanctuary to live out their lives under the care of ornithologists and specialised researchers from Uppsala

University. The representative they sent to check the condition of the birds had actually been quite enthusiastic about them. She said they had a unique plumage that looked as though it might have been the result of interbreeding with a now-extinct species from the Faroe Islands. Kjeld said he thought he'd heard his grandfather say something similar. Regardless of their genetic worth, they were going to be taken care of. And while Kjeld didn't think his father could understand that, he thought he would approve.

'Of course. Don't worry about the birds, Dad. I'll take care of them for you.'

'Thank you,' Stenar said, turning a page in the book.

Kjeld glanced at the time. He had one more stop he had to make before he could leave. An appointment with Erik Norberg to accept Peter Lindqvist's inheritance as well as his share in the recent sale of Norrmalm Industries. Kjeld didn't know how much it was exactly, but Erik assured him it was a two-digit number followed by a significant trail of zeros. Didn't matter. Kjeld wasn't planning on keeping much of it. He was going to put most of it in a trust for Tove, as well as an account for Sara's children when they were older. He also planned on asking Erik to set aside a sum to help Valle find himself a proper place to live. He thought that was something his father would have done if he could. The rest he would invest in the protection and preservation of Jämtland's forests. For his dad.

He stood up from the bed and picked up the cat carrier where Oskar was sleeping off another can of herring.

'You know, I was thinking maybe I'd bring Tove up here for Christmas. Would you like that?'

'Who?'

'Your granddaughter.'

'Yes, yes. That's a fine idea. Your mother would enjoy that.'

'I'll see you around, Dad.'

Stenar looked up from his book. A flash of unfamiliarity crossed his eyes and then he smiled. 'Don't take so long coming back, son.'

390

# Epilogue

The sun peeked through the clouds on the E45 southbound and despite the fact that it was yet to officially arrive, Kjeld felt like he'd left winter behind him. Oskar howled in the back seat, carsick and starved for attention. Kjeld's mobile phone dinged on the passenger seat and he glanced over to see that Esme had left him another voicemail. He'd barely been on the road for a few hours and this was already her third attempt to get ahold of him. He would call her back the next time he stopped for petrol.

It was still early and the road was all but deserted. Kjeld spent the straight stretches of highway thinking about Tove. He wanted to spend more time with her when he got home. He wanted to apologise for being absent. Not just to her, but to Bengt as well. He didn't know how that would go. There was still a lot of animosity between the two of them, but Kjeld had the feeling that a lot of that resentment and bitterness had been on his part. A part of him hadn't been willing to let go and it built up more bad blood between them than there had actually been. Perhaps if he had been able to accept that he'd made more mistakes in the relationship than Bengt, they would still be together. Instead he'd skewed his own perception and gave himself a reason to blame Bengt. He just hadn't realised it until now. He knew he'd have to work at it. Bengt wouldn't make it easy on him. He was protecting their daughter, after all. And, as much as Kjeld hated to admit it, Bengt was right. She'd needed protecting from Kjeld and his inability to dedicate his time to her.

But Kjeld was ready to change. He was prepared to make things good between them. It scared him, this desire to take on parental responsibility, but it scared him even more to think that there would come a time when it wasn't necessary anymore. When it wouldn't matter. He wanted to be her father before she was too old to realise she didn't need him.

The icy shimmer of Lake Orsasjön beamed from the right and Kjeld slipped on a pair of sunglasses to block the glare. Just before reaching Mora he took the third roundabout exit and followed Route 70 instead. It would add a few hours to his trip home and possibly delay the official witness statement he was supposed to give on the Aubuchon case, but he'd made a promise that he'd drop off a business card at the Nordea Bank in Västerås. And it was time that Kjeld started fulfilling his promises. All of them.

He pressed the play button on the CD player. The whining blare of a solo trumpet rang out above the lilting backdrop of a piano and the slow thunking beat of an upright bass. When the rest of the band joined in at the refrain, Kjeld caught himself humming along with the rhythm. He'd listened to this song a hundred times before, but this was the first time he'd heard it. As far as smooth jazz went, it wasn't half bad.

## THE END

# Acknowledgements

I still feel like this is a dream.

When I wrote this novel it was with the hope that just one person would read past the first page. I feel incredibly grateful that Sarah Goodey was the editor who not only gave this novel a chance, but helped turn it into something better than it was. As well as working on a very tight schedule to bring more depth to the characters and the story, she welcomed me into an amazing new family during one of the most challenging years of my life. A sincere thank you to Abigail Fenton for finding me in the open submissions pile and passing me on to her amazing team. A huge thanks to everyone at the HQ HarperCollins team for showing such an outpouring of enthusiasm and support for this novel, with specific thanks to those who worked on it directly to bring it to readers all over the world – Belinda Toor, Chris Sturtivant, Audrey Linton, Anna Sikorska, Kate Oakley, Anneka Sandher, Jo Kite, Becca Joyce, Kelly Webster, Sara Eusebi, Aisling Smyth, Tom Keane, and Lisa Milton.

To my first grade teacher who taught me how to read, my second grade teacher who helped me improve my reading, my third grade teacher who introduced me to stories above my reading level, and every teacher that followed who helped foster in me a love of reading and encouraged me to write.

Although I've been writing stories since before I can remember, it was my creative writing courses at various universities that put me on the path to finishing this book. To Robert Pope who saw merit in my early writing and taught me two of the most important lessons of the craft: 1) always include an animal in your story and 2) write because you love to write not because it'll get you a job. The animals in this book are for you, Bob. To Jane Alexander and Miriam Gamble who were my dissertation advisers on what would become the first act of *Where Ravens Roost*. Without your inspiration and criticism this book never would have made it past the initial draft.

As much as a story is written in isolation, it is not improved by it. My utmost thanks to everyone who read the book in its earliest form and offered their suggestions for improvement. Particularly Rebecca Barker, who has not only been my best friend, but one of my strongest confidantes both in writing and in life. To Christine Delano, who has seen more versions of Kjeld than anyone else, and yet still took the time to read one more version of him and give me the hard truths of what was and wasn't working well. To Pine Irwin, who has been reading my stories since the beginning and is still with me. You motivate me to keep going, even when I have trouble finding the words. To Zeena Price who not only offered me sincere advice on improving the plot, but also helped me adjust to my new life in a new country. To the 2019 graduating class of the University of Edinburgh's MSc in Creative Writing by Distance Learning programme for critiquing two and a half years of my short story westerns only to have me switch genres in the last semester. A special thanks to two of my classmates, Melissa Dudek and Dayle Furlong, who stuck with me after the programme ended and convinced me to rewrite half the book. You were both right. Those chapters had to go.

Without my family's support I don't know if I would have ever gotten this far. To my mom who has been telling me since childhood how much she loves my writing. (Even though I know she's just saying that because she's my mom.) To my dad who has supported all of my crazy career decisions over the years. (I promise I'll try to stick with this one for a while.) To Ronaldo who taught me to trust in other people. To Bonnie who has always treated me as one of her own. To my sisters, Kelly and Kristina, for challenging me in a way that only younger sisters can. To my cousin, Jessika Björklund, who answered my Swedish language questions. To my family in Norway and Sweden who opened my eyes to new cultures, languages, and landscapes that I fell in love with. To my family in the Netherlands, for supporting me during the most difficult adventure of my life and helping me find myself again.

A huge thanks also to the scientists, medical professionals, and researchers working tirelessly to find a cure for Alzheimer's Disease. And to those, like myself, who have lost loved ones waiting for that cure.

But mostly thanks to Feiko, who loved me even at my worst, and made it possible for me to follow this dream.

And to my cat, Watson, who sat on my lap long enough for me to write a book.

Dear Reader,

Thank you so much for taking the time to read this book – we hope you enjoyed it! If you did, we'd be so appreciative if you left a review.

Here at HQ Digital we are dedicated to publishing fiction that will keep you turning the pages into the early hours. We publish a variety of genres, from heartwarming romance, to thrilling crime and sweeping historical fiction.

To find out more about our books, enter competitions and discover exclusive content, please join our community of readers by following us at:

🐦 *@HQDigitalUK*

📘 *facebook.com/HQDigitalUK*

*Are you a budding writer?*
*We're also looking for authors to join the HQ Digital family!*
*Please submit your manuscript to:*

*HQDigital@harpercollins.co.uk.*

*Hope to hear from you soon!*

ONE PLACE. MANY STORIES

If you enjoyed *Where Ravens Roost*,
then why not try another gripping
novel from HQ Digital?

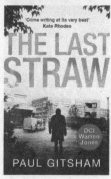